Praise for *The Ho*

'Sizzling . . . a joy to read' *Irish Independent*

'A glitzy, glamorous rollercoaster of a romance – hugely entertaining and so satisfying . . . Sheila O'Flanagan at her sparkling best' Veronica Henry

'A riveting story, strong characters, great settings and a satisfying dose of romantic adventure' Roisin Meaney

'Another satisfying contemporary novel from the author of *Three Weddings and a Proposal* and *The Missing Wife*' *My Weekly*

'A compulsive read from the master of the page turner' *Irish Mail on Sunday*

'A brilliant story' *Bella*

SHEILA O'FLANAGAN

The Honeymoon Affair

REVIEW

First published in 2024 by HEADLINE REVIEW
An imprint of HEADLINE PUBLISHING GROUP LIMITED

This paperback edition published in 2025

1

Cataloguing in Publication Data is available from the British Library

Paperback ISBN 978 1 0354 0288 5

Typeset in ITC Galliard Std by Palimpsest Book Production Ltd, Falkirk, Stirlingshire

Printed and bound in Great Britain by Clays Ltd, Elcograf S.p.A.

Headline's policy is to use papers that are natural, renewable and recyclable products and made from wood grown in sustainable forests. The logging and manufacturing processes are expected to conform to the environmental regulations of the country of origin.

Headline Publishing Group Limited
An Hachette UK Company
Carmelite House
50 Victoria Embankment
London EC4Y 0DZ

The authorised representative in the EEA is Hachette Ireland, 8 Castlecourt Centre, Dublin 15, D15 XTP3, Ireland (email: info@hbgi.ie)

www.headline.co.uk
www.hachette.co.uk

I am no bird; and no net ensnares me: I am a free human being with an independent will, which I now exert to leave you.

Charlotte Brontë

Chapter 1

Iseult

Tears are words that need to be written.
                                    Paulo Coelho

At the exact moment our plane touches down at the island airport in the Caribbean, my ex-fiancé is posting photos of a drinks reception from an art gallery in Florence. I know this because I turn on my phone and check his social media while I'm standing with Celeste at the carousel waiting for our luggage to arrive.

I hadn't planned on looking at my phone. In fact, unlike nearly all the other passengers (my cousin included) who were, by now, staring intently at their mobiles, I ignore mine for at least two minutes before fishing it out of my bag and switching it on. It pings with a flurry of notifications, and every one is a post from Steve. I take a deep breath and open Instagram.

Steve is a keen amateur photographer and likes to fill his feed with moody black-and-white pictures – usually of himself looking equally moody and intense. But that's OK, because he's the kind of guy who looks good in a moody photograph. In fairness, he looks good in real life too. And it was his ripped body, smouldering dark eyes, and black hair shaved at the sides (but falling over his forehead in a fringe of glossy curls I'd give an arm for myself) that first made my heart do somersaults. It still somersaults every time I see him, although that hasn't been for some time. In any event, that same heart is now broken into a million pieces.

He hasn't posted any photos of himself in the Italian art gallery, and I assume that's because he's working and not a guest; but if he's wandering around taking photos of people wearing tuxedos and cocktail dresses, I bet he's not in his preferred gear of frayed black jeans and black leather biker jacket. Maybe he bought some appropriate designer clothes in Florence. I picture him in a suit walking through the stunning baroque room where the reception is taking place, with its ceiling fresco, tall tables decorated with rose-filled gold vases, and line of gilt framed paintings on the walls. It's the kind of setting where you'd expect to see James Bond sipping a martini as he waits for an opportunity to drop a witty remark to the latest megalomanic hell-bent on destroying the world. I can easily imagine Steve rocking Dolce & Gabbana there, even if he's only ever bought one T-shirt by them, and that was in TK Maxx.

He's used the hashtags #LaDolceVita #PeroniAndProsecco #LoveItaly with his photos.

My broken heart is beating faster just thinking about him, and I have to remind myself that I'm looking at the timeline of my ex. Yet no matter how many times I tell myself this, and despite living my life without him ever since that awful day, I'm still having a hard time believing it.

The carousel judders into life, and Celeste nudges me,

because the very first case that appears is the brand-new pink and yellow Samsonite I bought specially for this trip. That was when I thought I was coming to the Caribbean to get married and I was shelling out money on fancy things because, well . . . #GettingMarried.

I drop my phone into my tote and grab the case. There's a slightly longer wait before Celeste's blue one arrives, but once we have both of them, we make our way through the customs area and out of the terminal building. A group of tour agents is waiting outside, and I find the one that Steve and I booked with. The agent smiles in greeting and points us to the taxi that's already beside the kerb. As we set off for the White Sands Resort and Spa (#BarefootElegance), I lean my head against the window and exhale slowly.

'We're going to have a great time.' Celeste squeezes my arm. 'Girls on tour.'

I don't say that I was supposed to be woman on honeymoon.

Celeste knows that already.

The drive to the hotel takes less than half an hour, and my spirits are lifted by the blue skies and aquamarine sea and the bright colours of the bougainvillea, hibiscus and other flowering shrubs that border the narrow road. It's hard not to feel uplifted too by signs with names like Pirates' Cove or Coconut Bay or Rum Runners' Beach. Nevertheless, I can't help thinking how much more exciting all this would have been if Steve was beside me and we were going to get married this week.

I manage another surreptitious look at Instagram when we arrive at the hotel and Celeste takes charge of checking us in. Steve has moved to a restaurant near the gallery for rigatoni pasta and chianti: #Friends #GoodTimes #Colleagues #BestMates #Firenze #Italia #LivingTheDream. I grimace.

'May I offer you a welcome drink?' A young waiter smiles at me and tells me that the exotic creations on the tray he's holding are called White Sands Experiences. They're mocktails, though, which is disappointing, because right about now I'm aching for a large gin and tonic, heavy on the gin and light on the tonic. But I'm thirsty so I take one anyway, and so does Celeste, who now has the keys to Room 501.

A porter, whose name badge identifies him as Janiel, has already loaded our cases onto a trolley and leads us from the reception area, with its high cathedral ceilings and lazy fans, through expansive gardens filled with highly scented tropical plants. The rooms at the hotel are located in a variety of small buildings, each with a magnificent view of the clear Caribbean Sea. Steve and I chose Room 501 because it was a corner room with its own private jacuzzi. When I wondered aloud if we weren't being over-extravagant, he told me that his princess deserved the very best for her honeymoon. I know it sounds saccharine sweet, and in all honesty I'm not a princessy sort of person, but it was lovely when he said it. After we split, Celeste insisted on listing all the royal princesses who have had a hard time of it, including Princesses Grace and Charlene of Monaco as well as Princess Diana and Princess Aiko of Japan. Meghan Markle too, if a duchess is also a princess. I'm not up to speed on titles.

'OK, not the best of circumstances, but – wow!' exclaims Celeste when we step into the room and Janiel opens the doors to the enormous balcony. 'This is absolutely stunning. No wonder they call it Paradise Island.'

I say nothing, but fumble the tip. Janiel, a supreme professional, manages to make it less awkward than it could have been. When he's gone, closing the door silently behind him, I follow Celeste to the balcony. She's opening the bottle of champagne that's been left on the small round table along with two glasses and a pretty flower arrangement. I suppose the champagne and flowers are left for everyone, not just wedding couples, though I can't help feeling that the rose petals that I noticed on the white bed linen (the room has two king-sized beds) are exclusive to honeymooners and have been put there by mistake.

'Come on, Izzy!' She hands me a glass. 'Onwards and upwards. Everything happens for a reason!'

I clink the glass against hers and take a long drink.

I think of the pictures on Steve's social media.

I finish the rest of the champagne in a single gulp.

Steve Carter became my ex-fiancé the day after I'd paid the balance of the money for our White Sands Five Star Exclusive Wedding Experience. We'd been alternating paying it off in instalments, him making one and me the next, and mine was the final payment. When he detonated his bombshell, he told me that he was happy for me to experience the White Sands by myself, as he planned to be in Florence that day organising the light installation for an art exhibition in a prestigious gallery. His boss had assigned the job to him as soon as he heard that Steve would be available owing to not getting married. It took a while for me to process that Steve's boss knew about my status as an ex-fiancée before I did.

I listened, speechless, as he told me that 'gifting' me the

honeymoon that I'd paid half of myself was the least he could do, because he knew that breaking off the engagement would be a big blow. He never wanted to hurt me – he caught me by the hands when he said that, and his dark brown eyes looked soulfully into mine – and said that it wasn't me, it was him. He loved me but he wasn't ready for marriage.

'I'll always love you, Izzy,' he said as he traced his finger along my cheek. 'But it would only hurt you more if I married you at the wrong time. I'm too young,' he added. 'Too irresponsible. I'm not good enough for you.'

As break-ups go, it was cinematic. As though he was reading from the script of a romantic drama. Even as my heart shattered into a thousand pieces, I was falling in love with him a little bit more.

'You're not too young,' I said. 'You're thirty-two.'

'But inside – inside I'm reckless, feckless and impulsive. I'm not marriage material. Not yet, anyhow.'

He was certainly impulsive the first time I met him. But so was I.

It was at a summer concert in Dublin's Fairview Park. The weather was glorious and the park was crowded with concert-goers, all singing and dancing beneath the blue skies. It was the kind of meet-cute moment that sometimes even happens in real life; when two people accidentally bump into each other, gaze into each other's eyes and fall in love for ever.

When Steve and I first looked at each other, I was smitten.

Then he kissed me and I was in love.

I know, I know. How can you love someone on the basis of a single kiss? When you don't even know their name?

So maybe I actually fell in love with him later, when he came back to my house because he lived on the other side of town and there wasn't a taxi to be had, while I live a mere ten minutes away.

'This is cosy,' he said when I opened the door. 'Is it yours?'

I explained, as I made coffee and brought it out to the patio table in the small west-facing garden, that it was our family home but that I was currently living there on my own. My parents had recently headed to New Zealand to see my brother, his wife and their newly arrived twin boys. As my dad was now retired, they planned to stay for a couple of months, although I already had the impression that they wouldn't mind extending their visit. Cori and Adrian live just outside Napier, and Dad, who's originally from Wexford, likes both the coastal town and the green spaces. Mum likes them too, but it was the lure of her grandchildren that made me think she was in no rush to come home.

Anyhow, my parents being away gave Steve and me time and space to get to know each other. He moved in, and I can honestly say there was never a moment when I wasn't ecstatically happy. We got engaged at Halloween – I know it was quick, but I was madly in love; besides, his proposal was romantic and original in equal measure.

I came home to find that he'd added a selection of orange and purple balloons to the rather terrifying decorations we'd put up earlier in the week.

'What's all this about?' I asked as I took off my heavy work jacket and sniffed the aroma of spicy chicken.

'A gesture,' he said. 'So that you know you're the best thing that ever happened to me.'

'Oh, Steve. How lovely of you.'

Despite his hard-man exterior, Steve likes cooking, even though most of his sauces (like mine) are from jars. But he pulls it all together better than I ever do.

'I'd have run you a bath if there was one,' he said. 'But maybe you'd like to take a shower and change anyway?'

He'd put spooky candles in the bathroom and had replaced my usual shower foam with a gel that called itself Spectral Slime. Much as I appreciated the nod towards the horror theme, I retrieved my rice milk and cherry blossom Rituals product from the shelf beneath the sink, then showered and came downstairs wearing my blue satin-look pyjamas.

'Best I could do to keep the Halloween vibe going,' I told him as I sat at the table.

'You can be my sultry spectre any time.' He kissed me and then put a plate of piri piri chicken in front of me. 'Eat up.'

After the meal, we went into the living room, where even more balloons were bobbing about.

'This is for you,' he said, producing a pin.

'What for?' I looked at him in surprise.

'You have to use it. On the balloons.'

'I hate bursting balloons. It's proper Halloween horror for me.'

'Oh, go on,' he said. 'This once? I promise you'll like it.'

I always found it impossible to say no to Steve. So I scrunched up my eyes and jabbed nervously at each balloon. The box with the engagement ring was in the purple one with the witch's face.

It was the most romantic moment of my life. Spooky, but romantic.

I still relive it.

Celeste was surprised that we'd got engaged so quickly, but even she said that we seemed ideally suited and totally in love.

Mum and Dad thought the same when they came home, sorry to have left their grandchildren but full of excitement at seeing me and meeting my fiancé. They liked Steve's easy-going nature and his quick humour, although Mum did remark that he was too handsome for his own good. He moved back to his own family home on their return, and I missed having him with me every day. But there wasn't an affordable rental to be had in Dublin and we were saving up, both for the wedding and to be able to get something suitable after we got married.

However, we were back together again sooner than I expected, as Mum and Dad decided to move to the Dingle Peninsula for the summer, a place we'd often gone to on holidays when Adrian and I were children, and where they'd found a picturesque cottage overlooking the sea. I said I hoped they weren't doing it on my account. Dad shook his head and said no, that he was taking advantage of his retirement package and they'd be back in Dublin as soon as the days got shorter and the nights longer.

So Steve moved back in and we settled into a happy routine together. With the possibility of both New Zealand and Dingle as potential retirement locations for my parents, I couldn't help wondering if they'd consider selling the house in Dublin to me and Steve, but it wasn't a subject I was ready to raise with them. I didn't want them to feel obliged to say yes. Then news came from Napier that Cori was pregnant again, and that her baby was due in a few weeks' time. We were all astounded, although apparently not as astounded as Adrian and Cori, who hadn't realised for ages that she was pregnant. She'd decided not to share the news sooner because she couldn't quite believe it herself. My parents booked return tickets to New Zealand for the birth, since Cori doesn't have any close family and Mum thought she might need some support. Adrian agreed.

Baby Azaria was born shortly after they arrived, and Mum fell in love with her straight away. New Zealand was definitely trumping Dingle in the possible retirement stakes for my parents.

Meanwhile, everything was on track for our winter wedding. We'd explained to family and friends that we were trying to save money by having it alone in the White Sands, and even though I know Mum was disappointed that there wasn't going to be a big day out at home, she was also pleased that she wouldn't have to leave the twins and Azaria to head to the Caribbean in November.

When Steve delivered his hammer-blow rejection, I completely understood why Cori had kept the news of her pregnancy to herself for so long. It was as though by not saying anything to anyone, it hadn't really happened. I told Celeste, of course, but begged her not to share it with Aunt Jenni and Uncle Paul until I gave her the go-ahead. I needed to tell my own parents first, but it took me a long time to feel able to break it to them.

Mum was shocked and upset for me, saying that he'd seemed such a nice young man she couldn't quite believe it. Dad was furious. I had to assure them that there was no need to race back to Ireland to take care of me (or, in Dad's case, 'knock that young pup's block off'). I said it was better that Steve had changed his mind now rather than later, and that although I was upset I'd get over it. I told Mum to concentrate on Cori and the babies and not to worry about me. She said that looking after her only daughter was as important as looking after her grandchildren, but I managed to persuade her that I was absolutely fine and that it was all for the best. I'm not sure how convinced she really was, but in the end she stayed put.

Of course I wasn't absolutely fine. I hadn't been from the moment Steve told me it was all off. Right then, all I wanted was to cling to him and say that I still loved him and would always love him and that I wanted to marry him whenever he liked and I'd do anything to make that happen. I thought of all the things I could do to change his mind, starting in the bedroom and ending up . . . well, probably in the bedroom too. But Steve doesn't respond well to clingy women. So I took off my engagement ring and handed it to him, then told him to get his things and move out. I applauded myself even though it was a struggle to keep the tears from falling.

'Right now?' He looked alarmed. 'I haven't got my stuff together. I thought we could be grown up about this. I hoped we could be friends. After all, I want you to go to the Caribbean, have a good time, chill out.'

'We can't be friends,' I told him, even though right then I was thinking that perhaps friends with benefits could lead back to what we had before. 'If you don't love me any more, you've got to leave. And I'd rather it was now.'

'I see that. I do. But . . . well, I couldn't start packing before I told you. Look, there's no need for us to fall out over this. Just because we're not getting married doesn't mean we have to hate each other.'

'Is there someone else?'

I had to ask even though I didn't know how he'd have time for someone else, because when he went out with the guys it was always to sporting events, and the rest of the time he was working or with me. But men and women have managed to cheat on those closest to them for centuries, and I told myself, no matter how little I wanted to believe it, that Steve was no different.

'No one else,' he assured me. 'Honestly. It's the whole go to the Caribbean, have an amazing wedding, being married thing . . . it's all so much and I'm not ready for it.'

'It's best you leave now, Steve.'

I didn't trust myself around him. I didn't trust myself not to throw myself into his arms and beg him to stay. He went upstairs and came down again ten minutes later, a black bin bag full of clothes in his hand.

'What about the rest of my stuff?' he asked.

'We'll arrange a time.'

'OK.'

He left.

I cried.

Inside, I'm still crying.

'You all right?' Celeste's voice, quiet and concerned, brings me back to the present.

I'm suddenly aware that the sun has almost sunk below the horizon and that the lights either side of the pathways from the individual two-storey blocks of the hotel are glowing gently. I can hear the chirp of cicadas above the distant sound of the waves breaking on the shore, and every so often a burst of laughter floats upwards on the evening air.

'Just thinking,' I say.

'Don't think,' she tells me. 'Enjoy yourself.'

'I was supposed to be getting married this week,' I remind her. 'I'm not sure enjoying myself is an option.'

'You came, didn't you?'

'Only because the insurance didn't cover my fiancé becoming my ex-fiancé,' I say. 'I wasn't going to cut off my nose to spite my face and stay home. Doesn't mean I have to enjoy it.'

'If you don't enjoy it, you'll definitely be cutting off your nose to spite your face.' She grins at our use of one of my mother's favourite sayings. 'Come on, Izzy. We're in the Caribbean. It's warm, summery and lovely. It's cold, dark and wintry back home. You've got to make the most of it.'

'I'll do my best.'

But my mind isn't in wintry Dublin. Or in the eternal summer of the Caribbean. It's in Florence.

'Do you want to get something to eat?' asks Celeste.

I can't remember the last time I was genuinely hungry, but I nod, and we lock the door behind us before making our way along the curving pathway, past the beach to the main hotel dining room. I've done this walk a thousand times on the virtual tour of the White Sands website, so even in darkness, everything seems familiar. The dining room is calm and spacious, divided up by tropical plants and with warm, intimate lighting.

One of the waiters brings us to a table in a corner, and I wonder if he's been given instructions to tuck us away out of sight, lest anyone realise I'm the woman who's been dumped. I know this is a ridiculous thought, but I can't help having it. I pick up the menu and look at it, although I'm really looking at the other diners, thinking that they're all on their dream holiday while I'm here being miserable.

My phone pings, and I glance at it, hoping for a moment that perhaps it's a message from Steve to tell me that he's sorry and that he's missing me and that he hates Florence and is on the way to the Caribbean right now. I picture him walking up to me and sweeping me into his arms, telling me he can't live without me and insisting that the wedding must go ahead as we'd planned. Even as those thoughts flicker through my mind, I wonder how I'd react. After all, no matter how badly I might be managing it, I'm trying to get over him. Besides, what would happen to Celeste, who's sharing the room with me? Where would she go? (Even if I'm hopelessly romantic about some things, I'm also eminently practical. Steve turning up would be a disaster. Though certainly something to write home about!)

The message is actually from my phone provider telling me about the extortionate charges for roaming services, so I switch off my mobile data, although I don't plan to venture further than the resort with its excellent Wi-Fi.

'Everything OK?'

I nod, though I'm a bit tired of Celeste asking me that. I know she means well, but I'm on my fecking honeymoon with her, so it's hardly going to be OK, is it?

'I think I'll have the red snapper.' She closes the menu. 'What about you?'

'The Caesar salad.'

'Why don't you try something a bit more substantial?'

'I'm more tired than hungry,' I tell her. 'It's been a long day.'

Which is true. We were up early this morning for our eight-hour flight, and of course we're now four hours behind GMT, so even though my watch is telling me it's 7.30, my body thinks it's half past eleven.

'I was tired until I started reading the menu.' Celeste grins. 'But it's so exciting!'

Celeste is a chef, and so the White Sands, with its reputation for fine dining and excellent cuisine, is like heaven to her. I know she's not happy that my engagement was broken off, but she's ecstatic about being on my honeymoon.

The food arrives, and while she attacks her red snapper with enthusiasm, I pick at the salad and check out our fellow diners. Most of the tables are occupied by couples; the White Sands isn't a couples-only resort, but with the whole wedding vibe thing it has going, it's very much geared towards romance rather than families. If you're having a big wedding, they provide private dining, keeping the public dining rooms from being taken over by groups of revellers. As Steve and I had planned to come here by ourselves, we would have had a room-service dinner on our balcony overlooking the sea, with our very own waiter for the evening. It would have been perfect.

Among the couples sitting in the restaurant, I decide that the youngest two, who only have eyes for each other, are newly-weds. They're both wearing very shiny wedding bands and her engagement ring is glittering in the light of the table lamp. I'm reckoning some of the older diners might be celebrating anniversaries; they're not quite as besotted as the newly-weds, but there's an empathy between them even when they're sitting in silence. Along with the couples, there are also a few intergenerational families, although no children. At what can only be described as the best table in the room, in a small corner that juts out over the sea, is the only solitary diner, a man who could be anything between forty-five and fifty-five. His face is tanned and his silver-grey hair far thicker and more luxuriant than you'd expect on someone that age. His eyes, behind heavy horn-rimmed glasses, are a surprising arctic blue. His navy linen shirt is open at the neck and the sleeves are rolled up, revealing a slim watch on his left wrist and a selection of leather bands on his right. He looks vaguely familiar, but even after staring at him for longer than is polite, I can't tell how.

'Well, I don't know.' Celeste shrugs when I wonder aloud where I've seen him before. 'Someone you stopped at the port, perhaps?'

I'm a customs officer, so I stop a lot of people at Dublin Port on a daily basis, usually truck drivers. And it's not that I can profile someone simply by looking at them, but this man doesn't look like a truck driver. Besides, I have a good memory for faces, and his isn't one of my regulars.

'I wonder why he's on his own?' I muse aloud.

'Maybe whoever he's with is joining him later,' said Celeste.

'Perhaps,' I agree. 'Or he could be a widower, returning to a place he and his wife once loved.'

'That's a bit sad,' says Celeste. 'Though I'm thinking if he's a widower, he's far more likely to be here with his new girlfriend than his melancholy thoughts.'

I tell her she has a heart of stone. I'm not sure why I'm so convinced he's alone, but there's something about him . . . I flinch as he looks up from the Kindle he's reading and his eyes meet mine. I don't shift my gaze, and pretend I'm not looking at him but at the blackness of the sea behind him. Then, thankfully, a waiter appears with more iced water and I turn to him instead.

Celeste has almost finished her red snapper and I've eaten more of the salad than I expected, along with one of the small warm bread rolls that accompanied it. When the waiter appears again and asks about dessert, Celeste chooses cheesecake while I opt for some fruit.

'If nothing else, I'd get into my wedding dress no problem now,' I observe when she comments on my healthy choices.

'You never had any problems with your wedding dress,' she protests. 'You looked fabulous in it.'

She was with me when I bought it. It's hanging up in my wardrobe at home. When we get back, I'll try to sell it online. I remind her it was always a bit tight but that it was very slinky.

She makes a face and scoops up the last of her cheesecake.

I pop a chunk of watermelon in my mouth.

We briefly ponder the possibility of having a nightcap before bed, but I'm suddenly exhausted and can hardly keep my eyes open. Celeste confesses to tiredness too. So we go back to the room.

For the first time in weeks, I fall asleep straight away.

Chapter 2

Ariel

I love deadlines. I love the whooshing
sound they make as they go by.

Douglas Adams

I'm watching the logo on my laptop go slowly round and round when the wall of heat hits me. Given that a horrible sleeting rain that really should be snow is hammering against the window, and that the temporary heater in my office has been cranked up to max for the past few hours with little discernible effect, I know the warmth is coming from within. I reach for the box on my desk and take out a tissue, mopping my now sodden brow, then my neck and finally (with an anxious glance out of the patio doors to be sure nobody is outside, although they shouldn't be, the mews is absolutely private) underneath my arms.

I throw the damp tissue in the waste-paper bin and lean back in my chair, furious with my body for doing its own thing yet again. Why do women have to put up with so much? First it's periods, which started for me on my thirteenth birthday and continued relentlessly, regular as clockwork, until my forty-fifth last summer. And now it's the menopause, a descent into the hell of unexpected sweating, brain fog and irritation levels that are off the chart. At least I hope it's the menopause that makes me feel one step away from exploding with rage at any given moment. Otherwise I'll really start worrying. Is there ever a time in a woman's life when she can just get on with it without having to think of how her body might ambush her? Honestly, it's a bloody minefield (pun not entirely unintended).

I have an appointment with my local doctor next week and I won't listen to any faff about natural remedies or lifestyle changes from him. I'll demand the best possible HRT immediately. I don't have time to be menopausal.

I catch sight of my reflection in the glass of the patio door and get up from my desk to inspect it more closely. My face is flushed, but despite my rosy cheeks and perspiring brow, I actually look reasonably good. Not just 'for my age', even if forty-five is the new thirty-five or whatever. I look good because I take care of myself. I've always done a good cleanse, tone and moisturise regime. I exfoliate regularly. I have facials every month. I do a thirty-minute yoga session before work every morning, I eat healthy foods whenever I can, though obviously there has to be a bit of leeway from time to time, and I try hard to only drink alcohol at the weekends, or if absolutely necessary for work. I know people will say there's no absolutely necessary time, but there is, I assure you.

Anyway, I don't look my age, and when I'm not doing my impression of someone battling Niagara Falls, I appear perfectly normal and well balanced. I pull my hair up from the nape of my neck, twist it and stick a pencil through it to hold it in a precarious bun. I was once a natural coppery brunette, but the greys started to appear long before the hot flushes, and now the colour is out of a bottle and needs regular touching up.

The hot flush ends as abruptly as it began, and I shiver. With impeccable timing, the boiler packed up this morning, which is why I'm using the hopelessly inefficient heater. The plumber I rang in a panic could barely contain his laughter when I asked if he could come out before the afternoon – he told me it'd be three days at the earliest. I tried alternative plumbers from the Local Heroes app, but there's nobody available to don a superhero outfit and come out any sooner. It seems that Dublin is a cesspit of broken boilers. If this weather keeps up, I'll be found, a block of ice, sitting frozen in front of my laptop while the intertwined ABA – Ariel Barrett Agency – logo still turns.

I rub my hands together and pull the heater closer to my desk. Then I look at my watch and subtract four hours. Charles will be having lunch now, stickler for routine that he is. I imagine him sitting on his balcony overlooking the sea, drinking a glass of wine – or maybe even a cocktail – his laptop open in front of him as he eats his chicken sandwich. (He's a stickler for his food routine too. Although the hotel is famed for the quality of its cuisine, I'm betting he's asking for chicken sandwiches for lunch and steak for dinner.)

I take out my phone.

Hope it's going OK

It's a few minutes before it pings in reply.

Wonderfully well

20

I'm glad to hear that. Do you want
to send anything to me?

No

Because the deadline is close

I know when the ****ing deadline is

I'm trying to help, that's all

Telling me about the deadline isn't helping

Sorry. I only meant

I stop as I see that he's continuing to type. I wait for the rest of his message.

It's pressure I don't need. You know I
don't work well under pressure

I'm not pressuring you

You damn well are

I hesitate for a while, then send a message that says I'll leave him to it. But it's taken me all my willpower not to actually phone him and tell him that he needs to get his arse into gear, and that his 'writing retreat' is hardly a retreat if he hasn't actually put any words on the page.

I grit my teeth, put the phone to one side and tap the

computer keyboard. I have other clients and other things to do rather than run around after Charles Miller. But I've always run around after Charles. Ever since the first day we met over fifteen years ago.

I was an ambitious young agent at Saxby-Brown, one of the UK's most prestigious literary agencies. Saxby-Brown has always had lots of big-name authors on its books, and it's a badge of honour for the agency that quite a number of them have won the Booker, or the Impac, or any one of the many literary prizes that are up for grabs throughout the year.

None of my authors at the time were prizewinners, because I generally looked after non-celebrity writers who sold enough to be profitable but not enough to get their books into the big promotions, the TV book clubs or the radio shows. Nevertheless, they were all wonderful, hard-working people and I was privileged to represent them. I truly hoped one day they'd be top-ten bestsellers and prizewinners too.

When Charles Miller's manuscript arrived on my desk (well, arrived by email as per our submission instructions, which was a positive start in itself; you wouldn't believe the number of hopefuls that ignore them), I began to skim through the covering letter, but it was so elegantly written that I started again and read it more slowly.

It was brief and concise, giving relevant information about his book while clearly conveying how much it meant to him. He said that he hoped he'd managed to write something that people would want to read, and added that he'd been writing for years but this was the first time he'd ever reached the end, and that in itself was so exciting he had to send it off to someone. And he'd picked me because he'd done some research and seen that I was looking for new voices and unique books and he hoped he fitted the bill on both counts.

I clicked on the attachment, hoping his novel would flow as fluently as his email. It did. I read all 90,000 words of it that evening.

I wanted to sign him right away.

Apart from the undoubted exquisiteness of his writing, the characters were real and alive. The story tugged at the heartstrings. I was absolutely convinced it would be a hit if it was handled in the right way by the right team. And I knew I was the right agent and Saxby-Brown definitely had the best team to find a publisher who'd support Charles and nurture his career.

Of course, the other part of potential success is the author themselves. If Charles had an engaging personal story, if he was attractive, if he got on well with people and could do a good interview, that would make it easier. The key was to sell him as well as his book. And that it was a poignant romance, skilfully portrayed by a man (fingers crossed, reasonably good-looking, articulate and not psychopathic), made it an excellent selling proposition. As I sat and planned, I realised I was getting too far ahead of myself. Right now, it was only about convincing a publisher that they'd have a bestseller on their hands.

I replied to Charles the next day asking if he could come and meet me at the office. His response was that he could, but not until the following week, as he'd have to take time off from his job as an accounts manager to come to London from Dublin, where he lived. I was surprised at hearing he was in accounts. He had the soul of a poet, not a number-cruncher.

In the days before virtual meetings were a thing, I told him I'd meet him wherever and whenever it suited him, and that if he preferred, I could come to Dublin.

I think I'd like to see your offices, he wrote. *Also, I haven't been to London for ages and I love the idea that I have to visit in order to meet my potential agent.*

I told him I was looking forward to meeting him.

When he turned up at the office, I knew I'd made the right call.

Despite my hopes for an interesting backstory (you know, like he'd recovered from a life-threatening illness, or a heart-rending divorce, always good for some column inches), Charles said his life was as dull as his accounting career. But it didn't matter. Because the only thing that did matter was Charles himself.

The man was a Greek god. The handsomest male author who'd ever walked into the Saxby-Brown office – and we've had our fair share. We've sold boy-band memoirs and biographies of actors and celebrities who've been filtered to within an inch of their lives. But Charles Miller, aged thirty-three and a half, wasn't a boy. He was a man. And the kind of man to make a woman go weak at the knees.

He had a lion's mane of thick golden hair, piercing blue eyes, and a jawline that was so square and strong it really did look as though it had been chiselled from granite. He was tall and broad-shouldered and he seemed to fill my small office both physically and with the strength of his character.

As I was a consummate professional, I didn't allow my knees to weaken. I told him to have a seat and I poured us both some water from the pitcher on my desk. (I needed the water. He was as cool as the proverbial cucumber.) I asked him about his book, what had inspired it, if he'd written it from his own experience, if he'd written anything else. And I asked him why he'd become an accountant.

He frowned slightly and scratched the red-gold stubble on his chin.

'Accounts manager,' he said. 'In a business. Not an actual accountant, though that's my qualification. I needed a job and I'm good with numbers.'

Most writers are terrible with numbers. I guessed I could spin something about a transition from facts and figures to romantic literature. But it would be nice to have something deeply personal too. I asked again about his inspiration. Had he had his heart broken like the hero of his novel?

'Not at all. I made it up,' he replied cheerfully. 'It came to me one afternoon when I was working on a spreadsheet.'

'I didn't realise spreadsheets could be so emotionally gripping.'

'Neither did I.' He smiled, and I was glad I was sitting down because my knees definitely would have buckled under his all-round hotness.

'It's a fabulous book, and if you allow me to represent you, I'll do my best to get it the success it deserves.'

'Wonderful.'

'But it doesn't always work,' I warned. 'You wouldn't believe how many books are published every year, and each author wants theirs to be a bestseller. Some very deserving ones end up selling only a few dozen copies. It's not fair, but it's the industry.'

'Life's not fair.' Charles shrugged. 'If it fails, I won't blame you.'

I couldn't help thinking that the perfect client had walked

into my office. Authors often do blame their agents when things don't go to plan, so having one say upfront that he wouldn't was refreshing. One way or another, I was going to try my hardest to make him a success.

Looking at him across the desk, the sunlight glinting off his magnificent hair, he reminded me of a young Hugh Grant without the stuttering awkward Englishness. Charles Miller was attractive, quietly confident and spoke in a smooth baritone that I knew would be ideal for radio. The whole package, of course, would be even better on TV.

But first I had to find him a publisher.

Which wasn't as easy as I'd expected, given how brilliant I thought his book was. However, the trend at the time was for complicated financial thrillers, and the charts were filled with novels with black-and-red covers and silhouettes of tall office blocks at night. Charles's was pure romance. If he'd been a female author, I would've brought it to a large publisher, suggested a floral cover with a breathlessly frothy blurb on the back, and marketed it as a chick-lit. But for Charles, I wanted to persuade publishers that it was a work of literature that would transcend genres.

Yet despite my relentless plugging, no one was biting. Eventually Graham Weston, the MD of Xerxes, a small independent publishing house, agreed to read it after I'd dropped him home, rather the worse for wear, from a launch party for one of Saxby-Brown's big-name authors. An author Graham really admired and wanted to poach from his current publisher. Which he ultimately did.

Graham read the manuscript and loved it. The rest, to overuse a cliché, is history.

Winter's Heartbreak was published in time for the following

Christmas, and it took off like Santa's reindeer on steroids. Readers loved it. Book clubs loved it. And reviewers were very, very generous with their praise. Charles ended up on every possible book programme, talking about it and sharing his insights into men with broken hearts as he wooed his audiences with his husky, mellifluous voice, his cool blue eyes and that amazing lion's mane of hair.

He knocked the financial thrillers off the charts, we sold the movie rights, he won the Booker, and Graham Weston bought me lunch at the Wolseley.

A couple of years later, no longer an accounts manager who wrote books, but a full-time author who was published in over forty languages, Charles was nominated for the Booker again, this time for *My Frozen Heart*, another heart-breakingly romantic novel. It didn't win any prizes, but it topped the bestseller lists for weeks and is currently in production with Netflix.

His life had changed by the time the movie of *Winter's Heartbreak* premiered, and so had mine. I'd become an agent that authors wanted to be represented by. My inbox was swamped with manuscripts and my confidence soared along with my career. I did my absolute best for every author I took on. None reached the dizzy heights of Charles Miller, but there were a lot of successes all the same. I celebrate every single publication day and every spot on the bestseller lists with all of them.

But Charles was, and always would be, my number one.

Not only because he was a brilliant writer.

Because he was also the man I was going to marry.

Chapter 3

Iseult

Women want love to be a
novel. Men a short story.
Daphne du Maurier

On the morning of what should have been my wedding day,
I wake up at six o'clock. I don't want to be awake this early.
I don't want to be awake at all. The only time I don't feel
that my heart has been ripped out and shredded is when
I'm sleeping. But I'm awake now and I know I'm not going
to fall asleep again, so I slide out of bed and pull on the
light robe that's lying over the back of a chair.

Celeste is out for the count, her head deep in the pillow,
muffling the tiniest gurgle of a snore that emits each time
she exhales. I slip on my flip-flops and gently ease the door
of the room open.

There's hardly any difference between the daytime and
night-time temperatures on the island. The air is warm
and balmy, and heavy with the scent of the flame-coloured
Barbados lilies and pure white butterfly jasmine that fill
the gardens. I can also sense the tang of the sea, and hear

the gentle thud of the waves upon the eponymous white sand.

As I arrive at the wedding gazebo, which is on a promontory and surrounded on three sides by the azure blue of the Caribbean, the sun rises and saturates the sky with golden light. A lone pelican dives, arrow straight, into the shimmering water, emerging a moment later and flying off towards the other side of the bay, his breakfast secure in his enormous beak.

The scent of the flowers and the beat of the waves is calming. Getting married here would have been romantic beyond words. Steve and I made the perfect choice of location. It's a pity we didn't make the perfect choice with each other.

I take my phone out of the pocket of the robe. I'd intended to leave it in the room, not wanting the temptation of it with me, but I reasoned that it might ring and wake Celeste, who'd worry about me because I never leave my phone behind. I convinced myself that was why I hadn't simply switched it to mute and left it under my pillow.

I unlock it and take a few photos, as if to further convince myself that the other reason I brought it was to photograph the sunrise. Then I check Steve's social media.

He hasn't posted anything since a photo at Florence airport last night (#HomewardBound #HeartInFlorence #BestTimeOfMyLife). Nothing about today. No pix of a deserted church or my returned engagement ring. No #WeddingDay #BigMistake #ShouldBeInParadise. Not that I expected anything from him to show that he knows what day today is. And not that he'd post anything even if he remembered.

I take a few more photos of the sunrise and post them to my own social media accounts. Steve still follows me, although I don't know if he looks at my posts. I'm not sure if he simply hasn't thought to block me from his, or if he wants me to know that he's having a great time without me.

I know I'm being silly. I know it's over and I shouldn't keep thinking about him. But I can't help it. You don't simply switch loving somebody off. Even if they've broken your heart. You can be furious and devastated at the same time. And you can want never to see them again and follow their socials at the same time too. But the fact that he's constantly in my mind makes me ask myself if I'm still in love with him despite everything. And if I'd take him back if he asked me.

I can understand why he got cold feet. It had all spiralled out of control a bit in the last few weeks before our split. Our conversations were entirely about weddings and houses – I was worried about where we'd live in the future, he insisted we'd find somewhere; I was juggling the constant emails from the White Sands, he was telling me he couldn't care less what kind of flowers were on the table; I wondered if we could livestream the wedding . . . actually he was quite into that and took it on himself to liaise with the IT guy at the hotel. Anyhow, there's no denying that planning the wedding meant romance had flown out the window and we were already bickering like an old married couple.

Maybe we could have fixed it.

Maybe it was never worth fixing.

I wish I knew.

I wonder will he look at my photos (#ParadiseIsland

#FeelingBlessed – I know, I know, it's complete bollocks, I'm feeling stressed more than anything!) and think he made a terrible mistake. I hope so.

I thought I'd be alone at this hour of the morning, but I'm not. I know everyone gets up early here, because Celeste and I have been out of bed by 7.30 every single day, and we've never been first down for breakfast. I didn't realise so many people were already out and about at dawn.

As I walk further through the gardens, with the sea framed by palm trees and hibiscus bushes, I notice a group setting up yoga mats beneath a large fabric sunshade strung between wooden pillars. A tall, very slim woman with cornrows in her hair asks if I'm joining them, and I shake my head.

'You can drop by any morning,' she tells me. 'No need to book at reception.'

'Sure.'

'We'll be happy to have you.' She flashes a wide smile at me before beginning to stream mellow music through speakers on the pillars.

'Let's start with sun salutations,' she tells the group, and they all raise their arms to the sky.

'Let's start with kickboxing,' I mutter under my breath, knowing that I don't have the power within me to be still and peaceful because my thoughts are far too turbulent to be cured by a bit of mindful stretching.

I continue along the path, which I discover leads to a small gathering of half a dozen more private villas. Steve and I considered booking a villa because they have spectacular sea views, a private beach and their own infinity pool, but they were very much out of our price range. Being completely frank, the entire hotel was out of our price range. But, you know, #NothingButTheBest #HappiestDayOfOurLives #NoExpenseSpared.

I lean against the picket fence that divides the villas from the rest of the hotel and remind myself that I'm actually very lucky compared to lots of other people in the world. I remember someone once telling me that whenever you have to remind yourself of your good fortune, you should also remind yourself that it's OK to feel your own unhappiness. But it seems horribly self-indulgent to be unhappy on Paradise Island.

As I contemplate degrees of happiness, a man wearing a pair of brightly coloured floral swimming shorts steps onto the decking outside one of the villas, stands at the edge of the pool for a moment, then dives in and swims the entire length underwater before surfacing again and shaking the droplets from his head. His body is toned and tanned, and it takes a moment before I recognise him as the same man Celeste and I saw on our first night, the one who was sitting alone at the best table in the restaurant and who's always at that table whenever he's there. He still looks vaguely familiar, and I rack my brains to try to remember where I've seen him before. As I stare at him, he looks directly at me, and even at a distance I blush with embarrassment. I give him a half-hearted nod and almost immediately turn away to walk quickly back to the room, where Celeste is up and dressed in shorts and a halter-neck top. She's pinned her dark hair up in a messy bun and looks casually stylish.

'Where were you?' she asks.

'Woke up early, went for a walk.'

'Everything all right?'

'Sure. Why wouldn't it be?'

I get dressed myself, then Celeste and I go to the restaurant, which, as always, is busy. I tell her about the enthusiastic guests swimming and doing yoga at 6.30 in the morning. Presumably, I add, they're the ones who get here first and bag all the good tables, and the sunloungers too. I don't mention our mystery man.

'You should've bagged a lounger with a towel yourself,' she says.

The hotel has a no-reservation policy for the abundance of loungers, but it's a policy that's ignored by most of the guests. So far each morning, much like the prized tables in the restaurant, the prized sunloungers have always been claimed by someone.

We're on our second cup of coffee when the man I saw swimming earlier walks in and is immediately brought to the secluded table again. We wondered if it was allocated to the guests at Coco Villa, the most exclusive accommodation in the resort, but now I know that's not the case and I say so to Celeste.

'Then how does he keep that table on permanent hold? He must have tipped them a fortune.'

'Maybe he likes his privacy. And I guess if you can afford to shell out to reserve it, why not?'

From a distance, I can observe him more keenly than before. He's wearing a cream polo shirt and maroon shorts, and there's no sign of the paunch that men often develop after the age of forty. He takes off his horn-rimmed sunglasses and props his iPad on the table in front of him.

'He must be an actor,' I say. 'I know I've seen him before, and not just here on the island.'

'Are you certain he's not a drug smuggler?'

'Never say never, but . . . never. He's very attractive, isn't he?'

'Too old for us.' Celeste pushes back her chair. 'Let's go. If we're much later to the beach, none of the sunloungers will be free.'

We find a relatively secluded spot at one of the White Sands' smaller coves, smother ourselves in Factor 30 and settle down with the books we bought at the airport.

Celeste, who likes to be challenged by her holiday reading, chose a Penguin Classic and is now engrossed in *The Portrait of a Lady* by Henry James. She tells me I'd like it because it's feministy. However, I'm happy with the latest Janice Jermyn page-turning crime caper, where every single chapter has both a suspect and a prospective victim. But much as I'm enjoying *The Mystery of the Missing Mallet*, my mind has wandered back to Steve's post, and I'm wondering what he meant when he said he'd left his heart in Florence. Did he meet someone there? Is he in love with another woman?

I reach into my tote and take out my phone. Out of the corner of my eye I see Celeste glance at me, but I keep my own gaze firmly on the phone's screen. It's none of her business what I'm looking at, and besides, most of the people on the beach are scrolling on their devices.

I open Find My Friends. Steve and I both allowed each other to share locations when he moved in with me, although I usually only used the app to see where he was when we were meeting up and he was late. He's a terrible timekeeper. I keep expecting him to change his privacy settings, but he hasn't. And OK, I know I shouldn't, but today was supposed to be our wedding day and I'd like to know what he's doing instead of marrying me. As the app zooms in on his location, I see that right now, four hours ahead of us in Ireland, he's at home at his parents' house in Templeogue.

It's kind of nice that he's stuck at home while I'm sunning myself in the Caribbean.

#StrongWoman #TheBetterBargain, I tell myself, and put the phone away again.

Chapter 4

Ariel

*The scariest moment is always
just before you start.*
                    Stephen King

An agent and her best client becoming lovers is probably a literary cliché, but it was impossible not to fall in love with Charles Miller. He was kind and thoughtful, clever and sympathetic, as well as being the sexiest man alive. I was astonished that he was still single, although I knew, because I'd quizzed him, that he'd had a couple of longer-term relationships in the past. However, none had become serious enough for him to live with the women involved. My questions about his love life were entirely professional – at least that's what I told myself – because I was trying to find interesting personal anecdotes that could be used for publicity.

The first time he came back to my apartment was after the Saxby-Brown and Xerxes teams had celebrated his Booker nomination in traditional fashion with champagne and cocktails at a trendy new Soho bar, and he was full of praise for me and all I'd done for him.

'You're my client,' I told him as I handed him the coffee I'd invited him in for (with the purest of motives, honestly; he'd muttered about needing to sober up before going back to his hotel). 'Of course I've done all I can for you.'

'I might be a client to you, but you're more than an agent to me.' His voice was huskier than ever. 'I mean it, Ariel. I . . . well . . . honestly, I don't know how I'd manage without you.'

And then we were in each other's arms and the coffee was forgotten as we stumbled to the bedroom and had hot, steamy sex with the curtains open and the lights of London cheering us on in the background.

It was as though a dam had burst. We couldn't keep our hands off each other. Charles was still living in Dublin, but he came to London every second weekend. We had sex in every room of my apartment, in the Saxby-Brown offices (late one evening, when the staff had gone home) and in the various hotels we took off to around the country. We were mad for each other, and it was the best time of my life.

We managed to keep our relationship under wraps for longer than I expected, but were eventually outed when another agent and his wife stayed at the same hotel as us one weekend. By then, though, I didn't care who knew. I was proud to be Charles's agent and equally proud to be his lover.

After that, when we were out together, we were the ultimate literary couple. I loved turning up to events with him, knowing I looked good, felt great and was well respected. I glowed from the inside out. My skin was dewy. And because I went to the gym every morning before work, my body was firm and lean.

I said all this, except for my body self-praise, one morning as we lay in bed together, exhausted from the publishing party we'd been to the night before and the great sex we'd had when we woke up.

'You make it sound as though we're a commercial arrangement.' He frowned.

'I've also just said I love you,' I told him. 'That's hardly commercial.'

'But you said it as though you were telling me to take an offer, not as though you really meant it.'

'After what we've just done, you think I don't mean it?' I raised an eyebrow and then burrowed under the light summer duvet, where I began to kiss him slowly.

'I . . .' He wasn't able to say anything else.

I'm even better at sex than at being an agent. After all, if a job's worth doing, it's worth doing well. One of my maternal granny's favourite clichés and one that I actually live by.

When we'd both regained our breath, he propped himself up on one arm.

'Move back to Dublin with me.'

I automatically glanced towards the full-length window, where I could see the Thames, busy with boats. I always considered the river to be the spine of the city, a proper working waterway, unlike Dublin's Liffey, which was under-utilised by comparison.

'I came to London to build my career,' I reminded him as I turned to face him again. 'Dublin's far too small a pond for me to fish in.'

'And yet you found me.'

'*You* found *me*.' I smiled.

'We found each other,' he amended. 'And I don't want to lose you. But we can't go on like this, commuting back and forth, seeing each other so infrequently.'

'We see each other twice a month. But perhaps I could come to Dublin the other weekends,' I suggested.

'It's still a peripatetic lifestyle, isn't it?'

'I wonder how many people use that word in actual day-to-day living,' I murmured. 'We travel back and forth because we want to.'

'What if I don't want to any more?'

He hauled himself out of bed and put on his shorts and a T-shirt. Then he opened the patio door and leaned over the glass balcony, staring into the distance.

I was worried now. He said he didn't want to lose me, but he didn't want things to go on like this either. We weren't exactly a long-distance relationship, but there were definitely stresses involved. I thought about this for a while longer before joining him and standing behind him. I slid my arms beneath his T-shirt, my fingers pushing through the hairs on his chest. He was the single most wonderful thing that had happened to me. I didn't want to lose him. But would I if I didn't go to Dublin with him?

I could see why he'd suggested it. After all, I'm a Dubliner by birth, although I moved to London after leaving college and rarely went back. There was no need. My parents sold the family home and retired to the island of Mallorca shortly after I landed my first job, thus instantly providing me with an excellent holiday location whenever I needed it. I don't have any close family in Ireland. So there was nothing to draw me back, although from time to time I missed the lilt of the accent and the easy wit and good humour of the city.

'I'm a London girl now,' I said as I rested my head against his back. 'Why don't you move here? It's surely a way more exciting place for a writer to be.'

'I don't need excitement,' he said. 'I don't write exciting books.'

'The literati are always very excited about your books,' I reminded him. 'Xerxes has made an excellent offer for the next one.'

'An entirely different thing,' he pointed out. 'As you should know.'

'I do. What,' I asked, 'would you expect me to do in Dublin? The company I work for is here.'

'There are publishers in Ireland,' he said. 'Agents too.'

'Not a lot,' I remarked.

'Of which?'

'Either, I guess.' I thought about it for a minute, the idea suddenly taking hold and bubbling up inside me. My long-term ambition had always been to have my own agency. I'd assumed it would be in London. But there was no reason I couldn't work from Dublin. It was a short flight, after all. Besides, communications were improving all the time. My heart began to beat faster. I could do it, if I wanted. And perhaps there'd be more space for me in Dublin, fewer other agents pitching to authors. Fewer authors too, of course.

'It's not like you have to be physically here,' said Charles, echoing my thoughts. 'You can Skype and conference-call just as easily as rushing off to someone's office. In fact, the way technology is going, I bet in a few years everyone will be working from out-of-office locations. Working from home has its advantages.'

'It's easy for you,' I said. 'Writers don't exactly need to

be in an office environment. But for me it's important to have face-to-face contact. I had to actually meet Graham Weston to interest him in your book, remember.'

'You could base yourself in Dublin and come to London every few weeks,' said Charles. 'Press the flesh and enjoy the social side of things. It's eminently doable.'

The more I thought about it, the more I thought he was right. And I loved the sound of the Ariel Barrett Agency – ABA. I'd picked the name years before. I accept it's not exactly original, but it has impact.

'Besides . . .' he turned around to look at me, 'I'd like the woman I love to share the amazing new house I've bought.'

I knew he'd been looking at property as a way to invest his earnings from *Winter's Heartbreak*, and he'd shown me images of some of the houses he was interested in. But I hadn't realised he was looking for a place to live. He always said he was happy in his rented apartment.

'I can't believe you've bought a house and you want me to live in it with you.' I couldn't keep the surprise out of my voice.

'You say it as though it's a bad thing.'

'Not at all. But it would be a big move for me. And . . . well . . . it'd be your house, not ours.'

'In the end I had to move quickly on the purchase,' he said. 'I didn't have time to talk it over with you. There was a lot of interest because it's in a lovely neighbourhood, so I just went for it.'

'Where is it?'

'Terenure.'

I nodded. I was probably more familiar with the area than

him, having grown up in Ballyboden, a mere 4 kilometres away, whereas his family home was in Waterford, which is about 160 kilometres from Dublin.

'You'll love it. Period. Detached. Double-fronted. Five bedrooms. Two reception. Lovely dining room. Massive kitchen.'

'You sound like an estate agent.'

'I'm trying to sell it to you,' he said. 'I do feel a bit bad about not bringing you to see it first.'

'You don't have to consult me about everything,' I told him. 'I'm your agent, not your wife.'

He walked back into the apartment. I followed him. He reached into the pocket of the jacket he'd slung over a chair the night before and took out a distinctive blue box, which he handed to me.

I opened it and looked at the Tiffany's solitaire inside.

'Ariel Barrett,' he said. 'I know you're a free-spirited, independent, successful woman who doesn't need a man in her life to be happy. But I'd be honoured if you'd become my wife.'

I was all those things. I was also a woman who hadn't planned on getting married at all.

But I was in love with Charles, and that changed everything.

So I said yes.

Our engagement was mentioned in the trade papers and briefly in the national media too. Everyone loved the romance of it, the unknown agent who'd turned an unknown author into a mega success and who'd fallen in love in the process. However, when I revealed that I planned to move to Ireland with Charles and open my own agency in Dublin, my closest friends worried that I was sounding the death knell of my career. Over drinks with Ekene, another Saxby-Brown agent, and Maya, one of my favourite book publicists, they outlined their concerns about the plan. But despite my initial reservations, I was excited. I told them times were changing and I didn't need to be tethered to a desk in London to do the best for my authors. I outlined my plans for the ABA and told Maya that I'd need someone to do PR work for me in London and that I hoped she'd be on board.

'We're all strong, confident women,' I said. 'We should support each other. Even if we might end up competing with each other sometimes.' I turned to Ekene.

'You're right,' she said. 'It doesn't matter that we're working for different agencies, we'll always be friends. Thankfully the book world isn't as awful as some other industries when it comes to friendships. If I hear of authors that might suit you better than me, I'll let you know.'

'And vice versa,' I promised her.

So Charles and I got married, I left Saxby-Brown, and I pitched ABA as a home for authors who wrote strong contemporary fiction, romantic fiction and thrillers. I guess I was basically covering almost all types of fiction except sci-fi, horror and erotica, though that didn't stop them arriving in my inbox anyway.

Some of my Saxby-Brown novelists came with me, others stayed safe in the arms of the bigger company. I understood and I didn't mind. In a relatively short period of time, ABA had secured a list of excellent writers who hoped I'd work the same magic for them as I had for Charles Miller. I didn't manage to get an author shortlisted for the Booker, but two of my new clients quickly established themselves as strong sellers. I'd deliberately chosen them because I thought they'd do well commercially. Janice Jermyn wrote cosy crime (a misnomer if ever there was one – anyone who's been a victim of a crime knows it's never cosy) and Lucy Conway was the author of glamorous romantic fiction that I reckoned would sell by the shelfload.

I was right in both cases. The high-body-count murders of Janice's books, which she now produces at the rate of two a year, always make the bestseller lists. And Lucy's exotic blockbusters are the mainstay of airport bookshops everywhere. I love both women, as much for their friendship as for their brilliant writing and their excellent contribution to the agency's bottom line. But back then they were only starting out, and my main income was from Charles's royalties as well as the massive advance I'd managed to secure for his next novel, even though he hadn't a clue what he was going to write yet.

Charles brought me to visit the Dublin house and I immediately saw why he'd bought it and why it would be perfect for us. Additionally, I thought as we walked around the garden, the mews at the back would make an ideal office for me.

Before I could lay claim to it, however, it became our temporary home, because wonderful though the main house was, it needed a lot of work to make it habitable. The builders had estimated five months for the renovations. It took double that, and as I said to Charles afterwards, the fact that we didn't kill each other during that time was a miracle. Working and living in the same space together while also trying to oversee the house makeover was harder than I'd anticipated. Charles has a habit of speaking his dialogue out loud, and it didn't matter to him that I might be on the phone trying to put together a deal as he wandered around the mews loudly quoting from his work in progress. When I'd first met him at Saxby-Brown, I'd thought he was one of the most practical writers I'd ever met, but his practicality extended only to the business part of it, not the actual writing, where his process was chaotic. He would often interrupt me, wanting my opinion on a particularly tricky paragraph, completely oblivious to what I might be doing at the time, arguing with me if I did come up with a suggestion and then arguing with himself about the merits of the entire book.

We were both getting tetchy by the time he decided to take himself off to a tiny cottage on the west coast of Ireland because he needed somewhere away from the sound of jackhammers and cement mixers to write. I was relieved, although it meant that Charles's interruptions were replaced by even more interruptions from the builders, with their daily questions about knocking down walls and plastering ceilings. However, the builders were easier to deal with than Charles, and as he was getting more writing done at the cottage, it was ultimately a win-win situation overall.

The cottage actually belonged to Charles's family, having been passed down by his great-grandmother, and the Millers shared time there among themselves. Although I was grateful for his absence during the week, I visited him at weekends, when we'd talk about his book, swim in the Atlantic Ocean and picnic in the cottage garden with its stunning view over Clew Bay. It was almost like our original courtship, when he'd travelled to London every fortnight to see me. Most of our time there was idyllic, the sex was fantastic, and the only fly in the ointment was the occasional weekend when Charles's mother, Pamela, joined us.

Pamela and I had, as the Irish expression goes, somewhat 'taken agin' each other when Charles had first introduced us. Initially I'd thought we might get on, as he'd told me that she was an avid reader and loved books. Also, she was as unlike the traditional trope of a doting Irish mammy as it was possible to be. She was stylish and businesslike, and very much used to getting her own way. I admired her and wasn't overawed by the force of her personality, which she seemed to take as a personal insult. I was also a little too London for her, too sassy, too metropolitan elite. She actually did use the words 'metropolitan elite' when we met. Over the years she would throw in 'woke' too, possibly because the agency supports a charity that champions ethnic voices in publishing. She also liked to tell me how I should run my business and how I should promote Charles's work. At first I gritted my teeth and nodded, but over time I began to point out, probably too sharply, that I knew how to do my own job.

The thing is, Pamela was, and still is, a very successful woman in her own right, and she believed she always had something useful to bring to the table. She was the one who added a proper restaurant to the family pub's more basic food offering, and when her husband died and Charles's brother, Nick, took it over, she further augmented the Miller business empire by opening a café a few doors down from it. After Charles's success with *Winter's Heartbreak*, she restyled the café as a literary hang-out, with framed posters of famous Irish authors on the walls. Charles is in pride of place, along with Yeats, Joyce and Beckett. So far, Edna O'Brien is the only female author deemed good enough for Pamela's gallery. She chairs a book club that regularly meets there, and has been quoted several times in the papers talking about the arts. She's also been a guest speaker at a number of businesswomen's functions as well as some literary events. She's a powerhouse, and not only for her age (she's nearly eighty). It's a shame we didn't hit it off.

Maybe that would have made all the difference.

Despite the chaos of the building work going on around me back in Dublin, my productivity soared and I felt confident about the growth of the agency, even if, as I said jokingly to Ekene, I was working out of a derelict house at the back of another derelict house. She was very encouraging and told me that ABA was becoming more and more respected for the calibre of the authors who had joined me. When I rang Charles to tell him this, he told me that it was exactly what I deserved because I was a human dynamo.

I've always liked the idea of being a human dynamo.

When the work on the house was eventually finished, I was very excited to move into the newly named Riverside Lodge. Given that I'd had a lot of input into the renovation and the decoration, it felt very much like my home, even though I hadn't been part of the purchasing process.

'At least it won't take as long to do up the mews,' I said as Charles and I looked down the garden from the window of the room he'd designated as his writing sanctuary in the main house. 'It's not a huge space and won't need much to bring it up to spec.'

'D'you know, I think it's fine the way it is,' he remarked.

'Haven't we been living there for nearly a year with no problems? I really don't want to be distracted by more building work. I'll need quiet time for my editing.'

I wasn't going to let him divert me from the renovation of the mews by talk of his book. I told him I couldn't possibly work out of a shed and that I needed a proper office. Charles kept suggesting different rooms in the house, while I continued to make the case for the mews, reminding him that it had always been earmarked for me.

'It's just . . . I was thinking . . . the mews might make a nice granny flat for Mum,' he said.

'You're not serious?' I looked at him in horror. 'You want her to live here? I thought she was happy with her café and book club. And isn't she close to your brother and his wife in Waterford?'

'I wasn't thinking about it for right now,' he said. 'But who knows what the future might bring.'

'Charles, I can't work in the same house as you, even a house this size,' I said. 'The mews was always supposed to be mine. If your mother eventually needs more care, we can have a family discussion about it then. Perhaps we should—'

'Please let me decide what's best for my own mother,' he said.

'Of course.' I backed off. 'But the mews—'

'I can't talk about this now,' he said. 'I'm supposed to be writing.' And he stomped out of the room, slamming the door behind him. I stayed where I was, my heart thumping and hardly able to control my breathing. There was so much going on in that conversation, in Charles's unexpected and unwanted suggestion, that I couldn't even process it.

An hour later, as I was sitting in the upstairs room of the mews, the one I'd thought would be a great place to keep my authors' published books and their manuscripts, Charles tapped on the door and came in.

'I'm sorry,' he said.

'What about?'

'Springing a change of plan on you.'

'The plan has been changed then?'

'No,' he said. 'It hasn't. It's just that when we were in Mayo, Mum talked about growing older and how she'd manage, and she mentioned the mews and . . .' He shrugged helplessly.

'You told her she could live here?'

'I'm not that daft.' He gave me a sudden smile. 'I told her it was falling down and we couldn't afford to do it up yet.'

'You don't want to renovate so she can't stay here? Or you don't want to renovate it as an office so she can?'

'I'm being silly,' he said. 'She put me under a bit of pressure and . . . You're right about this, Ariel. When the times comes, we should all sit down and talk about it.'

'But in the meantime, we have to pretend we can't do up the mews?'

'No,' he said. 'It was meant to be your office and that's what it'll be.'

'And when she visits and sees it?'

'We'll tell her it was cheaper to do it up as an office than a granny flat.'

'I *do* love you, you know,' I said. 'Even if you're a bit mad sometimes.'

'I love you too,' said Charles.

I pulled his polo shirt over his head and he unbuttoned my blouse, and we made love on the space where my office desk is now.

I sometimes relive that moment when I'm sitting here looking at my Agent of the Year awards (I've won twice) and my lovely shelves packed with my authors' books.

Despite everything, the memory still makes me smile.

An intense squall of rain hitting the patio window startles me. I look out at skies that are even greyer and more laden with clouds than before. The east-facing mews is lovely in the summer, when it gets the morning sun and stays warm all day, but can be miserable in winter, when the days are short and the skies leaden. I forward a few emails to my part-time assistant, Shelley, who mostly works from her home in Greystones, a seaside town not far from Dublin. She's super-efficient, and the fact that we only meet in person once or twice a month doesn't impact on the excellent personal and professional relationship we have.

The sleet has turned to snow. I shiver violently and envy Shelley's more benign working conditions. I've an appointment with a potential client in an hour and originally told her to come to the office, but the lack of heating and the weather outside means that it's less than inviting. I don't want Francesca Clooney thinking my business isn't doing well enough to heat the place. I want my office to radiate confidence and success, and sitting here freezing our buns off certainly won't do that.

I pick up my phone and send her a text telling her I have an electrical problem at the office and suggesting we meet in the Shelbourne instead. Seeing your prospective agent in the elegant surroundings of one of Dublin's best-loved hotels is what every aspiring author dreams of, so hopefully she'll feel excited about that. Of course, it's not always elegant surroundings and exciting meetings, but at least it's a good start.

I pull on my red parka and leave the freezing office, locking the door behind me while glancing towards the red-brick house at the far end of the garden. Despite its undoubted grandeur, it looks forlorn in the winter gloom. The only light is from the upstairs landing, glowing gently through a frosted window. One of the bathrooms, I know. With lovely underfloor heating.

I shiver again, then turn away and unlock my car, an electric Mini, perfect for around town. I love it, and I think it reflects the more creative side of my work, even though when I walk into a meeting I always want to appear as polished and professional as possible. Which is why I keep a bag full of make-up and serums in the glove compartment, and why I plan to change from my lovely warm boots and toasty parka into fashionable heels and my Prada jacket as soon as I get to the hotel.

I arrive early, assuming Francesca will be early too and wanting to have time to fix my face as well as change my shoes. I spend ten minutes in the Ladies' trying to make myself look as great as I did fifteen years ago (and obviously failing, though things could be worse; at least I haven't sweated all the make-up off), and am sitting at a table in the bar with a glass of sparkling water and my iPad open in front of me when my prospective client arrives. My heart sinks when I see she's accompanied by an older man, who, judging by their likeness, is probably her father. Francesca is in her mid twenties, and it's my experience that people of her age seem to rely a lot more on their parents than I did in my twenties. My father wouldn't have dreamed of coming to a business meeting with me. I wouldn't have dreamed of asking him.

I stand up and give a small wave to attract their attention.

She walks over to me and smiles, a wide, attractive smile that I think will look good on jacket covers, then introduces the man as her dad, Raymond.

'Nice to meet you, Mr Clooney.' I extend my hand and he takes it, gripping it too firmly and shaking it too hard. 'Can I get you anything?'

'A soda water for me, as I'm driving the soon-to-be bestselling author today. But Francesca will have a glass of champagne. To celebrate.'

There's nothing to celebrate yet, but I order the water and the champagne anyway. I'm really keen to sign Francesca, who has a lot of raw talent and who's written a very readable historical police procedural set in Ireland during the Second World War (a time known somewhat prosaically in Ireland as the Emergency, the title Francesca has chosen for her novel). It has all the classic tropes – a hunky police officer whose wife has left him, a superior officer more interested in the politics of his position than catching culprits, a feisty secretary who's secretly in love with the handsome hero, and a clever plot with a couple of unexpected twists.

I know I can sell this book. And I'm confident that it could be successful.

'So.' Raymond Clooney takes an old-fashioned Filofax and a heavy ballpoint pen from the briefcase he's set down beside him. 'Let's get down to business. How much will my little girl make from this venture?'

'Before we talk about money, we need to talk about what I'll do to make sure your book has the best publisher possible.' I speak directly to Francesca.

'Any publisher would be lucky to get her,' Raymond Clooney says before she has a chance to open her mouth. 'It's a brilliant read.'

'Absolutely.' I nod in agreement and then tell him that it's never a smooth road to publication and that even the most amazing authors have been rejected more than once. 'Stephen King got thirty rejections for *Carrie*,' I add for emphasis. 'But he's a legend now.'

Raymond is having none of it. He insists that Francesca is a literary genius and it will be entirely my fault if she's not recognised as such from the get-go.

'I will do my absolute utmost to ensure that she gets the right publisher for her lovely book,' I assure him.

'That's not good enough,' he tells me. 'We want guarantees. Guarantees of a bestselling book and guarantees of the amount she'll make.'

If only there were guarantees in publishing. But there aren't. I try to explain this, but it's like talking to a brick wall.

'I looked you up.' Raymond Clooney smooths down the page in his Filofax while Francesca shoots me an embarrassed look. 'You're rather succeeding downwards, aren't you?'

'Excuse me?'

'Well, you've got that Charles Miller bloke. I never rated him. Saw him on the *Late Late* blabbering on about his novel years ago. Tried reading it. Absolute tripe.'

'Charles Miller won the Booker prize,' I remind him. 'And—'

'And I heard he was suffering from writer's block and hasn't written a book in more than five years.' Raymond goes on to tell me the many ways in which my best client has failed and how I'm responsible.

'What do you do yourself?' I ask, instead of trying to argue with him.

'Sales and marketing,' he replies. 'So I'll be a great asset to Frannie. I'll be able to run a campaign for her.'

Oh God. He truly does think he's an expert.

I turn to Francesca. 'And what do you want from an agent?' I ask.

'Whatever's best for my book.'

She's lovely. She really is. I'd like her as a client if it didn't seem to be a package deal with her dad.

'Do you trust me to deliver that for you?'

'I . . .' She looks hesitantly at Raymond.

'Come to us with a list,' he says. 'Tell us who's interested. We'll choose and you get eight per cent.'

I take my standard agency contract out of my bag and put it on the table.

'Any agreement is between me and the author,' I say. 'And as you can see here, the author is Francesca. And my fee is fifteen per cent.'

'Eight and a half.'

'I'm sorry, but—'

'It's clear you know nothing about business and nothing about negotiating and you won't get the best deal for Frannie.'

I'm on the verge of losing my temper, something I've never done with a prospective client before, when he stands up and says he's wasted enough time with me.

'But Dad . . .' Francesca looks doubtful.

'You know I'm the only one who'll do their best for you,' he tells her. 'You can trust *me*, not her.'

Francesca looks at me apologetically before following her father out of the bar. She hasn't touched her champagne.

I take the glass, decant the golden liquid into my own, swallow it in a single gulp and remind myself that it's always important to take the rough with the smooth.

Nonetheless, from start to finish this has been a shitty day.

Chapter 5

Iseult

The beach is not a place to work;
to read, write or to think.
Anne Morrow Lindbergh

The first wedding at the White Sands since we arrived is taking place today. From the balcony of Room 501, I'm watching the staff carry armfuls of flowers to the gazebo where the ceremonies are held. I try not to imagine how my own wedding might have been, but I can't help picturing me and Steve standing in the bower together, vowing to love each other till death us do part.

Thinking you'll be together for life is pretty optimistic, isn't it? For me and Steve, that could've been more than fifty years. I wonder if we'd have stayed the pace. Well, clearly not when we didn't even get to the starting gate. So perhaps he did me a favour. I've got to look at it like that.

The women carrying the flowers are joined by another couple of staff members, this time carrying flute glasses and silver champagne buckets. They're laughing and chatting, although I can't hear what they're saying.

'I wonder if they become blasé about it,' remarks Celeste as she joins me on the balcony. 'Weddings are practically an industry here.'

'Love isn't an industry,' I protest.

'Hah!' She gives me a sceptical look. 'Valentine's Day, anyone? An excuse for restaurants and florists to hike up their prices.'

'OK, OK, I'll give you Valentine's.' Though I'm remembering Steve bringing me to a gorgeous wine bar in the docklands and sharing a lovely meal overlooking the river, and it was so romantic I didn't care about the price. Not that I had to. We normally split the bill when we went out but for Valentine's Day he insisted on paying.

'I'm sorry,' says Celeste. 'Love isn't only about performative gestures in public.'

'No.'

Now I'm thinking of the proposal balloons again. I was so sure then that he was the one. And I was sure he was sure I was right for him.

If something had happened, if there'd been a massive row or he'd found someone else, I might have understood it better. But his vague 'I'm not ready' makes me feel that it was more about me than him. I wish I knew what it was. Why I wasn't good enough for him. I get some comfort from the fact that there hasn't been one post on his social media of him with another woman, not even in Italy, but I still feel as though I've let myself down somehow.

'Are you sure you don't mind me heading off without you?' It takes a moment for Celeste's words to filter through. She booked a catamaran trip around the island earlier. As I'm not keen on being on the water, I decided not to join her and told her I'd be perfectly happy on the beach, but with the wedding due to take place later, I think she's worried I'll have some kind of bridal meltdown. If she knew I'd been thinking about Steve's proposal, she'd be even more worried.

'I'll be fine,' I promise her. 'I'm going to read my book and work on my tan.'

'Because I won't go if you don't want me to.'

'Of course I want you to. I'll be fine here. I want to read my book, honestly.'

I walk with her down to the beach, where other guests are already awaiting the arrival of the catamaran. I stand at the edge of the sand, allowing the water to wash over my toes and thinking that perhaps I should have gone after all.

Then the catamaran arrives, bobbing up and down dramatically, and I'm happy with my decision again. The crew members help their passengers on board, and I take photos of Celeste as the boat moves slowly away from the beach, then turn back towards the hotel and head to the room.

This is the first time I've been properly alone since we got here. I don't count the day of my early-morning walk because Celeste was nearby. Now she's sailed off and I feel . . . well, a bit liberated, if I'm totally honest. Because of course she's been kind and generous and lovely, but that's made me have to be brave and strong and outwardly cheerful all the time. And it's been hard.

I know I said I was going to lie on the beach and work on my tan, but I'm not in the mood to do that right now. I feel the need to be active. So I slap on some more sunscreen, pop a baseball cap on my head and retrace my steps from earlier in the week, past the private villas where I saw the man dive into the pool. Other than in the restaurant, where he continues to sit alone at the same table, I haven't noticed him anywhere in the resort. He's never on the beach during the day, or in the bar at night. I've decided he's some kind of recluse. Or else he's a golfer and out all day, although he's not part of the group of men and women who regularly leave the hotel in the mornings with their bags and clubs, and who are generally very sociable.

I wave at one of them, a woman in her sixties who Celeste and I got talking to last night. She's a widow, and she and her husband used to come here every few years to play a couple of local courses and chill out. He died less than a year ago, but she chose to come again anyway, and has joined up with the group. She's friendly and optimistic and doesn't show her grief outwardly, but I'm sure it's there.

She continues in one direction and I go the other, towards the less developed part of the resort, where there are a number of small rocky coves. According to the website, people can fish there, but I'm not sure why any of the guests would. It's not like they'll cook the catch for dinner.

The first cove I reach is more of a narrow inlet, and there's no beach, merely shingle that crunches underfoot. The second is wider, but also mainly shingle, and I'm thinking that I've done enough Famous Five exploring when I see yet another cove, this time with a small beach. I think it might be a nice place to sit and contemplate life, even though I have to access it by scrambling over some rocks. As I jump from the last, I land awkwardly and cry out in shock.

It takes me a moment or two to catch my breath, and then I tentatively test my ankle, which definitely twisted in my fall. It's a bit sore, but nothing too awful, which I'm thankful for, because I'm trying to imagine clambering over those rocks again and getting back to the hotel with a dodgy ankle, and thinking that coming to this isolated spot on my own was actually quite stupid. I walk slowly to the water's edge and allow the cool waves to wash over my feet.

When I turn around, I realise it's not as isolated as I thought. I'm not alone.

Restaurant man is here, half hidden behind a twisted palm tree. He's sitting under a parasol, a small folding table in front of him. On the table is a thin sheaf of paper. He's not looking at the paper, though, he's looking at me.

'Hi,' I say as cheerfully as I can. 'Sorry if I'm disturbing you.'

He says nothing, and I walk slowly up the beach, keeping my weight off my bad ankle.

'I'm going to sit here for a few minutes until my ankle is OK, then I'll be out of your hair,' I tell him. Closer to, I'm guessing he's in his fifties rather than his forties. Pretty fit with it, though. He's wearing a light T-shirt that allows his muscles to show, and it's obvious he works out.

'This is a private beach.' He's clearly irritated. 'I come here precisely because it's private.'

'It's part of the resort,' I respond. 'So not private if you're a guest. And I am too.'

'I know,' he says. 'I've seen you.'

Is it good to have been noticed? Or has he noticed me in a 'how the hell can she and her friend afford to be here' kind of way?

'Iseult O'Connor,' I say. 'I've seen you too.'

'After the poet or the legend?'

'Neither,' I reply when I realise he's asking about my

name. I'm actually named after my great-grandmother, who I never knew and who was once arrested for throwing a stone through the window of a government office as part of a votes-for-women campaign. But I do know the legend of Tristan and Iseult (or Isolde, as she's also known) and I also know that the poet is Iseult Gonne, who would have lived around the same time as my great-grandmother. Not that any of this is of the slightest interest to the man sitting at the folding table.

A puff of breeze rustles through the palms, and as I feel it reach my shoulders, the pages in front of him rustle too, and are then gently lifted and float on the air, spinning in all directions.

'Oh bloody fucking hell!' he cries.

I wasn't sure earlier, because his accent held a mid-Atlantic twang that could be from anywhere, but his unapologetic swearing is pure Irish.

He gets up from the table, which topples over, and begins to rush after the pages. I manage to collect the ones that have blown in my direction, but at least half a dozen end up in the sea and are almost immediately carried out of sight.

'Now look what you've done,' he says as he returns and rights the table. 'An entire morning's work wasted.'

'I hardly think it's my fault,' I protest. 'I don't control the wind.'

'You distracted me.'

'You should've put a stone on them or something.'

'So it's *my* fault?'

'Yes.'

He glares at me, and I shrug. I don't know what he's getting so worked up about. I'm sure he's got all his data on a computer somewhere. Although I notice as I glance down at the top page in my hand that it's full of handwritten comments. I hand the sheets to him.

'A whole morning ruined.' He groans.

'It's not completely ruined,' I say. 'You've got most of the pages. A few are probably on the way to the Bahamas or something, but I'm sure you can replicate whatever notes you made.'

'I can't replicate them.' He's practically snarling now. 'They came from somewhere deep inside and I don't know if I'll ever find that place again.'

I've no idea what he means, so I stay silent.

'I can't do this any more.' He puts the pages on the table and this time weighs them down with a large stone. 'I thought I could, but I can't.'

'Do what?'

He doesn't answer, but instead puts his head in his hands and then rests both on the table.

'Are you all right?' I ask.

He remains silent.

To be honest, I'm a bit worried about him now. And about me. I wouldn't have put him down as some kind of crazed killer or anything, but you never do know, do you? Women and girls trust men all the time before realising they shouldn't have.

'Well,' I say, 'I'll be off. Ouch.' The ouch is because a sharp twang of pain has shot through my ankle. 'Um, I'll be off in a minute.' I sit on a nearby tuft of grass and rotate my ankle gently. It isn't even swollen, so I know it'll be fine, but it obviously needs a little more TLC before I take it walking again.

'What part of Ireland are you from?' he asks suddenly.

'Dublin. Marino. And you?'

'The south side.' He gives me a half-smile when I tell him I won't hold that against him.

'Do you ever get stuck?' His tone is far more conciliatory now, mellow and actually quite soothing.

'Stuck where? How?' I'm wondering if he's talking about Dublin's notorious traffic, or about Northsiders and Southsiders preferring to stay on their respective sides of the river, but he tells me he means work. He wants to know if I ever don't know what I should be doing.

'Not really,' I reply. 'I follow procedures and the outcome is inevitable.'

'Do you think about work all the time?'

'My line of work is all about a single day. Of course repercussions can happen later, but basically I go in, do my job and go home. It's why I love it.'

From his original pose of seeming to look past me, he now removes his sunglasses and stares straight at me.

'What do you do?' he asks.

He looks startled when I tell him. People often are. In the same way they'd be startled, I think, if I said I was a tax inspector. Because everyone has a moment where they've brought home too many cigarettes or too much booze from a holiday, or made a slightly suspect claim on their tax return. Minor things that nobody gets too exercised about, to be honest. It wasn't the job I expected to get when I was transferred from Agriculture to Revenue, but when the opportunity came up, I thought it might be interesting. Besides, I don't like being stuck behind a desk. I like being out and about.

'I can't see you in Dublin Airport calling stressed passengers to one side,' he says.

'I don't work at the airport,' I tell him. 'I'm based in the docks. I check maritime traffic, not people coming home from their jollies.'

'You mean freight?'

'Mostly,' I say. 'Lorries coming in from everywhere. It's a dirty job but somebody's got to do it.' I smile at this. I love my job, even if I do get a bit grubby from time to time. But you know how it is, you say things to people to keep the conversational ball rolling. Not that I'm entirely sure I want a conversation with him.

'I see.' He's looking at me appraisingly now.

'And you?' I ask. 'What do you do that has you working when you should be on your holidays? Because don't tell me you've come to the White Sands to work. It's a place for total relaxation.'

'Not for all of us.'

I wait. He waits. I think he's expecting me to say something, but I'm not sure what it is. And then I realise that I thought he was familiar before and he's definitely familiar now. It's his mid-Atlantic accent that's ringing a bell. But he's not a movie star, crap as I am at recognising them. I know most of the older ones and I can't place him in anything. A singer, perhaps? One of those tenor trios that were all the rage years ago? Something like that?

'I'm working on my novel,' he tells me. 'I came here for peace and quiet.'

'Your novel?'

'Charles Miller,' he says.

And now I remember. He was on *The Late Late Show* a while back, talking about the movie of his bestselling book.

'Oh, right. Pleased to meet you.'

'You don't know who I am, do you?' He puts the question after a moment's pause.

I tell him that I saw him on TV.

'Have you read my books?'

This is awkward. I think about faking it, and then shake my head.

'I'm more of a crime and thriller reader,' I admit.

'I see.' He says this as though I've just admitted to murdering kittens. 'I suppose in your line of work it shouldn't come as a surprise.'

'I like crime,' I tell him. 'It's satisfying. Mostly the bad guys get what's coming to them, which isn't always the case in real life.'

'You have a point,' he concedes.

'I'll go and leave you to your muse,' I say eventually, standing up and wiping sand from my shorts. I'm still hobbling a little, but my ankle is much better now, something I tell Charles Miller when he asks if I'm all right.

'Nice talking to you,' I say, even though it wasn't.

He's concentrating on his notes and doesn't reply.

I limp back the way I came.

When I get back to the room, I change into a swimsuit and do what I told Celeste I'd be doing: lying on the beach with my Janice Jermyn, where there's a satisfyingly high body count and the murderer is always revealed at the end.

But after a while, I take out my phone and google Charles Miller. It seems his rise was pretty meteoric after his debut won the Booker and was made into a movie; his second novel is 'in development', whatever that means. His most recent books don't seem to have been as popular, because they've neither won prizes nor appear to be in development, but he's clearly done pretty well nonetheless. There's very little under personal information in Wikipedia, just that he was born in Waterford, graduated from UCD and is forty-nine. I do a little more digging and see some photos of him accepting his Booker Prize, and others at the movie premiere over ten years ago. There's a good-looking brunette by his side in these, and I wonder if she's a girlfriend or partner or wife. A further search brings up a piece headlined 'An Agency Romance', which says that Charles and Ariel Barrett, the agent who discovered him, have become engaged. It goes on to say that they're the hottest couple in London right now. I wonder where she is while he's alone on Paradise Island. If I was his fiancée or wife, I wouldn't be too keen on being left behind in London while he pretended to work beneath tropical skies.

I abandon Google and open Find My Friends instead. Steve is currently travelling along the M50 motorway that circles Dublin. I take a photo of the view in front of me and post it to my Instagram #PeacefulParadise.

I pick up the Janice Jermyn again, and next thing I know, the smell of meat on the barbecue wakes me up. I've been asleep for almost an hour, which is unheard of for me on a sunlounger. But I feel surprisingly rested, and surprisingly hungry too, even though I had an enormous breakfast earlier. I remind myself that it was six hours ago and so I'm entitled to be ravenous. If nothing else, this holiday has seen me regain my appetite, and probably a few of the kilos I lost after Steve and I split.

I haul myself off the lounger, pull on my patterned

sundress, and make my way towards the main building, where a queue has already formed at the barbecue. I check in at the restaurant and am allocated a table, then I order a glass of wine and join the BBQ line, where I opt for grilled fish, chicken wings and a selection of salads. Yes, those kilos are most definitely on the way back.

I'm about to tuck in when I see Charles Miller making his way to his usual table. He's wearing a maroon polo shirt and shorts, along with deck shoes and a panama hat. I quite like the hat. It makes a statement that the baseball caps more usually worn by the male guests don't.

I don't want him to see me staring, so I open my book and start to read, though it's actually very difficult what with the sauce from the chicken wings making my fingers sticky as well as rolling inelegantly down my chin. When it comes to BBQs, I'm a messy eater. I'm aware of him walking through the restaurant with an empty plate, but then I get to an engrossing part of the novel (an unexpected additional murder in Chapter Fifteen) and am startled when I realise he's standing beside my table. This time his plate is loaded with food.

'Are you eating alone?' he asks.

I swallow some potato salad before I can answer.

'Yes. My cousin's on a trip.'

'Your cousin?'

'The girl I'm on holiday with.'

'Oh yes. The pretty one.'

Never let it be said that Charles Miller is tactful. Perhaps my expression gives me away, because his look is apologetic. 'I'm not making comparisons,' he says hastily. 'Just that she's stereotypically pretty.'

But he should. I do all the time. Celeste is the glossier version of me. Her hair, dark brown like mine, although with lovely russet undertones, is long and curly, while mine is short and spiky, and her skin is flawless, whereas I'm prone to breakouts. She's taller, better proportioned and was always the heartbreaker.

'You've more character.' Charles Miller digs the hole a bit deeper.

'For someone who's supposed to be good with words, you're doing a terrible job,' I say.

'Sorry. I'm . . . Look, would you like to join me? I'm on my own too and it would be nice to resume our conversation of earlier.'

It was hardly a conversation; it was him being annoyed with me, and I'm really not in the mood for people being annoyed with me. However, I tell myself he's being conciliatory and I should be nice about it. So I nod, then pick up my plate and follow him. A flurry of waiters and waitresses gather around to transport my wine, my book and my bag and set them down on Charles's table. I'm amused when one of them calls him Charlie-boy.

'Well,' he says when we're settled. 'I think we got off on the wrong foot. And then I put the other one in it by implying that your cousin is a beauty queen and you're average when actually you're quite striking.'

I'll take striking as a compliment today and say so.

'In that case . . . we're OK?' He sounds relieved.

'Of course.' I take a sip of wine. 'I suppose this could be the opening of your next book. A boy-meets-girl comedy? Although we're obviously not a boy-meets-girl comedy. I'm sure you have a significant other in your life.' I'm not going

68

to let on I already know about him being part of one of London's hottest couples.

'Not any more.' He frowns. 'Also, I don't write romantic comedies. Do you know anything about my books? I won the Booker Prize, even if it was a long time ago now.'

'I know.' I nod while taking on board the fact that his agent-slash-fiancée-slash-maybe-wife is now his agent-slash-ex. 'They should give you a little badge you can wear to proclaim your brilliance. I got the impression earlier you weren't writing much of anything, romantic or otherwise. Didn't you say you were stuck?'

'A badge would be nice.' He gives me a wry smile. 'Though I'd feel like a fraud wearing it at the moment.'

'Have you got writer's block?'

'Norman Mailer says that writer's block is a failure of the ego,' he says. 'My agent often tells me I have an enormous ego. Makes the failure even worse, I guess.'

I want to ask if that's the same agent who discovered him and became his fiancée-slash-ex, but that's a bit too personal. It could be a sensitive subject.

'I wouldn't know,' I say. 'I struggle to write a report, let alone anything longer, even when it's nothing more than a list of procedures.'

'I love writing lists of procedures,' he says, and this time he's wistful. 'I used to do it all the time when I worked in an office.'

'I'm sure writing novels is better fun than writing reports.'

'So was I once.' He shakes his head. 'Sorry, I'm banging on about myself. Tell me about your job.'

I do my best to explain what it's like to stand in the rain and stop a six-axle articulated lorry that's been driven from

Turkey to Ireland by an irritated driver who just wants to get the job done, and he listens with interest. He's a really good listener.

'And do you enjoy it?' he asks.

'Love it.'

'It sounds confrontational.'

'Part of the skill is *not* being confrontational,' I tell him.

'I could've done with that myself over the last years.'

'What have you been confrontational about?' I ask. 'It doesn't say in your bio.'

'What bio?' He looks startled.

'Your Wiki bio, of course.'

'I wasn't aware I had one.'

'Don't you google yourself?'

'No.' He shudders. 'I don't. Nor do I look at my Amazon reviews or other stuff like that. I did at the start and it nearly killed me.'

'Why? Weren't they good?'

'Lots were. But definitely not all of them. And I never remember any of the good ones, only the awful ones.'

'I've read some of them,' I tell him. 'Most people think you're amazing.'

'You're only as good as your last book,' he tells me. 'And when that's a flop, it's a difficult place to come back from.'

'*Was* your last book a flop?'

'It was critically acclaimed.' He makes a face. 'It's what we say when we get positive reviews and nobody buys it.'

'But you *did* win the Booker, even if you don't have a badge,' I remind him. 'Surely that means loads of people bought it. It's like a gold-star recommendation, isn't it?'

'That was a lifetime ago,' he says. 'And yes, a lot of people did buy *Winter's Heartbreak*, but that doesn't mean they'll buy everything I write. They bought my second because it was shortlisted too, but fewer bought the third, even though it took me an age to write and the *Irish Times* said it was "emotionally engaging at a fundamental level". My fourth was a novella to keep the publisher happy, and now I'm trying to figure out if the idea I had that sounded so good when I pitched it to my agent will actually turn out to be a book that no one at all wants to read.'

'Why did you come here to write it?' I ask. 'I mean, it's a stunning location but it's hardly a get-away-from-it-all type of place. I thought all you great writers needed to find perfect solitude to work: no internet, no people, nothing to distract you. A house in the hills or the forest or the wilds of Connemara or something.'

'Yes, well.' He shakes his head. 'The wilds of Connemara were booked up. Besides, I'm not that sort of writer. I didn't do English literature in college. I wrote my earlier books mostly in my lunch hour at work. I shouldn't need solitude to be able to write.'

'And you've compromised by coming to a luxury hotel where you hired a private villa and reserved a table to yourself so that you don't have to mix with the common people?' I can barely hide how funny I find this.

'Sort of.' He looks embarrassed.

'It's the kind of failure I could manage,' I tell him.

He laughs. He's a completely different person when he laughs. His faint air of superiority disappears, and because his laughter is so deep, it's infectious. I laugh too.

'You're a tonic,' he tells me.

'I'm not sure about that.'

'And you're right.' He nods 'I'm being precious about my book and my writing. I need to get on with it and stop tearing myself apart.'

'What's it about?' I ask.

'Someone who retreats to a backwater island to find themselves,' he says.

'This definitely isn't the best place to imagine a backwater.' I look around. The restaurant is busy with holidaymakers. There's lots of laughter and animated conversation, and people are having a good time.

'That's why I go to the cove,' he says. 'Although I should be able to imagine a backwater island for myself. It's just . . .'

'What?'

'I'm not a hundred per cent sure what I'm trying to create.'

I wipe my sticky fingers on the crisp linen napkin and pour myself a glass of water because I've finished my wine and I don't want him to think I'm a lush.

'I know you were dismissive of it earlier, but what about a crime novel?' I suggest.

'I don't do crime.' He's clearly aghast at the suggestion.

'It doesn't have to be as good as this.' I pick up the Janice Jermyn book and hand it to him. He's been glancing at it from time to time during our talk.

'That's not the sort of thing I write.'

'Have you read it?'

'No. Of course not.'

'Then you don't know if it's your sort of thing or not.'

'My themes—'

'You've said you're writing about someone who wants to find themselves,' I tell him. 'In this, the detective inspector is going through a very personal trauma. The first victim was running away from her family. The second . . . well, no spoilers, but there's a lot of finding oneself going on.'

'I really think—'

'You could write a crime novel and make it sort of literary,' I say. 'Use your flashy way with words. Start at the beginning and keep on going till the end.'

'You're giving me writing advice?' He shoots me an amused look.

'I'm not really offering advice on writing,' I say. 'I'm offering advice on how to get things done. That's something I'm good at.'

'Right,' he says.

'Read the book,' I tell him. 'I haven't finished it myself yet, but your need is greater than mine. I'm pretty sure whodunnit at this point, though as Janice always keeps a few twists for the final chapters, I could be wildly wrong.'

He hesitates, then reaches into the backpack beside his seat.

'I'll do a swap.'

He hands me his Booker Prize-winning book, *Winter's Heartbreak*. The cover is grey and silver and says that more than five million copies have been sold. I wonder if he carries it around with him all the time, to remind him how good he is at writing.

I don't say that some kind of tragic romance is the last thing I want to read.

Chapter 6

Iseult

We cannot choose where to start and stop.
Chris Cleave

The wedding takes place at four o'clock in the afternoon, when the heat of the sun has abated enough for everyone in the wedding party not to melt. The men are in proper suits and have been waiting for a good twenty minutes in the gazebo before the bride arrives. She's wearing a traditional white dress and a long veil that's fixed to a garland in her hair and is lifted gently into the air by the warm breeze. The music of the reggae band wafts towards the beach, where everyone has turned to look at the bridal couple, because you do, don't you, when there's a wedding? You can't help yourself. I imagine what it would have been like for me, walking along the flagged path to the gazebo, standing among the tropical flowers and making my vows with Steve, knowing that we were the centre of attention, and although I don't want to cry, the tears flood my eyes all the same.

I didn't go for a blingtastic dress in the end, despite Celeste's encouragement. I chose mid-length white silk, with

74

spaghetti straps and pearl buttons down the back. I thought it was very sophisticated but also casual enough for a beach wedding. The bling was on my wedge sandals, which had diamanté straps and silver heels.

There's a burst of laughter from the gazebo, then the sound of clapping and the pop of a champagne cork. And then the guests walk back to the hotel while the bride and groom have their photos taken. I wipe my eyes, take out my phone and check Steve's location.

He's on the M50 again.

I lie on my sunbed and take a picture of my legs stretched out, the beach and the sea in the background, and immediately post it: #HolidayBliss #CaribbeanMagic #LuckiestGirlInTheWorld.

It's nearly an hour later and I'm four chapters through Charles Miller's bestselling book when the catamaran floats in to shore and I see Celeste jump down and walk along the beach. I put the book to one side and wave at her. When she reaches me, she flops down on the vacant lounger nearby.

'Good day?' I ask.

'Fun,' she replies. 'How about you? Did you see the wedding?'

'Hard to miss it.' I don't want to talk about someone else's wedding. 'Tell me about the trip. Did you stop off anywhere interesting?'

She says that the most interesting part was the snorkelling, which she loved, and that the views of the shore from the catamaran were stunning. She hands me her phone and I flick through various shots of the green island rising from the aquamarine sea and the pristine beaches in secluded coves, as well as the people on the boat enjoying the sun, sea and cocktails. I pause at one of the photos. The cove it shows looks very like the one where I met Charles Miller earlier, although there's no sign of either of us in the photos. I tell her about it, and about having lunch with him at his reserved table.

'Look at you.' Her eyes widen. 'I leave you alone for a few hours and you're hobnobbing with the celebs.'

'Hardly a celeb,' I say. 'A bit up his own arse, to be honest.'

'I should have recognised him but he looks different in real life.' She glances at the book on my lounger. I've left it open at the page I was reading. 'He gave you a copy of his book?'

I explain about swapping it for my Janice Jermyn and she laughs.

'I read *Winter's Heartbreak* when it first came out,' she says. 'It was lovely. The second one wasn't bad either. I don't think I've read the others, though.'

'He said they didn't sell as well,' I tell her. 'All the same, he doesn't really have to worry if this one sold five million copies. Only thing is, I want to shake the male character. He's completely self-obsessed.'

'Sounds realistic.' Celeste grins.

We gather up our things and head back to our room, where Celeste takes a shower and I sit on the balcony with a cup of mint tea. I'm tempted to check on Steve again, but I restrain myself. I'm aware my cyber-stalking is unhealthy. I'll stop after today. I will. But in the meantime, it fills the unfillable hole in my heart.

We're later than usual to dinner, and even as we're led to our table, I can't help glancing towards Charles Miller's usual spot. There's no sign of him. I wonder if he's too engrossed in *The Mystery of the Missing Mallet* to eat. I bet he's enjoying it, even though it's so completely unlike his own book. It's a great holiday read. I suppose the only problem for Charles is that he's not on holiday. Honestly, though, what kind of world does he live in where he can afford to come to a luxury resort to write? The last payment I made for the White Sands took me to within ten euros of my credit card limit.

'Earth to Iseult.' Celeste clicks her fingers in front of my face. 'You're miles away.'

'Sorry. Just daydreaming.'

'What about?'

'Random things. Not Steve,' I add.

'That's progress.'

'I guess so.'

The reggae band is playing in the bar after dinner – maybe it's a double gig, the wedding earlier, the bar now – and quite a lot of people are dancing to the music, which, in fairness, makes me want to dance too. I don't, because I have all the natural elegance of a herd of drunken hippos on the dance floor. Celeste and I sit at a table on the outside terrace, where we can see the moonlit sea as the waves break gently on the shore. It's indescribably beautiful and I feel as though I'm on a movie set – perhaps one of those Agatha Christie mysteries where everyone is in evening dress and drinking cocktails and having a lovely time until someone is murdered.

'Meeting Charles Miller has sent your imagination into overdrive.' Celeste looks at me in amusement when I say this. 'However, I do like the sound of cocktails. I'm going to the bathroom, so I'll order on my way. What would you like?'

'Strawberry daiquiri,' I say, and she nods.

Sitting alone at the round table, I feel even more like someone in a movie set, although this time the lone female in the slinky dress who's found face-down in the pool. I'm actually wearing a slinky dress tonight; it's one of the outfits I bought in a swirl of wedding preparations, and it's a gorgeous emerald green with silver sequins around the simple scoop neckline. It fits perfectly, thanks to my current slim-line figure, and falls in a gentle swish of silk to just above my ankles. It was my night-after-the-wedding dress. The rest of my clothes are far more casual.

My hair is too short to style elegantly, but I've gelled it, and it shows off my lovely Pandora drop earrings, my 'something new' wedding gift to myself. Funnily enough, though lots of things make me emotional about my cancelled wedding, wearing the earrings doesn't.

I sit and wait for Celeste to return, trying to look as though I'm thinking profound thoughts and not at all conscious of actually being on my own. Then I see Charles Miller walk through the dining room to the bar, where they already have a drink waiting for him, even though this is the first time I've seen him here since we arrived.

He takes the drink and walks past me. And not that I'm expecting him to join me for some more literary conversation or anything, but it's as though he's never seen me before. The words of greeting that had formed on my lips remain unsaid. I'm shocked by his rudeness.

Then, in one of those series of connected events that end in disaster, a couple who have been dancing slowly together to the reggae version of 'Lady in Red' decide to do a dramatic spin. The woman's outstretched arm bangs into Charles's drink, it sloshes onto my table and I leap out of my chair like a startled gazelle to avoid getting gin and tonic or whatever he's ordered all over my beautiful dress.

'I'm so sorry!' the woman apologises to Charles, absolutely ignoring me. 'I should've looked where I was going.'

'My fault,' says her partner. 'We were trying a *Strictly* move and made a mess of it.'

'It's fine.' Charles's tone can't quite disguise his irritation. 'I'm fine.'

'We'd better go,' the woman says with a giggle. 'I've clearly had too much already.'

She and her partner disappear into the night, leaving me watching the drink pool on the table. Which is when Celeste comes back with two strawberry daiquiris.

'What happened?' she asks.

'Some idiot barged into me,' says Charles, at the same time as I say that he's spilled his drink on the table. He turns to look at me for the first time, and squints.

'Oh,' he says. 'Sorry. I didn't recognise you.' He takes his glasses out of the pocket of the jacket he's wearing and puts them on, just as a waiter appears and begins to mop up the drink from the table.

'Lucky it didn't get you, Izzy,' says Celeste.

'My cat-like reflexes,' I tell her.

'May I get you another drink, Mr Miller?' asks the waiter. 'A martini with an olive, yes?'

'Yes, please,' says Charles.

'Are you going to join us?' asks Celeste, when he stays standing beside the table.

'He's just waiting for his drink.' I'm the one being rude now.

'Do you mind if I sit here?' he says.

'Not at all,' Celeste tells him.

She sits down, and Charles takes an empty chair from another table and sits beside me.

'So,' says Celeste. 'You're the famous author. Izzy's told me all about you.'

'Have you read my books?'

I wonder if he asks that of everyone he meets.

'A couple,' replies Celeste, and he looks pleased though also a little disappointed. I suppose he wanted her to say she was his number one fan.

'Are you enjoying it?' He turns to me, and I tell him that he writes really well before asking him how it's going with *The Mystery of the Missing Mallet.*

'It's . . . intriguing.'

'Have you worked out who the murderer is yet?'

'It's either the carpenter or the husband,' replies Charles.

'Why?' I ask.

'Because the victim has been having an affair with the carpenter,' he says.

'That's a red herring. It's definitely not the husband.'

'But the affair—'

'The affair is irrelevant.'

'Affairs are never irrelevant.' His words are heartfelt, and I wonder if that's what happened with the agent-slash-ex.

'In this case, I'm betting it is.'

'So you think . . . one of her colleagues?'

'I haven't read far enough to be sure yet, but I'll write my guess down and you can check later.'

'You're on,' he says, as the waiter reappears with a fresh martini.

'Cheers, ladies,' Charles says.

We clink glasses.

Celeste looks at me over the rim of her cocktail glass and winks.

Charles starts talking about books again, but it's Celeste who replies this time, because the genre has switched from cosy crime – my specialist subject – to far more literary novels. Celeste holds her own in the conversation, most of which is going over my head because I haven't read any of them. I listen to them debate the merits of one of the books Celeste has brought with her, and I'm amused to hear Charles's rather acerbic take on the author, Cosmo Penhaligon.

'He thinks he's better than he is,' he tells Celeste. 'Believes all the good reviews, ignores the bad ones.'

'Don't you think you're quite good yourself?' I join in again. 'You do seem to expect everyone to know you're a prizewinning author.'

'God knows why. Nobody really cares but me.' His sudden vulnerability is disarming.

'I'm sure you'll write something great,' I tell him. 'Especially if you follow my advice and turn to crime.'

'I couldn't write anything like the woman you gave me,' he says.

'Because it's too difficult?' I ask.

'No.' He shakes his head. 'Because . . . because it's not me.'

'Why don't you write literary crime?' suggests Celeste. 'After all, John Banville did and they're bestsellers.'

'I haven't read his crime output,' says Charles.

'It's not as fast and twisty as Janice Jermyn,' I tell him. 'You've read them?'

'A couple.'

'But they're not as good as Janice?' Charles's face lights up.

'Not for me,' I say. 'But then I've never read any of his other books, so maybe I'm just a hopeless what-d'you-call-it, who hasn't a clue about art or culture.'

'Philistine,' supplies Celeste.

'Those Philistines get a bad press,' I say.

Charles smiles.

The band, which had briefly stopped playing, starts up again, and we have a short debate on reggae music and culture in which we all agree that the music is great, although Charles insists you can't compare it to Mozart or Wagner or even (and he grimaces as he says this) Strauss.

'I like Strauss,' I say. 'He was easier to play on the piano.'

'You can play the piano?' He looks surprised.

'Badly,' I admit. 'I stopped after the Grade 4 exam.'

He looks impressed all the same.

'So not a total philistine after all,' I add.

'I never thought you were.'

But he did. He does. I can tell. And although Celeste is more knowledgeable than me about the literary world, he probably thinks she's a philistine too. He's definitely up his own arse. And yet he can suddenly look quite lost. Mostly, it has to be said, when we start talking about popular culture and streaming services, stuff that he appears to know very little about.

That's the thing about holidays, isn't it? You get to meet people you'd never normally meet. They distract you from your day-to-day life. And then, thankfully, you never see them again.

Chapter 7

Ariel

You know what I did after I wrote my first novel? I shut up and wrote twenty-three more.
Michael Connolly

I'm at the Globe in London, where Graham Weston is hosting a reception to celebrate his father's ninetieth birthday. George Weston founded Xerxes sixty years ago, so it's a double celebration. Xerxes are good at celebrating things. They had a fiftieth birthday bash the same year I won an industry award. My cup was overflowing with joy and my champagne glass was overflowing with Veuve Clicquot. It was a great night: *Snow in Summer*, Charles's third book, had just been published after a tortuous writing experience, and he was seen as the glittering jewel in the Xerxes crown.

It doesn't seem like ten years ago. Life, and the industry, has changed a lot since then.

There are lots of well-known Xerxes authors here. Unfortunately, Charles is a notable absentee, being holed up in the Caribbean working on his next book, the deadline for which is the end of the month. He's been writing and rewriting for over a year without getting anywhere. However, when he's totally immersed, he can get a messy first draft down on paper quite quickly, so I'm keeping my hopes up while also being terrified that he won't have anything at all.

I'm conflicted about him being away, because this is a high-profile event and it would be good, on many levels, for him to be here, but it's actually more important to get some work out of him, especially as even a synopsis is like trying to prise an oyster out of its shell. But I got him to record a video of his best wishes to George and Xerxes, which Graham plans to show later. I had to make him record it three times, because the first two had the gorgeous Caribbean Sea in the background (once directly, once reflected in a mirror) and I didn't think a video of him apparently living it up in the tropics when he was supposed to be in the grip of his muse would go down well in dark, gloomy London, where Graham, and Charles's editor, Sophia, are waiting impatiently for his manuscript.

Anyhow, his video is excellent – he can totally turn on the charm when he wants to – and I'm relieved he's working hard, so I can allow myself to relax a little and enjoy myself tonight. I have two other authors here, and they deserve some of the time and attention that Charles seems to monopolise whenever he's around.

Penny Blackwater is one of the new wave of writers from Northern Ireland who've been taking the literary scene by storm; she's been shortlisted for a few literary prizes, and although she hasn't actually won anything yet, I'm very hopeful. Her debut was great, but her next book is even stronger, so my fingers are crossed. My other author, Avery Marshall, writes quirky literary comedies that sell really well and that Graham Weston himself particularly likes. In fact, I see the two of them together now, talking animatedly, and I make my way over, glass of champagne in my hand.

'Two of my favourite men,' I say as I join them. 'How are you both? What a fabulous night, Graham. Your father must be delighted.'

Although George handed over the reins of the company to Graham years ago, he continues to take a keen interest in the book world and loves nothing more than to be in the company of 'his' authors.

'He's thrilled,' says Graham. 'It's lovely to have so many of our best-loved authors here. And quite a few of them brought to us by you, Ariel.'

'Always glad to find the right home for them.' I smile.

'Is Charles around?' Avery, tall and thin and looking very much like a stick of liquorice in his tuxedo, raises an enquiring eyebrow.

'He's sequestered himself while he writes his latest,' I tell him.

'I didn't think he was the sequestering sort.'

There's always been a bit of needle between Avery and Charles, possibly because the first time they met, Charles pretended he didn't know who Avery was. The second time, Avery had won the Wodehouse Prize for comic fiction, and Charles congratulated him so effusively I knew he didn't mean a word he said.

I smile now at Avery and tell him that Charles always locks himself away when he gets to a certain point in a novel.

'I'm delighted he did the video, though it would've been nice to have him with us in person,' says Graham. 'He was our first Booker winner after all.'

Their only Booker winner, though I don't say that out loud.

'And I'm your Wodehouse winner.' Avery raises his glass.

'Indeed you are.' Graham clinks his against it, and so do I.

'Xerxes did really well this year,' I remark. 'Your sales have been excellent.'

'Thanks to Avery here,' says Graham. '*Black Ivory* was a fantastic seller for us.'

Avery smirks.

'And, of course, poor Maura,' adds Graham. 'Her dying so tragically was a real boost to sales.'

Maura Mulholland, one of Ekene's authors, wrote mid-list sagas. When she died earlier in the year while on holiday in Italy, her latest book and her entire backlist went stratospheric. Ekene was thrilled. Though obviously sad about Maura's passing, she conceded that it was great publicity.

The book world can be very harsh.

I see Penny Blackwater alone on the other side of the room and excuse myself. I don't like to see her by herself, although Penny is one of those people who would be perfectly happy on a desert island. Being alone, even in a throng of people, doesn't seem to bother her in the slightest.

'Hi,' I say. 'Here long?'

'I arrived a minute ago,' she replies in her distinctive Derry accent. 'There's a big crowd.'

'I guess it's a kind of pre-Christmas party event,' I say.

'Oh, aye. I was delighted to get dressed up.'

'You look fabulous.'

She's wearing a gold lamé dress that clings to her perfect figure, while her long blonde hair is twisted into a loose plait that hangs down her back.

'Thanks,' she says. 'So do you.'

Well, yes, I do. I'm wearing black, which always suits me,

and I've gone for a kind of sixties cocktail look to embrace the spirit of the evening. I'm wearing red shoes and long red gloves, although I'll have to get rid of the gloves soon, because as more and more people join the party, I can feel myself getting hotter and hotter. I'm hoping that's just the heating system and not me, because I started the HRT the day I got the prescription from the doctor and so far it's been miraculous – the hot flushes have stopped and I'm feeling a lot more energetic which is a good thing for sure.

'Charles not here tonight?' asks Penny.

I give her the same reply as I gave Graham and Avery.

'I wish I had the time to sequester myself away,' she says.

I give her a sympathetic smile. Although her book has had rave reviews and prize nominations, and sold reasonably well too (a welcome bonus!), Penny can't afford to give up the day job yet. Her main income is from her work at an online travel company. She's great at social media, though, and such a lovely writer as well as a lovely person that I'm convinced she'll soon have a massive breakthrough.

'Have you posted anything yet?' I ask.

She grins and shows me a few pix of the evening, with various hashtags that include #Celebration #BookNight #BookLovers and, of course, #NotSoGentleKisses, the title of her book.

'Do you want me to take a photo of you?' I ask.

'Let's do a wee selfie,' she says, and pulls me towards her.

She gets the angle of the phone exactly right so that we both look glamorous and sparkling, although it's very clear that she's sparkling with youth whereas I'm entirely dependent on my make-up, which needs a bit of refreshing. I find a place to deposit my champagne glass and tell Penny I'll be back to her shortly.

It's surprisingly quiet in the bathroom, and I sit in one of the stalls to cool down for a moment. I remove my gloves and take out my phone, and even though I'm totally not a fan of using the phone in the loo, I send a text.

Are you still working?

I'm not really expecting a reply, but the answer comes straight away.

Researching

How's it going?

The effects of multiple cocktails on the human body are very interesting 😊

Are you drinking?!?!?!?!

Not as much as I could

FFS, Chas, I've told everyone you're sequestered and working hard

I am. This particular research is essential to the plot

I replace my phone in my bag, give the loo an unnecessary flush, leave the cubicle and wash my hands. I reapply my lippy and mascara before brushing my hair. Then I walk outside and find a quiet place in the lobby before FaceTiming Charles's number. He answers as a voice call with no video, and I can hear the sound of calypso music in the background.

'Is everything all right?' I ask.

'Of course. There's no need to keep checking up on me. I told you that before.'

'I know. It was you talking about cocktails that made me . . . well . . .'

'You're like my mother, you know that, don't you?'

I shudder. Charles's mother might be eighty years old, but she's an absolute witch. Or perhaps a word that rhymes with witch.

'My only concern is that everything's working out for you. It was a big gamble taking six weeks away.'

'What you really mean is that you hope I didn't simply splurge on a six-week holiday in the sun when my deadline is looming.'

'Sort of,' I admit.

He laughs. I haven't heard him laugh like this in ages. I feel myself relax.

'I'm writing like a madman and I hope you'll be happy with the result,' he tells me.

'I hope so too. I'm sure Graham's fingers are crossed. I'm at the party tonight.'

'What party?'

'For heaven's sake, Chas! His dad's ninetieth. The one you recorded the message for.'

'Oh, right. I'd forgotten.'

How could he forget? It's on our shared diary. It's been there for months.

'Penny and Avery are here too.'

'Of course they are. How *is* dear Avery?'

'Looking well.'

'Still reminding you of a pipe cleaner?'

'A liquorice strip,' I say. 'I'm too young to know what a pipe cleaner looks like.'

Charles chuckles. It's nice to hear. He's sounded despairing for so long that I've worried about him. And then I hear voices in the background, and a female voice telling him that his random order was a mojito, and I ask if he's at a party himself.

'The manager's cocktail party,' he says. He adds that it's nice to think we're both having a good time and drinking cocktails, even if we are about seven thousand kilometres apart.

'I'd better get back to mine,' I tell him. 'Obviously I want to make sure that people know you're Xerxes' most important author and that you're devastated not to be here tonight but you're being driven by the muse.'

'Or the mojitos.'

'You really are writing your book?'

'I really am.'

He says that quite seriously, so I decide to believe him. Because if he's not writing the book, if he's just living it up on Paradise Island . . . well, I don't even want to contemplate that disaster.

'Talk soon,' I say. 'Enjoy the rest of your evening.'

'You too. Tell George I wish him all the best. Tell Graham he'll have the new manuscript soon.'

'I will.'

'Goodnight, Ariel.'

He ends the call before I have time to say goodnight in return.

Chapter 8

Iseult

What I like in a good author is not
what he says but what he whispers.
Logan Pearsall Smith

The manager's cocktail party is great fun. I'd imagined a stiff reception with people standing around being polite, but it turns into a beach barbecue with music and dancing and everyone having a good time. We've all had way too much to drink, but Celeste and I agree that the cocktails aren't very heavy on alcohol so it's OK to mix and match. Although two hours in, I'm not entirely sure about that.

'Your random order is a mojito, sir.' I approach Charles Miller with a frosted glass only to see that he's on the phone. He smiles at me and nods towards one of the small tables on the wooden decking overlooking the sea. Then he mouths the word 'work' and makes a face before telling whoever he's talking to that he's at a cocktail party. I glance at my watch as I move away to give him a bit of privacy and calculate that it's nearly midnight back in Ireland so a bit late for him to be having a work conversation. Though I suppose a writer is a writer 24/7. I think, suddenly, of my own workmates, who'll be on the night shift now, and I take a photo of the hotel, looking pretty with the coloured lights strung around it, and send it to Natasha, who I know is the team leader tonight.

Her reply is instant.

Feck off

I grin and send another, this time of my mojito.

Feck right off

I send a thumbs-up.

I hope you're having a fabulous time

I am. How're things there?

Intercepted some coke yesterday. Very happy

Yay! Well done you

All down to Fish and Chips

Chips is one of the sniffer dogs. He's a gorgeous, playful English springer spaniel. His handler, Brad Flisch, is naturally known to us all as Fish. Between them, they have a great detection rate.

Give Chips a hug from me. Tell
Fish I'll see him next week

Will do

I put my phone in my tiny handbag, which actually only has space for it and the card key for the room. Charles has his back to me while he keeps talking on his mobile. Celeste is chatting to the widow who plays golf. She's a lovely woman, I've discovered, really strong and determined to live her life to the fullest even without her husband.

'He wouldn't want me moping about the place,' she told me as we swam in the sea this morning. 'Besides, I was never the moping sort.'

'But you miss him?'

'Every minute of every day,' she replies. 'All the same, it is what it is. I can't change the fact that he's gone and I'm here. He'd want me to make the most of life.'

I admired her fortitude and resolved to be more like her myself. As a result, I haven't checked on Steve's location all day. In fact I've decided never to do it again. I'm giving myself a pass on wanting to know where he was on our wedding day, but I don't want to turn into an actual stalker.

I move away from the main group and head back towards the beach. There are a few couples strolling hand in hand along the water's edge, and I make a determined effort not to imagine me and Steve doing the same. I glance back towards the party and see that Charles has finished his phone call and is now in conversation with one of the male golfers. I turn away again and walk to a small outcrop of rocks at one end of the beach. I sit there and watch the waves lapping against them.

It's about ten minutes later when Charles joins me. He has a cocktail in each hand.

'All alone?' he asks as he offers me another mojito.

'Happily.' I accept it from him.

'Am I interrupting?'

'Not at all.'

He perches gingerly on an adjoining rock.

'I wrote about people doing this,' he says with a grimace. 'I made it seem romantic. I didn't realise how bloody uncomfortable sitting on a rock is.'

I laugh.

'Seriously.' He grunts as he tries to find a more comfortable position. 'I have a new respect for models who make it look easy when they're showing off swimsuits.'

'Especially as those photo shoots are usually in the winter,' I remark. 'And anyone modelling a bikini in Dublin in the winter deserves a medal.'

He chuckles, and we sit in companionable silence for a while. I continue to look out to sea, not that there's anything to look at except the silver-white light of the moon on the rippling water.

I'm not thinking of anything, simply enjoying the music that's wafting on the night air, the warmth of the breeze on my shoulders and the proximity of Charles Miller, who doesn't seem bothered by our lack of conversation. Then I'm aware of someone approaching us, and I see Celeste.

'Hi.'

'I came to say goodnight.'

'Huh?' I peer at my watch in the moonlight. 'It's early yet.'

'Bit of a headache,' she confesses. 'I shouldn't have had those vodka martinis. I don't have your iron-clad constitution, Charles.'

'Do you want me to come up with you?' I ask.

'No. Stay. Have fun. I just need to lie down.'

'Are you sure?'

'Absolutely.'

'Would you like me to walk you to your room?' Charles stands up and brushes sand from his linen trousers. 'Those pathways aren't best lit, and I'd hate you to stumble in those fabulous heels.'

Celeste thanks him and slips her hand around his arm. 'Don't go away,' he says to me as he walks with her.

I feel a little guilty for not leaving the party too, but I'm not tired and haven't had as much to drink so am good for a while yet. Besides, the fire torches on the beach and the music of tonight's calypso band are enticing. I sit on the edge of the jetty and allow my feet to dangle in the warm seawater.

It's not long before Charles returns to join me.

'Is Celeste all right?' I ask.

'Fine,' he assures me. 'She's going to bed. She says she probably had one martini too many.'

'I'm beginning to think they mix them stronger at night,' I remark.

'Oh well, it's not a holiday until someone has a hangover. Thankfully, it's not me.'

'Because you're not on holiday,' I point out. 'You were having a late-night conversation about work earlier. What do you mean by work? Writing your book? Or other stuff?'

'Talking to my agent, mainly.' He grimaces. 'She's agitating for a manuscript. Or at least a few chapters.'

'Have you had the same agent all the time?' I ask.

'Yes.'

'So she was also your significant other?'

'Jesus.' He looks at me with a touch of irritation. 'You're

95

like the hairdresser in Janice Jermyn's book. Investigating things that don't need to be investigated.'

'All I did was read your bio and a couple of news pieces online.'

'Yes, I've had the same agent for ever. Yes, we were together for a while. We're not any more but she's still my agent. Does that satisfy your inner sleuth?' His tone is mild, though I think he's put out that I know so much about him. But honestly, does he really not google people himself?

'I didn't mean to sound like I was quizzing you,' I say, although I'm itching to know if they got married and divorced, or if one of them broke off the engagement. In which case we'd have something in common. I ask him as casually as possible if there's anyone else in his life.

'For crying out loud! What's this, the Spanish fecking Inquisition?'

I don't say anything. I don't want him to think I'm harbouring ideas about him, given that we're sitting apart from the rest of the guests, dangling our feet in the moonlit water in what can only be described as a romantic setting. It's not like I'm feeling romantic. About him or anyone. All the same . . .

'Sorry.' He shrugs. 'I'm not good at answering questions about my life unless it's an actual interview. Anyhow, it's all about the work these days. She's one of the best agents around. I like to work with the best.'

'You must have loads of manuscript to give her,' I say, thankful that we've moved on from the inquisition accusations. 'Haven't you been locked up in your room for the last few days writing?'

'Yes,' he says. 'Twelve hours a day. I'm motoring along.' He sounds both surprised and enthusiastic.

'In that case, send her something to read and give yourself a break.'

'I don't want to send anything at all until I'm sure of what I'm doing,' he says.

'You're still not sure?' I'm shocked. 'But if you've written loads . . . well . . . what happens if you're not sure?'

He doesn't answer.

'If you send it to her, won't she be able to tell you whether it's OK?'

'I've taken a fresh approach. Maybe I need fresh criticism.'

'Surely if it's good it's good,' I say.

'You're so naïve. Come on.' He holds out his hand.

'Come on where?'

'With me.'

He pulls me towards the pathway. There's an unexpected firmness in his grasp; I feel the dryness of his palm and a surge of electricity between us. Not sexual electricity. He's old enough to be my father. (Although not really. Dad is sixty-five. According to Wikipedia, Charles is nearly fifty.) Nevertheless, there's a connection that's real. I don't know if Charles feels it too.

He pushes open the white gate that leads to his private villa, then slides the patio doors apart and shows me inside

It's gorgeous, all marble tiles, modern furniture and mood lighting. The sort of decor I'd love to have in my own house, if only I could afford a place of my own. There's also a small kitchen, divided from the living area by a granite counter. Charles's laptop is perched on top, still open. There's a pile of printed paper beside it.

'I get the hotel to print out the draft every day,' he tells me.

'I'd've thought it'd be safer to read it onscreen,' I remark, remembering the incident in the cove.

'I like to see hard copy,' he says. Then he thrusts the top pages at me. 'Here.'

'You want me to read it?' I look at him in astonishment. 'Your actual book?'

'Not the entire book,' he says. 'The first chapter.'

'This is what you were working on in the cove?'

'No,' he says. 'Well, yes. But I've reworked it.'

I take the pages from him and sit on the comfortable sofa.

'I'll make coffee,' says Charles.

'Decaf,' I tell him. 'Otherwise I'll be awake all night.'

He says nothing, but busies himself with the machine.

I look at the first page and begin to read.

I'm still reading when he brings the coffee and puts it on the glass-topped table in front of me. I glance up, but carry on until I finish the chapter.

'Well?' he asks.

'Not bad.'

'Not bad!' He sounds affronted. 'Just not bad?'

'It's very different to *Winter's Heartbreak*.'

'Of course it is,' he says. 'It's a crime novel. Like you suggested.'

I nod. It's crime, but not my sort of crime. I don't know what to say.

'Not as good as Janice Jermyn?' He looks at me enquiringly.

'Well . . .' I put the pages on the table and take a sip of coffee. 'It's much . . . much wordier than her books.'

'Of course. Because I'm creating characters and atmosphere.'

'But we're nowhere near the murder yet.'

'It's the first chapter. I'm setting the scene.'

'Janice always has a murder in Chapter One.'

'Janice hasn't won the Booker.'

'Janice sells a lot of books.'

'What would you do differently?' he asks.

'I'm not the writer.'

'But as the reader?'

'You've read *The Mystery of the Missing Mallet*. I'd make it more like that.'

'Then I'd be copying someone else.'

'Not exactly the same,' I say. 'Just . . .'

'More murders,' he says.

'One, anyhow.'

He laughs. Then he gets up and hands me some more printed sheets.

'Try this.'

I read without stopping, and then I look up at him.

'Did you write it?'

'It's the same story. The same characters. Of course I did.'

'I love it. I love that they're all going on holiday together. I love that everyone has a reason to hate the grandmother. I've no idea who the murderer might be.'

'Oh good.' He looks pleased. 'I thought that was an essential part of the whole thing.'

'It is.'

'I'm glad you like it. The first chapter I gave you was how I started the rewrite. And then I realised that it *was* too wordy. You're right about that. So I changed it.'

'It's great,' I say. 'Obviously you've a long way to go, but it's a page-turner for sure.'

'I think it's good too,' he says. 'And I have to thank you for your advice. You know what you like and you speak your mind. I'm so used to people talking around me, speaking in code, not saying what they really mean. You're refreshing.'

'Thanks, I think.'

'Seriously, Iseult. You're my saviour.'

'I'm glad I helped.'

'You really did.'

He smiles at me, I smile at him, and then somehow I'm in his arms and he's kissing me.

I hadn't thought there was a sexual electricity between us. I was very wrong.

Because this feels very, very right.

He's the one who breaks away first, and he looks at me with those amazing blue eyes that aren't icy any more.

'I'm sorry,' he says. 'That was particularly inappropriate.'

'It was wonderfully inappropriate.'

'I wanted to thank you. I got a little overenthusiastic.'

'So this isn't how you usually thank people?'

'No.' He smiles, then frowns. 'I've actually wanted to do that for . . . well, quite some time, to be honest.'

'Really?'

'Yes.'

'Wow.'

'But better if we don't do it again,' he says.

I'm disappointed, but I say nothing.

'I should write some more.' He breaks the silence. 'I'm on a roll. It's very exciting writing this way,' he adds. 'Usually I draw up a detailed plan, but I have the old manuscript to work on and I'm having such fun turning everything on its head that I don't need one. It's wonderful to feel murderous instead of angsty about all my characters.'

'In that case, I'll leave you to your murderous intentions.' He doesn't seem to notice the chill in my voice.

'Thank you.' He puts his hands on my shoulders. 'Thank you for pulling me out of the hole I'd dug for myself. Thank you for telling me I should write something different. Thank you for being you.'

'You're welcome.' My tone isn't quite as chilly now.

He leans forward, and so do I.

We're kissing again.

And he forgets all about the exciting new developments in his book and concentrates on the exciting new developments with me instead.

It's much later when I gently open the door to Room 501, take off my shoes and tiptoe across the tiled floor. I think about doing my cleanse, tone and moisturise routine but decide it would be better not to wake Celeste, who's curled up beneath the sheet of her bed. So I slide out of my dress and drape it over the nearby chair, then slip beneath my own sheet in my underwear.

Celeste rolls over.

'You took your time,' she says.

'I thought you were asleep.'

All that trying to keep quiet and she was faking it!

'Drifting,' she says. 'That must be the latest a party has ever gone on in this hotel. Usually everyone's tucked up before midnight.'

I glance at my watch. It's nearly one.

'I was talking to Charles Miller,' I say.

'Only talking?'

'He's an interesting man.'

'Only talking?' she repeats.

And kissing. Talking and kissing. But not anything else. Because even as we were lying on the super-king-sized bed in his gorgeous villa and I was wrapping my legs around his body, he suddenly swore and muttered about not having condoms and really not wanting either of us to suffer unforeseen consequences of what was happening.

'I'm on the pill,' I murmured. Which was enough for Steve when I first went to bed with him. He confessed that he hated condoms and never enjoyed sex wearing one.

'You may well be.' Charles Miller disentangled himself from me. 'And I trust you completely on that score. But I've got to this point in my life without being responsible for an unplanned pregnancy and I'm not going to start now. I like to be part of the protection plan.'

'Oh.'

'We don't know each other,' he says.

'Well, no. But—'

'I'm sorry, Iseult.' He sat up and pulled on the shirt and shorts he'd been wearing earlier. 'I didn't mean for us to have this conversation. I didn't expect this to happen at all.'

'They don't make male authors like they used to,' I said as nonchalantly as any woman who's been pushed away twice by a man can possibly be. 'I thought all you guys were like Hemingway and . . . and . . .' I stopped there, as Hemingway was the only author I remembered from school who was portrayed as a womaniser.

'I'd be pleased to be compared to him as far as success with my books goes,' said Charles. 'It's just that . . . well, I'm not really the kind of man who'd meet someone and sleep with them straight away. I know that probably sounds daft to you. My niece once told me that hopping into bed with someone isn't any greater deal than a kiss these days, but I grew up with the Catholic guilt, you see, so I'm not quite as good at it.'

'OK . . .'

'That aside, though, I don't want to have a one-night stand with a beautiful young woman who's about half my age. You realise that turns me into a trope. Middle-aged man runs off to tropical island and falls for younger woman.'

'If you've fallen for me, it's not a one-night stand. What about your ex-significant-other who's your agent?' I asked. 'You said it was all about the work these days, but is it?'

He hesitated, and I felt my heart sink.

'It's a very long time since we loved each other,' he replied. 'We don't have a personal relationship any more.'

'So if there's nothing between you and I'm OK with it, it's no big deal.'

'I'm sorry,' he said. 'I need a bit of time to process this. And . . .' he looked at me sheepishly, 'as I was kissing you, I thought of a great plot twist.'

'You've got to be kidding me.' I clambered off the bed and started to get dressed. 'I'd better get back. Celeste will be wondering what's happened to me.'

'I'm sorry,' said Charles. 'I . . . You're a lovely person.'

'Thanks for letting me down gently. Twice,' I added for good measure as I picked up my bag and walked to the door.

'Iseult.' He stopped me opening it. 'It's not that I wouldn't . . . it's . . .'

'It's fine.'

Our eyes locked and we gazed at each other for what seemed like an eternity. I could feel the electricity surge all over again.

And then I opened the door and walked out.

'Crikey,' says Celeste, when I tell her this. 'You would've had sex with him?'

'I haven't had sex with anyone since Steve. I haven't wanted to have sex with anyone since Steve,' I say. 'But I so wanted to with Charles Miller.'

'Wow.'

'And I realise that he's an older man, but he doesn't seem older when I'm with him.'

'Izzy! You don't seriously fancy him, do you?'

'Physically he's amazing,' I say. 'And he was nice to talk to. And his murder mystery book was great.'

'I never thought you'd rebound like this,' says Celeste.

'I'm not rebounding. I'm . . . well . . . I'm interested in someone. As a holiday romance,' I add quickly. 'Nothing more than that.'

'In *Charles Miller*.'

'It's not like he's Timothée Chalamet,' I tell her. 'He's a writer, not a celeb.'

'And yet we recognised him.'

'Anyhow, it's irrelevant.' I lie back on my pillow. 'He thinks it's inappropriate.'

'Do you?'

'Honestly?' I pause. 'I haven't a clue.'

Chapter 9

Ariel

Books are mirrors. You only see in them
what you already have inside you.
Carlos Ruiz Zafón

Already this winter is being likened to some of the big freezes over the past decades, and there's an appreciable accumulation of snow outside the patio doors of the mews. Fortunately the boiler has been fixed and I have the heat up high, but it's still chilly. At the other end of the garden, the solitary light in the big house is glowing gently. It comes on at sunset, and sunset in December is at four o'clock in the afternoon, although the bank of grey clouds in the sky is making it feel as though it's almost midnight.

I can't concentrate. It's been a horrible few weeks and I don't know if that's because Charles has been away for so long and I'm panicked about what he might be working on (if he's working at all) or because, along with my failure to sign Francesca Clooney, I also missed out on a young writer who I thought had great potential after reading his short story in a magazine. But when I made contact with Bernard Loughlin, he told me that he didn't want the pressure of having an agent and being tied to a publisher and that he was going to do it for himself. I then discovered that he'd signed with Martin Hellman at my old agency. And not that Martin isn't a good agent, but he used to be my effing assistant when I worked in London, and it's annoying to be thrown over for your assistant. Also, my current assistant, Shelley, dropped in earlier to let me know she'll be heading off to Naples in the summer, where she hopes to get a job, as she speaks fluent Italian.

'I'll be sorry to lose you,' I said.

She flicked her dark curls back and smiled at me.

'I've really enjoyed working for you, Ariel. It's been so interesting. But it's time for me to do something different. I don't want to stagnate.'

I can understand that. I felt the same way when I was her age. I was grasping life with both hands when I went to London. I wanted to make a name for myself and be a roaring success. And I *am* successful, I remind myself. I'm good at my job, I love my authors, and over the years I've had some great offers from other agencies to join them. But I like the freedom of working for myself, even if, right now, I'm in a bit of a slump. Terrifying though they may be, I can deal with slumps. They've happened before and I've always bounced back.

I finish the email I was composing and print off a few spreadsheets. Then I close my laptop, pull on my wellies and take a bottle of red wine from the walnut sideboard that runs along the wall behind me. I put on my jacket, heave a couple of bags over my shoulder and let myself out of the office, locking the door behind me, before trudging up the thirty-foot garden to the house.

A blast of warm air hits me when I let myself in, and I almost purr with satisfaction. It's been incredibly difficult not to come up here to work over the past six weeks, but I would have had to change the programming on the central heating for that to happen, and I've never been good at programming the central heating. I'm glad today's pre-set has worked perfectly.

I remove my boots and take my stretchy jeans and a pair of Skechers from one of my bags. I change into them, then walk through the kitchen to the storage room beyond. Hauling out two large cardboard boxes, I carry them upstairs, leaving one in the front reception room and the other in the living room. Then I return to the reception room, where I open the box and look at the Christmas decorations.

Charles and I have always decorated two trees for Christmas. One for the front bay window, mainly to impress the neighbours, and the other for the living room at the back at the house, strictly for us. Even since we split up, I decorate the trees. I don't want people to think Charles is a Christmas Grinch, but I know if I leave it to him, he won't bother.

I listen to an audiobook while I work on the bay window tree. The decorating is reasonably quick, because each year when I take down the decorations I place them neatly in individual boxes within the main storage box and I know exactly which decoration goes where. When I'm finished, I switch on the fairy lights and smile with satisfaction. I'm pleased with the effect, which like every year is cool and sophisticated. The theme here is silver and blue, which goes with the pale greys and blues of the reception room.

In the living room, things are a little different. It's always been a wonderful place to relax – south-west-facing so it gets whatever sun might be available through the painstakingly restored windows, and with heavy drapes to keep out the chill. The high ceilings allow for an impressive chandelier (which is hardly ever switched on, because the side lamps are more restful) and the decor of reds and golds is very inviting.

It's a grown-up room in a grown-up house that's full of atmosphere and the hidden lives of the people who've gone before. Though, being honest, I rarely think of the people who've gone before. I'm more interested in the here and now. Which is what I get in my own apartment, a modern build about three kilometres away that overlooks the Dodder river. Walking distance from here in the summer. Not quite as inviting on days like today.

The living-room tree is always decorated in warm shades of red, gold and green. The audiobook ends just as I finish. I turn on the lamps and uncork the wine. But before I pour it, I take a black wool dress and my black stilettos from another of my bags. I run a brush through my hair and let it flow loosely around my face, refresh my lipstick, then flop onto the sofa and stretch my legs out in front of me, leaning back against the deep cushions and gazing at the tree. There's something about a Christmas tree that's joyful even when you don't feel particularly joyful yourself. But I'm finding my joy again in lying here looking at it.

Where did it all go wrong? I sip my wine and ask myself that question over and over again, even though I already know the answer. We wanted the same thing until we didn't. We loved each other until we didn't. We were good together until we weren't.

Until the day I had to choose and I didn't choose him.

The warmth and the wine make me sleepy, and it's the sound of the front door being opened that jerks me out of the doze I've fallen into. There's a scuffling in the hall, a muttered cursing, and then the door to the living room is opened.

'Jesus Christ,' he says as he sees me. 'What the hell are you doing here?' And then, 'Oh. You've decorated.'

'Welcome home, Charles.' I lift the bottle of red from the table. 'Freedom Friday. I brought a bottle of Monastrell. Didn't you notice the tree in the front?'

He takes off his leather jacket and slings it over the back of the sofa. Then he sits down beside me.

'Now that you mention it, yes. But the street is festooned with trees and lights, so it didn't seem like anything out of the ordinary. Thanks, though. You know me and decorating.'

I do.

I pour him a glass of wine and raise mine to him.

'Season's greetings,' I say, then give him a quizzical look. 'Has Santa brought a manuscript?'

He hesitates, and I feel my stomach sink. Then he grins.

'He absolutely has,' he says, and clinks his glass against mine. 'And he's very, very happy with it.'

'Very, very mysterious, too.' I take a sip of wine. (Not a sip. A gulp of relief.)

'I needed to be,' he says. 'It's different. But you're going to love it.'

'Am I?'

'I know it's a very tentative first draft and needs work, but it's got bestseller written all over it.'

'Gosh.' I take a more modest sip and replace the glass on the table. 'You're not usually so gung-ho.'

'I'm in a gung-ho mood. A gung-ho-ho-ho mood, in fact.'

He sounds so remarkably cheery I feel the tension leave my shoulders.

'So . . . are you going to give it to me?' I ask.

'I have to print it out first,' he says. 'The hard copy I have isn't complete. The hotel printer decided to throw a hissy fit. I'll do it now while I change into something more comfortable.'

He leaves the room and I hear him go up the stairs, and then the sound of his footsteps overhead. Most of the floorboards in the house were salvaged in the great makeover, but they creak a lot. Then I hear the printer whirring into action and allow myself a relieved smile. I wasn't a hundred per cent sure Charles really was working in his island paradise, and I'm very glad he was.

I pour myself another glass of the rich red wine, and this time I drink appreciatively, enjoying its tangy blackberry flavour. I've always been a red wine drinker, even in the summer, when most people like to switch to whites or rosés. I'm more of a full-blooded-flavour person myself.

It's about twenty minutes before he comes downstairs again. He's changed into a pair of grey Hugo Boss leisure pants and a matching grey sweatshirt. He looks great in them. That's the annoying thing about Charles. He always looks great.

'Manuscript?' I ask as he sits beside me and pours himself some more wine.

'Is that all I am to you?' he asks. 'The man with the manuscript?'

'Of course not,' I say. 'I'm eager, that's all.'

'It's still printing,' he says. 'So while we're waiting, tell me how things have been.'

And then, because I always tell him everything, I say that it's been pretty shit and I admit to not having signed Francesca Clooney and missing out on Bernard Loughlin too. I say that Lucy Conway is pregnant and so probably won't write her usual book next year, and that it looks like a small independent publisher will fold while owing money to authors, including mine. And I tell him about the boiler being on the blink, that I've been working in a fridge while he's been sipping cocktails and that my assistant is leaving me. Rather to my surprise, I hear my voice wobble at the end.

'Hey, hey, Ariel.' He obviously hears it too. 'You've had a bad few weeks. But you always come out on top.'

'Do I?'

'Of course you do. Remember that time Sven Bergensson insisted he had writer's block and he couldn't finish his book and you held his hand through the whole process and in the end he won a PEN America award? And it was a major bestseller. If it wasn't for you, that would never have happened.'

'I'm glad you think it was me, but it was Sven himself,' I say as mildly as I can.

'He hasn't done that well since,' observes Charles. 'What's he at these days?'

'He's writing,' I reply. 'Slowly.'

'Even slower than me?' He laughs, and I do too.

'Here.' He fills my half-empty glass, then frowns. 'You forgot the peanuts.'

I usually bring peanuts on Fridays. Or Bombay mix. It's become a tradition of ours and I've missed it while he's been in the Caribbean. I've missed him.

I slide along the sofa and lean my head against his shoulder. He stiffens for a moment, then relaxes.

'I think I'm fed up because of the weather,' I murmur. 'It's been so bloody cold here. I've been thinking of you enjoying yourself beneath tropical skies, and I guess I've been jealous.'

'I was working,' he says.

'Every day?'

'I have a manuscript for you, so yes, every day.'

'But there must have been some fun times too?' I sit up straight again and take another sip from my wine glass. 'You know, cocktails and canapés on the deck.'

'I wasn't on a boat.'

'I seem to remember you were at a party when I called you last. And I'm betting there was a deck somewhere.'

'There was,' he concedes. 'And beachfront dining. And calypso bands.'

'How lovely.'

'It was very therapeutic,' he says. 'It put me into a different space.'

'A creative space, obviously.'

'Eventually.'

'Meet any interesting people?'

'Some,' he says. 'But I was working.'

'And listening to calypso bands . . .'

'Not really my sort of music.'

'True. Hey, Siri,' I say. 'Play jazz.'

The room is suddenly filled with the mellow sound of Chet Baker's 'I Fall in Love Too Easily', which is one of our favourite songs. Any time I ask Siri to play jazz, that's the first thing that comes up.

We sit in silence for a while and I feel myself begin to unwind for the first time in weeks. It shouldn't be because Charles is beside me, but it is. There was a long time after our split when I wondered if we could even maintain our professional relationship. But after a tricky few months when we didn't work together, we adapted. Even though I'm based at the bottom of the garden, we rarely see each other during the week, but since late last year I've come to the house with a bottle of wine and some nibbles most Fridays, and we talk about the stuff we used to talk about before. Charles outlines his creative thoughts and I give him encouragement and advice.

We've got to a good place in our relationship. When he ran into a block in putting his latest idea down on paper, it was me who suggested he should head off somewhere for a few weeks to write without interruption. I proposed a few weeks in the Mayo cottage, but apparently his sister Ellis had taken up temporary residence there, as she frequently does. I then suggested rural France as an ideal alternative, but Charles had already decided on the Caribbean. For a complete change of scenery, he said. Something to challenge his senses. And I told him about the hotel that Corinne Doherty had gone to years ago and from which she'd written her smash Jemima Jones hit, the one that had been made into a movie followed by an Apple TV series featuring the female detective. I pointed out that he already had the movie and the TV series, so he was way ahead of Corinne, but he was in the depths of anxiety at that point and didn't really listen to me. However, it appears the blue seas and skies, and the white sands and calypso bands have worked their magic.

I can't wait to read his book.

I need some good news this month.

Chapter 10

Iseult

*I don't want just words. If that's all
you have for me you'd better go.*

F. Scott Fitzgerald

My house was like a fridge when I got home from the Caribbean, but now it's warm and toasty and I can walk naked from the bathroom to my bedroom without feeling at all chilly. I put on my M&S Autograph bra and pants, then plug in the hairdryer. While we were away, I allowed my hair to dry naturally, and put gel in it for a carelessly spiky look, but today it's minus five outside and I don't fancy icicles on my head.

I'm excited to be going out. Ever since returning home, it's been nothing but work, except for the occasional text from Charles Miller. Because my walking out of his room at the White Sands wasn't the end of whatever there was – or is – between us. I was pissed off with him at that moment, for sure. After all, there was a definite spark and there was no reason we couldn't have lit it, even for one night. We were on holiday, after all. It's practically mandatory to have a no-strings relationship on holiday, isn't it? I couldn't believe he had rejected me for a plot twist.

He didn't appear at breakfast the following morning. His table was free at lunch too.

'Avoiding you, maybe?' suggested Celeste.

'If so, he's an idiot,' I said.

It wasn't until after dinner that he showed up at the cocktail bar. He was talking to one of the golfers. I made it my business to ignore him. But after a while he came over and asked if he could join us.

Celeste gave me an enquiring look. I shrugged, so she nodded and he pulled one of the wicker chairs up to the table.

'How was your day?' he asked.

'I finished the Janice Jermyn,' I told him.

'But *I* have the Janice Jermyn,' he said. 'And I finished it too.'

'I got it from the library.'

The White Sands had a library of books left behind by guests. *The Mystery of the Missing Mallet* and *The Mystery of the Drowning Fish* (Janice's previous book) were among them.

'Oh,' he said. 'Well . . . we had a bet about the murderer. I wrote down my guess. Did you?'

'Actually, yes.' I opened my glittery evening bag, took out a piece of paper and handed it to him.

'Of course you could have written this after you'd finished the book,' he pointed out as he unfolded the paper. 'I won't pretend I got it right myself. I thought it was Becca.' He looked at the name I'd written. 'Dammit. Maura. How did you know?'

'I told you. I read a lot of murder mysteries. I'd guessed

116

before I even gave you the book. Chapter Twenty-Five confirmed it for me.'

'But there's no mention of Maura in Chapter Twenty-Five,' he said.

'Exactly.' I winked at him.

'I underestimated you.' He raised his glass to me.

'Never underestimate Izzy,' said Celeste. 'She always comes out on top.'

I spluttered into my margarita as she nudged me in the ribs. Fortunately the reggae band struck up and the music saved us from talking. Celeste was the first to make a move. She said she was going to refresh her lipstick. Charles and I were left alone.

'I really am sorry about last night,' he said as soon as she was out of earshot. 'I messed up.'

'You didn't mess up,' I retorted. 'You led me on.'

'Seriously?' He raised an eyebrow. 'You think?'

'Charles, we were naked in your bedroom,' I reminded him. 'I had reasonable expectations of what would happen next.'

'I suppose you did.'

'But I also think it's sweet that you were thinking of our sexual health,' I told him. 'And possibly even my reputation.'

'I don't know what I was thinking.'

'Actually, it was your book,' I reminded him. 'A plot twist. I do hope it was worth it.'

'I wrote two chapters after you left. Good chapters.'

'Never in my wildest dreams did I think that I'd inspire a great romantic novelist to write crime by not sleeping with him,' I said.

'Are you being sarky with me?'

'A bit.'

'You're very confident.' Charles frowned. 'Why do I always go for confident women?'

'Your agent-slash-ex was confident too? Well, she must have been if she had her own business.'

'I used to call her Annie-Get-Your-Gun,' he said. 'She'd shoot anyone down if they deserved it.'

'And me? What would you call me?'

'My muse,' he said, very seriously, as he folded my hand in his.

By the time Celeste returned, we were gazing into each other's eyes.

'I'm in the way,' she said. 'I'm going back to the room.'

'Don't,' I said. 'It's fine.'

'I came on this holiday to be emotional support, not a gooseberry,' she told me.

'I'm so sorry.'

'Don't worry,' she said. 'Get whatever emotional support you need from Charles. I'm off to read a book. Not one of yours,' she added, looking at Charles as she picked up her drink. 'I'm going to bed with John le Carré.'

Charles and I remained at the table.

'I should go up too,' I said.

'Probably,' he agreed. 'But I'd much rather you came to my room first.'

So I did.

This time he had protection. I wonder if he'd visited the resort pharmacy or made a trip into town. Either way, I was happy. He was so much better in bed than Steve. He asked me exactly what I most enjoyed and wanted, and his touch was gentle but confident.

I had a great time.

It was a pity Celeste and I were going home the next day.

But he's texted me a few times. At first his messages were quite formal, but now he's getting into emojis and GIFs and is calling it a new way of expressing yourself. I told him it's the way I've always expressed myself, and he sent back a string of emojis, some of which I had to explain to him later. I think it was an eye-opener for him. All the same, I'm not sure what he expects from me, or indeed, what I expect from him. It was great, but it was only a fling. Yet every time a text arrives, I feel a thrill. But will meeting up again in a cold, snowy Dublin put a freeze on the tropical heat that's smouldering below the surface?

I pick up the dryer and switch it on, blasting my hair with hot air. Then I pause. Because I think I've heard a noise downstairs. Which is impossible, especially over the noise of the hairdryer, but you know how it is when you're on your own. You're sensitive to unexpected sounds. It's probably someone outside, but I switch off the hairdryer nonetheless and stand silently in the bedroom. And then I hear it again, the muted thud of a door being opened and closed.

I'm so still I'm almost a statue – I can't believe someone has broken into my home. I've always felt very safe here, sandwiched between the O'Reillys on one side and the Castles on the other. Mr and Mrs O'Reilly are contemporaries of Mum and Dad; they've been my next-door neighbours all my life. The Castles are blow-ins, as they've only lived here for ten years. They're a young family, mum, dad and two small children. Both couples look out for me, and I look out for them.

I look around me and swear softly as I remember I left

my phone in the kitchen so I can't even ring for help. My statue mode of earlier is crumbling. I'm beginning to shake.

And then I hear footsteps on the stairs. The intruder is halfway up. I know, because the sixth stair always creaks and he (I'm assuming it's a he) has stepped on it.

I feel like I'm in the pages of one of Janice Jermyn's cosy crimes. Only it's not so cosy when you think you're about to be a victim. I'm conscious that in my bra and pants I'm the perfect female murder for Chapter One. I imagine my lifeless body stretched across the carpet, the diamanté jewel in my bra twinkling under the lights while Crispin Devereux, Janice's hunky DI, looks at me appraisingly. Despite this mental image, I'm hoping that whoever has broken into my house isn't planning to murder me. I begin to worry about what they might do instead, though, and I look around for something with which to protect myself. There's nothing but the hairdryer. It's a lightweight ceramic Remington and I'm not sure how much good it will be as a weapon. But it's all I've got.

When my bedroom door is pushed open, however, I hear a surprised voice say, 'Izzy!' and I drop the hairdryer and reach for my dressing gown instead. I don't have the belt tied before he's standing there in front of me, one eyebrow raised in amused appreciation.

'You're looking well,' he says as he takes his ear buds from his ears and puts them in their case.

'What the hell are you doing here, Steve?' I demand. 'How did you even get in?'

'I have keys,' my ex-fiancé tells me. 'I was going to leave them behind.'

'You could've posted them through the letter box.' Relief

at not being accosted by a potential murderer has allowed the tension to escape as absolute fury.

'I had to collect my stuff first,' he says.

'What stuff? You came back and took all your stuff ages ago.'

'I left a toolbox behind,' he said. 'Under the stairs.'

'No you didn't. I saw you bring it with you.'

'The main toolbox, yes,' he says. 'But not my smaller one. I completely forgot about it.'

'And you only remembered tonight?'

'Yesterday,' he says. 'I needed one of the attachments. But I couldn't come yesterday. I let myself in tonight because I thought you were still away.'

'How could you possibly think that?' I demand. 'You knew the dates of our honeymoon, for heaven's sake.'

'Yes, but we talked about spending a few days in London. I assumed that's what you'd do.'

There were no direct flights to the Caribbean island from Dublin and so we'd been routed through London. And yes, we did talk about staying there, but changing the connecting flight to Dublin would have been outrageously expensive, so we decided we'd leave it and go another time. I remind Steve of this.

'I was driving by,' he says. 'It seemed as easy to pop in.'

'And it never occurred to you to knock first?'

'Only when I'd actually opened the door,' he admits. 'The house was in darkness, so I assumed you weren't back. Though I was surprised the alarm wasn't set.'

It was in darkness because I'm energy-conscious. The only light on downstairs was a table lamp in the living room. All the same, he should have known I'd never go away without

121

setting the alarm, and he should have copped that it was warm inside the house too. And surely he would have heard the hairdryer – although with his ear buds in and probably playing one of his heavy-metal mixes, maybe not.

'I decided to make myself a cuppa,' he explains. 'I came up because the water pressure was low, so I thought I'd check the pump. I was trying to be helpful, Izzy.'

'For heaven's sake! It was low because I was in the damn shower.'

'Yes. Sorry. All the same, it's lovely to see you.' He grins. 'Looking fit and tanned and very sexy.'

'Shut up!' I tighten the belt of my dressing gown. 'How I look is none of your business any more. Now get your stuff and go.'

'Ah, don't be like that.' His voice softens. 'I didn't mean to give you a fright. I'm really sorry. And I'm glad to see you looking well. Did you have a good holiday?'

All memories of the Caribbean had been pushed from my mind by Steve's appearance, but now I think again of the beautiful island, of the White Sands, and of Charles Miller. Who certainly wouldn't ever be standing in front of me in a pair of Snickers work trousers with holster pockets and a quilted fleece over a black T-shirt. In fairness, Steve looks great in his work gear. I'd almost forgotten how very fit he is.

'It was a lovely holiday.' I keep my own voice steady. 'Lots of fun things to do.'

'Did you meet anyone?' His joking laugh shows that he thinks that's a highly unlikely scenario, and I really want to tell him that yes, I did, and that I had amazing sex with a man who was far more mature and handsome than him, but it's not a discussion I want to get into. So instead I give him a dismissive look and tell him again to get his toolbox and go.

'I really am sorry, you know,' he says as I follow him downstairs. 'Both for . . . well, maybe I didn't go about breaking up the best way, and I regret that. But also for turning up without checking. It was stupid.'

It wasn't stupid. It was entitled. But then he always acted entitled when he was with me. It's another thing I decide not to say.

'Would you mind if I had that cuppa?' he asks now. 'I've been out all day and I'm gasping for a brew.'

I glance at the clock on the wall.

'While I dry my hair,' I say. 'I'm going out.'

'Out?' He switches on the kettle. 'Where to?'

'Town.'

'With Celeste?'

'What on earth business is it of yours?' I demand. 'I'm going out, that's it. And I have to finish drying my hair or I'll be late.'

'Don't let me stop you.' He takes a mug out of the cupboard, drops a tea bag into it, then removes his phone from his pocket. 'I have a few messages to deal with. I'll be done in a couple of minutes, knock back the tea and go.'

'Steve . . .' I look at him, but he's already engrossed in his phone. So I go upstairs and continue drying my hair.

My hair is done and I'm wriggling into my dress when he walks into the bedroom again.

'Don't you ever knock?' I demand as I tug it around my waist.

123

'I know you well enough not to knock,' he says. 'You must be going somewhere nice. That's your posh dress.'

It's one of my only dresses, and if not posh, it's the prettiest one I possess. It's a cerise Ted Baker with a sheer neckline and a full skirt with prints of multicoloured butterflies, and I always feel cheerful when I put it on. I wear it either with my solitary pair of stilettos (when I'm going full dress-up mode) or with a pair of mid-heeled black ankle boots, which is a bit more my style. As I don't want to go full dress-up, but mainly because it's still snowy outside, I pull on the boots while Steve stands there watching me.

'It isn't a date, is it?' he asks.

'It's none of your business.'

'Well, if it is, I'm glad you're moving on.'

'Steve, get out of my bedroom. Get out of my house.'

'I want to be friends, Izzy. Why don't you?'

'Because you broke my heart!' I whirl around from the mirror, which I've been using to check how I look. 'You broke my heart, you broke off our engagement – what am I saying, you cancelled our wedding! You don't love me, but I love you . . .' I stop as I see the expression on his face. 'Loved you,' I amend. 'I loved you and you let me down.'

'Oh, sweetheart, no.' In two steps he's beside me and his hands are on my shoulders. I can smell his aftershave, a subtle woody scent that will always make me think of him. 'I know I was a prat and I wish I'd behaved better.'

'Forget it.' I try for dismissive but only succeed in sounding mulish. 'It's fine.'

'It's not.' He leans towards me and brushes my lips with his. 'It's not, and I'll always regret that I hurt you.' And then he kisses me again, and I don't know why I kiss him back, but I do, and before I realise what's happening, his hand is on my leg and pushing up my dress.

'For God's sake!' I can't believe it took me all of five seconds to come to my senses. 'What the hell d'you think you're doing?'

'OK, OK.' He removes his hand and shrugs. 'I'm sorry. I didn't mean to . . . I'm out of here.'

He turns away and clatters down the stairs. A moment later, I hear the front door slam. I peep out of the window to make sure he's gone before I sit on the edge of the bed and rest my head in my hands.

What on earth just happened? Did I encourage my ex-fiancé to kiss me and touch me and make me feel . . . well, I don't know how I feel, to be honest. I'm actually shaking, but I'm not sure what emotion is causing my hand to tremble and my eyes to fill with tears. I don't want my eyes to fill with tears, because I don't have time to redo my make-up, so I sniff a couple of times, then blow my nose and finish getting ready.

I pause before I go downstairs again, checking myself in the mirror and thinking that I look good in my cerise dress, black jacket and black boots. I look strong and capable.

It would be nice if I felt that way too.

Chapter 11

Iseult

Why can't I try on different lives, like dresses,
to see which fits best and is more becoming?

Sylvia Plath

The Shelbourne Hotel is a blaze of light and Christmas decorations, and the doorman greets me with a welcoming smile as I walk up the steps and into the warm, busy foyer. I take a deep breath and turn towards the bar, which is heaving with people. There's a lot of expensive suit-wearing going on from the men, while the women are in dresses that clearly cost a lot more than my Ted Baker. They're chattering and laughing and clinking cocktail glasses, and I think that this is very much out of my comfort zone. When I go out for a drink, it's usually to my local pub in Marino, which is cosy and nice but not the sort of place you dress up for. And when I come into town, not that I do often, I don't usually venture as far as St Stephen's Green but go to the older, grungier bars like O'Neills or the Stag's Head, where there may indeed be cocktails but you're more likely to see people drinking pints of Guinness (as an aside, I hate

126

Guinness, but I'm quite good at knocking back a pint of lager if challenged).

I scan the crowd and then I see him, sitting at the bar, looking distinguished and very literary in a dark jacket over a black roll-neck top. As I approach him, I'm suddenly afraid that I'm wearing the wrong thing. The Ted Baker is super-pretty, but it's not exactly sophisticated, and Charles Miller looks very sophisticated indeed. He's different to the man I first saw at the White Sands in his shorts and polo. He looks like he belongs here. I'm not sure I do, and I suddenly wonder what on earth made me say yes when he sent the text asking if I'd like to see him again. Holiday romances are best kept on holiday. But Charles said that he wanted to celebrate finishing the book and handing it over to his agent, and that as I was the one who'd inspired him to write it, he thought it would be nice to celebrate with me. It seemed a perfectly nice and normal thing to do, but now I'm wondering if I should simply turn around and leave.

As I hesitate, he looks up from the book that's open on the bar in front of him and sees me. He smiles, and I push my way through the crowd.

'Iseult. You made it.'

'Of course I made it. I'm sorry I'm late. I was . . . unavoid-ably detained.'

He raises an eyebrow.

'Sorry,' I say again, not prepared to tell him about Steve.

'No matter. You're here now.' He raises his hand to the barman, who, without Charles saying anything, places a glass of bubbly in front of me.

'Thanks.' I sit on the stool he kept free for me and take a sip. It's crisp and cool and utterly delicious. 'Congratulations on the book,' I say as I raise the glass to him. 'I've been thinking of you lying on the beach sipping cocktails while I trudged to work in the snow.'

'I wasn't sipping cocktails. I was writing all day every day. The words simply poured out of me. I've never written a book so quickly.'

'What does . . . your agent think of it?' I want to use her name, but that feels too personal. He always spoke about her as though their relationship was entirely professional and there was never a personal aspect to it. I can't help thinking it's a bit odd that they seem to be able to work together when he's clearly scarred by whatever happened between them.

'I don't know yet.'

'What?' I stare at him. 'I thought she was buzzing to read it.'

'I gave it to her and she got a migraine.'

'From reading it?' I give him a puzzled look, and he laughs.

'No. When she got home with it. She gets them a couple of times a year and is absolutely flattened for a few days. She has to lie in a dark room and can't even move her head. She certainly can't read. Even after the headache is gone, it takes her a day or two to get back to normal.'

'The poor woman,' I say with real sympathy. 'That must be awful.'

'It is.' He nods. 'The first time I saw her with one, I honestly thought she was having a stroke or something. She couldn't keep her eyes open and she could hardly speak. It was frightening. Yet when she recovers, she's absolutely fine.'

'I'm very glad I only get normal headaches,' I say. 'And

if I'm being honest, most of those are self-inflicted due to alcohol.' I glance at the tapered glass in my hand. 'Though not this alcohol. It's lovely.'

'Champagne doesn't leave you with a hangover,' he says.

'I've heard that before, but I've never drunk enough to find out.' I smile at him.

There's a sudden surge in the crowd around us, and then it subsides. It appears that many of them are here for a private function and it's time for them to leave the bar. I'm thinking that their departure should give us some space, but almost immediately more people arrive, equally well dressed.

'It's invariably busy here at the weekend,' says Charles. 'Especially at this time of year. I should have thought of that when I suggested it as a meeting place, but it's where I always come when I'm in town.'

'No worries.' I take another sip of champagne.

'I've reserved a table for dinner,' he says. 'We should go ourselves.'

'Where?' I ask.

'Oh, here. No point in heading out into the cold again, and it's a nice place to celebrate, don't you think? Elizabeth Bowen wrote about it, you know.'

I've no idea who Elizabeth Bowen is or was. I say nothing, but glance towards the window, through which I see soft white flakes gently falling from the sky. They've been doing that on and off all day, but fortunately the snow hasn't settled.

Charles and I make our way to the dining room. I've never eaten at the Shelbourne before, and I'm a little taken aback by the formality of the room, with its dark wallpaper and gloomy paintings. Starched white tablecloths are laid with shining cutlery, and each table has a small floral centre-piece. It's not really my thing, but with the wintry weather outside, it kind of works.

'A far cry from the beachside restaurant at the White Sands,' remarks Charles as a waiter pulls out a chair for me.

'It's different,' I agree. 'I did like the White Sands, though. Everyone was so lovely there.'

'On the one hand, I enjoyed myself immensely,' says Charles. 'On the other, I'm not really such a warm-weather person that spending nearly six weeks away was a good move. I missed the rain.'

The wine waiter comes to the table and asks if we'd like to order something from the cellar. Charles does this without even looking at the list. I think of all the times I went out with Steve when we studied the wine list carefully, trying to identify wines we knew and always making sure not to choose the least expensive in case the wine waiter thought we were cheapskates. Steve knows as much as I do about wine, which is absolutely nothing. On the rare occasions when we were with people who knew a little more than us, he would always say that thing about not knowing much but knowing what he liked. He would then say he'd be happy with anything except a Tempranillo. This wasn't because he'd know a Tempranillo from whatever isn't a Tempranillo but because it made him sound as though he actually did know a little. I bet he's drunk it loads of times totally unaware.

Charles, however, seems to know quite a lot. On the occasions we ate with him at the White Sands, he used to have discussions with the staff about the wines and where they'd originated. He always chose something nice. When

Celeste and I ate alone, we asked for glasses of the house wine. It was included in our package, so we saw no point in ordering anything else.

I pick up the menu and look at the choices. I wish I could see the prices. I'm sure they reflect that this is a luxury hotel, but I feel uncomfortable knowing that Charles is paying for the meal, and for the undoubtedly pricey wine as well as the excellent champagne. He insisted on this when he first asked me out, saying that the evening was entirely his treat. Nevertheless, I'm used to splitting the bill.

'What's wrong?' he asks.

'Huh?'

'You're frowning at the menu. Don't tell me nothing appeals to you.'

'It's not that.'

'What then?'

I explain about the bill, and he looks at me incredulously.

'I told you this was a celebration, a way of saying thank you,' he says. 'I wouldn't dream of you paying.'

'I appreciate that. But . . .'

'What?'

How can I say what I'm thinking? That if I allow him to pay for everything, he might have expectations about where the night will lead. And that although I slept with him on the island, it was a very different proposition to sleeping with him now. It's not that I haven't thought about it. It's not that I might not want to. But I don't want to feel obliged.

I look at him wordlessly.

'It's different,' I say eventually.

'What is?'

'Here. With you. It's different to the Caribbean. We were on holiday then. It was fun. You weren't paying for me.'

'You're worried that me paying for you shifts the balance between us? Despite my reasons for asking you?' He zones in on the main problem.

'Yes. But the thing is, if I was paying for myself, we'd probably be in Nando's.'

He laughs, and I feel my mouth twitch.

'That's perfectly reasonable,' he says. 'And if we ever go out again, we'll go to Nando's and I will stiff you with a bill for chicken butterfly and sides as well as halloumi, followed by a salted caramel brownie.'

'You're a Nando's fan?'

'It used to be my favourite treat,' he says. 'I sometimes still order it online.'

'Oh, Charles.' This time I'm the one who laughs, then he joins in, and we're both chuckling away happily when the waiter comes to take our order.

It's all wonderful. The meal, the setting, the company – especially the company. I did wonder how weird it might be to see him in Dublin. I wondered if I'd ask myself what on earth I'd been thinking by sleeping with him in the first place. I wondered if he'd think the same. But I don't. And I don't think he does either. And now we're in a taxi together, going back to his house for a nightcap. Of course, it's not at all convenient for me to go to Terenure for a nightcap. It's the complete opposite direction to where I live. And I'm doubtful that 'nightcap' means only a drink. But I don't care. Along with the (fabulous) wine, I've had another glass

132

of champagne, and after the trauma of Steve turning up at my house, scaring me half to death and seeing me in my underwear, being with Charles is calm and lovely and grown up. He held the door of the cab open for me when I got in, and I saw him unobtrusively tip the doorman of the hotel who'd whistled it up for us. He's a world away from Steve and I'm happy to be here with him.

When we arrive at his home, my eyes widen. It's a detached red-brick house with a bay window either side of the front door, which is painted pillar-box red. Ivy is growing up the walls, but it's kept under control, only covering part of the brick. There are five upstairs windows and a stained-glass fanlight over the door, illuminated by an internal light. A large Christmas tree decorated in silver and blue takes up one of the bay windows. The steps up to the door, where an enormous holly and ivy wreath is hanging, are granite, and two large stone statues of lions (at least I think they're lions, they're very decorative) stand either side. Their mouths are open, showing their teeth.

'Temple dogs,' says Charles when I comment on them. 'They protect the house from harmful influences.'

'Hope they don't bite me so.' I watch him open the door, then follow him into the house.

It's gorgeous, in a kind of old-fashioned way. The high-ceilinged hallway is painted in navy and grey, and the floor is parquet wood with a carpet runner running the length of it. The light that I saw from outside comes from a tiered chandelier, although there are also a couple of gently glowing lamps on two well-polished tables on either side of the hall.

'Jeepers,' I say. 'Writing books is a profitable thing.'

'More precarious than profitable,' says Charles. 'I was

probably a bit foolish sinking all my money into this house, but at least I have a lovely home to retreat to.'

'You totally do.' I continue following him, this time into a kind of living room that has a clubby feel with its red and green decor and squishy sofa with oversized cushions. There's another Christmas tree here, with a more traditional feel to it, and I'm impressed that he's had the time to put up two trees and a wreath and fill the house with diffusers that give off a slightly spicy scent. If I'm honest, given that he lives on his own, I was expecting more of a man-cave than this elegantly decorated home.

'I say foolish, but actually I was lucky.' Charles walks to a cupboard and takes out a bottle of wine and two glasses. 'Even if I am, as they say, asset-rich and cash-poor, this is a good area and house prices have increased steadily.'

'Your entire generation was lucky.' I sit on the sofa. 'It's really hard for someone my age to buy a house. And I doubt you've run out of cash. You spent six weeks on a beach, after all.'

'It's all relative.' He uncorks the wine, a deep ruby red, and pours it into the glasses.

I'd like his sort of relative, I think as I take a sip. I thought when I saw him at the White Sands that he was well off, given the gorgeous villa he was staying in, but this is another level altogether. I wish I'd paid more attention in English class and written a bestseller instead of joining the Civil Service and ending up stopping trucks at Dublin Port. I glance at my watch and then out of the window, where snowflakes are still drifting lazily from the sky. Even though it's late, ships will continue to arrive and unload their cargo while my friends and colleagues stand in the freezing night and look for signs of contraband. I'll be joining them in the morning. I'm looking forward to it.

'You OK?' Charles sits beside me, and I nod and tell him I was thinking about work and how cold it is down at the port.

'It's chilly in here,' he remarks, which is partly true, because it's a big room and the heating doesn't entirely eliminate the draught coming from beneath the door. 'When I did the renovations, I tried to make it as snug as possible, but as it was a listed building there were some things I couldn't quite manage.'

'It has a cosy feel, though. Do you live here on your own?'

'Since the break-up of my marriage,' he replies.

'What happened?' I ask, at the same time registering that he and his agent did actually get married in the end and wondering how well they really get on professionally. I think of my colleagues Sian Collins and Peter Tominey. They were offered a chance to move to different sections after they got divorced, but neither wanted to, although they're never on the same shift. Nevertheless, if it works for them, I guess it can work for Charles and his ex too.

'Oh, there were a variety of reasons it went pear-shaped, but the truth was, I was jealous, and she, rather understandably, couldn't put up with me.'

'Jealous of what?'

'Her other male authors mainly.'

'Oh.' I mull this over. 'Did she give you a reason to be jealous?'

'If someone wants to be jealous, they can always find a reason.' He gives his head an impatient shake. 'It's not important. What matters is we messed it up.'

All the same, he sounds forlorn. And I'm thinking that they bought this house when they were full of hope and expectation and it must be awful to be still here when all that has gone. And that it's definitely amazing they still have a working relationship. I wonder if he still loves her.

'You don't have children?'

Wikipedia didn't mention any.

'No. One good thing at least.'

'Did you want them?'

'We decided to put a family on hold. One of our better decisions,' he adds.

I presume the lack of children is why he kept the house and she's not here instead, although even with children she'd be rattling around in it. I wonder if Charles feels he's rattling around. It's a big place for one person.

I ask him if he finds it lonely here.

'Lonely? No.' He seems a little surprised at the question. 'I find it peaceful, to be honest.'

'I like living on my own, but I'm not sure I'd be as keen on it in a house like this where there are probably all sorts of nooks and crannies. My entire home would fit in this room.'

'You're exaggerating.'

'Only slightly.'

'Would you like a tour?'

'Yes please.'

I place the glass of wine on the dark-wood coffee table and stand up.

'This is my living room. Obviously.' He gestures around. 'And through here . . .' he opens connecting doors to the room with the blue and silver tree, 'is my library.'

'Oh, wow.' The only furniture is a couple of comfortable-looking armchairs and a coffee table. The walls are taken up entirely with bookshelves, which themselves are crammed with books. 'It really is a library. How many books?'

'Thousands,' he says. 'I've more in my study, of course.'

I thought I was quite a good reader, with my overflowing IKEA Billy bookcase, but this is a whole new level. I walk over to one of the shelves and see that there are little numbered tags on them, while the books themselves are arranged in alphabetical order. I congratulate him on his organisation. My books are simply shoved on the shelf as I finish reading them.

'My sister did it,' he said. 'She worked in a library for a time. So they're arranged using the Dewey system.'

That goes completely above my head, and he explains that it's a way of classifying books into groups and then subdividing the groups to make it easy to find any volume. I tell him I don't need a system to know where all my Janice Jermyns are, and he smiles and confesses that he hasn't read all the books on his shelves.

'I do read a lot,' he admits. 'But when this room was finished and had so much space for books, I bought loads of old editions to fill the shelves. Of course, now I actually need more space again. I have an entire set of Dorothy L. Sayers,' he adds, and walks over to them to show me 'So I'm not totally hopeless when it comes to crime, even if hers are classic murder mysteries.'

'Maybe yours could be the start of a series.' I take out a couple of the books and smile at the old-fashioned covers before putting them back in their correct places. 'After all, your detective is a very sexy character.'

'I didn't try to make him sexy.' He looks appalled.

'Imagine that! He writes sexy without even trying.' I grin. 'Come on, show me more.'

He brings me to the kitchen next, which is at the lower level and, in contrast to the studied yet faded elegance of upstairs, is relentlessly modern, white and clinical. It connects to a smaller room which is set up as a home gym, with a Peloton bike and a rowing machine. No wonder Charles looks so fit! I think of my own lapsed gym membership and vow to renew it.

Then we go up two flights to his study, which is a lovely, comforting space with big armchairs, more bookshelves and quite an impressive desk with a vintage-style desk lamp with a green glass shade and a gold base. Dozens of framed quotes from famous writers are hung on the walls.

'So this is the creative hub,' I say. 'Cool.'

'The allegedly creative hub,' he reminds me. 'I had to decamp to the White Sands to write, remember.'

'What was stopping you here?'

'I don't know.' He perches on the edge of the desk. 'Perhaps . . . perhaps it was having such a great place to write.'

I look at him curiously.

'I wrote my first book in my office at work,' he says. 'I wrote the second in my tiny one-bedroom apartment. The builders were in here when I was writing my third. Now that I have the perfect space, it intimidates me. To be honest, I got it done up like this for photographs.'

'Photographs?'

'You know, when I do TV or newspaper interviews. It's good to have a place that looks the part.'

I laugh. I can't help it.

'You think I'm a complete arse, don't you?' he says.

'Not a complete one,' I assure him. 'But there's a certain arse-ness about it all right.'

'It looked great when RTÉ did that programme about Ireland's prizewinning authors.'

'I'm sure it did.'

'The fact that you obviously didn't watch it has stripped me of all arse-ness,' says Charles, and I smile.

He suggests we go downstairs again.

'Nothing else to see up here?' I ask.

'Another room with books and bits and pieces. Not for the public, though. It's more of a dumping ground than anything else. And bedrooms.'

I nod.

'Would you like to see the bedrooms?' he asks.

'How many?'

'Five.'

'That's a lot when you're on your own.'

'I do have people to stay,' he protests. 'My sister whenever she's flying out of Dublin. And my mother occasionally. My nieces when they're in town too.'

'Your sister is the one who worked in a library?'

He nods.

'Do you have many brothers and sisters?'

'One of each,' he replies. 'Ellis is now involved in arts and crafts. She's two years younger than me. Nick is married with children. Well, I say children, but they're in their twenties now. Louisa is at college in Cork. Emily's working in Singapore.'

'And your parents?' I didn't ask him about his family when

we were at the White Sands. Other people weren't important then. But I'm interested now.

'My dad died a number of years ago and Nick took over the running of the pub we own. He lives in the house that comes with it while my mother has a nice modern bungalow just outside the town. Ellis divides her time between staying with Mum, a house with a studio she rents in Enniskerry and the cottage we own in Mayo. Which is where I decamp to write from time to time.'

I'm dying to ask more, but as I don't want to appear too nosy, I ask him to show me one of the guest rooms.

He opens one of the doors. The room is decorated in the same dark colours as elsewhere in the house, but it's very cosy and I'm entranced by the original cast-iron fireplace and the old floorboards, partially covered by a large faded green rug. There are views over the long back garden, which is well lit by outside lights and has a renovated mews at the end.

'Does anyone live there?' I ask.

He shakes his head, and I think that if it all goes pear-shaped he'd get a great price for renting it out. I don't say that out loud, though.

'It's lovely,' I tell him. 'And you've obviously worked really hard for it. So congratulations.'

'Do you want to see my room?' he asks.

'Your bedroom?'

'Yes.'

I hesitate.

'Just to see it,' he says. 'I'm not . . .'

'You're not?' I raise an eyebrow.

'I don't want to pressurise you.'

I think for a moment about Steve and his lips on mine earlier. His assumption that it would be OK. And I smile at Charles.

'I'd love to see your room.'

He smiles and takes me by the hand.

#ThePerfectMan, I think as I accompany him.

Chapter 12

Ariel

A good book is an event in my life.
Stendhal

I place the last page of Charles's manuscript on the coffee table, then gaze across the city from my apartment window. I'm on the fourth floor, and the view towards the bay is beautiful. One of the things I definitely prefer about Dublin as opposed to London is being beside the sea. I allow my eyes to rest as I gaze into the dusky light and think about my client's latest book.

I started reading first thing this morning, when I woke up and realised that my migraine had finally lifted. I raised my head cautiously from the pillow, half expecting the blinding pain that takes residence behind my right eye to return, but I was perfectly fine. I was equally cautious getting out of bed, but by the time I'd made it to the kitchen to make myself a cup of tea, I knew I was back to normal.

I cursed the inappropriate timing of getting a migraine at the same time as Charles's manuscript. No matter how much I wanted to read it, I simply couldn't. My migraines have become less frequent over the last few years, but when one does arrive, I react by immediately posting an out-of-office message on all my media before getting myself into a dark place and taking a couple of pills. Then I lie down and wait for it to pass. I'm always relieved when it does.

I rub the back of my neck before picking up the manuscript again.

It's good. Really good. *A Caribbean Calypso* is well written, very witty, cleverly plotted (despite some glaring errors, which can be fixed) and the characters are hugely engaging.

But it's not the novel Charles was contracted to write, which was tentatively titled *Springs Eternal*. It's not the novel his readers will expect. Many people who read pacy crime novels also read Booker Prize winners; however, the kind of people who read and review Booker Prize winners don't usually admit to having popular murder mysteries on their shelves (or if they do, they murmur that it's a guilty pleasure).

My phone buzzes.

How are you feeling?

Better

Have you been able to read the manuscript yet?

Yes, I'm letting it sink in

In a good way?

In an agent-y sort of way

This time my phone rings.

'What do you mean, "in an agent-y sort of way"?' demands Charles. 'Can't you just give it to Graham and tell him how brilliant it is?'

'Obviously this is a very different kind of book, and not what he'll be expecting from you, so it'll require some additional discussion with him.'

'Is it *too* different for Xerxes?' Charles sounds anxious. 'I know they don't do crime usually, but the characters *are* from *Springs Eternal* and the plot follows the plan I had for it in a weird kind of way.'

'I don't recall three murders in the outline you gave me,' I say in amusement. 'Or a poisoned pineapple, fun though it was to read about. What on earth possessed you to write a murder mystery anyway? You were gung-ho about *Springs Eternal* in its original format.'

'Until I got writer's block and discovered another side to myself.'

'A homicidal side?'

'Maybe.' He laughs.

'Well, leave it with me and let me persuade Graham he has a bestseller on his hands. But there'll have to be some editing, Charles. You've dropped clues that give away the murderer early on.'

'Dammit, have I really? It's so hard not to do,' he says. 'But it's not something to worry about just yet. Let's see what Graham and Sophia have to say. I'm sure we'll work it out. Have you eaten? We could have a late lunch and talk it over.'

Sophia, Charles's editor, is in her sixties, very experienced, and has worked with him ever since *Winter's Heartbreak*. They get on really well together.

'I have a . . . Oh, all right. I'm at home right now. Will I come to Riverside Lodge?'

'If you're OK with bread and cheese.'

'I'll stop off at the deli on the way,' I tell him.

'You're a gem,' he says, and ends the call.

It takes about ten minutes to drive from my apartment to Charles's house, but stopping at the deli delays me, and it's over half an hour later before I'm pointing the remote at the sliding gate that leads to the parking space beside my mews. The snow of the previous few days has melted, although it feels cold enough to start again at any minute.

I walk past my office and up the path to the kitchen door. It's unlocked. I step inside and made my way into the hallway.

'Anyone home?' I call. 'I come bearing gifts.'

I hear the sound of footsteps, and a minute later Charles appears. He's wearing a light blue sweater over his oldest jeans. His eyes flicker to the shopping bag in my hand. 'What did you get?'

I take out smoked chicken, salads and some crusty rolls, and he smiles appreciatively.

'Excellent choices, thank you.'

'Give me credit for knowing your favourite lunch,' I say as I begin to butter the rolls. 'Haven't you done any shopping since you got back?'

'No time.' He shrugs.

I did all the food shopping when we were together because Charles is utterly hopeless at it. He eats out or orders in whenever he's on his own.

'Wine or water?' he asks.

'Water is fine, thanks.'

'So.' He puts a glass in front of me, then sits on the opposite side of the counter. 'I'm really excited about *A Caribbean Calypso*, Annie. I believe in it completely.'

Apart from my parents, he's the only one who ever calls me Annie, and that's usually only when he's trying to make a point. Mum named me Anne, after her godmother. But Anne isn't a stand-out sort of name, and I wanted to stand out. So when I went to London, I changed it. Nobody else knows my given name and I never, ever tell anyone. It was a statement of trust in Charles that I told him.

I sip my water and then ask him about his inspiration for the book.

'The Caribbean didn't put me in the right frame of mind for a heartbreaking love story,' he says. 'But it was perfect for a murder. I had it read by an expert,' he adds.

'An expert?'

'At the resort,' he says. 'There was a girl who read lots of crime.'

'Someone you didn't even know read your manuscript?' I'm shocked. Early on in his career, he showed a first draft of *Winter's Heartbreak* to his sister-in-law, Rachel. Fortunately, despite her lukewarm response to the main character, he persevered, but since then he hasn't let anyone bar me and the Xerxes team see his work before the advance reading copies are ready.

'I wanted feedback from someone who knew the genre,' he says.

'OK . . .' I can't help sounding doubtful.

'And she was right, you said so yourself. It's a good book. She's a fan of Janice Jermyn, by the way,' he continues, 'I told her I'd get her some signed copies of her books.'

'You did, did you?'

'Why not?'

I'm stunned by Charles's confidence. He was at a low ebb when he left for the White Sands, but now he reminds me of how he used to be when I first met him. He believed in his writing then, in what he was trying to say. He believed in it when he wrote *My Frozen Heart*, too. I think it was the time I was most in love with him. When everything stretched before us, bright and promising. The sunlit uplands of literary success in which we both would find eternal happiness.

There's no such thing as eternal happiness. If one of my authors wrote that in a manuscript, I'd tell them that our time on earth is finite, and that strictly speaking our happiness ends with the end of our lives. They'd probably argue that it could carry on in the afterlife, and then we'd have an existential discussion about it and I'd still insist on them editing it out.

However, despite me and Charles no longer being romantically involved, we're still good friends and professional partners. I'll be behind him every step of the way with his new book. He wouldn't expect anything less from me and I wouldn't expect anything less from myself either.

Chapter 13

Iseult

Half my life is an act of revision.
John Irving

I'm standing on my plinth, freezing in the biting easterly wind that whistles around the buildings and the cargo crates of the port, when the final truck rolls off the ship. It's a six-axle articulated lorry and the container is painted green with the logo of a transport company I've never heard of. I hold up my hand to tell the driver to stop, and I can feel his irritation as the air brakes engage.

'Hello,' I say as he lowers the window. 'Where have you come from?'

He's a heavyset middle-aged man with a weathered face, and he gives me an irked look from below the black baseball cap pulled down close to his eyes.

'UK,' he says, and then nods back at the ferry. 'Where d'you think?'

I keep my voice pleasant. 'And what goods are you carrying?' I ask, although I already know the answer because I've seen the manifest. It's machine parts.

'I don't know,' he says. 'I picked it up, that's all.'

You'd think he'd be fully aware of what the load is, but a lot of the documentation is sent electronically now, and sometimes drivers are the last in the chain. Brexit has made things a million times more complicated. We've taken on more staff simply to deal with the digital paperwork.

'That's OK,' I say. 'Would you mind driving into the next lane and they'll direct you. We need to do an additional check.'

'Why?' he demands. 'I've driven all over Europe and nobody ever stops me. Only here in this little island. Who do you think you are?'

'I'm a customs official,' I reply. 'And I'm doing my job.'

'And I'm doing mine.' He glowers. 'I don't need to be delayed.'

'We'll be as quick as we can,' I say. 'Thank you.'

When the last of the vehicles has left the port, I walk over to the large covered shed where the lorry is now parked. The driver is talking to Katelyn, who tells him she needs him to open the container. He grumbles as she breaks the seal, but says nothing more. There's a certain frisson of tension in the team as he swings the doors open to reveal dozens of tightly stacked crates.

'Are you going to check them all?' His tone is sarcastic.

'No,' says Katelyn.

The driver taps his foot, then rubs his arms. Despite some drifting flakes of snow, he's only wearing a gilet over his Meat Loaf T-shirt, and he must be cold. The customs team, me included, are all well wrapped up in thermal fleeces, hats and boots, as well as our hi-vis jackets. We talk quietly among ourselves as we wait for Fish and Chips. When they arrive,

Brad signals to Chips to jump into the container. Tail wagging enthusiastically, the dog climbs onto the crates, although his lack of interest in them makes us exchange anxious glances. But after a good rummage around, he sits down and barks, indicating he's detected something.

'X-ray?' I suggest. The crates would be a nightmare to unload and open.

Ken nods, and I tell the driver to move the lorry to the mobile X-ray unit. I like the X-ray unit. I like looking at the images, figuring out what they might be and deciding if there's anything worth investigating further. With Chips having indicated for drugs, I'm sure we'll find something. The question is whether it'll be a big haul or just a spliff the driver has managed to drop in the container. I ask him if he has a jacket to put on while he waits in the designated area for us to X-ray the container. He grabs a fleece from the cab, grumbling all the while.

Mateusz Bernaki, another team member, is already in the unit when I open the door and walk in. He begins the scanning process, and the contents of the truck start to appear on the screen. We both study the image, changing the colour and contrast in an effort to spot anomalies. There's no shading that would indicate anything that shouldn't be there, and yet there's something not quite right.

'See that?' I point to the roof of the container.

'Yup.'

'Any chance we're talking lead-lined?'

'Could be.'

I use my walkie-talkie to ask Robbie if he or Ken saw anything that might have been a false panel in the container.

'No,' he replies.

'Get the driver to bring it to the yard,' I tell him. 'We're going to search it.'

I walk outside and explain to the driver what's happening. He seems resigned now, and asks if he can get coffee while we're searching the container. I say I'll see what we can do. We're not great on guest comforts at the port. He gets back into his cab, and we follow him in our customs cars, making sure he parks the lorry in the designated bay. I bring him to a room where I tell him he'll have to wait. As I leave, I hear him ask another one of the officers for coffee.

Back in the bay, Ken and Katelyn climb onto the crates and begin checking the container itself, running their hands over the roof, which, to be honest, looks perfectly all right to me. I worry that we've got it wrong, that we're wasting our time and the driver's.

'Anything?' I ask Ken when he jumps down.

'I want to have another look at the scan.'

I stay beside the container while he goes back into the unit. Fish and Chips have long since returned to the office building, Chips in good form because as far as he's concerned it's job done and time for a bit of fun. I check the lorry's digital paperwork again.

My mobile vibrates. I glance at the message. It's Charles saying that Ariel (though he still only refers to her as 'my agent') has read the book and that they're currently talking about it. But he thinks she really likes it. Charles and his issues are inhabiting a world a million miles away from my current concerns. I send a short text saying that I'm at work. My phone pings with a reply, but I don't get to look at it because Ken has returned with a large flashlight. I replace my mobile in the back pocket of my trousers while he concentrates the light on the roof, shining it into the corners. Then he gives a grunt of satisfaction.

'We need cutting equipment,' he says. 'And I'm thinking it's time to call the Gardaí.'

Usually the drugs are smuggled in the crates themselves. We've found cocaine in furniture, packed in sofas and chairs, we've found drugs in tyres, in plaster statues and animal feed. (Not obviously in the actual feed itself, or Ireland would have some very chilled-out cattle. In bags of the same size and appearance.)

It's another hour before Ken finally accesses the space in the roof. As he lowers the hatch he's made, we can see the carefully bundled packages of powder. I start taking photos, absorbing the scale of what we've uncovered. By the time we're finished, we've unloaded multiple slabs of what we reckon is cocaine. I feel very proud of the team and our efforts.

The Garda drug squad, who arrived earlier, are also busy taking photos. A female officer goes inside the building to arrest the driver, who may or may not have known what he was transporting along with the crates of machine parts. It's not a good day for him, but it's a great one for us.

'Who's the man!' Ken beams at the senior garda.

'The dog, I believe.' The garda grins. 'Great job, though.'

'Yay our team!' I high-five everyone.

This is going to be an item on the news later.

Obviously I don't post anything about it on social media. But if I did, it would be #LoveMyJob.

We're all totally buzzing when our shift finally ends, and the whole team heads out to celebrate. The pub across the inlet of the bay is busy with locals, but we find a big table and order drinks all round.

'Excellent teamwork from everyone concerned,' I say.

'Here's to us!' Ken lowers his voice to imitate a narrator in a reality programme. 'Keeping our borders secure, one gram at a time.'

The team laughs. We're suckers for watching *Border Patrol* episodes, although they mostly concentrate on individuals coming through airports with drugs concealed in their luggage or on themselves. I much prefer the more industrial nature of the port, which is an entire ecosystem on its own.

My phone buzzes and I think of Charles's last message. The one I neither read nor replied to. Oh well, he'll know I was too busy to get back to him.

Hey. I hear there was a drugs bust at the port today

It takes a moment before I realise the text is from Steve rather than Charles. I'm not sure I want to answer it. But eventually I do, because I can't believe he knows about it already.

How did you hear that?

Breaking news

Seriously?

Information gets out quickly these days. It's not as if we keep things secret, but if the Gardaí were hoping to locate the actual importer of the drugs, having a news story about today's find probably isn't going to help.

Apparently they've arrested a couple of
people who are 'known to the Gardaí'

Steve uses the euphemism for career criminals.

That was quick

According to the report it's worth about €5 million

I couldn't say

I knew it would have a high street value, but €5 million
is an excellent haul.

You must be pleased

Thrilled

Well done

Thanks

Are you in the pub?

He knows us too well.

Yes. But leaving shortly

I'll be going past. I might see you there

What the hell? I don't actually type this, but I think it.

Steve dumped me with weeks to go before our wedding, and now he's saying he'll meet me where I'm having a drink with my colleagues. Plus he called to my house without asking and scared the living daylights out of me. Then he kissed me. We're over. He wanted it that way. So what's he playing at?

I type quickly.

I'm leaving now sorry

How about seeing you at yours?

Am going out

Where?

None of your business!!!!!

Chill out, Izzy. I want to be friends, that's all

When I told Natasha that Steve wanted to be friends, she said that an ex asking to be friends is like a kidnapper asking to keep in touch after they've released you. It made me laugh, but she's right. He broke my heart, for heaven's sake. But this is him all over. He only sees things from his point of view, which in my case seems to be: I didn't want to marry you but I'm quite happy to go out with you. I'm not in love with you but I expect you to be there for me. The truth is that a few weeks ago I'd have been over the moon at hearing from him. Those first days at the White Sands I'd even been wondering how I might get back with him. But now . . . now I have other options.

I look at my phone again and click Charles's message. It's brief and to the point:

Will I see you later?

It's probably too late to reply. When he didn't hear back from me earlier, he'll have found something else to do. Or perhaps he's working on his book again and won't welcome an interruption. Besides, certain as I am that I don't want to see Steve, I'm not sure about Charles either. Although we had a fabulous time at the Shelbourne and an even more fabulous time at his gorgeous house, I'm really uncertain about where this is going. I love being with him, but he's not the sort of person I've ever imagined dating, and I'm pretty sure he'd say the same about me. I wonder if he simply feels obliged to keep thanking me for helping him unlock his writer's block.

I start to tap the keypad.

Sorry. Busy day at port. Couldn't get back to you earlier. I'm free later if you are. X

As I press send, I wish I hadn't added that bit about being free. It sounds a bit needy. I definitely don't want to come across as needy.

I finish my non-alcoholic beer and tell the team I'm going home.

'Stay for another,' says Ken.

'I'd love to, but I've got to go. Might have a hot date tonight.'

'Really?' Katelyn's eyes widen. 'A new man? I'm delighted for you.'

'Early days.'

'Have a great time.'

'Absolutely.' I haul my bag over my shoulder and carry my electric scooter outside. I often use the scooter to get to work, depending on my shift, but I don't like using it when there's a lot of traffic around. It's busy this evening, so I head home on foot. When I get to Bram Stoker Park, I stop to check on Steve's location. He's in Baldoyle, about twenty minutes away. He's obviously decided not to call to the pub after all.

It looks like I'll have the evening to myself unless Charles calls, which is very unlikely. But I don't mind either way.

After all, who needs a man when you've had the best day at work?

Chapter 14

Ariel

Tomorrow we will run faster,
stretch out our arms farther.
F. Scott Fitzgerald

The clouds roll in as dusk falls, and Charles switches on the table lamp in the living room, where we're together again, this time discussing the next steps towards publication of *A Caribbean Calypso*. He's opened a bottle of wine, but I'm driving so I've asked for sparkling water. He pours it for me and adds ice and lemon. He always likes to do things properly.

I made a few more suggestions, including getting rid of the massive clue to the murderer early on, and he's reworked those parts of the novel. So now it's ready to go to his publisher.

'I'll bring it to Graham myself,' I tell him. 'I'll make a big deal of delivering it personally and make sure he knows he has a real commercial bestseller on his hands.'

'He has,' says Charles.

I laugh. It's always fun to see him when he's super-confident.

'What?' He looks momentarily aggrieved, and then laughs himself. 'Oh, look,' he says. 'It won't be a disaster if he doesn't like it. There are other publishers, after all.'

'It won't be ideal,' I say. 'You'll still owe him a book and you'll have missed the deadline.'

'Even if it isn't what he expected, it's a good story. A family of desperate women, an enigmatic man and his younger lover, and a dark, festering secret, all coming to a head in a tropical paradise. It's got Netflix or Prime written all over it.'

'You have a point.' I take a sip of sparkling water. 'Tell me a little about your beta reader.'

'My what?'

'It's a term for early readers,' I tell him. 'You must know that, Charles.'

'I've heard it,' he admits. 'But I thought it might actually be some kind of publishing algorithm.'

I grin. 'So tell me about her.'

He sits back on the sofa and gazes into his glass. 'She was on holiday with her cousin. The cousin had, thankfully, read me. Beta girl was the Janice Jermyn fan.'

'I truly can't believe you gave your manuscript to a complete stranger to read.'

'Like I said, she was an expert. So I thought, why not?'

'And you don't think *I'm* a crime expert given that I'm Janice Jermyn's actual agent?'

He looks at me with an expression of surprise. I say nothing as he takes a slow drink. 'I . . . I suppose I was afraid,' he says finally.

'Afraid?' I frown. 'Afraid of me?'

'Afraid you'd say it was terrible. If someone I didn't know hated it, that was one thing. But if *you* hated it . . .'

159

'You're such an eejit, Charles Miller.' I lean across to him and squeeze his hand. 'You'd never write a book I hate. I'm always on your side, no matter what. You know that.'

'I know I *should* know that,' he says. 'But sometimes . . . well, I wouldn't blame you if you'd lost a little of your respect for me.'

'Absolutely not,' I say. 'You're one of the best writers I know.'

'Respect for me as a person, not as a writer.'

'I'll always respect you,' I say. 'Always.'

'That's not what you said when you left me.'

'The past is the past and we've moved on,' I tell him. 'We're in a much better place than we were a couple of years ago.'

'Do you ever wish we'd done things differently?'

'I don't think we could have,' I say after a moment's silence. 'I think we did our best.'

'Whatever about anything else, I was lucky the day I sent my first manuscript to you.' His tone, which had been wistful, suddenly becomes positive again.

'I know.'

'We did great things together.'

'We still can. And who knows, you may even get nominated for both the literary awards and the crime awards. A double whammy.'

He laughs and hugs me. I hug him back. Then I lean my head against his shoulder and savour the moment. We sit together in a silence so complete that the only sound I hear is my own breathing.

This is what I missed when our marriage started to go wrong. When I was growing my business and signing hot new clients, and collaborating with a media agent to look after movie and streaming deals and building up my list of overseas agents so that my authors would have access to a global market. When everything seemed to be coming together but in fact we were setting it up to fall apart.

It wasn't inevitable, I suppose. But there were competing pressures on us, and Charles couldn't quite get his head around the fact that my other authors were as important to me, professionally at least, as he was. Backed up by his interfering mother, who seemed to think she knew more about the business than I did, he wanted to know what deals they were getting and what they were writing and how I thought they were doing, even though I told him that this was confidential information between me and them. He didn't like the amount of time I spent with them, especially Cosmo Penhaligon, an up-and-coming author in his mid thirties who lived in a picture-perfect clifftop house in Cornwall. I occasionally stayed there for a few days while we worked on his manuscripts together. Charles hated the fact that I was staying in another man's house and made his feelings clear. I told him not to be so childish. Nevertheless, I understood it. Cosmo was younger than him, almost as attractive, and even if he wasn't as successful as Charles, he was doing very well. I knew he was going to be an important client for me and I was giving him a lot of attention. I told Charles that he had to trust me, even though, when Cosmo turned on his own brand of charm, it wasn't easy to trust myself.

'It's hard to believe it's all about work when you've bought at least six new outfits for your visit to Cornwall,' said Charles one day when I was heading off to the airport.

'Because there's a heatwave in England and I need to dress for it.'

'In shorts and crop tops?'

'For God's sake, Charles, stop being so silly.' I glanced out the window. 'My taxi is here. I'm off.'

'When are you back?'

'I already told you. The weekend.'

I leaned towards him to kiss him, but he turned away so that my lips glanced off his cheek.

I heaved a sigh of relief when I got into the taxi. My mind was already on Cosmo's book. I didn't need Charles's petty jealousy distracting me.

The kiss Cosmo greeted me with when I arrived at his home just outside St Ives was a lot warmer than the cheek-grazing I'd had with my husband. And it wouldn't have taken much for my stay with him to have crossed the line. After all, Cosmo's books were very erotic, and we were sitting side by side talking about sex scenes as well as sharing glasses of wine in his gorgeous garden overlooking the sea. If I'd been a character in one of Charles's novels, I'd definitely have slept with Cosmo Penhaligon, but I couldn't afford the fallout.

When I got back to Dublin, I discovered that Charles had decamped to Mayo. He hadn't texted, but simply left a note on the kitchen counter, and a bundle of laundry in the basket. I was so annoyed that if I could've caught a flight back to Cornwall right then, I would have. But I was meeting Janice Jermyn the following day and I certainly wasn't going to stand up one of my favourite authors for an affair with another. When I finally did speak to Charles, he told me that his mother and sister had joined him for a few days, but that he was sure I had better things to do than come to Mayo. I spent the next two weeks rage-working my way through more admin than I normally did in a month, and comparing and contrasting Cosmo and Charles as clients and as men. It was Charles who kept falling short.

However, when he eventually arrived home, he was in much better spirits and I'd worked off most of my anger. We didn't talk about my visit to Cornwall or his stay at the cottage, and although things weren't back to normal, the atmosphere between us slowly improved. I thought we'd dodged a bullet.

We had, but the damage was already done.

A couple of weeks later, Charles heard me on the phone talking to the organiser of a prestigious literary festival in Canada about Cosmo's availability for an event. He wasn't free for the slot they were interested in, but he told me he'd be able to do it later in the week, and hoped I'd be able to swing it for him because he really wanted to go. Although the organiser was keen to have him, she said that switching the date would be difficult and suggested that if Charles was available instead, he'd be a good alternative.

'If you can't change the date, I'll discuss it with Charles,' I told her. 'But I think it would be of real benefit to your festival to have Cosmo.'

When Charles realised what was going on, he came and stood in front of me flapping his arms and saying that he'd be happy to go to Canada, while I mouthed at him to go away.

'Why are you favouring Cosmo bloody Penhaligon over me?' he demanded when I ended the call. 'That woman was perfectly happy to have me.'

'You've done this event before,' I reminded him. 'Cosmo hasn't.'

'So what!' he exploded. 'You know, with you running off to St Ives at every available opportunity and now pushing him ahead of me, it's very clear to me where your loyalties lie.'

'It's not a case of favouring him over you,' I insisted. 'I'm working for both of you.'

'You certainly *are* working for him,' he said. 'I saw your laptop the other day. It was open on the flights page.'

'So what?'

'So you're not long back and you're looking for an excuse to go again.'

'Oh for God's sake, Charles. If my client needs me, I'll go. And I'll remind you that you weren't even here when I came back last time. So I could've stayed longer.'

'And done what?'

'Had a good time,' I snapped.

'Have you already had a good time with him?' demanded Charles. 'Sitting in his lovely living room reading his soft porn together.'

'It's not soft porn,' I objected.

'It bloody is. And I can just see it, him asking you if a woman would really like what he's describing and then you—'

'Stop it!' I cried. 'You're being ridiculous.'

Though only partly ridiculous, because the scene he was sketching out was uncannily accurate.

'You're different every time you come back from him,' said Charles.

'And you're different every time you come back from

164

Mayo,' I retorted. 'Doesn't mean I suspect you of having an affair with the woman in the cottage next door.'

'Because Mrs Mahon is eighty-five. And because my *mother* was with me in Mayo. But I've seen the way Cosmo Penhaligon looks at you. I've seen the way you look at him. I'm not a fool, Ariel.'

'Yes you bloody are,' I said. And I stormed out of the room.

The following day, Charles told me it was him or Cosmo.

I said it wasn't an either/or situation. And that in case he'd forgotten, I was married to him, not Cosmo. I was sleeping with him, not Cosmo.

'You sure about that?' he asked.

'Of course I'm sure. But I'll tell you something, Charles Miller, if the opportunity arises to hop into bed with Cosmo Penhaligon, I'll seriously consider it. I might as well be hung for a sheep as a lamb. And at least when you're ranting on at me, I'll be able to think it was worth it!'

We stared at each other in grim silence. I wished I could take back those words, but it was too late. Charles cleared his throat. Then he said I still had to choose.

'As I said at the start of this . . . discussion, it's not a case of you or Cosmo,' I said as calmly as I could. 'I don't love Cosmo.'

'You want to have sex with him.'

'Can't we—'

'Drop him,' he said. 'Or it's over.'

I always thought it was possible to have it all. I always thought I had the power to fix anything that was wrong. But I couldn't fix this. Love doesn't truly conquer everything. I loved Charles, but I'd already compromised my career by moving to Ireland for him. I wasn't going to let him tell me who could or couldn't be my client. And I wasn't going to let him make me feel guilty every time I went away.

So I moved out.

He didn't try to stop me.

While I was in Canada with Cosmo (whose book was a roaring success and went to number one there), Charles met with other agents. I knew that by walking out on him I'd lose him as a client, but I also knew that my heart wasn't in it any more. I still loved his books, but our tangled relationship would make things too difficult. Somehow neither of us could recapture the joyful moments that were ours alone: sitting in the garden together, spending weekends at the cottage in Mayo or heading off to Europe for short breaks he insisted were research even when the most research we did was finding the nearest bar. It hadn't always been about books and his career.

And until his Mayo trip without me, he had stuck up for me every time his waspish mother complained about my relentless ambition.

I'm sure Pamela Boyd-Miller was thrilled at our split.

I said as much to Ekene when I went to London for a visit. I didn't have any business meetings. All I wanted was to talk to my friend about my messed-up marriage.

'Charles is an absolute fool, and his mother always sounded like an interfering old bat to me,' Ekene said. 'She's convinced him you should be running around after him the whole time, and that's why he thinks you should be putting him ahead of your other authors. I'm glad you didn't. Cosmo Penhaligon is a great writer.'

'He's not Charles, though.'

'I know.' Her voice softened. 'But I know you. You'll get over Charles.'

'I still want the best for him. I wonder who he'll find to represent him?' I gazed thoughtfully at her. 'I wonder if he'll go for a female agent and if she'll fall for him too. If she'll become the next Mrs Miller.'

'Now you're just being silly,' said Ekene, and she ordered more drinks.

When Charles asked to meet a few weeks later, I wondered if he wanted us to reconcile. After all, no matter how close I might have come to it, neither of us had been unfaithful; our problem was all about a lack of trust and balance, and I couldn't help feeling that it was something we could work on. I insisted on a neutral venue, so we decided on the elegant surroundings of the Merrion Hotel, where we were served tea and coffee in silver pots and where the serene atmosphere lulled us into being almost pleasant towards each other. However, Charles didn't want to reconcile. He wanted a divorce.

He said he'd been writing a lot since we'd separated and he realised that this was a good thing. He said perhaps he was one of those writers who was better off without the distractions of domesticity. I was proud of myself for not saying that he didn't have a clue what domesticity was.

And although part of me was sad about making our split permanent, I was prepared for it.

He asked if we couldn't sort it out between ourselves without involving legal teams. I agreed it should be possible for us to do most of the heavy lifting – after all, negotiation is my business – but I also warned him we might need advice at the later stages. I asked what he wanted from our separation.

Not surprisingly, he was worried about having to sell Riverside Lodge. I told him there was no need for that. I asked to keep the mews as my office and said I'd buy an apartment of my own. Charles, clearly relieved that I was being reasonable, said that he'd make a contribution to the cost of my new home.

We had it all sorted in less than half an hour. I couldn't help thinking that if we'd managed to have the same kind of civilised conversation over the past few months, we wouldn't be getting divorced at all.

I ordered two glasses of champagne, and when they came, I raised my glass.

'I only drink champagne on two occasions,' I said, quoting Coco Chanel. 'When I'm in love, and when I'm not.'

'And which is it now?' asked Charles.

'Sadly, the latter.'

'What about Cosmo?'

'I'm not in love with Cosmo.' I gave him an exasperated look. 'I was never in love with him. I'm not in love with anyone.'

'I hope you still like me, even if you don't love me,' he said.

'I'll always admire you. I'll always want you to do well and I'll always cheer when I see you at the top of the best-seller lists. How are you getting on with your search for a new agent, by the way?' I kept my voice even as I asked the question, and followed it with a gulp of champagne.

'A lot of people are interested in representing me, naturally enough,' he replied. 'I haven't made a decision yet. And you? Any new authors?'

I said I wasn't really looking for new talent right now. He reminded me that it wouldn't be easy to replace him. I'd been feeling a little sentimental about my soon-to-be-ex-husband-and-client. Now I simply drained my glass and said that nothing good in life was ever easy but I was sure I'd manage.

'So given that you're buying an apartment here, you're not thinking of returning to London?' He gave me a quizzical look.

I wasn't, but his question got me thinking. Perhaps this was a chance to make a radical change. To be back in the heart of things again. I told him I'd consider it, but that it wasn't an immediate plan. He said that whether I bought in Dublin or in London, he'd still contribute to the cost. I thanked him, then got up and left him to finish his glass of champagne alone.

When I got home, I opened a bottle of my own. This time I toasted myself with a Marlene Dietrich quote: 'Champagne makes you feel like it's Sunday and there are better days around the corner.'

There would be better days. I was sure of it.

I hoped they'd come quickly.

When everything was finally agreed between us, we sent the document to our solicitors and told them we didn't want to change a thing, although in conversations long afterwards, we laughed at the fact that both our legal representatives had suggested we could do better out of our agreement. But we didn't waver. I was proud of both of us.

To my surprise, Charles then brought up another subject. Whatever about our personal lives, he said, we were good for each other professionally, and what did I think about being able to work with him again now that we had all the messy personal stuff out of the way. He didn't feel the same connection with the other agents he'd met as he did with me. And he knew that no matter what he might have said in the past, I always had his best interests at heart.

This time I was completely unprepared. I thought he was enjoying meeting different agents, but of course I was pleased that none of them seemed to measure up to me. Nevertheless, I'd already told myself that working with Charles would be impossible. And although I believe in making the impossible possible, I wasn't sure how good an idea this would be. At the same time, I had to admit that keeping an author of his calibre at the agency would send an excellent message. I didn't want him to go back to Saxby-Brown, or, even worse, to one of the big conglomerates. He wasn't a conglomerate type of person. I told him I'd think about it. In the end, despite my uncertainty, I agreed. After all, I had a possible streaming deal for one of his books and I didn't want to lose it. So we stayed together professionally, and it's been surprisingly smooth sailing ever since.

The boundaries, which were very strict at the start, have become a little more fluid as we live our new reality. And if sometimes we stray into more personal moments, we're always very clear that I'm his agent and he's my author and the personal is really just the professional with the edges rubbed off a little.

We were, for a time, the perfect married couple.

Now we've become the perfect break-up couple.

I feel tears prick the back of my eyes. It's just the emotion of remembering everything we've gone through, but I don't want him to notice. I get up and walk over to the window. A dusting of frost means that the garden sparkles beneath the light.

'Thanks again for doing the decorating.' He comes to stand behind me and puts his hands on my shoulders. 'You know I'm grateful for everything you do for me. And I very much appreciate that you're taking this book and running with it. I know you'll make it a real success.'

'No pressure,' I say.

'I always put pressure on you,' he says. 'I can't help it.'

'I put pressure on myself. I remember you coming to my office all those years ago and me telling you what might or might not happen, and you listened and nodded and put your career in my hands, and I felt huge pressure to deliver.'

'I didn't know any better.' He smiles.

'We're a good team,' I say. 'Despite everything.'

'Of course we are.'

He turns to me and I turn to him, and I don't know how it's happened, but we're kissing each other just as we used to kiss. I can't deny it's wonderful. It's happened before, in moments of celebration, but each time we've pulled away from each other very quickly. This time I don't want to pull away at all.

I wonder if we should get back together.

I wonder if he thinks so too.

Chapter 15

Iseult

*The writer wrote alone and the reader read
alone and they were alone with each other.*

A. S. Byatt

I'm still thinking about the drug interception as I make myself a mug of coffee and take out a tin of biscuits. We've had big hauls before, even bigger than this, and it's always the same. You want to punch the air and jump up and down and say again how flipping fantastic you and your team are and how great your job is, even on days when you're outside freezing your buns off.

The last time we intercepted a large quantity of drugs, I was so pumped up that when Steve came home I couldn't wait to get him in my arms. We made love on the kitchen table, which was probably not the most hygienic thing in the world. Oh well. My table. My germs. All the same, the memory means I give it a quick spray of Dettol before I sit down with my coffee and biscuits, even though the actual event was months ago and I've both used and cleaned the table many times since then.

I take out my phone. Charles hasn't even seen my previous message, so I send another one.

Sorry. Very busy earlier. Is it too late to meet now?

He still hasn't seen it by the time I've finished my coffee. I wonder if he's sitting at the desk in his study pounding the keys of his computer. I fondly imagined that the manuscript was finished when he typed 'The End', but he told me that that's just the beginning of another phase of rewriting and editing that can take ages. He'll certainly have to change the big giveaway to the identity of the murderer early on. There's another bit in the middle I'd change too. I didn't tell him when I read the manuscript that I'd guessed who it was because of it. I didn't want to puncture his bubble of joy.

Although I'm usually perfectly happy with my own company, I wish I hadn't left the pub so early, even though the others probably didn't stay that much longer after me. I scroll to my mum's name and try FaceTiming her. I let it ring for ages before deciding she's not up yet, but as I'm about to end the call, her face fills the screen.

'Izzy.' She beams at me. 'How are you?'

'Great.' I go on to tell her about the drugs haul, and she's suitably impressed. She and Dad weren't initially supportive of my move into Customs. Dad was a teacher and Mum a tour guide – what she doesn't know about Dublin's historical sites isn't worth knowing – and I have a sneaking feeling they wanted me to have a somewhat more intellectual career when I joined the Civil Service. A diplomat maybe. Or something in the arts. Mind you, they probably wanted the same for Adrian, and he's ended up as a farmer on the other side of the world, so if they did have other ambitions for us, we've disappointed them.

'How's everyone there?' I ask when I've milked my drug seizure success as much as I can. Mum tells me that Azaria is thriving and the boys are holy terrors. The love and adoration in her voice is evident. Then Dad takes over the call. New Zealand life suits him. He looks younger than before he left, and healthy in a rugged, outdoorsy sort of way. He's been googling the drugs seizure online and tells me that he's proud of me, which unaccountably makes me well up.

'You OK, sweetie?' he asks when I sniff.

'Of course. It's been a long day.'

'Your mum and I are driving into town and meeting some new friends later,' he says.

'I'm glad you're making friends.'

'Tarquin and Jonelle,' he tells me. 'They run a sailing school. Or at least they did. Their son runs it now.'

'Are you coming home soon?' I ask.

'Are you missing us madly or planning to do something with the house while we're not there?' He replies with a question of his own.

'Missing you, of course,' I say. 'And I don't have any plans. I just wondered. I know you're trying to manage your stays in New Zealand so you can go again next year.'

'Your mum thinks our services are required here for another couple of weeks at least. But we have a plan for afterwards if you don't mind.'

'What plan.'

'A cruise.'

'How lovely. Where?'

'Around Asia.' Mum's face appears on the screen again.

'But if you want us home first, we can do the cruise next time we come here.'

'Of course not. There's no need to rush back for me, honestly. I think it's great you're living your best lives now.'

'I'm glad we brought you up to be independent,' says Dad.

'Me too.'

We exchange a few more pleasantries, then he passes the phone back to Mum and I talk to her for a little longer before we all say our goodbyes.

It's only later that I realise I never said a word about Charles Miller.

He still hasn't answered my text by the time I go to bed. #AllByMyself

He does, however, call me the next day, although as I'm at a meeting about the drugs interception, I don't answer him until later. When I do, he's absolutely intrigued by it and peppers me with questions. I tell him I'll give him the full run-down next time we meet, and suggest it might be a great scenario for his next murder mystery. He asks if I'm free to go for a coffee, and I'm wondering if he's thinking of research and whether it's me or the drugs haul that's more important to him. When I say this, he says that not everything is research and he wants to meet me because he enjoys my company. I feel a warm glow at that. We arrange to meet later at Kavanagh's, an old-style pub at the end of the Malahide Road that's within easy walking distance for me.

When I get home, I change into jeans and the Christmas jumper that Adrian sent from New Zealand and that arrived far too early. It's bright green with a red-nosed kangaroo pulling Santa's sleigh.

'Very festive,' says Charles when he arrives at the pub a few minutes after me. He's wearing another of his fine-knit polo necks teamed with dark trousers, and doesn't entirely fit in with the local seasonal fashion vibe that echoes my jumper.

'I thought I should get into the Christmas spirit,' I say.

'Being totally honest, I'm a bit of a Grinch when it comes to Christmas,' he admits. 'I had my heart broken on Christmas Day.'

'Like in *Winter's Heartbreak*?'

'Not exactly.' He smiles. 'I was six, and the girl next door wouldn't let me kiss her better when she fell off her new Barbie scooter. She told me she didn't need kisses from boys, she could get better all by herself. I was devastated.'

I laugh. 'I thought it might have been your agent-slash-ex.'

He looks slightly uncomfortable at the mention of her, and I decide not to pursue it. Instead I ask if he knows anything about the girl next door now.

'Not a thing,' he replies cheerfully.

'It's funny how you can feel so deeply for someone and then suddenly it's over,' I remark. 'Thanks,' I add, as the gin and tonic I ordered earlier is placed in front of me. I ask Charles what he'd like to drink, and he asks for a G&T too.

'Are you over your ex-fiancé?' he asks.

I'd told him all about Steve when we were at the White Sands.

'Definitely,' I say, ignoring the fact that I haven't deleted him from my contacts yet. 'I wish I hadn't wasted so much of my time on him.'

'How was it wasted?' asks Charles.

I consider this for a moment before telling him that I'd thought Steve and I were putting in the work for something long-term. If he hadn't asked me to marry him, I could've been out there looking for someone else.

'There has to be someone else, does there? You're not interested in simply living your life as a unique person?'

'I was perfectly happy being a unique person before I met him,' I reply. 'He changed everything. And not that I'm looking at every man as a potential partner, but there could've been someone out there who passed me by because I was with Steve. I realise it does make me sound a bit needy,' I add, after a brief pause when Charles says nothing. 'But I'm not, honestly.'

'I was just curious. You seem to be a very independent person. There's no need to explain yourself to me.'

'What about you?' I ask, when I've finished processing the fact that I felt it necessary to explain myself to him at all.

'What about me?'

'Do you feel you wasted time on your marriage, or was it worth it?'

He thinks for a moment before replying.

'Obviously the whole thing is a bit tricky because of knowing her professionally first,' he says. 'That part certainly wasn't a waste of time. She's amazing.'

I say nothing.

'I thought we were in love,' he continues. 'I wanted us to be in love. I think she did too. I'm just not entirely sure we really were.'

'You mean you liked the idea of it?'

'It seemed right, that's all.'

'Were you happy?'

'We broke up, which speaks for itself. But for a while we were happy,' he concedes. 'So I suppose our marriage wasn't a waste of time either.'

'She's an attractive woman,' I say.

'What?' He looks at me in astonishment. 'How do you even know what she looks like?'

'Google,' I said. 'You really are hopeless about googling people, aren't you? I found her website. And earlier I saw a picture of you and her at an awards ceremony. There isn't much out there,' I add. 'I guess she's not as important as you. Though information on you is surprisingly limited for someone so famous.'

'It's a little disconcerting to think of you googling me,' says Charles.

'Why wouldn't I? You're famous.'

He looks pleased at that, then asks whether if he googled me he would see pictures of me standing on top of a pile of seized drugs.

'Nope,' I reply. 'But there are probably some awful ones of me on social media.'

'I never think to check people out,' says Charles. 'At least not people I meet socially. Other authors, yes, of course, to see if they've sold more than me, but random acquaintances . . . never.'

'Surely everyone checks out anyone new they meet.' I'm not sure if I'm insulted at being called a random acquaintance. 'It's one of the flaws in your book. Nobody googles anyone else and they would.'

'Oh.' He looks startled. 'You should've said.'

'Not up to me to say. I'm sure your publisher or your

agent-slash-ex or your editor or whoever it is who looks after these things will mention it.'

He glances at his watch. 'All of them probably,' he says. 'In fact, my agent is on her way to London to talk to my publisher about it right now. Hopefully it'll go well.'

'Even with the lack of googling and a few other fixable glitches, it's a proper page-turner,' I assure him, but he looks suddenly unconvinced. I like this about Charles. He can be so confident one minute and then, in an instant, completely insecure. I wonder are all authors like him, or is it only the Booker Prize winners. And do they all spend their time googling each other to see how successful they are? I smile at the thought.

'What's so funny?' he demands.

I shake my head.

'I hope you're not laughing at me.'

'Wouldn't dream of it,' I say, though I'm not sure he believes me.

The door of the pub opens and a group of young men wearing GAA jerseys walk in. They're also wearing shorts, even though it's still freezing outside. I shiver involuntarily. The men sit at one of the high tables and order food. Charles looks at them with interest.

'OK, I know you live in a rarefied literary world, but you must have seen Gaelic football players before,' I murmur.

'Of course.' He gives me an impatient glance. 'I played for the local team when I was younger.'

'Seriously?' He's fit, but not bulky enough for a football player.

'Under twelves,' he confesses. 'I was very fast. But too light. I came off worst in every physical encounter. Broke my collarbone twice.'

I look at him in surprise.

'So you can revise your preconceptions,' he tells me. 'I support Waterford and always will.'

'Better not say that too loud here,' I say. 'This is a Dublin pub.'

'The signed jersey on the wall is a giveaway.' He grins.

I laugh, and suddenly the atmosphere between us lightens and I don't feel like he's a fish out of water any more. We chat about Gaelic football for a while, and he's a lot more knowledgeable than me, because while most of what I know comes from the guys at work, he actually follows the Waterford team. Then the subject veers towards family, and he asks me what my Christmas plans are given that my parents are on the other side of the world.

'I'm spending it with Celeste,' I reply. 'Her family being my family too, of course. What about you?'

'I'm not sure yet,' he replies.

'But it's only a few days away.' I look at him in horror. 'Surely you've made plans.'

'I'm not much of a Christmas person,' he says. 'If you hadn't had anything on, I was going to ask you to join me.'

'Will you be on your own otherwise?' I really am horrified. I can't bear to think of him alone on Christmas Day. I wonder if I should invite him to my uncle and aunt's. But that would be unfair on Aunt Jenni, who's already got her entire schedule worked out and has stuck it to the notice-board in the kitchen.

'Don't worry about me,' he says. 'I have a standing invitation to my sister's if nothing better pops up. We're both loners, so it suits us. But,' he adds, 'I always have a get-together at home on New Year's Eve, which is great fun. I hope you can come. Bring Celeste. We might have a tropical island theme, for the cocktails at least.'

I look at him doubtfully.

'Unless you already have a party to go to?'

'No,' I say.

'That's settled then.' He looks pleased, and I don't say anything else. However, it seems the right moment to take the narrow gift-wrapped box out of my bag and give it to him.

'It's not much,' I warn. 'A token really.'

He smiles and expertly begins to ease off the green and gold paper while I watch in anticipation. Inside the box is a silver bookmark with his name engraved on it. I saw it at a local craft and jewellery shop that offered the engraving for free, and bought it even though I wasn't a hundred per cent sure we'd even see each other before Christmas. I thought the engraver might recognise Charles's name, but he made no comment whatsoever. I won't tell Charles this if he asks, though!

'Thank you,' he says, 'It's lovely.'

'You probably have loads of bookmarks.' I'm suddenly concerned that it's a rubbish gift.

'Yes, I do. But none like this.'

I smile at him. He puts the box into his coat pocket. And now I'm wondering if I've embarrassed him, because he might not have bought me a present. It doesn't bother me if that's the case. I'm not exactly expecting one.

We sit in silence for a moment, and then he takes a wrapped package from his other pocket. It's the same shape as the one I gave him, and I have a sudden horrible feeling that he's bought me a bookmark too.

'Are you going to open it?' he asks as I turn it over in my hand.

Unlike him, I'm not one of those people who can unwrap a gift without reducing the paper to shreds, so the exquisite wrapping is a mess by the time I've finished. He hasn't bought me a bookmark. He's bought me a watch. A gold-faced Gucci watch with a pink leather wristband. My eyes widen and I look at him.

'It's way too much,' I say. 'You can't buy me presents like this.'

'Don't you like it?' He looks disappointed.

'Of course I like it. It's beautiful. But it's an expensive watch, Charles. You can't give me an expensive watch for Christmas when I've only bought you a bookmark.'

'It's the thought that counts, isn't it?'

'Even so . . .'

'I'll be upset if you don't accept it.'

I examine the watch more closely. It's really pretty, with a gold bee motif in the centre of the face. I like bees. I like their fuzzy little bodies and their industry in producing honey and looking after their queen.

'It's beautiful,' I say, fastening it round my wrist.

'It suits you.' Charles nods approvingly.

And it does.

I love it.

And I have all the feels for him too.

Maybe there's something more to me and Charles than I first thought.

#ChristmasPresents #FestiveRomance

Chapter 16

Ariel

*Inspiration comes of
working every day.*
Charles Baudelaire

I stride into the offices of Xerxes Publishing, with their views over Lincoln's Inn Fields, wearing my favourite purple dress, an almost matching purple coat and a pair of black platform boots to add height and presence. I'm a vibrant splash of colour among a lot of black and white, because the Xerxes office is smack in the heart of the legal district. When Graham's dad set up the business, he rented space from his older brother, who had a law firm, and they've been here ever since. Graham sometimes jokes that there's as much fiction in the law as in his own business. One of his most successful authors – after Charles – writes legal thrillers. Sadly not a client of mine, though.

Graham gets up from behind his large old-fashioned desk with its green leather inlay (a gift to his father from his barrister brother) and walks around to shake my hand and offer me coffee. We share pleasantries as we wait for it to arrive. As yet, he hasn't said anything about *A Caribbean Calypso*. I feel a trickle of nervous perspiration on my back and breathe slowly and evenly.

Effie, his PA, comes in with a pot of coffee, milk, sugar and two cups on a red lacquer tray. She places the tray carefully on the desk and pours the coffee.

'Milk no sugar?' she says as she looks me.

I nod.

Graham takes his coffee black with three lumps.

'Well,' he says, when Effie leaves, 'Charles has certainly provided us with an interesting read.'

'More than interesting,' I say. 'Riveting. Compelling. Exciting. Completely enthralling.'

'You think?'

I feel my stomach tense.

'I absolutely do, and I hope you do too,' I say.

'I do, actually.' He stirs his coffee. 'It's great fun. And beautifully written.'

'No more than anyone would expect from Charles.'

'But it's clearly not a literary novel. Not by any stretch of the imagination.'

'It's literary crime in the tradition of P. D. James,' I say. 'I think it's a great direction for him to have taken and it will bring lots of new readers to his books.'

'It's nothing like what I was expecting.'

I tell Graham that we can do great things with it, raise Charles's profile even higher and maybe even win the Golden Dagger or another crime award. Then I list all the things Xerxes can do to make that happen.

He smiles. 'You're a born saleswoman, you know that, Ariel?'

'I'm merely pointing out the advantages of having a book like this from him.'

'I think he should work with a different editor,' says Graham.

I'm not sure how Charles or Sophia will feel about that and say so.

'Sophia agrees that someone who specialises in crime might be a good idea,' Graham assures me. 'We have a recent hire who's a better fit for this book. Sydney Travers.'

'It'll be a different experience for Charles to work with a man,' I say.

'Syd is a woman,' says Graham. 'She joined us earlier in the year. She's edited crime before. So perhaps it's a seren-dipitous moment for us all. I wanted you to meet her anyhow, because I've earmarked her for Avery's latest. As you know, his own editor is off on sabbatical next year.'

I wince. Given the edge between Charles and Avery, the idea of them sharing an editor isn't exactly compelling. On the other hand, Graham is committed to publishing the book, which means that Charles will get paid and so will I. The most important thing is making sure Charles has the right editor, but I can't ignore the commercial reality of the situation. Besides, Avery's next book isn't due for ages yet, so he and Charles won't be being edited at the same time. Honestly, keeping tabs on these guys and their fragile egos is a juggling act in itself.

'Sounds great,' I say.

'I'll call her now.'

Graham picks up the phone and has a brief conversation. A moment later, a young woman, ebony hair in a severe ponytail and wearing a black skirt and white blouse, walks into the room. She looks as though she's lost her way from the barristers' offices.

'Syd, meet Ariel. Ariel, this is Sydney Travers. She's read the book already.'

'And I love it.' Behind her black-framed glasses, Syd's brown eyes light up. 'So clever and refreshing and smart. It does need quite a bit of work to make it the best it can be, but I'm sure we will get there.'

'Excellent,' I say. 'Graham says you've edited crime before?'

'For Strychnine Books,' she replies.

Well, that's a positive. Strychnine is a niche crime publisher and has published some great novels.

'I'll talk to Charles and we can set up a Zoom. I doubt we could do an in-person meeting this side of Christmas,' I say. 'He's very excited about the novel and definitely wants the best possible people working with him.'

'I look forward to meeting him. I'm thrilled at the chance to work with him.'

I get the feeling she'll handle him well. And I think he'll like her.

Syd goes back to her desk, and I tell Graham that I'll chat to Charles but that I'm sure he'll be eager to receive Syd's editorial notes and push on with the rewrites.

'Great,' says Graham. 'It's a bit of a gamble for us, you know.'

'It's a sure thing, Graham,' I say.

'I love your confidence.'

'My confidence is in my author and in you.'

He laughs. 'Always a pleasure to see you, Ariel,' he says.

'And you.'

We shake hands again and I leave his office. I wait until I'm out of the building and leaning against the wall before punching the air and reminding myself that I'm a brilliant agent.

I meet Ekene and Maya for dinner that evening. We go to a modern Spanish restaurant in Soho, where we order paella Valenciana and more cocktails than we should, given that it's a weekday. But it's also nearly Christmas and the restaurant is buzzing with people drinking even more than us. There's an end-of-season feel about things, as though nobody cares about tomorrow. And I don't care either. Because Graham has accepted Charles's book and a weight has been lifted off my shoulders.

I FaceTimed Charles from my hotel, and because I couldn't keep the beam off my face, he knew immediately that everything was OK.

'He loves it but is suggesting a different editor.' I made my tone and my expression excited and positive. 'A young woman named Sydney Travers. She has experience in the genre.'

'I thought we were transcending genre?'

'It's a crime novel, Charles. That's a genre.'

'But it's *my* crime novel. Not any old crime novel.'

He was back on the horse of confidence, obviously.

'Of course. But better to have someone who's good at it, don't you think? After all, you had your beta reader look at it precisely because she had experience.'

'You're right.' His voice softened. 'Thank you so much, Ariel. You're a superb agent. You really are.'

'I do my best.'

'I couldn't manage without you.'

'I know.' I laughed.

'So tell us about the book,' demands Ekene as the waiter arrives with the bottle of champagne I ordered.

I give them a brief résumé.

'Sounds interesting.' Maya takes a sip of champagne. 'How are Xerxes going to publicise it?'

'We haven't talked about the campaign yet.'

'I'd be happy to work on it,' she says.

Maya has done work for Xerxes in the past and would be a good choice for Charles's PR, as she's experienced with crime novels. I tell her I'll talk to Graham.

'Congratulations to you and to Charles.' Ekene raises her glass. 'The poster people for civilised break-ups and working brilliantly together.'

'We seem to get on better apart,' I say. 'It was too hard to separate the personal from the professional when we were married. Leaving aside the entire Cosmo Penhaligon episode, Ma Miller was always there sniping away in the background. Which was a bloody cheek when you consider I invited her to all his book launches *and* the premiere of the movie. I'm glad not to have her in my life any more.'

'You don't need that negative energy.' Maya also raises her glass. 'Nothing but positivity tonight, Ariel.'

I'm full of positivity. I'm delighted to be out with my friends and delighted that everything's going to work out for Charles and *A Caribbean Calypso*. After all, despite everything, he and I are still a team. We know each other better than anyone. Even though there have been bumps on the road, we always want the best for each other.

We always will.

Chapter 17

Iseult

Romanticism is the abuse of adjectives.
Alfred de Musset

Christmas at Aunt Jenni and Uncle Paul's is fun. Nana O'Connor, who's eighty-eight and is now in a lovely care home nearby, joins us for the day, and so does Celeste's middle brother, Frank, who lives and works in Cork. We do a Zoom call with her older brother, Jack, who's currently in California, working for a tech firm. We also Zoom with Mum, Dad, Adrian and Cori, whose Christmas Day is almost over. We talk so long and so loudly that nobody really hears what anyone else is saying, but the gist of the news from Napier is that the twins trashed the house with excitement and baby Azaria was as good as gold the whole time.

They all looked great, I think later that evening when we've eaten and drunk far too much and are imitating beached whales in front of the TV. I'm so lucky to have family who get on, even if New Zealand makes it difficult to be physically close. Maybe next year I'll get a chance to visit my brother and his wife and get to know my niece and nephews. It's being able to build up enough holiday time from work that's the issue. I'd love to go for a month if I could. But unfortunately my job isn't like Charles's. I'm tied to a schedule and can't work just anywhere in the world.

I glance at my phone. He's sent messages throughout the day wishing me happy Christmas and telling me silly jokes from crackers. I haven't seen him since our evening at Kavanagh's when he gave me the watch. Celeste spotted it on my wrist earlier and said that it was a pretty extravagant gift that surely meant Charles was serious about me. I batted that away and reminded her I'd only bought him a bookmark.

The phone in my hand pings again. This time it's a selfie of him and a tall, well-built woman with strawberry-blonde hair falling in loose curls around her shoulders. Even if he hadn't told me, I'd have guessed this was his sister. The resemblance to him is evident. They're in what seems to be a small but very Christmassy room. Less stylish than Charles's own home, but warm and welcoming all the same, with a fat barrel of a madly overdecorated Christmas tree.

I message him back with a pic of me and Celeste in party hats.

My phone pings again almost immediately, and I assume it's a reply from Charles, but it's not.

Hope you're having a lovely Christmas.
You deserve the best. Sx

For crying out loud! What's Steve doing sliding into my messages again?

I show it to Celeste, who tells me to block him, but it's

Christmas and I can't make myself do that. In the end I simply send a generic Season's Greetings GIF.

I'm so over Steve. I must put my wedding dress up for sale.

#NeverWorn #MyMendedHeart

That could be the title of Charles's next novel.

I stay at Aunt Jenni's for two nights, then return home. The house feels bare because my festive decorating was minimal. All the family Christmas stuff is in the attic and I'm not a fan of going up to the dark, dusty space under the roof with its eerie shadows and unexpected bits of bric-a-brac from past times. Instead, I bought a little potted tree from the garden centre and put it on the sideboard along with a tiny wooden crib (also from the garden centre). Then I strung some indoor lights around the room, which I reckoned was enough to make it look festive. But it's not the same, that's for sure.

I sit by the gas fire, and for the first time since Mum and Dad went away, I feel alone. I know I'm not really alone; I could go back to Aunt Jenni's and stay there if I wanted. I also know that if I asked her, Mum would come running home to me. She wanted to when Steve broke up with me, and I was very firm about being perfectly OK, even though I really wasn't. All the same, I managed. But I'd give anything for her arms around me tonight and a whisper that she loved me. I allow a tear to leak from my eye and then pour myself a Baileys. If Christmas isn't a time for drowning maudlin thoughts in a sweet, creamy liqueur, I don't know when is.

The ring at the doorbell when I'm two thirds of the way

down the glass startles me. The first thought that goes through my head is that it's Steve, and even though I'm not sure I want to answer the door to Steve, I open it anyway.

Charles is standing there, bundled against the cold in a black leather jacket and a tartan scarf.

'I thought you weren't going to answer,' he says.

'I didn't think it was you.'

'There are people for whom you don't answer the door-bell?'

'Sometimes. What are you doing here?' And then, realising that I'm being rude, I tell him to come in.

'I got back from Ellis's early and thought I'd surprise you.'

'I could've still been with my aunt and uncle.'

'You could. But I made a bet that you wouldn't. Family is all very well, but most of us can only last a couple of days with them.'

'Like you and Ellis.'

'She lectures me,' says Charles. He unwinds the scarf and hangs it over the newel post before taking off his jacket and hanging it there too.

'About what?' I ask, leading him into the living room.

'Everything. Nice tree,' he adds.

'Don't sneer.'

'I'm not.' He grins. 'I like it.'

'Can I get you a drink?'

'Wine?'

I produce a bottle of red from the cupboard. As I unscrew it, I realise that Charles is probably a cork-in-the-bottle kind of man. Oh well, this is a Lidl special, it got great reviews and they were limiting stocks to customers, so he'll have to do his best to like it.

He makes no comment on the wine, either its taste or the screw top. I sit opposite him and raise the remainder of my glass of Baileys. 'Happy Christmas.'

'Happy Christmas,' he echoes. 'Was it good?'

I tell him how much I enjoyed being at Aunt Jenni's and how great a cook she is and how much fun it was to talk to Mum and Dad and Adrian and Cori.

'How about you?' I ask. 'Fab pic, by the way.'

'Ellis and I had fillet steak and chips,' he replies. 'We didn't talk to anyone.'

'No turkey and ham? And not even a call to your mum?' I'm shocked.

'We texted. She always goes to Nick and Rachel's for Christmas.'

As he tells me more about his family, I can't help wondering if it's him or his mum who's the most distant person in it, and he laughs and says that they're both very independent people.

'What about your brother? Do you get on OK with him?'

'I get on OK, as you put it, with everyone. I just don't see the need to be in their pockets all the time. Nor they in mine. I like doing my own thing.'

'I guess that comes with being a writer. Being solitary and stuff.'

'It comes with my family,' he says. 'But the writing too.'

I decide not to follow up on his comments, as he thinks I'm inquisitive enough, but instead remark that he must be excited that his book was accepted.

'I'm very pleased,' he admits. 'I was more anxious than I should have been.'

'It's a great book.'

'Thank you.' He raises his glass. 'And thank you for being such a good beta reader.'

'I'm an ordinary reader,' I say as his glance flickers to the bookshelves in the alcove by the fireplace. He stands up and looks at them. My entire collection of Janice Jermyn and Agatha Christie. Dad's Harlan Coben and Lee Child. Mum's Patricia Scanlan and Ciara Geraghty, as well as the wide selection of random books that we all love, none Booker winners, but all great stories.

'I liked Agatha Christie as a boy.' Charles takes out *The Murder of Roger Ackroyd* and flicks through the pages. 'I enjoyed working out who the murderer was.'

'And did you?'

'Sometimes.'

'I rarely did with hers,' I admit. 'There was always a sneaky twist, particularly in that one.' I nod at the book in his hand, and he laughs.

'I hope my sneaky twist is as good.'

'It's pretty good,' I acknowledge.

We slip into silence, but it's a companionable, easy silence. Every so often I glance at Charles, who's gazing into the fire, seemingly deep in thought. I love being here with him, but I have to ask myself what on earth is going on between us. He's an older, divorced man, and in a million years I would never have imagined myself sitting in my living room with someone like him. I'm wondering what he's thinking about me. How is he framing the relationship, if relationship is even the right word, between us? Has he called over for some festive sex, as a quid pro quo for the watch? Is that it? I nibble on the end of my nail and then whip it out of my mouth, because I had them shellacked for Christmas and I don't want to ruin them. (They're a glittery gold. I love them.)

'What are you thinking?' Charles breaks the silence.

'It's usually women who ask that question.'

'Ah, but I'm a man in touch with the emotions that women feel. That's a quote from *The Times*,' he adds. 'So I'm allowed to ask.'

'I was wondering about us,' I say.

'Us?' He looks surprised.

'If there even is an us,' I say. 'Which I feel there might be. And yet I don't know.'

'Of course there's an us,' says Charles.

'And what are we?'

'Two people who care for each other?'

'OK . . .'

'What do you want, Iseult?'

When my parents call me Iseult, I feel like I did when I was a little girl and in trouble over something. When Charles does, I feel like a proper grown-up.

'I thought we were a holiday romance, but now you're saying we care for each other and I don't know what that really means. Don't panic, though,' I add. 'There's no pressure. I don't want anything from you.'

'I want you,' says Charles. 'You make me feel . . . inspired. Renewed. Spirited. Wholehearted. Actually, wholehearted is best,' he continues. 'You make me feel wholehearted about my life and about my work. You unblocked me.'

'You're making me sound like Dyno-Rod.'

'Are you always this . . . this down-to-earth?' he asks.

'Yes. I'm sorry if that's not spiritual enough for you.'

'Spiritual?' He laughs.

'Um . . . I don't know the right word. But you're all creative and whatever. Your first thought when you heard my name was that I was named after a poet. But I'm not creative and I'm not poetic and I'm not really your sort of person at all.'

'Are we having our first row?' asks Charles.

I don't say anything.

He gets up from the chair and puts his arm around me.

'Don't overthink it,' he says. 'I like you just the way you are.'

I recognise that line. I can't imagine Charles has read *Bridget Jones's Diary*, though.

I lean my head on his shoulder. He puts his fingers beneath my chin and tilts it so that we're face to face.

'I never expected to meet anyone like you,' he says. 'You've completely knocked me out of my groove. But I love it.'

I love it too.

Chapter 18

Ariel

Champagne arrived in flutes on trays and we
emptied them with gladness in our hearts.

Roman Payne

I stride past the baggage carousel at Dublin Airport, happy
that I only needed carry-on luggage for my trip to my
parents in Mallorca. It was the first Christmas I'd spent with
them for a few years, and it was more enjoyable than I'd
expected. We have a complicated relationship. My dad is an
absolute sweetheart but lives in a world of his own. Mum
is . . . well, not a million miles away from Pamela Boyd-
Miller, if I'm honest. There's the same spikiness about her.
The same way of telling it like it is when sometimes a white
lie would be better. And just as Pamela apparently criticised
Charles when he was younger, Mum was always on my case
to study harder, do better, live up to my potential. She never
really indicated what she thought my potential was, but
maybe she was right, because I always try to do that anyway,
and (this rather shitty year aside) I generally succeed.

In Mallorca, she's mellower, more chilled and prepared to

go with the flow than before. When I was a child, she wrote lists. Lists of chores. Lists of achievements. Lists of where we had to be and when. She was a relentless list-maker. But all that has changed, and when I arrived at Villa Hibiscus with its picturesque views of Palma Bay, she greeted me with a glass of cava and told me to leave unpacking till later. She and Dad have a whole new network of retired friends whose main aim in life is to have a good time, so there were plenty of lunches and dinners and parties to go to. On Christmas Day itself, we ate at a restaurant on the promenade of their local beach, and I didn't once think back to the Christmases Charles and I spent together curled up in the living room of Riverside Lodge, drinking red wine and thinking that life couldn't get any better. I messaged him, of course, as I always do, a photo of me wearing a Santa hat with the Mediterranean as a backdrop, and he sent one back of himself and Ellis at her house.

As much as his mother and I locked horns, I got on reasonably well with Ellis, who's very much her own person. Like Charles, she's creative, although her creativity comes in painting and pottery. Her home is in Enniskerry, a picturesque village about 30 kilometres to the south of Dublin, and she works from a shed in her back garden. When we first met, she was also working in a library, but shortly after Charles and I married, she bought the house and set up her own business. She's sharp and smart and good at communications, and she's also very talented. I have two of her paintings in my office, and in my apartment a long, slender vase that she made for my birthday one year. We used to meet up quite a lot when Charles and I were married, and I considered her to be a friend. I still do, even though I haven't seen her in ages. I should've sent her a Christmas card.

I'm getting into a taxi when my phone buzzes.

What time are you home?

On the way now. Anything wrong?

No. Just checking you're coming to my party

I always come to your party. I ORGANISE your party!

I'll see you this evening. Don't be late

I'll be there before midnight!

Honestly, Charles is like a baby sometimes. And when he says 'my party' as though I'm a casual invitee, he's being disingenuous. The reason I do the organisation for him is because he uses it as a kind of promotional thing. He invites a few of the better-known reviewers along, and they always come, even if only for a short time, because Charles is an excellent host. Despite the hassle of being in charge, I enjoy it myself. I like our status as a civilised ex-couple who are still best friends. And occasional lovers.

Although that hasn't happened in quite a while.

Should my New Year's resolution be to make it less occasional? Or would that be an absolute disaster?

I remind myself that I don't make New Year's resolutions. I'd never keep them anyway.

I am, as always, the first to arrive at Riverside Lodge. I need to be there to make sure that the caterers and bar staff have arrived, that everything has been set up, that there's enough booze and non-booze for everyone, and that Charles himself is prepped for the onslaught.

I first had the idea of the party the year of Charles's Booker win. *Winter's Heartbreak* was topping the bestseller lists and I thought it would be a nice way to celebrate his success, thank everyone for all their hard work and have a good time. It was great fun and Charles was happy to make it an annual event. We've had the same caterers every year. The MD of the company, Ash O'Halloran, contacts me in October to run through the plans, and updates me regularly, so I already know that everything is in hand and there's nothing for me to worry about. She's even dealt with Charles's last-minute request to have a Caribbean theme (I should have thought of it myself, to be honest) by introducing new canapés and adding pina coladas and tropical sunsets to the cocktail list.

Now, standing beside Charles and looking around the two rooms with the interconnecting doors open so that the already big space is even bigger, I feel myself relax. The food is prepared, the bar staff are ready for the influx that will shortly descend on us, and he and I are sharing a well-deserved glass of champagne. (I'll be sticking to fizz despite the tropical cocktails.)

'I don't say it often enough, but you're a real marvel,' he says as we clink our glasses together.

'I know.'

'Thanks for this, and for everything you've done for the book. I know the change of direction was a gamble.'

'It was a challenge.' I smile. 'But all's well that ends well, and hopefully we'll have a massive hit on our hands next year.'

He puts his arm around me and squeezes my shoulders just as the doorbell rings and our first guests arrive. The literary set are always on time, afraid the wine will run out if they're late. It never has, of course. I always order more than enough. The journalists arrive promptly too, although they'll feck off to other events before midnight. But it's good to get a piece in the paper about how great the party is and how much Charles is loved. I haven't got him named as a national treasure yet, but sooner or later somebody will use the phrase.

It's a more relaxed party than the Xerxes celebration. Maybe that's because most of the guests are Irish and aren't treating it as a work event. As far as they're concerned, it's a good night out. We always invite Graham, but he only ever came to the London parties. Sydney Travers, Charles's new editor, was a late invitee. I was surprised when she accepted, but she said it was a good opportunity to meet him in person, and when she arrives, I introduce her to him straight away.

'I'm so looking forward to working on your book,' she tells him. 'I enjoy your work and I definitely want to make you as successful a crime writer as you are a literary genius.'

Charles is melting under the gaze of her enormous brown eyes, which are positively smouldering without the barrier of her glasses. Mind you, they're the only thing about her that is smouldering, as she's channelling that black-and-white vibe again – if her hair was in plaits instead of a loose bun on the back of her head, she'd be a ringer for Wednesday Addams. I hide a smile at the thought and leave them to their discussion as more arrivals walk into the room.

Within half an hour, the atmosphere is loud and jovial.

The champagne is doing its job and I'm doing mine by chatting to everyone and telling them all how much we appreciate them. The waiters bring around trays of food, and I'm glad that Charles actually remembered to roll up the rugs, because otherwise he'd be paying for professional cleaning.

'Ariel! Ariel!' Brandon Heath, the organiser of one of the country's biggest literary festivals, waves me over. 'Ariel, sweetheart, is it true? That the king of literary fiction has written an actual thriller?'

Brandon also contributes to the literary pages of the newspapers, highlighting the 'books of the season' a few times a year. He always picks the most obscure titles it's possible to choose. And not that I don't think lesser-known books shouldn't get lots of lovely publicity (I have a few authors who'd kill for a mention from him), but I do think it would be nice if he made an occasional mention of an author readers have already heard of. He's never given Charles the nod in any of his pieces, although I sent him an advance copy of *Winter's Heartbreak* before it came out. After that, of course, Charles was too famous to merit his attention.

'A literary thriller. It's brilliant.' I take a fresh glass of champagne from a passing waiter, along with a delightfully named island spice profiterole from another.

'I'm not hugely keen on writers diluting their talent,' says Brandon.

'Hardly diluting.' My words are muffled due to my having stuffed the entire profiterole into my mouth. 'More expanding,' I add as I swallow it. 'And hopefully bringing his work to a wider audience.'

'I'd have thought his audience was wide enough already.' Brandon's eyes narrow. He's jealous of Charles, naturally.

'It's a fun but thought-provoking read,' I say as I glance around the room to see who I can palm Brandon off onto. I spot Sydney on her own and wave her over. At the same time, I see Charles talking to someone I don't know, a young woman with spiky hair wearing a green silk dress and an uncomfortably high pair of heels. She must be a new bookseller. I'll introduce myself later.

I leave Brandon and Sydney together and make my way around the room, stopping to talk to all the people who need to be talked to. I take a moment to wonder about the last time I went to an event that wasn't in some way work-related. In all the years of our relationship, Charles and I only ever socialised with literary people, and since our split, the only times we're together in public are for book-related things too. Even before Charles, all my socialising was literary because I was trying to make a name for myself. I've never really thought about it before, and even if I had, it wouldn't have bothered me, but right at this moment, I wish there was a part of my life that was just for me.

I need to go out more with people who don't give a toss about the written word. And then I remind myself that I'm back from a few days in Mallorca, where we didn't talk about books once. It's the whole New Year thing that's making me feel maudlin. My only non-fiction author, a celebrity psychologist, who's a friend of a friend, wrote a book about seasonal depression, pointing out it often peaks on New Year's Eve. It's all to do with reflection on the year past, and high expectations for the one to come. If we feel we haven't achieved as much as we should, if we set the bar too high and think we've failed, all the enforced jollity can be a bit much.

But if any of the guests here tonight are feeling seasonally depressed, they're hiding it well. The buzz of conversation and bursts of laughter are fuelled by the limitless champagne and brightly coloured cocktails. Apparently one of the things that triggers seasonal depression is concern about finances. Charles spends an absolute fortune on his New Year's Eve party. I do hope it's tax-deductible. I look after many things for him, but not his accounts. Given his previous career, he does that himself. He says he finds it therapeutic.

I continue to work my way around the room, stopping to talk to various guests before looking for Charles again. I can't see him, and nor can I hear his distinctive voice over the hubbub of conversation. The champagne has loosened people's tongues and their inhibitions. Myles McGuigen, a mid-list writer of historical fiction, has his arm around Bettina Boyle, whose bookish podcast has been one of the year's successes. Seán Óg O Faolain (Irish history) and Briain MacCártaigh (Irish genealogy) are having an animated argument about the 1916 Rising, and Shane Wilson, curator of a summer literary school, is actively kissing PR guru Kate Collins. It's all a bit bacchanalian, but it's also fun, and it makes me feel a bit less stressed too.

I glance at my watch. Twenty minutes to go. I'd better find Charles before the fireworks start.

Chapter 19

Iseult

Quiet people have the loudest minds.
Stephen King

Celeste's dad is dropping us to Terenure for Charles's NYE party. He said he couldn't leave us at the mercy of Dublin's taxi service on the busiest night of the year, and told us to call him no matter what time it is if we struggle to get a cab later. I came to Celeste's earlier so that we could glam up together and help each other with hair and make-up – not that she needed help with her hair because she'd it done earlier and it's swept high on her head with a dinky little plait across the front of it, like a hairband. I've gone for my spiky look again. When we're finally ready, we take a selfie of ourselves and post it to our socials with lots of #PartyReady and #NewYear hashtags. Celeste looks great in the silver-sequinned mini dress with fringed skirt and spaghetti straps she bought in the sales, teamed with dangly earrings and sparkly shoes from Zara. I'm grateful I can still fit into my emerald-green silk. It doesn't matter that I've worn it multiple times this month. It was expensive, and at least I'm getting the wear out of it.

It's unusual for me to go out on New Year's Eve, as it's never been my favourite night of the year. I normally volunteer to do the late shift at work, preferring checking cargo to drunk-kissing and hugging at midnight. However, Charles's event is sure to be different. The invitations said black tie!

'Ready?' Celeste turns to me.

'As I'll ever be,' I say. 'I wonder will there be any single men there tonight?'

'Apart from Charles?' She arches a perfect 3D eyebrow.

'He's not . . . well, he is, but . . .'

'Have you decided if you're in a relationship with him?' she asks.

'I'm in something with him,' I admit. 'But a proper relationship . . . oh, Celeste, I don't know.'

'As long as you're having fun.' She gives me a quick hug. 'Don't let him hurt you, that's all.'

'Absolutely not,' I assure her. 'My heart is like a rock these days.'

'Any more texts from Steve?'

'Thankfully not a word since the Christmas Day message.'

'Good.' Celeste does a shimmy that made her dress glitter beneath the light. 'Let's have fun tonight.'

We clatter down the stairs and rouse Uncle Paul from his comfy seat in front of the telly.

It's forty minutes after the party was due to start when we arrive at Riverside Lodge. I was terrified of being too early (whenever Steve and I went to parties, nobody even thought of turning up before the pubs closed), but I can see through the lighted windows that there are already plenty of people inside. There's an actual red carpet leading up the steps to the hallway, where there's also a real-life doorman. Seriously, how much money has Charles Miller made from writing books?

'Have fun, ladies. Stay safe,' says Uncle Paul as we get out of the car.

'Don't worry, Dad. If we're stuck, we'll definitely call you,' says Celeste.

We walk up the steps to the house, and the doorman checks our names off a printed list.

'Have a great evening,' he says as we step inside.

For a moment I'm reminded of Steve's posts from the art gallery in Florence. Not that the house is anything like the art gallery, but it's evoking the same vibe of glamour and sophistication and potential for a James Bond lookalike to knock back a shaken-not-stirred martini before quietly disposing of the villain, though I don't know who would be the villain in this crowd of tuxedos and cocktail dresses. Celeste and I have barely taken a couple of steps into the room when a waiter offers us champagne, and have hardly gone any further when another puts a plate of mini bagels in front of us.

I'm absolutely starving, so I grab two and shove one into my mouth. Celeste takes a couple as well. We smile at each other.

'It's very flash, isn't it?' she says.

'Oh, not flash. More . . . refined.'

'It won't be refined by midnight,' she observes. 'It'll be the usual heave of drunken lunatics.'

'Probably,' I admit. It doesn't matter if you're in a tux or jeans. Once you've tipped yourself over the edge, you've tipped yourself over the edge.

We wander through the interconnecting rooms. Celeste is awestruck by the decor, even if it's been taken over by Christmassy stuff.

'I feel like we're in a TV show,' she murmurs. 'Or maybe even a movie, where we've been transported to somewhere amazing.'

'There's a touch of *Grand Designs* about it all,' I agree. 'Though this is more of a grand restoration than anything.'

'Both of our houses would probably fit on the ground floor,' she observes.

'I know.'

'I wonder who owned it before Charles.'

'I think he said it was a wine importer. Or maybe it was a tobacco importer.'

'Gosh, you could've stopped the wine or tobacco at customs.'

'Before my time, but you never know.'

We both laugh at the thought.

'Ladies, you came.' Suddenly Charles is standing beside us, and the noise of conversation and laughter seems to disappear. 'I'm so glad,' he says.

'Thanks for asking us,' says Celeste. 'This is an absolutely fabulous house.'

'Would you like a tour?' he asks.

'Oh, yes please.' She beams at him, and I can't help thinking that he really does know how to turn on the charm.

'I've seen it already,' I say. 'I'll stay here.'

'Are you sure?' He frowns.

'Yes. I want to eat a few more of those yummy bagels.'

'I'll bring some with us.'

He grabs a platter from a passing waiter and leads us into the hallway. We do the same tour as he did with me, although this time without going into his bedroom. Celeste loves it, especially the hi-tech kitchen.

'Feel free to use it any time,' says Charles. 'I could do with some home cooking.'

'What do you make mostly?' asks Celeste as she opens the door of the top-of-the-range Miele oven and peers inside.

'Oven chips,' he replies. 'And pizza.'

She looks at him in horror, and I laugh.

'Seriously,' he says. 'I don't cook. I get stuff delivered.'

'How are you so fit?' she demands.

'I get good stuff delivered. I work out too, although not as often as I should. Anyway,' he says, 'let's get back to the madding crowd.'

We follow him upstairs, and he's immediately accosted by a man who he introduces as Myles, another author. Celeste is interested when he says he writes historical fiction, and they move slightly to one side as he tells her about his latest novel, set during the Second World War.

'Are you having fun?' Charles asks me.

'Yes. Thanks for asking us.'

'I wanted you here.' He reaches out for another glass of champagne and hands it to me. 'You look lovely, by the way. That dress suits you.'

'Thanks.'

'Though it'll always remind me of almost dumping drink over you in the Caribbean.'

'Me too.' I grin.

'I was so lucky to meet you there.'

'I enjoyed spending time with you.'

The conversation between us isn't exactly flowing. Every time we meet, the first few minutes alone are awkward.

'There'll be fireworks later.'

For a moment I think he means between us, but then I

see him glance out of the window, where a couple of men are setting up the display.

'I thought private firework displays weren't allowed,' I remark.

'Not strictly,' he concedes. 'But it's only a few, and none of the neighbours have dogs so they don't mind. In fact, they usually come out to have a look themselves.' He slides his arm around my waist and pulls me towards him. 'Come on. Let's introduce you to a few people.'

We plunge into the crowd, where I meet men and women whose names I instantly forget. After a while, Charles abandons me and I wonder if he's going to come back. I look around for Celeste, and see she's talking to a very tall, very skinny red-headed man. She's laughing, he has a big grin on his face and the chemistry between them seems good. I don't want to interrupt them, but I don't know anyone else, and besides, they're all involved in deep discussions. I do what everyone in these circumstances does and take out my phone. I've missed five messages, all early Happy New Year GIFs from my work WhatsApp group. I send one back, and then another message comes in.

Wishing you all the best for the coming
year and hoping it's good to you. Sx

I should have bloody blocked him at Christmas. Annoyingly, he's going to know I've seen this message now. So I send one back saying *Same to you*, and then my phone rings.

'How are things?' he asks.

I'm struggling to hear him over the noise, so I walk into the hallway. It's equally noisy here, and I open the door to the dining-room where the waiting staff are loading up trays with more glasses of champagne. I apologise, take a glass that one of the waiters hands me, and return to the downstairs kitchen, which is blissfully quiet. Even as I do, I wonder why I'm bothering. Why I don't tell Steve I'm busy and can't talk to him. Instead, I say I'm at a party.

'Where?' He sounds peeved.

'Terenure.'

'Terenure! You don't know anyone in Terenure.'

'Obviously I do.'

'Workmate?' he asks.

'No.' I shake my head even though he can't see me. 'Look, Steve, why are you texting me and calling me? We're not a couple any more and it's really disconcerting.'

'We're friends, though,' he says. 'I told you. We'll always be friends. So I'm texting you in a friendly way.'

'Well stop.' My determination comes from the large gulp of champagne I've taken. 'I've moved on.'

'You have a new boyfriend?' He sounds shocked.

'I have new friends.'

'In Terenure? I find that hard to believe.'

'Why?'

'I've never met anyone as . . . as . . . conservative as you, Izzy. Everything in your life is always the same. You hate new things. You don't do anything that takes you out of your comfort zone. You—'

'When you're finished insulting me, let me know,' I say.

'It's not an insult, it's an observation.'

'And is my conservatism, as you put it, the reason you dumped me?'

'Partly,' he admits.

I end the call without saying anything else. My phone rings again and I silence it. I sit on the sofa (the kitchen has a relaxing space with a sofa!), and as I sip my champagne, I think that Steve is very wrong about me. Yes, there are ways in which I like things to stay the same. But I went to the Caribbean without him, and I slept with a man who's the complete opposite of him. A man who invited me to a posh party in his huge house. I'm hardly in my comfort zone now, am I? So what does Steve Carter know about anything.

The kitchen door opens and Charles walks in,

'There you are,' he says. 'I was looking for you.' His eyes narrow as he sits down beside me. 'Are you OK?'

'Yes.' I put Steve to the back of my mind and smile. 'Just sending a few New Year messages. Thanks for the invite to your party. It's nice to have something good to do on New Year's Eve.'

'You thanked me earlier. And you don't need to. I wouldn't have enjoyed it without you.'

'Oh. Well, I'm enjoying myself too.'

'And yet you're down here alone.'

'Like I said, checking messages.'

'People who are having fun don't need to check messages.'

'I do.' I smile.

He puts his arm around me and draws me close. His kiss tastes of champagne and smoke. I say so.

'I had a cigar earlier,' he confesses. 'I smoke two at this time of the year. One on New Year's Eve. The other on New Year's Day. Oh, and I have one whenever a book comes out. It's my only vice.'

'Oh, I dunno.' I find his lips again. 'I'm sure you have others.'

*

It's quite a while later before we go upstairs again, and Charles is immediately accosted by a man who tells him there's only fifteen minutes till midnight and we should all be outside for the fireworks. Charles nods and asks if the man has spoken to Ariel. Why would she have anything to do with the fireworks? I wonder. It's Charles's party, after all, and she's only his agent. Slash ex.

'I'd better get involved,' Charles says to me. 'See you shortly.'

He leaves me standing in the hallway and joins the revellers, where he shouts at everyone to gather up and get outside. There's a general movement, and a stylish woman wearing what even I can see is a very expensive dress in midnight blue catches Charles by the arm and demands to know where he's been. She has a beautiful solitaire diamond on the third finger of her right hand, a multicoloured ring on her left, a diamond tennis bracelet on her wrist and a silver chain with a blue stone that matches the blue of her dress around her neck. It takes me a moment to recognise her because she's older than the photographs I've seen and, quite honestly, more glamorous.

It's Ariel.

She's gorgeous.

Dammit.

She puts her hand on his back as she ushers him down the stairs, and I stare at the ring she's wearing on the third finger of her left hand. The multicoloured stones gleam richly beneath the lights. I wonder if she's engaged, and if so, to whom. Charles never mentioned it. Though in fairness, he does his best never to mention her. It's usually me bringing up the agent-slash-ex issue.

The partygoers follow them down the stairs. I do too.

It's freezing outside, and I wish that I'd been smart enough to find my jacket, because my green dress is backless and I've a large amount of skin exposed to the elements. I tell myself that the cold is invigorating, and besides, I'm surrounded by people so I'll warm up quickly enough.

Charles jumps onto a box and shouts at us all to be quiet for a moment. Then he begins a countdown to the new year. As he reaches zero, a huge rocket bursts overhead in a shower of golden stars. He leads the applause, and Ariel kisses him. On the mouth. In a very non-agent-slash-ex way. I feel my stomach tighten and look around for Celeste. She's being kissed by the guy with red hair. Charles's editor is also being kissed, although somewhat more platonically, by a man who I think is an author.

I'm not being kissed by anyone. Platonically or otherwise.

The woman beside me turns and wishes me Happy New Year, and I say the same to her, then I push my way towards Celeste and tap her on the shoulder. She throws her arm around me before introducing me to the redhead. His name is Darragh Mackey and he's a bookseller. He gives me a peck on the cheek and asks me if I'm cold. I'm guessing that beneath my red lipstick, my lips are actually blue, but I say, 'Not at all' and Celeste tells me I look amazing in my dress and I say that she looks amazing in hers and Darragh says that we both look amazing and it's great to meet new people at Charles's party. I'm trying to think of something other than 'amazing' to say in return when I feel a hand on my own shoulder. It's Charles. He does the Happy New Year thing with Celeste and Darragh and then manoeuvres me away from them and from the mass of people who are now making their way back into the house.

We're standing beneath a tree that's covered in fairy lights.

'Here.' He slips his jacket around my freezing shoulders and I breathe a sigh of relief even as the breath turns into mist in front of me. 'That's the problem with women coming to parties in gorgeous dresses,' he says. 'We guys are OK. Shirts and jackets.'

'You're being very gallant in giving me yours. We should go inside.' My teeth are chattering.

'Wait a moment,' he says.

I stand beside him in silence, watching the rest of the party disappear indoors.

'I've been thinking,' Charles says. 'A lot.'

About Ariel, I suspect. Because that was hardly a platonic kiss they shared. He's been lying to me about how ex she really is.

'What have you been thinking about?'

'Me. And you.'

'Oh. Not you and Ariel.' I can't help myself. 'She's beautiful, by the way.'

He looks startled. 'Were you introduced?'

'No, but I recognised her from the online photos,' I reply. 'And she clearly means a lot to you still, despite everything. That was a very intimate kiss you shared.'

'Hardly intimate given that it was in front of a crowd of people.' He shrugs. 'Besides, she kissed me, I didn't kiss her.'

'It didn't seem that way.'

'Are you jealous?'

'No.'

But I am. Of course I am.

'Look, Iseult—'

'I know that's my name, but I told you before, everyone calls me Izzy.'

'I like your proper name,' he says. 'Though if you prefer Izzy, that's what I'll call you from now on.' He gives me an impatient look. 'I didn't bring you here to talk about names.'

'What then?'

'I suppose I should start by saying that I'm older than you and have lived longer and have more experience and wisdom.'

'Jeez, way to make me feel like a child,' I say, sounding like a mulish teenager.

'I don't mean it like that,' says Charles. 'What I mean is – this isn't something I would've done years ago. I'd have thought it through, waited patiently, weighed up the options . . .'

'Have you created a bucket list for next year?'

'No,' he says. 'I've created a priority list. And I only have one priority on it.'

'A number one bestseller spot for *A Caribbean Calypso*.'

'Not that,' he says. 'Although perhaps that's in second place.'

'So what's top of your list?'

'This.' He clears his throat. 'Iseult O'Connor, Izzy, I love you. Will you marry me?'

I think my jaw literally drops.

And I look at him without saying a word.

Chapter 20

Ariel

Old words are reborn with new faces.
Criss Jami

It's a more raucous party than usual. People are chugging back the champagne like lemonade, and part of me wishes I'd ordered a cheaper Prosecco instead. But I dismiss the thought. People expect the best at Charles's New Year's Eve party, and that's what they'll always get. I want them to have a great time with good vibes and remember it when his book comes out. I know he's an award-winning author, but I'm leaving no stone unturned.

It's nearly midnight and I've done enough schmoozing. I need to find Charles and get people out into the garden for the fireworks. If we don't go now, half of them will be stuck inside when the clock strikes twelve. But then I see him and he's shouting at everyone to move outside. I hurry over to him and ask him where the hell he was, say that I was beginning to worry, and he tells me to chill out, that everything's fine. I follow him to the garden, where he jumps up onto the box (my heart is in my mouth, it's not very sturdy) and begins the countdown. When we get to midnight, the fireworks go off and everyone claps, and Charles jumps down again and kisses me.

He's such a good kisser. He always was. He kisses you like you're the most important person in the world. And no matter what we've gone through, I hope I'm still the most important person in his world. Because even with all the changes in our lives, he's still the most important person in mine.

'Did you make any resolutions for this year?' I ask when we part.

'Maybe.'

'To write a series of murder mysteries?'

'God, no.'

'To write another Booker winner?'

'If only.'

'To get another screen adaptation?'

'That's your department, not mine.'

'If I made New Year's resolutions, that would definitely be one of them,' I assure him. 'Absolutely. Hopefully we'll close the TV deal on *An Autumn Story* soon. As well as which, *Snow in Summer* is great mini-series material. I have some irons in the fire there and Shelley's totally on top of it, but I don't want to count our chickens until they're strutting down the road with Amazon Prime seared into their chests.'

He laughs. It's such a lovely, rich laugh.

'I'm going inside,' I say. 'It's bloody freezing out here.'

'I'll be in in a moment.'

'New Year's cigar?'

'You know me so well.'

I leave him to it and go into the house. The atmosphere

is slightly more subdued now, but the waiting staff begin circulating with the champagne again, along with a lovely selection of petits fours, and it doesn't take long for the hum of conversation to get going.

I spot Sydney Travers and join her.

'This is fun,' she says. 'Thanks for inviting me.'

'You and Charles have had time for a quick chat?'

'Yes. It's nice to meet and talk in person. He's charming, isn't he?'

'He is.' I smile. People always say that about Charles. Well, women do. I'm not sure that men think of him as anything other than a competitor.

'He said he was willing to make some structural changes,' Sydney tells me. 'Which is a relief. Some authors are so precious, they don't want a word changed. However, he's accepted that the issues on page two and in Chapter Twelve need solving, among others.'

'Yes, I've spoken to him at length about Chapter Twelve.'

'And there's the fact that one of his red herrings is blatantly misleading to the reader.'

'Misleading is OK, though,' I say.

'But not something that's gratuitously misleading,' says Sydney. 'Anyway, not to worry, we'll sort it.'

'Grand,' I say.

She takes her phone out of her bag and looks at it.

'My cab is here,' she says. 'I'll get going now.'

'Well done you on managing to book one for tonight.'

'The hotel did it for me as soon as I arrived.' She smiles. 'Years of experience of not being able to get cabs on New Year's Eve means I pulled out all the stops. To be honest, I usually spend it at home these days.'

'I would too if it wasn't for the party. But at least I don't have to worry about cabs, because I can stay over.'

'You and Charles seem to have a very close personal relationship despite not being together any more,' she says.

'We have a bond,' I tell her. 'And even though it wobbles from time to time, it's unbreakable.'

'How lovely.' She smiles again. 'I wish I had a bond like that with my ex. But I hate the sight of him and I think the feeling is mutual.'

'You're divorced?' I look at her in surprise.

'We got married stupidly young,' she says. 'Everyone warned me against it. Live with him, they said, but I wouldn't listen. I thought he was the love of my life. A few months later, I realised he wasn't.'

'We all make mistakes.'

'Anyway, I'd better go,' she says. 'It was great to meet you again.'

But before she has a chance to leave, Charles claps his hands and silences the crowd.

'A quick word,' he says. 'To usher in the new year.'

I frown. He doesn't usually do quick words. He's very aware that at parties (at least Irish parties), people are quite happy to drink the drink, eat the food and amuse themselves without the need for any other interventions.

'I know we all make resolutions at New Year,' he continues. 'Even if they don't last. And we promise ourselves we'll make changes in our lives. That doesn't always work out either. But I'm making a massive change in mine, and I wanted to share it with you.'

What the hell is he talking about? I glance at Sydney,

who's clearly peppering to get away but feels obliged to listen to whatever it is Charles has to say.

'I'm getting married!' The words burst from him, and for a moment I don't understand what he's saying. Married? What is he talking about?

'This evening a wonderful woman has made me the luckiest man in the world by agreeing to become my wife,' he goes on. 'And here she is – Iseult O'Connor, soon to be the new Mrs Miller, and I couldn't be happier.'

He turns around and grabs the hand of the person standing behind him. I gasp as I recognise the girl in the green dress. She looks rather like a rabbit caught in the headlights as she stands beside him. He puts his arm around her and kisses her, and I feel my stomach flip over. It's all I can do not to vomit on the floor.

'Gosh,' says Sydney, who's still beside me. 'I wasn't expecting that. Were you?'

My mouth is so dry I can't speak. I simply shake my head while keeping my eyes fixed on the two of them.

'She's quite young,' observes Sydney.

Yes, she is. A lot younger than me. And therefore a hell of a lot younger than Charles. Who on earth is she? What in God's name is he thinking? And what on earth has he told her about us?

Meanwhile, people are applauding and raising glasses to the . . . what, newly engaged couple? A few men are patting Charles on the back while the girl stands there looking embarrassed. She's suddenly embraced by a young woman in a sequinned dress. They were together earlier. They must be friends. And Charles was obviously the one to invite them, because I haven't a clue who they are.

I try to push my way forward, but there are too many people in the way.

'Tell him I said congratulations,' says Sydney, who's heading towards the front door. 'And I'll be in touch about the edits.'

'Sure.' I hope I sound like a professional agent and not someone who feels as though she's been kicked in the stomach. Or stabbed in the back. Or both.

I can't believe Charles has done this to me.

Not after everything. And not in front of everyone.

Iseult

I said yes. I'm in shock at saying it, but even as the words left my mouth, I was sure I was doing the right thing. I knew deep down it wasn't just a holiday romance. There's something between us that I can't even explain to myself. I know we haven't been together long, but when he's not with me, I feel as though something is missing. Being with him makes me feel as though I'm part of someone's life in a way I never did with Steve. My emotions are more mature. I feel more mature too. I've moved on to being someone else, Iseult instead of Izzy. A woman who knows what she wants from life.

'I love you so much,' he said, when I accepted his proposal in the freezing garden, along with the small opal ring that he said was temporary until we could go into town and buy the one I wanted. 'I know we were meant to be. I really do.'

'I was afraid to be in love with you,' I said. 'I thought it was just a brief thing. That it didn't really matter. That *I* didn't matter.'

'Iseult.' He looked at me with those amazing blue eyes. 'You matter more to me than anyone else in the world. I'm overwhelmed by how much you matter. It took me some time to realise that I've never loved anyone the way I love you. And I'm going inside right now to tell everyone, so this is your one and only chance to back out.'

'Why would I do that?' I asked. 'I think I fell in love with you the moment I first set eyes on you.'

'Really? When was that?'

'When I saw you at the White Sands. Sitting all alone at your table.'

'Don't tell me you wanted to mother me?'

'No.' I grinned. 'I wanted to fuck you.'

'If only I'd known.'

He laughed as he took me by the hand and led me back into the house.

'Before you make a big announcement – if you truly want to do that – please let me tell Celeste,' I begged. 'She'll never forgive me if I don't give her a heads-up.'

He shrugged, and I went looking for my best friend. She was alone in front of a sideboard laden with strawberries dipped in chocolate.

'I'm eating far too many of these,' she said. 'But hey, the diet starts tomorrow.'

'The best day for a diet to start,' I agreed. 'Listen, I've something to tell you.'

'Shoot.'

As I spoke, her eyes opened wider and wider and she put her pina colada on the sideboard.

'You're kidding,' she said eventually, grasping my hand and looking at the ring.

'Nope.'

'Are you sure?'

'Yes.'

'Really sure? Because—'

'Don't give me all the reasons why it might not work,' I said. 'I've thought of them myself. Give me the reasons why it will. Because he's going to tell everyone in a few minutes and there's no going back after that.'

'There's always going back,' she said. 'Oh, Izzy, he's lovely, he really is. If you're sure, I'm sure. If you're happy, I'm happy.'

'I really am,' I said.

'In that case . . .' she flung her arms around me, 'con-bloody-gratulations. But honestly, you could have stiffed him for a better ring.'

I'm looking at Ariel as I stand beside Charles, feeling a little bit like his Booker Prize award. Obviously I won't feel like that all the time, but right now, with everyone's eyes on me, it's a bit embarrassing. But that'll pass. I wish I'd thought of calling Mum and Dad before Charles said anything, but my only thought was to tell Celeste before he announced the news to everyone else. I expected a few doubts from her. I'd have said the same if our roles were reversed. But I know she's happy for me. *I'm* happy for me. I never expected this to happen, but now that it has, it feels (despite my current embarrassment) absolutely right.

His agent-slash-ex walks up to him. She can't keep the shocked expression from her face.

'What on earth are you doing?' she asks.

'Ariel.' He says her name like a warning. 'Time and place.'

'You think this was the time and place?'

She's angry, I realise. Probably because he didn't tell her before everyone else. And I understand that. It's why I told Celeste.

'It seemed right.' He shrugs.

I step forward. 'I'm sorry if you've been taken by surprise,' I say. 'But I hope we'll all get on well together.'

'You hope . . .' She stares at me. 'Who *are* you exactly?'

'Iseult O'Connor,' I say. 'Charles's fiancée.' I add that bit to cement my status in her head. Because even though their relationship is over, I can feel her shock. I'd be shocked too if Steve told me he was engaged to someone else, even though I don't love him any more.

'I had no idea.'

I'm not sure if her words are directed at me or at him. I want to give the two of them a moment, but even as I turn away towards Celeste, he reaches out and grabs me by the wrist.

'No need for you to go anywhere,' he says. 'Ariel's being rude, but that's because she's been caught off guard. She's always rude when that happens.'

'I am not,' she protests.

'We'll talk later.' And he walks away from her, bringing me with him towards the other side of the room.

'Is she all right?' I ask.

'She hates being the last to know about anything,' he murmurs, and then smiles as people start congratulating him though mostly ignoring me.

'Unfortunately my new editor seems to have gone before we got a chance to chat with her,' says Charles when we've finally accepted all the good wishes there are to accept.

'I talked with her earlier,' I say. 'She's nice. She has some cool ideas about making it more difficult to spot the murderer.'

'You've been having editorial conversations about my book?' He looks amused. 'I suppose you have a proprietorial interest in it, after all.'

'I certainly have a proprietorial interest in you,' I murmur.

He draws me close to him and smiles. 'Our married life will be so perfect. I'll write books and you can tell me what I'm doing wrong.'

'Sounds like a plan,' I say.

And it does.

It's about an hour later when the crowd starts to thin out. Charles is saying goodbye to various people while Celeste and I sit on the comfortable sofa and discuss my newly engaged state.

'You had a thing for him from the start,' she says. 'I could tell.'

'Maybe.'

'When you came back to the room after not having sex with him . . .'

'Hmm. I did think that was a deal-breaker.'

'But then you did.'

'I did. And it was wonderful.'

'It's funny how life works out. I wonder would you have noticed Charles Miller at all if you and Steve had been at the White Sands together.'

'No! Because I would've been at my own wedding.'

'But if you had . . .' Celeste looks thoughtful. 'Gosh, can you imagine – falling for someone else on your wedding day!'

'Just as well it wasn't my wedding day so,' I say.

'I suppose we'd better make a move.' She glances around the now rapidly emptying room. There are a few people engaged in deep conversation, probably the ones who are always last to leave any party, but the majority have now gone. Celeste opens her phone app and searches for a taxi.

'Half an hour.' She sounds surprised. 'Not bad if it actually shows up and we don't have to emergency-call Dad.'

'Fingers crossed.'

I look for Charles. He's talking to Ariel. Hopefully smoothing things over with his agent-slash-now-very-much-ex.

Ariel

It's ages before I get the chance to talk to Charles, and now that I'm in front of him, I don't know what to say. I start off with 'Have you lost your mind?' and not surprisingly, it goes downhill from there, especially when he tells me that she's his beta reader, the girl he met in the Caribbean.

'Far be it from me to call out a blatant holiday romance,' I say. 'But for feck's sake, Charles. You let her read your book. She said nice things. You were flattered. It's understandable.'

'All those things may be true,' he says. 'But what's also true is that I love her and she makes me happy.'

'Even if that's the case, you seem to have forgotten—'

'She's exactly what I need.' He interrupts me. 'And I think I'm what she needs too.'

'Maybe so,' I say. 'I'm quite sure her youth and adoration are both very appealing.'

'She's a grown-up,' he says. 'Don't talk about her as though she's a child.'

'She's half your feckin' age!' I retort.

'She's twenty years younger than me. That's nothing these days.'

'Oh for crying out loud, Charles. None of that is the issue, is it?'

He looks at me mutinously.

'You haven't told her, have you?'

'We can sort it very quickly,' he says.

'So I'm right.' I shake my head. 'You've asked her to marry you in front of a whole room of people, and you're still married to me.'

His lips tighten. 'Only legally,' he says. 'We're separated. We've been living apart for years. It's a technical thing,' he adds. 'We did all the paperwork when we first split up. I'm sure it can be done and dusted in a matter of weeks.'

I say nothing. It should have been done and dusted a long time ago, when we worked out the financial agreement and then handed it over to the legal people. But it was around then that his novella was published and the Netflix deal was in the pipeline. I was working so hard to make sure both the book and the deal were going well that I told my solicitor I didn't have time to worry about finalising a divorce. Charles wasn't too worried either. He hates legal stuff. After a few abortive attempts by the solicitors to push things along, the divorce papers have been gathering dust.

'She'll go mad,' I tell him.

'She'll understand.'

She won't. And there's another thing she won't understand either. I'm not sure I want to mention it to Charles right now, but the fact that we've occasionally slept together since our separation doesn't bode well for the future Mrs Miller. Not that we'll ever sleep together again if this marriage goes ahead. I'm shocked at how suddenly bereft I feel at that.

'OK, don't hit me or anything, but . . .' I take a deep breath. 'Don't you think you're living one of your own books? You've written about a holiday romance, and it doesn't turn out well.'

That was *Snow in Summer*, the book I'm hoping to get a mini-series deal for. It's set in Italy, and Italy is having a moment right now. I haven't told Charles that there's talk of changing the ending. It's something he doesn't need to know yet.

'My relationship with Iseult is nothing like the relationship in my book,' he protests.

'Yes it is,' I say. 'A holiday romance between an older married man and a younger woman.'

'It's quite different,' insists Charles. 'There was a thirty-year age gap in that book. There's only twenty between Iseult and me. And their relationship wasn't a bit like ours.'

'Don't be naïve,' I say. 'The media—'

'All publicity is good publicity, isn't that what they say.' He makes a face. 'I suppose someone will unearth the fact that you and I are not actually divorced yet. Everyone assumes it, and I know I never disabuse them, because in my own head we are. Oh, it doesn't really matter,' he adds. 'People get engaged before their divorces come through all the time.'

'*Are* you doing this for the publicity?' I ask. 'It's not entirely a bad idea if so, but you should have talked it over with me. And I'd have spoken to Shelley or Maya so we could finesse it.'

'What d'you take me for!' He looks annoyed. 'I've fallen in love with a lovely woman, I want to marry her, and you should be happy for me.'

'Is it research?' It suddenly occurs to me that this is a more likely reason. 'Are you planning another novel with a younger female character? Charles, you can't pretend you're in love with her just for research. That would be horrible.'

'It's not research, it's not publicity and it's not some moment of madness either.' He sounds exasperated, and I wince. 'I love her and I want to marry her and that's it.'

'But she's so young and innocent and—'

'Not at all,' he says. 'She's actually a very smart, very sexy woman.'

His words drop like stones.

'And she's looking at me somewhat anxiously now, so I'm going over to talk to her. And I'll fill her in on our marital status. Maybe not tonight. That'd be unfair. But tomorrow for sure. She'll understand. I'd like you two to get along in the future and for you not to be a complete bitch to her. Will you say hello now?'

'I'll talk to her,' I say. 'I'll be as sweet as candy. And I won't tell her that she might be your fiancée but I am actually your wife.'

We walk over to where Iseult and her friend are standing, consulting their phones.

'We've ordered a taxi,' she says to Charles. 'If we're lucky, it'll be here in half an hour or so.'

'You're going?' He looks surprised. 'I thought you'd stay the night.'

'I can't stay the night,' she says. 'I have work tomorrow. I need to get home and get some sleep.'

I'm pleased to see he looks disconcerted. Maybe the fiancée isn't as under his thumb as her wide-eyed ingenue look implies.

'Hello.' I extend my hand to her. 'I'm sorry we didn't get a chance to talk earlier. I hope you two will be very happy together.'

'Thank you. I'm sure our announcement was as much of a shock to you as his proposal was to me. I'm sorry it didn't work out for you guys, but I'm happy that you're his agent-slash-ex.'

'His agent-slash-ex,' I echo.

'He's told me a lot about you.'

'He has?'

'I'm glad you two have a good working relationship,' she goes on. 'He depends on you a lot.'

'More than you think.' I can't stop myself.

'Ariel.' Charles's voice holds a warning.

'I'm sure you'll soon find out everything you need to know about me and my agency's first client,' I say.

'I'll make him happy,' she says.

'I hope he makes you happy too.'

'Oh, he does,' she says, and she smiles.

She's pretty in an unsophisticated kind of way. Her eyes are big in her oval face and her spiky hair is very on-trend. She's shorter than I first thought, but that's because she's discarded her heels and is barefoot. I dread to think what she's picking up on her feet. It's impossible to have a party without a lot of horrible debris ending up on the floor.

'If you need tips on managing him, just ask,' I say.

'Izzy can manage anyone and anything,' says her friend. 'I'm Celeste. We're cousins, though more like sisters really.'

'Pleased to meet you,' I say.

'The taxi is on Morehampton Road,' Celeste tells Iseult. 'Should only be ten minutes if the driver doesn't pick up a street fare and leave us in the lurch.'

'I hope there's no delay, especially not if you have to be at work,' I say to Iseult. 'Shame you have to go in on New Year's Day.'

'Iseult is a customs officer,' says Charles, his voice bursting with pride.

I'm rarely completely surprised, but this does surprise me. Like me, Charles doesn't know anyone outside of books and publishing these days. Though obviously his Caribbean sojourn meant he met a variety of people.

'I'm sure that's a very interesting job,' I murmur while wondering if he's thinking of another crime novel, this time set in the world of drug smuggling. She'd be perfectly placed to give him good material for that.

'Five minutes for the taxi,' says Celeste, who's monitoring its progress on her phone.

'Will you call me tomorrow?' Iseult asks Charles.

'Of course. I was hoping we could go shopping for a proper engagement ring.'

'When I have my next day off.'

'I want to get you something spectacular,' he says.

'I don't need a flashy ring.' She looks at the opal ring on her engagement finger. 'This is lovely.'

I glance down at my own engagement ring, the diamond solitaire I wear on my right hand. Then I look at my other ring, the rainbow of garnets, sapphires and emeralds I chose instead of a more traditional wedding ring because I liked it so much. I wear the diamond occasionally, but I wear my wedding ring all the time – not because Charles and I haven't divorced yet, but because it's my favourite piece of jewellery.

'Of course you want something spectacular,' Celeste tells Iseult. 'You're not properly engaged until you have a decent ring.'

'I wasn't properly engaged when I had one either,' she remarks.

'Huh?' I look at her bewildered, but Charles laughs and his eyes meet mine.

'It's not her first rodeo,' he says.

'You've been married before?' I stare at her.

'Engaged,' she says.

'And very recently too.'

'Well.' I reach out and grab a glass of champagne from the tray a waiter left on one of the side tables earlier. 'Nothing is ever as it first seems.'

'Don't worry,' Charles says to her. 'We'll get you a perfect ring and make an official announcement.'

'I rather think that news will be out before you have a chance to do any jewellery shopping,' I say. 'There were journalists here tonight, after all. As for social media . . .' I take out my phone and see I already have loads of notifications. 'Yup. It's all over social. So you need to have everything in the open, Charles. Everything.'

'I will,' he says.

'I'll call my parents as soon as I get home,' Iseult tells him.

'Taxi's here,' says Celeste. 'C'mon, Izzy, let's go.'

Charles wraps his arms around her and kisses her, and I have to turn away. I stare at the fairy on the top of the tree. The lights around her are going on and off so that it looks like she's winking at me.

Chapter 21

Ariel

Realism can break a writer's heart.
Salman Rushdie

I'm surprised Iseult left. I'm sure Charles is too. He must have expected that his newly proclaimed fiancée would stay the night with him. The night he and I got engaged, we couldn't keep our hands off each other. We made love three times. But she's heading home with her cousin and doesn't seem to care what Charles might want. Everything about this engagement is weird. Everything about this relationship is weird.

Since our split, both Charles and I have seen other people. He went out for a few months with a singer he'd met at an arts festival, and was seeing a music critic for a short time too. But there was certainly no suggestion of him being in love with either Daria or Rowena, and both times the relationship just fizzled out. As for me, I've had a busy social life and have met lots of men. But despite going on occasional enjoyable dates, I've always compared them to Charles and found them wanting. He once said the same to me.

Maybe that's why we never actually got around to finalising the divorce. Maybe, deep down, we always expected to get back together.

But if that was ever the case, it's not now.

He walks back in from the front door, where he was saying goodbye to his new fiancée. I leave him in the living room with a glass of whiskey while I supervise the departure of the catering staff, who've already packed up all their equipment. When I return, he's sitting in one of the comfortable armchairs, his shirt unbuttoned and his bow tie abandoned.

'One of us had better get a solicitor to file those papers asap,' I say.

'That'll be me,' says Charles. 'I'll get on it right away.'

He's bursting with the kind of excitement he usually only has on publication day. As for me, I'm still in shock. Perhaps I was wrong to think, however fleetingly, that one day we might get back together, but being married to him, connected to him, has meant we've had each other's backs in a way that no other relationship between us would. There'll be another relationship now. Him and Iseult. Husband and wife.

But not until we get a divorce.

'Well, you've certainly brought the new year in with a bang.' I pour myself a glass of red wine from the bottle beside me. 'I wish you'd warned me.'

'I didn't know myself.'

'You didn't know?' I can hardly keep the disbelief from my voice.

'I mean, I wasn't sure I'd actually do it. Not because I don't love her,' he adds quickly. 'Because I didn't think she'd like a fuss. But it was such a lovely opportunity . . .'

'For her not to say no.'

'She wouldn't have said no.'

'She might have if she knew you were still married,' I observe. 'She might change her mind when she learns you weren't truthful about it.'

'Stop going on about it. I told her about you. The divorce itself is a technicality.'

'If you say so. I'm not convinced she'll see it like that. You should have told me before you pulled that stunt.'

'I didn't think you'd care. It's hardly going to affect us, after all. We've made it work between us, haven't we?'

'Well, yes. But making it work hasn't stopped us sleeping together, has it?' I say this in as offhand a tone as I can, and add that it will never happen again.

'Obviously.' He looks at me as though I'm crazy. 'I wouldn't cheat on her with you, Ariel. Those other times were . . . well, they were lovely and all that, but it was just sex, wasn't it?'

I say nothing.

'It kept us close,' he adds.

Did he think that sleeping with me from time to time made me work harder on his behalf? That I did things for him I wouldn't otherwise have done? If that's the case, he doesn't know me at all.

'When did you decide you wanted to marry her? It's awfully sudden.'

'I know it's sudden, but I also know it's right,' he says.

'Why didn't you tell me about her?'

'I didn't want to jinx it.'

'Oh, for heaven's sake, Charles! Why on earth—'

'Stop.' He interrupts me. 'It's none of your business. You're not in charge of my personal life.'

'Christ Almighty, I've been in charge of your personal life

for years. Before, during and after we were married. I organised tonight, didn't I?'

'You wanted to organise tonight. Same as you want to organise everything I do. You selected my new editor for me. You talked to Maya about PR. You didn't ask me.'

'Because they're professional things!' I cry.

'They're personal too. My books are personal to me, if not to you.'

I grit my teeth. This is not the time to get into an argument about what's personal and what's professional.

'Besides, she needs me,' he says.

'In what way?'

'In a way that you don't. You don't need anyone.'

That's true. At least I've tried to make it true. I've always preferred to depend on myself. It doesn't mean I didn't need Charles when we lived together. When you love someone, you need them. But, of course, we don't love each other any more.

'What do you know about her?' I ask.

'Now you sound like my mother.'

'Does *she* know?' I wonder what Pamela Boyd-Miller will have to say about her son's new fiancée. Iseult seems to be significantly more malleable than me. Perhaps that's why Charles has fallen for her. Perhaps Pamela will too.

'Nobody knows,' he replies.

'Except everyone who looks at social media.'

'It's New Year's Eve.' He shrugs. 'Social media will be overloaded. Nobody will notice.'

'Don't be ridiculous. Of course they will. I suppose we could spin something for the PR rounds about falling for your beta reader.'

'This is my life, not a PR stunt.'

'I'm shocked you asked someone to marry you, stunt or not!' I exclaim. 'Charles, seriously, listen to me, because this comes from a place of caring for you – do you really love her?'

'She's amazing,' he says. 'She says things like they are. She doesn't tiptoe around me. She told me the manuscript I first showed her was crap. She said that Janice Jermyn's books were better than mine. She doesn't care what I do or who I am.'

'You're a writer, not a celebrity superstar!'

'She's young and forward-looking and she has her own career,' says Charles. 'And it's good that it has nothing to do with publishing.'

'A customs officer?' I shake my head. 'Honestly, Charles, it's—'

'I'm sick of everyone I know being involved in publishing,' he says. 'You should be too, Ariel. I'm supposed to be a writer and in touch with the world, yet ever since we married, our world has become book launches and reading events and awards dinners and we never do anything that isn't about a bloody book.'

He's saying the same thing I've often said to myself. Yet I love this world and everybody in it. Besides, bookish friendships aren't all about work. Ekene and Maya are proper friends as well as colleagues. Lots of the people I meet in the course of my job are friends too. Just because I don't know engineers or gardeners or even customs officers doesn't mean I'm not living the life I want to lead.

'She was part of that huge drugs find mentioned on the news recently.' The pride in his voice as he continues makes it sound as though he was involved in it himself. I find it hard to imagine the girl in the green dress and ill-fitting shoes managing to confront drug smugglers, but I guess we all have our strengths. However, I'm perfectly sure that no matter what he might say, the main strength she has as far as Charles is concerned is that she's young.

'How old is she?' I put the question casually.

'Twenty-nine,' he replies.

When I was twenty-nine my name was mentioned in one of the trade magazines as one of the Thirty Under Thirty to watch. And of course when *Winter's Heartbreak* went on to be so successful, there was another piece about me, talking about how I'd fulfilled my potential.

There aren't any articles about me these days. There are younger, hungrier people snapping at my heels, hoovering up the good talent, doing spectacular deals, and they're the ones who make the pages of the trade magazines now. It's not that being in your forties can't be about success and challenges; it's simply that nobody remarks on it any more. They expect you to have done everything you're supposed to by now. And they've moved on to fresher talent.

Exactly as Charles has done. He's found a younger, more vibrant replacement for me. He's moved me from personal to professional, and I have a horrible feeling that eventually he'll try to move me out of my professional role too. Or if not him, her. Because will she really want me working with my not-yet-ex-husband? Will she want me phoning him with details of deals I've done? Will she want me celebrating with him?

Like heck she will.

I feel a sudden spurt of fear. Then anger.

She will not push me away.

Whatever about him marrying someone else, Charles and I have something special together.

A twenty-nine-year-old in a hi-vis jacket isn't going to change that.

Not now, not ever.

Chapter 22

Iseult

There are very few innocent sentences in writing.
David Foster Wallace

Celeste congratulates me again as I get out of the taxi outside my house. She's been nothing but supportive, but I'm not entirely sure she's a hundred per cent convinced I've done the right thing in getting engaged to Charles. I understand her hesitation. I'm only just over my break-up with Steve. I haven't known Charles that long. He's older than me. We're from different worlds. Yet there was a connection between us from the moment I first saw him sitting alone at his table at the White Sands, and it's become stronger with every passing day. I've never felt more sure of anything in my life.

I let myself into the house and make myself a cup of tea. I'm light-headed from champagne and cocktails, and I don't want to appear drunk to my parents. They'll think I said yes because I'm pissed, not because I'm in love. I drink the tea and eat two chocolate Hob Nobs. Then I FaceTime mum's number.

It's mid-afternoon in Napier, and she's sitting at the garden table with a mug in front of her and baby Azaria on her lap. They're both wearing wide-brimmed hats to protect their faces from the sun.

'Hello, sweetheart,' she says. 'Happy New Year. Isn't she a dote?' She holds the phone so that I can see my niece more clearly. Mum is right. Azaria is gorgeous, with her dark eyes, perfect button nose and soft rosebud mouth.

'Cuter than cute,' I say. 'Happy New Year to you too. Where's Dad?'

'Helping Adrian in the barn. Well, I say helping. He's probably getting in the way.'

I grin. Dad has a vision of himself as a handyman, but his approach to DIY is patchy at best. After a decent interval of living with his efforts, Mum usually gets 'a man' in to do a proper job.

'Everything OK with you?' she asks. 'Was the party good?'

She'd been pleased to hear I was going to a New Year's Eve party. She always complains that I volunteer to work at the end of December far too often.

'It was excellent.' My heart is beating more rapidly. 'And . . . well . . .'

'What?'

'I'm starting the new year with a bang.'

'How?'

I hold up my finger with the opal ring. She looks at it in puzzlement.

'A gift?'

'Temporary,' I say. 'It's an engagement ring. I'm engaged.'

She's silent for so long that I think the screen has frozen. It's only Bo, Adrian and Cori's adorable miniature dachshund, running around behind her that confirms we still have a connection.

Azaria coos at the dog and Mum resettles her on her lap. Only then does she look at the screen and at me. 'Have you got back with Steve?' she asks. 'That's not your proper ring.'

'Not Steve,' I reply. 'I'm engaged to Charles.'

'Who the hell is Charles?'

'I told you about him. The writer I met in the Caribbean.'

'Charles Miller?' Mum can't keep the shock out of her voice. 'Charles Miller the author? Are you mad? He's old enough to be your father.'

'No he's not. And I'm not mad either. I love him.'

'Izzy. Iseult.' She can't keep the anxiety from her voice. 'You hardly know the man. You met him on holiday. I don't want to even think that you had a fling with him, but if you did, it was a holiday thing. You can't possibly be serious about marrying him.'

'Why not?'

'You were there for a fortnight and you're only back a few weeks. You're on the rebound.'

'I'm not.'

'Izzy, please.' Mum sounds really stressed. 'Please tell me that at least you won't rush into marrying him.'

'We haven't set a date yet.'

'He was married before, wasn't he?'

'Yes. To his agent. She handled his business affairs and they became close and I'm sure they both thought that getting married was a good idea. Clearly it wasn't.'

'Did he tell you everything about it?'

'We haven't discussed it much.'

243

'You should.'

'I don't need to. You should have confidence in me to know my own mind, Mum.'

'I do have confidence in you. Honestly I do. But you're in a vulnerable state. Steve treated you terribly. That'd leave any girl a bit shaken.'

'I admit I was very shaken, as you put it, over Steve. But that doesn't mean I can't fall in love with someone else.'

'You deserve someone to love you the way you should be loved,' says Mum. 'And I truly want to believe that Charles Miller is that man.'

'He is. I promise you.'

'Darling, if you're happy, I'm happy. I don't want you to think otherwise.'

'You do, though.'

'I'm concerned for you, that's all. You're my only daughter.'

'Your engaged and very happy only daughter,' I assure her. 'Trust me, Mum, Charles is a wonderful man. Please don't worry.'

'Mothers always worry about their children.'

'Did you worry when I got engaged to Steve?'

She's silent.

'Did you?' I repeat.

'I liked Steve,' she says slowly. 'He was a very attractive man. All the same, a little bit of me thought that perhaps you could've done better.'

'Mum!'

'I know, I know.' She sounds harassed. 'I mean . . .'

'It doesn't matter.' I put her out of her misery. 'After all, we split up. And I've done much better now, haven't I? I promise I'm not on the rebound. Please don't worry about me.'

'If you're happy, I'm happy,' she repeats, this time with more conviction.

'I'm very, very happy,' I tell her.

'Well then, lots and lots of love and congratulations.'

'Will you tell Dad or will I?'

'I will. It'd take a while to get him from the barn.'

'That's fine.' I glance at my Gucci watch. 'I have to be at work in a few hours from now. I'd better get some sleep.'

'OK.'

'I'll talk to you again soon. Give Dad a hug from me. And a big kiss to the boys and Azaria.'

'Take care,' she says. 'I love you.'

'I love you too.'

I do love my mum. She's always looked out for me, even if sometimes we see things differently.

But now I'm looking out for myself.

#Engaged ♥ #Again

The reaction to my news at work is far more satisfactory. I get a group hug from the team, and all the girls want to try on the opal ring, even though I tell them it's not my real ring.

'It's so romantic,' says Natasha. 'I never thought you'd bounce back from Steve like this.'

'Neither did I,' I say as I replace the ring on my finger. 'But there you go. When you're not looking for love, you find it.'

'I'll keep that in mind.' Natasha, who's been through a recent break-up herself, gives me a wry smile.

'You'll find the right person,' I assure her, even as I

remember her saying exactly the same to me when we were in the pub and I was sobbing into a glass of Heineken.

'In the meantime . . .' She picks up the walkie-talkie that's crackling with Ken's voice. 'The ship is in. We'd better get down there.'

I pull on my anorak and hi-vis jacket and we hurry out of the building and into one of the cars. It's a long enough trek from the building to the dock, so the cars are essential. I'm checking the foot passengers this evening. We got an alert about one of them, and when he walks through, Ken and I bring him to one side. The other passengers give us curious glances but carry on to collect their baggage. The passenger we've tagged is very relaxed and answers all our questions without any issues. We've no reason to detain him, and as the shuttle bus to the city will be leaving shortly, I tell him he can go.

My day-to-day life is very different to champagne receptions in grand houses, I think. But very soon I'll be living in a grand house myself. I'll have to talk to Charles about redecorating. Gorgeous as it is, I want to feel like Riverside Lodge is *our* home and not his home with the agent-slash-ex. I'm sure he'll agree.

Minor details, I say to myself as I get back into the car and return to the customs building. The important thing is that I've never been happier in my life.

I'm home by 7.30 and Charles arrives half an hour later. I hear the gate creak open and his footsteps on the path before the security light comes on. I'm at the door before he rings the bell.

'Eager,' he says as he puts his arms around me and kisses me.

'Very.' I kiss him back.

The kissing lasts quite some time before we make it to the living room, where he takes off his heavy wool coat.

'It's bloody freezing out,' he remarks as he drapes it over a chair. 'This is the coldest winter I can remember.'

'Ooh!' I smile at him. 'The opening sentence to *Winter's Heartbreak*.'

'You recognise it.' He looks pleased.

'Of course I do.'

He sits in the armchair nearest the gas fire and holds out his hands to the flames. I tell him that I'll make some tea, and he raises an eyebrow and tells me to take the bottle of wine out of his coat pocket. It's another red I'm not familiar with, and I'm betting it's expensive. Also, there's a cork. I rummage around in the kitchen drawer looking for the corkscrew. I use it so infrequently that it's always hidden beneath other bits and pieces. But eventually I find it and uncork the bottle. I'm quite pleased that I manage to do this efficiently, as I'm so out of practice. I take the IKEA glasses from the cupboard and pour us both a generous measure.

'I probably should've brought champagne,' says Charles. 'So we could celebrate again.'

'I drank too much champagne last night,' I say. 'And I'm only having one glass of this. My poor liver has been put through the mill these last few weeks.'

'Mine too,' admits Charles. 'I'll cut back a bit soon, but not yet. January is far too long a month to survive without a decent glass of wine.'

I nod in agreement and take a sip. It's very good.

'So.' He settles back. 'Have you announced the news to your friends and family?'

'I told my mum,' I reply. 'She's a bit shocked.'

'Not surprising,' he says. 'She'll get used to the idea.'

'Of course.'

'It was fun to make it a thing at the party,' he says. 'There are one or two pieces on social media about it.'

'Have you suddenly become social media savvy?' I grin.

'No, but I did check for mentions,' he says. 'Everyone was very kind, which is nice, and it's good PR for *A Caribbean Calypso* too.'

'Tell me you didn't ask me to marry you so people would talk about your book?' I'm not sure if my question is serious or not.

'Darling Iseult, of course I didn't. I asked you to marry me because I'm madly in love with you and I can't imagine my life without you and I want to grow old with you. Older,' he amends. 'One of the pieces did mention that you were half my age. Idiots.'

'Age is just a number,' I remark.

'They mentioned Ariel, too.' He squirms somewhat uncomfortably on the chair. 'I thought you might have read the comments.'

'I don't have time to check social media at work,' I tell him. 'And I'm not surprised she got a mention. You two have a working relationship and she's very glamorous.'

'You think she's glamorous?' He looks surprised.

'Charles! She's beautiful. So stylish and confident.'

'Ah, well. I'm not sure she'd say that herself.'

I'm pretty sure she would.

'There's something I need to explain about Ariel and me,' he says.

Despite the warmth of the fire, I feel a sudden chill.

'It's our divorce,' he says. 'It's not finalised yet.'

'What! You told me she was your ex when we were on holiday.'

'She *is* my ex,' says Charles. 'Couldn't be more ex. Just not, well, legally ex.'

'You asked me to marry you when you're already married?' My heart is pounding.

'Iseult. Izzy. You know yourself Ariel and I aren't living together. You've stayed in my house. I told you she has an apartment of her own. And we can hardly be less together than me going to the Caribbean without her for six weeks. You must see that.'

Well, true. I'd go ballistic if my husband went to a tropical island without me.

'It really is a technical thing,' says Charles. He goes on to explain that when they'd got everything together and were ready to send the papers to the courts, a whole heap of deals for him had come up and they'd both been overwhelmed with signing various documents. And that Ariel, as the applicant, had told her solicitor not to bother about it for a while, and Charles himself had put the papers to one side and forgotten about them. And that every so often one or the other would talk about sending them in, but they hadn't done it yet because there didn't seem to be any rush. 'But now we will,' he says. 'And given that it's uncontested, it won't take long for it to be finalised, I'm sure.'

I'm trying to come to terms with the fact that Charles is married. He might not be living with Ariel, but he's married to her. And that changes everything.

'No it doesn't,' he says when I say this. 'It changes absolutely nothing. Both of us have had relationships since our separation. Nothing serious, certainly on my side. I don't know about hers.'

'And the ring she wears?'

He looks at me in confusion.

'On her wedding finger.'

'It was her wedding ring.'

'She's still wearing her wedding ring! Even though you're supposed to be getting a divorce.' I'm having to work to keep calm here.

'From the minute she saw it, she wanted that ring,' he says. 'It doesn't look like a wedding ring, so it's not really an issue if she wears it. It was a very expensive piece of jewellery, after all.'

I say nothing.

'Anyhow, we're getting our respective solicitors on the case right away,' he continues. 'I want nothing more than to marry you. You've got to believe me.'

'And Ariel?'

'She's happy to get the divorce over with too. She's certainly not going to throw a spanner in the works. I promise you our relationship is purely professional.'

'OK,' I say slowly.

'I love you,' says Charles. 'I couldn't love you any more than I do.'

'I love you too,' I tell him, and then I kiss him.

He carries me up to the bedroom, although the stairs are so narrow I bang my head on the wall.

Maybe that's why I see stars when we make love.

Chapter 23

Ariel

Some editors are failed writers.
But so are most writers.

T. S. Eliot

I have a hangover. I never have hangovers, but I'm starting this year with gritty eyes and a mouth that feels like the bottom of a birdcage. I'm also raging with thirst, but at least I don't have a migraine. I roll out of bed and walk unsteadily to the kitchen, where I drink the half-litre bottle of water that's on the countertop. I'm remembering last night, although remembering isn't exactly the right word, because every moment of it is seared into my consciousness and it's like a continuing reel in my head. Charles and his new fiancée. The woman he plans to marry. The slip of a girl in the green dress and high heels.

He's lost his mind, of course. He does this from time to time, gets wild enthusiasms and drops them again. Like the time he got into golf, joined a club and bought all the gear. He spent an absolute fortune on drivers and putters and electric caddy cars and stormproof jackets and trousers. As far as I recall, he played twice. Not that getting engaged is the same as playing golf, but with Charles, well . . .

My feet hurt. It takes a minute to remember that I ended up walking home from the New Year's Eve party. The fiancée and her friend had clearly bagged the last available taxi in Dublin, because no matter which app I tried, all I got were chirpy messages saying that their drivers were 'super busy' at the moment.

'You don't have to walk,' Charles said to me as I fumed. 'It's late and it's cold. Stay over.'

'You've got to be joking.' I stared at him. 'Stay over? When you've announced your engagement to somebody else?'

'Oh, it's fine. She'll understand. It's you, Ariel, not some random woman. You can use a guest bedroom.'

He said it as though sleeping in the master bedroom was an option. As though I was actually considering it. Naturally, I'd no intention of staying at Riverside Lodge. Did he really think Iseult would be happy with her fiancé's not-quite-ex-wife staying in his house overnight? Was he that naïve?

'Charles, it's highly inappropriate for me to stay here and I wouldn't dream of it.'

'Look, I know you're upset—'

'Upset?' The word came out as a squeak. I cleared my throat. 'I'm not upset. I'm angry that you didn't have the common courtesy to tell me what you were planning. Not because it matters to me, but because . . . because . . .' I couldn't finish the sentence. Mainly because I was lying. I *was* angry, yes. But despite what I'd told him, I was upset too. Who wouldn't be? And even though there was a part of me that was tempted to stay and seduce him from under his brand-new fiancée's pert little nose, I'm not that sort of woman. I might want to ensure there's no change to our working relationship, but that's it. At least, I think that's it.

I turned away from him and went to the utility room, where I knew there was an old pair of my boots that I'd never bothered taking home with me.

'Honestly,' he said, when I clumped back up the stairs wearing them. 'This is madness. How can you walk in them?'

'They're flat,' I pointed out.

'But your dress. It'll drag along the ground.'

'I'll get it cleaned.'

'Ariel—'

'It's fine,' I told him. 'I'd be home by now if we weren't spending so long talking about it.'

And so I put on my coat (not warm enough for the bitterly cold temperatures) and stepped into the night air. My breath immediately misted in front of my face. Charles stood at the door and didn't shut it behind me until I walked out of the gate. I heard the thud of it closing.

It was a bloody cold walk, and although there were plenty of taxis on the streets, none of them were free. By the time I let myself into my apartment a little over half an hour later, I was frozen to the bone and had blisters on my toes. The boots might have been flat, but I was wearing fine stockings and not the woolly socks that would have been far more suitable. I eased the boots off and noticed that my expensive stockings were laddered and useless. I swore softly, then made myself a hot whiskey with lots of cloves and honey, which I drank standing barefoot at my patio window, allowing the underfloor heating to warm my sore feet. My heart was pounding and I couldn't tell if it was from the exercise of walking home, the throbbing of the blisters or the sheer rage I felt at Charles, both for getting engaged and for blindsiding me in his announcement of it.

I turned away from the window and opened my laptop. The wallpaper on the screen was of me and Charles shortly after he won his Booker Prize. He was holding his award in one hand; the other was around my waist. I allowed myself to remember that night, how great it was and how I felt that everything in my life was as perfect as it was possible to be. I didn't for a second allow myself to think that ultimately it had all been downhill from there.

I banged at the keys and changed the wallpaper to a picture of me getting my Agent of the Year award. Then I burst into tears.

I drink another bottle of water as I walk back to the living room, locating my discarded tights beside the sofa and chucking them in the bin. I allow myself an additional moment of rage, then blow my nose and wipe away the stupid, stupid tears that fill my eyes before checking social media to see if there are any more posts about Charles's party, and more importantly, the announcement of his engagement.

There are plenty of pix from the party – mostly tight-shot selfies, and quite a few of Charles and his young fiancée hashtagged #NewYear and #NewWoman. Or #NewYear and #EngagementSurprise. There are also a couple of Google Alerts linking to short online pieces about the engagement. Truth is, most of the journalists had left before midnight, and although the story is cute if you like that sort of thing, it's not real news. And Charles is too old for it to pop up on any celebrity sites. There's one brief story about him and me, saying that we separated a number of years ago but remain friends. It doesn't suggest that we didn't get divorced.

I craft a post for Charles's accounts saying that he's delighted to have finally delivered his next book to his publishers and hopes that readers will love his foray into intelligent crime writing. I add that as well as writing books, he's also found time to fall in love and that he's delighted to announce his engagement to . . . and here I have to stop, because my mind is a total blank. I can't remember the name of the girl in the green dress. All I can think is that she was his beta reader. But I can't call her Beta Girl, can I? I feel the glow of a hot flush start at the tip of my head and work its way through my body. I forgot to take my HRT last night. For feck's sake, though. Is it menopausal brain fog, or did I actually decide to blank the name of my husband's twenty-nine-year-old fiancée?

In the end, I post it without her name and use the hash-tags: #NewYear #NewBeginnings #CrimeFiction #LiteraryFiction #Bestseller and finally #SoInLove. I nearly gag at the last but shove it in anyway. Then I slam the lid of the laptop closed and get into the shower. I lean against the tiled wall and allow the warm water to massage the top of my head. I want it to relax me, but of course it doesn't. I'm still on edge when I get out again.

I'm not going out today, so I dress in my sloppiest track-suit bottoms and fleecy top before sitting at the table with Charles's manuscript and my red pen. I'm going to edit the shit out of his crime novel. Hopefully Sydney will too. And he'll be so damn busy rewriting it that he won't have time for his young lover. Even hearing the words 'young lover' in my head makes my heart pound again.

Seriously, what's he thinking? Oh look, I don't need to ask myself that question. She's vibrant and pretty and those dark doe eyes looked at him with such love and admiration I'm not surprised he fell for her. All men want to be admired and it's obvious she admires him. But she hasn't seen him first thing in the morning with his gold and silver stubble and his eyes bloodshot from being up too late writing without stopping. She hasn't seen him in a temper because the book isn't working out the way he expected. And she hasn't had him shouting at her to find his white shirt – 'no, not that one, the one with the better buttons' – before he goes off to a book event or a TV appearance. She's only seen the professional Charles, not the domestic Charles. She thinks she loves him, but she only loves the idea of him.

I, on the other hand, love all of him.

Even if I left him.

Loved all of him, I mean.

Although right now, I'm furious with him.

Sydney calls me the following day saying that she has some editorial notes for Charles and will forward them to me too in the next few minutes.

I download the document as soon as it arrives. Her notes are very comprehensive. Charles will go ballistic at the amount of work they entail, as she's made some very clever suggestions around some of his too-easy clues that will mean extensive rewriting. He hates rewriting.

She's done well, though, with lots of ideas about how he can make it a little more Charles Miller while keeping the best of his Janice Jermyn experience. If he does as good a job as I know he can, I'm absolutely sure we'll have a winner on our hands. Although, I concede, as I get to yet another note about the orange-blossom scent the murderer wears, Janice would never have let such an obvious tell slip through.

I'm so intent on what I'm doing that the sound of my mobile buzzing is an unwelcome distraction. I glance at the caller ID and feel my eyebrows rise in surprise.

'Hello, Ellis,' I say as I answer it. 'It's good to hear from you. Happy New Year.'

'Same to you,' she says. 'Ariel, what the hell is going on with Charles?'

I like that she gets to the point straight away. I used to think Ellis was a little bit airy-fairy, what with chucking in her library job and opening an art studio in her shed, but she's quite hard-nosed when it comes to business. And possibly when it comes to her brother, too. We used to have some great chats about him, among other things. I can't believe we've allowed our friendship to drift.

'He told me when we were together at Christmas about this girl he met in the Caribbean,' she says. 'Said she was bright and intelligent and that she and her friend were good fun. He didn't say anything about getting engaged to her. He still hasn't. I saw it on social media. What the actual fuck, Ariel?'

'It's a question I've been asking myself,' I say.

'Have you met her? What's she like?'

'I've no idea. The party was the first time I set eyes on her. The first time I knew anything about her.'

'Ariel!'

'It knocked me for six,' I admit.

'What on earth is wrong with him that he simply sprang it on you without a word?'

It's quite pleasing to hear how furious she is with him. It makes me feel less like a raging old hag.

'It doesn't matter,' I say. 'We're practically divorced.'

'Though in reality married,' says Ellis. 'I've got to say it, Ariel, I always thought you guys would get back together. I think he did too, and that's why he didn't chase you up over the divorce. Plus, you continued to represent him despite everything.'

'It's hard to believe we work so well together when we couldn't live together,' I admit. 'Quite honestly, it was easier being his agent when I wasn't being his wife. And I do care for him, of course I do. But whatever either of us might have thought about one day getting back together, it's not going to happen now.'

'It was a mistake to give him the best of both worlds,' Ellis tells me.

'What d'you mean?'

'You working in his back garden meant he could see you any time he wanted. You socialise together. You have each other's backs. You're one of those married couples who live in separate houses and have wild sex every time they get together.'

'We're really not.' I keep my voice as steady as possible. 'I have to keep things civil because he's my client, not because he's my husband.'

'And the wild sex?'

'OK, OK, so we've slept together a few times. It didn't mean anything.'

'Didn't it?'

I sigh. I don't know if it did or didn't. It was usually on a Freedom Friday and after a bottle of wine. So it was drunk sex. Or friends-with-benefits sex. Or just ordinary casual sex. But it wasn't enough to make us decide to give being married another go. So in the end, it was still break-up sex.

I tell Ellis that I really don't want to talk about my sex life with her brother, and remind her that the only thing that matters is that he's now engaged to someone else.

'What's the fiancée's name, by the way?' I ask. 'He introduced us, but only after he'd made his announcement, and I've completely forgotten.'

'Iseult O'Connor.'

I nod, even though we're on a voice call and she can't see me.

'I do think he's completely bonkers in getting engaged,' I concede. 'I can understand him having a fling with her, but marrying her? What on earth's going on in his head? What's *she* thinking?'

'I bet she sees him as a ticket to a great life. The house, the glamour . . .'

I laugh. Even Ellis is seduced by the so-called glamour of Charles's life. But she only sees one side of it. I'm sure Iseult sees the same. I point out that it isn't all parties and having a good time, and she admits I'm right. But she feels sure Iseult is only in it for the money.

'Do you really think so?'

'Why else?'

'I know he's your brother and therefore you're blind to his charms, but he *is* quite a desirable man,' I point out.

'Not for a twenty-nine-year-old girl.'

'Twenty-nine isn't a girl,' I say, even though that's exactly how I've been thinking of her. 'She's a grown woman.

Although . . .' I grit my teeth before continuing, 'she's certainly younger and perkier and livelier than me.'

'I'm quite certain he's making a massive mistake,' says Ellis. 'It's infatuation, not love. Can you . . . well, can you string out the divorce thing? Give him time to come to his senses?'

'It's been strung out enough already. We need to move on.'

'I've every confidence that you can move on in whatever way you want,' says Ellis. 'You're a strong woman with your own business. But he's . . . well, he's always been a bit vulnerable. He pours it all into his books. He can't afford to make a terrible mistake with this girl.'

'You haven't met her yet,' I say. 'You might actually think she's perfect for him.'

'Is she?'

I snort. I might be good at arguing a point, but I'm not going to say that Iseult is perfect for Charles.

'Is she drop-dead gorgeous?' asks Ellis.

'She's pretty enough, with her smooth skin and dark brown eyes that look at him devotedly.'

'It's the devotion, isn't it? All men want women to look at them as though they're gods, when the reality is that most of them are children.'

I laugh. Then I tell her that Charles reminded me of a Greek god when I first met him.

'Don't make it easy for him, that's all I'm asking,' she says. 'If it's the right thing for him, make him work for it.'

I've always made things easy for Charles. It's my job, after all. But I don't say this to Ellis.

When we end the call, I sit with the manuscript in front

of me and the red pen in my hand. Then I draw a line through two long, unnecessary paragraphs. I tell myself that whatever about his personal life, when it comes to his novel, I'm certainly not going to make things easy for him one little bit.

Chapter 24

Iseult

Writing is like getting married.
One should never commit oneself
until one is amazed at one's luck.

Iris Murdoch

There's a part of me that doesn't quite believe Charles and Ariel are completely over, despite his promises that the divorce will happen quickly. But then he takes me shopping for an engagement ring in Warren's, the very exclusive jeweller's near Grafton Street, where every single ring is exquisite and breathtakingly expensive. I've often stopped and looked at the window displays, but I've never been inside the store in my life.

When Charles says we're looking for an engagement ring, the saleswoman brings a tray of sparkling diamonds along with two glasses of champagne.

Charles likes their signature ring, the Snowdrop, which is a diamond solitaire in a white-gold setting. It's gorgeous, but too imposing for me, and I ask for something smaller. The saleswoman seems slightly horrified by the idea of someone wanting a smaller ring, but brings another tray of neater, more modern designs.

My favourite is the Ice Cube, which is an arrangement of small square diamonds in a white-gold band. As I slide it onto my finger, I feel my eyes fill with tears.

'What's wrong?' Charles notices me wipe them away.

'It's this. I love it.'

'Oh good.' He sounds relieved. 'I thought you hated it, and I was afraid we'd be here all day.'

The saleswoman goes to get a box for the ring, even though she knows I'll be wearing it out of the shop because it fits perfectly. While she's out of earshot, I ask Charles if he bought Ariel's engagement ring here too.

'Why would you even . . .' He shakes his head. 'No, I didn't. I bought it in London.'

When the saleswoman returns, I give her my mobile and she takes a photo of Charles and me holding hands, and then one of me holding a refilled glass of champagne, my ring very visible. That's the one I post to my Instagram account: #Engaged #LuckiestGirlInTheWorld #ForeverInLove.

It only takes fifteen minutes for my phone to buzz with a message. It's an unknown number and the message is brief.

What the actual fuck?

I know it's from Steve.

I send him a reply when Charles and I are in Davy Byrne's pub having more champagne to celebrate our engagement. (I've become a convert to champagne over Prosecco. It seems I'm already growing accustomed to higher standards.) Charles has gone to the Gents', so I message to say that

I've met someone and am engaged to him. A second later, my phone rings.

'Are you off your trolley?' he demands. 'A few weeks ago you were going to marry me.'

'Whose phone are you using?' I ask in return.

'A work one,' he says. 'You blocked me after New Year's, Izzy. That was a horrible thing to do.'

'Because you kept contacting me and we're not together any more.'

'I was being friendly.'

'You were being stalkery. It's like you didn't want me yourself but you don't want me to be with anyone else either.'

He's silent for a moment, then tells me I'm talking rubbish, yet I can't help feeling I've touched a nerve.

'There's no need for you to be friends with me any more,' I say.

'OK, OK, I'm sorry if you feel hassled. I didn't mean it. But before we stop being friends, I have to point out that you've gone from being engaged to me to being engaged to someone else in jig time. Are you sure you know what you're doing? And who on earth is he?'

'His name is Charles Miller. He's a writer and I love him. That's all you need to know.'

'I'm saying this because I care about you. You're on the rebound.'

'If you cared about me, you wouldn't have dumped me. And FYI, I'm not rebounding from anything.'

'I admit I messed up,' says Steve. 'I told you why. I'd have been wrong to marry you feeling the way I did. It was because I cared for you that I broke up with you, and it's because I care now that I'm telling you not to do this insane thing.'

'Stop trying to make excuses,' I say. 'I'll do whatever I damn well please.' I end the conversation at the same time as my fiancé returns to the table.

Everyone oohs and ahhs over my latest ring at work.

'I prefer it to your previous engagement ring,' Katelyn says, as she extends her hand in front of her and watches it sparkle beneath the office lights. 'Not that that one wasn't lovely, of course, but this is stunning.'

'You make me sound like I get engaged every week.' I make a face at her.

'Hey, as many times as you need to find the right person,' says Natasha.

'I thought I had with Steve,' I tell her. 'But I *know* I have with Charles.'

'You'll have to bring him to the pub some night so we can all meet him.'

'I will,' I promise. 'He's very impressed by my job. He might turn it into a book one day. We X-ray a container and find a body. Can you imagine! I must suggest that one to him. In the meantime, though, can I have my ring back?'

When the Ice Cube is safely on my finger again, Natasha and I head for the car and drive to the docks to do our inspection on the most recent arrival. I might be #TheHappiestGirlInTheWorld, but I still have a job to do.

When I tell Celeste my ring is from Warren's, she's impressed.

'I don't think you can walk out of there without dropping five figures on a piece,' she says.

'You can,' I say. 'Just about. But we didn't.'

'It's absolutely stunning.' She spins it around on her finger. I don't ask what she's wished for, although the tradition is usually for a lovely mother-in-law.

'And to think how devastated I was when Steve dumped me.' I smile when she hands it back. 'I was heartbroken in the Caribbean. Life's amazing, isn't it?'

'Will you go back there for this wedding?' she asks.

'We haven't talked about it yet,' I reply. 'But I'm thinking that a massive do in Dublin this time, with you as my bridesmaid, would be perfect.'

'Oh, Izzy.' She flings her arm around me. 'Thank you. That's exactly what I wished for just now.'

'What can I say?' I grin. 'I'm the girl who makes wishes come true.'

Now that we're officially engaged, and my fiancé and his agent-slash-hopefully-soon-to-be-officially-ex are pushing ahead on the divorce, Charles turns his attention away from engagement rings and back to his book. I thought he could take his time about editing it, but apparently there's another deadline for this.

'Maybe I should read it again for you,' I suggest. 'I'm your beta reader after all.'

'But not my editor.' He says this dismissively and I frown. 'Sorry. Sorry. I'm a bit stressed at the moment,' he adds when he sees my expression. 'I'm always stressed by this part, and the worst this time is that Sydney's damn changes have meant rewriting three bloody chapters. Three!'

'If it makes it harder to figure out who the killer is, that's a good thing,' I console him.

'You're not the one doing all the work.'

'Janice Jermyn—'

'I'm not Janice bloody Jermyn,' he snaps.

'I know. Sorry.'

We sit in silence for a while. It's Sunday and my day off, so I'd asked him if he'd like to meet. We haven't seen each other much since we bought the ring, and we're having lunch in an airy café within walking distance of his house. It's packed with families, and I get the feeling that Charles doesn't find this very restful.

'Let's go,' I say.

'What about coffee?'

'We'll have it back at the house. You've a brilliant machine in the kitchen.'

'All right.' He's still grumpy, but he pays the bill and leaves a generous cash tip on the table.

When we get back to Riverside Lodge, he makes us both coffee and we sit at the island in the kitchen. I move my hand so that the diamond in my ring splinters into a prism of colours. Charles laughs, and the dark mood between us lifts immediately.

'You love doing that, don't you?'

'Yes.' I'm a little embarrassed that he's noticed.

'It looks lovely on you,' he says. 'I'm very happy you like it.'

'Like it? I love it.' I slide from the bar stool and put my arms around him. 'I love you too, Charles Miller.'

'And I love you,' he assures me. 'I'm sorry if I'm a bit tetchy. I'm always like this when I'm editing. Ariel says it's my worst writing phase.'

'Does she help with it?' I'm madly keen to talk about her

and their relationship, but I haven't known how to raise the subject. I don't want to appear obsessed; I tell myself I'm not, but I can't help remembering the look on her face when she met me. It's unsettling that she's still a part of his life, and will be even when they're properly divorced. I'm hoping that once he's finished the book, she won't have any need to be in touch with him for ages.

He tells me that Ariel's original notes on his manuscript, before he even gave it to the publisher, ran to twenty-two pages. And since then, his editor, Syd, has sent even more.

'You need a break,' I tell him.

'We've just been out to lunch.'

'A proper break,' I say. 'I'm going to bring you to the port.'

'But I . . .' He hesitates, then smiles. 'I'd love to come to the port with you,' he says.

The traffic at the port isn't as heavy on a Sunday, and I drive him around the various warehouse and storage areas. It's always impressive to see the huge stacks of freight containers, and I explain about the X-ray machine and the other things we do. I also tell him that I have the best view in the world from my desk, and he asks if he can see it.

I phone the officer in charge today to ask if I can come in with a visitor for a nanosecond. He agrees, and soon Charles and I are standing at the window, looking out at the bay.

'You're right,' he says. 'The view is amazing.'

Katelyn, who's also working, walks in, and I introduce her to Charles.

'I love your books,' she tells him.

'I'll give Izzy some signed copies for you,' he promises.

And then they're chatting away, and I think how Charles has some great people skills, even if he doesn't always use them.

'Absolutely hunky,' Katelyn whispers to me as we turn to leave, and I wink at her and link my arm through my fiancé's.

#LuckyMe

We go back to Marino for a cup of tea after the port visit, but unsurprisingly end up in bed first. I'm impressed by his stamina and say so, which makes him look pleased until he asks if I mean for his age.

'Are you mad?' I sit up and push my hair out of my eyes. 'You're way better than . . . well . . .' I don't really want to mention my ex-fiancé. Or give him the chance to mention his nearly-ex-wife either. It's time to put our past lives behind us.

'I'd better call a cab and get home,' he says when we've had the tea. 'I want to do some more editing.'

'On a Sunday?'

'Need to keep going,' he says.

'I suppose you have to work hard to get those good Amazon reviews,' I tease.

'Bloody Amazon.' He snorts. 'One-star reviews because the book arrived a day late or the cover is torn.'

I laugh. I can't help it. He laughs too and puts his arms around me. 'If I was giving you a review, my darling Iseult, it would be a five-star one. You're my total inspiration.'

'I am?'

'Of course you are. I've based Carolyn on you. Didn't you guess?'

Carolyn is the murderer.

I'm not sure how I should feel about that.

Chapter 25

Ariel

Authors and lovers always suffer
some infatuation, from which only
absence can set them free.

Samuel Johnson

I haven't seen Charles face to face since his grand engagement announcement, but I'm too busy to care. I return to London to meet with some publishers, have a girls' night out with Ekene and Maya (they're stunned by the news of Charles's engagement) and also drop in to Xerxes to see Sydney and Graham. Sydney says she hasn't heard back yet from Charles on the edits other than that he's currently working on them, while Graham talks about the publication date: if Charles gets the edits back quickly, Xerxes will publish in the early summer, because who doesn't love a juicy murder mystery set in an exotic location when they're about to set off on their own holidays?

I've stayed away from the mews office since the party, but the day after I return from London, I go over there. The weather has turned milder, and with the sun shining, it feels positively spring-like, and a lot more welcoming than it was before Christmas. I pick up a bundle of late-arriving Christmas cards and put them, unread, into the recycling bin. Then I make myself a cup of coffee and look towards the main house while I drink it. I haven't heard back from my solicitor following the email I sent her on New Year's Day, and I should probably chase her up, but I'm not in the mood.

I wash the cup and return to my desk. As well as the hard-copy manuscripts that arrived during the week, another fifty have been sent by email. There's always an uptick around New Year, when unpublished writers who've had some time on their hands over the holidays work like crazy to get their manuscripts off to an agent as part of a New Year New Me push.

I read without stopping until four in the afternoon. There's a slight stretch in the evenings now, more noticeable today because of the clear skies. I debate with myself for a few moments, then open the cupboard behind my desk and take out one of the bottles of Merlot that Penny Blackwater sent me as a Christmas gift. I go into the bathroom and refresh my make-up, then slip into my heels and walk up the garden path to the house.

The back door is unlocked, which means Charles is at home. I walk into the kitchen and call out to make my presence known. There's no reply, but if he's in his study, he won't have heard me, so I go up the stairs. He's not in the living room either, and it's only now that I think perhaps he might be in bed with Iseult. The thought makes me feel light-headed. And then I hear his footsteps on the stairs, and I move into the hallway again.

'I thought I heard you,' he says.

'I called out. I'm sorry, I should've texted you before coming up.'

'Wouldn't have mattered. My phone is on silent.'

It always is while he's working. Annoyingly, he often forgets to change it back again.

'How's it going?' I ask.

'Grim.' He frowns. 'Between you and that Sydney woman, I'll be a wreck before this book is finished. Three whole chapters to rewrite, for God's sake.'

'I offer my sympathies.' I hold up the bottle. 'And a decent bottle of red?'

'Excellent idea.'

We walk into the living room together. He takes the bottle from me and opens it with the fancy silver corkscrew I got him for our fifth wedding anniversary.

The gentle glug of the wine into the glass is welcome and relaxing after what has been a long, busy week.

'Where's Iseult?' I ask when we're sitting on the sofa. This time I don't kick off my shoes and curl my feet under me. I keep them on and cross my legs primly at the ankles.

'Working. She does shift hours.'

'I guess that suits when you're working hard yourself.'

'At the moment, yes. It'll be different when the book's finished, though.'

'And will that be soon?' I use my most sympathetic tone.

'I bloody hope so. Iseult can't believe it's taking so long. When I told her that Sydney's suggestions meant rewriting three effing chapters, she was shocked.' He runs his fingers through his hair. 'I'm in two minds about it. Iseult wasn't half as worried as Sydney about those clues, and she's the crime expert after all.'

'Maybe she should write a book herself,' I suggest.

He looks at me in horror. 'It was bad enough when you started writing one. I can't possibly have another wife who thinks she's an author.'

I try not to take his words to heart. My own effort didn't come to much. It's a lot harder to put something down on a blank sheet of paper than it is to criticise what someone else has done. I still secretly harbour the hope that one day I'll write my own novel, but it's a dream that's in the distant future. I don't say this to him, though. He took it as an insult that I thought I could write at all.

'So will she be here later?' I ask.

'Maybe.'

I top up our glasses.

I know I should leave, but the wine is lovely and calming, and besides, I want to find out more about his fiancée. All the same, I have to go about that casually. I don't want him to think I'm quizzing him too much. I settle back in the sofa, but I still don't curl my legs underneath me.

Iseult

It's been a long, frustrating day and what I'd really like to do is go home and put my feet up. But Charles texted earlier asking if I was going to drop over to Terenure and I said I might. I should really ask him to come to me instead, but Riverside Lodge is my future home and I want to spend time there with him. I also want to bring up the subject of redecorating. It's very elegant, but I have some modernising ideas of my own. So when I've finally finished at the docks (all routine checks, none of them turning up anything illegal, although one of the drivers was really mouthy and nasty to me, which normally I shrug off but which got to me today), I message Charles to say I'll be with him a bit later, then scoot home to have a quick shower and change into a pair of jeans and my favourite jumper, a soft cashmere in deep purple that brings out the brown of my eyes.

I've timed it so that I can walk to the Malahide Road and catch the cross-city bus that stops about five minutes away from Charles's house. When I arrive, I see that the hall chandelier is glowing gently through the fanlight over the door. I press the old-fashioned enamel bell in a brass setting and hear the loud buzz echo along the hallway. It takes a minute before Charles opens the door. As always when I see him, I catch my breath at how damn good-looking he is. Even in what he laughingly refers to his 'lounging around' casual trousers and zipped top, he looks urbane and sophisticated.

'Hello, darling.' He pulls me close and kisses me. 'I've missed you. And I'm sorry for dragging you across town,' he adds as I follow him to the living room, 'but I was working like crazy all day.'

I'm about to say I was working like crazy too, but then I see he's not alone. And I recognise the woman who's sitting on the sofa as his agent-slash-not-quite-as-ex-as-I-thought.

She's tall and lithe and confident as she stands up and greets me, reminding me of who she is, as if I could forget. Her copper hair gleams in the light thrown by the standard lamp and her make-up is impeccable. She's wearing a black top and a short tartan skirt that shows off legs encased in patterned black tights. Her shoes are Louboutin – the red soles go with the red in the skirt. She's still wearing the multicoloured ring, although there's no jewellery on her right hand today. I tuck my hair behind my ears simply so that my own ring flashes in the light.

'Nice to meet you again,' I say, even as I glance at Charles and raise my eyebrows to signal my uncertainty at her being here.

'The pleasure is all mine.' Her voice is confident and a little husky.

'We're having book talk,' says Charles. 'Those bloody edits! I told her you'd be good at looking over them, given that you were such an inspiration in the Caribbean. Wine?' He holds up a half-empty bottle of red, and even though it's not my favourite, I nod.

Ariel sinks back onto the sofa and Charles sits beside her. I suppose that's where they were seated before I arrived, but I'm irked at being the one in the high-backed armchair while they relax together.

'So how was your day?' asks Charles.

I say it was one of our more routine days, with too much form-filling and one particularly rude driver, and he sympathises.

'It must be a very interesting job,' says Ariel in a tone that implies the complete opposite.

'It usually is,' I tell her.

'A bit of a nuisance for you to come here from the port.'

'I came from home,' I say. 'It's the same bus, just a longer walk.'

'You got the bus?' She sounds shocked.

'What else?'

'A cab. An Uber.'

'The bus is just as quick,' I say, even though I reckon a cab would take half the time. But I'm not splashing out for taxis when I don't need to.

She says nothing and takes a sip from her glass. Her eyes, a dark hazel, are looking at me speculatively. I feel like she's assessing me, seeing if I'm a suitable partner for Charles. I also feel like she's finding me wanting.

My throat is suddenly dry, and I take a rather larger mouthful of wine than I intended, which leaves me coughing uncontrollably. Charles gets up and puts his arm around me, but Ariel stays where she is, quietly watching me with those appraising eyes.

'You OK?' he asks, when my coughing fit subsides.

'Fine.' I clear my throat. 'Sorry.'

'That Merlot should be savoured,' says Ariel. 'It's an excellent vintage.'

'I *was* savouring it,' I say. 'A bit too much, obviously.'

'Maybe you're more of a cocktail girl.' Charles grins. 'Never saw you having a problem at the White Sands.'

'I don't have a problem with alcohol generally,' I say. 'Neither swallowing it nor drinking too much of it.'

'Hmm.' He grins again at that. 'I seem to remember one or two mornings when you were less than bright-eyed and bushy-tailed.'

'I was fine every morning.' My words are sharper than I intended, and he looks startled. Ariel, on the other hand, smiles.

'So tell me more about yourself.' She leans her head to one side and looks at me enquiringly. 'Charles has been very sparse with the details, except for crediting you with turning him into a crime fiction author.'

'I didn't. He decided on that himself.'

'You recommended Janice Jermyn to him. He'd never have listened to me if I'd done that. She's one of my authors, you know,' she adds. 'I'll get you a signed copy of *The Mystery of the Missing Mallet* if you like.'

'Would you?' I'm taken aback by her offer. Charles never returned my *Missing Mallet* copy to me. 'I have a signed copy of *The Mystery of the Drowning Fish*, but I'd love one of the *Missing Mallet*.'

'Ah, the *Drowning Fish*.' She looks pleased. 'Six weeks at the top of the bestseller list.'

'Really?' Charles looks at her in surprise.

'Yes,' says Ariel. 'Apple TV is interested too.'

'Seriously?' This time his voice is tight. He told me before that Ariel was working on a streaming deal for him.

'We're in conversation with them,' she says. 'I shouldn't have said anything, though. It's not signed, sealed and delivered yet.'

'Who'll play Claude?' I ask. 'He's such a great character.'

'Probably a newcomer, but definitely someone handsome,' says Ariel.

'Charles's detective is very handsome too.' I wink at him. 'I can't wait to see him on the screen.'

'Those kinds of deals take ages,' he says.

'I'm sure Ariel is working really hard on your behalf,' I tell him, and then turn to her and thank her for the offer of the signed Janice Jermyn.

'My pleasure,' she says. 'So, Iseult, what d'you think of Charles's effort? Really? Between ourselves.'

'I think it's great. Good characters, good plot and perfect for TV.'

'I like your loyalty,' she says.

'It's definitely a great read. A bit . . . wordy,' I add, 'but I think that'll suit his fans.'

'You know what his fans want?' She gives me an amused look.

I shrug, and tell her that my cousin is the literary one in the family and she loves Charles's books, and that I know she'll love *A Caribbean Calypso* too.

'She was at the party,' Charles says, looking at Ariel. 'Do you remember her? Brunette, silver dress. Spent a lot of time talking to that bookseller . . . um . . . Darragh somebody or other.'

'Mackey,' I supply.

'Of course I remember her,' says Ariel, who looks a little surprised at me remembering the bookseller's name. I don't tell her that Celeste has been on two dates with him since New Year. She's quite smitten. Well, as smitten as Celeste ever gets. It's a long time since she's lost her heart to anyone.

'Anyway, Iseult . . .' Ariel settles back in her chair and sips her wine. 'Tell me all about you and Charles. It was such a big surprise.'

'Nothing to tell,' I say. 'We met, we fell in love, we're getting married. As soon as you guys get divorced,' I add. 'Which from what he says won't be an issue as you have the papers all ready to go.'

She flinches at that, and I can't help smiling to myself at getting under her skin. And then I feel a spark of anxiety at the fact that she clearly cares.

'Have you heard back yet?' Charles asks her.

'No, but you know yourself what it's like over Christmas and New Year. I'll give Sheedy a buzz next week and tell her to move it onto the priority list.'

'Good,' I say. 'Because getting married is on mine.'

Charles laughs. Ariel smiles, but it's a tight smile.

'I'm happy for you,' she says to him. 'Truly. And I think you and Iseult make a lovely couple.'

'Izzy,' I say. 'Everyone calls me Izzy. Except Charles, because he can't help being pompous.'

There's a sudden glimmer of amusement in Ariel's eyes, but it disappears quickly.

'I meant to say to you, Charles, that Graham is considering a slightly earlier publishing slot if you get the edits back in time.' Her tone is suddenly brisk and businesslike.

'This is a completely different process and I want to get it right,' he tells her. 'Izzy says that the worst thing in mysteries is the author taking the reader for granted. I don't want to do that.'

'You're not,' I assure him.

'Thanks.' He smiles at me, then opens another bottle of red and refills my glass. I didn't realise it was empty.

'I'm delighted you're having such a good influence on him,' says Ariel. 'It was so nice that you were able to take a break at the White Sands. It's lovely to get away to the sun in December.'

'Yes.'

I can feel Charles watching me.

'Izzy was due to get married there,' he says, emphasising the 'Izzy' and smiling at me. 'Thankfully, she didn't.'

'You left your fiancé at the altar!' Ariel sounds both shocked and slightly impressed.

I'd like to let her think that's what happened, but I admit that we'd split up before then and I went to the resort with my cousin instead.

'I might pass that plot line to Lucy, if you don't mind,' she says.

'Lucy?'

'Conway. She's my romance author. She's always looking for new ideas.'

'I'm not sure,' I say. 'There are plenty of couples who break it off.'

'But not that many where the jilted bride-to-be jets off to the luxury resort where she was due to be married and gets engaged to a world-famous author there instead,' she returns.

'Please don't let someone turn my life into a book,' I beg her.

'If you're going to live with Charles, you'll learn that he turns everything into a book,' Ariel says. 'Every little thing, no matter how trivial.'

'No I don't.' Charles shoots her a dark look.

'I'm giving her fair warning,' she tells him. 'Your first book was based on your own failed romance. Your second on our early relationship, and the third—'

'You wrote books about being with Ariel?' I interrupt her and stare at him.

'Not at all,' says Charles.

'Oh, come on.' Ariel shakes her head. 'That scene with Emilia and Jonny in Sorrento—'

'I brought them to a place we went to,' says Charles. 'It's hardly describing our relationship.'

'But afterwards—'

'Stop,' he says. 'I may occasionally use situations from real life, but they're always fictionalised in the books.'

I haven't read *Snow in Summer*. If it's about Charles and Ariel, I'll have to.

'And then *An Autumn Story*,' she says. 'A study of a marriage.'

'A failing marriage.'

They seem to have forgotten I'm here. The conversation is entirely between the two of them.

'And then you went to the Caribbean to write *Springs Eternal*,' she continues. 'And of course there's an older man with an interest in his younger colleague, although when the book turns into *A Caribbean Calypso* she ends up murdered. In fact three of the female characters end up dead. Which might be saying something about all of us.'

I think of the plot and wonder if the first victim, Amanda, is based on Ariel. He describes her as a dark-haired, long-faced woman with hazel eyes and a superior look. When she was offed in the book, I wasn't at all surprised. She was a sarky, sniping sort of person, and I can't help feeling that Ariel is too. But then she turns to me and apologises for descending into stupid book talk and says that they always do that, which is probably why they split up in the first place, and that I must be getting a totally wrong impression of her. Then she gets up and retrieves her coat and says that she's heading home.

'You're not driving!' Charles looks aghast.

'No. I walked over here today. I'll get a cab.'

'Fine.' He leans back on the sofa.

I'm still sitting in the armchair opposite.

'I love your ring,' I say.

She glances at it, and then at me.

'So do I,' she says. 'It works as a statement piece, even though Charles and I are no longer together.' She looks at her phone. 'I'd better go. It was a real pleasure to meet you again, Izzy, and I'm absolutely thrilled for you and Charles.'

She sounds so genuine and her smile is so wide that I believe her. I tell myself that I've been foolish and paranoid to think otherwise. Even if she's still wearing her unconventional wedding ring.

'Charles, sweetheart, do please get those edits to me as soon as you possibly can, and don't get distracted by your wonderful fiancée. You *are* wonderful,' she adds, turning back to me. 'You're exactly what he needs.'

Charles follows her out, and I hear the front door opening and then a quick murmur of voices before it closes again.

'Sorry,' he says, coming back into the living room. 'She sometimes calls to the house on a Friday evening to talk about my work in progress. We usually share a glass of wine. She stayed because she wanted to meet you properly. It was a bit fraught the last time.'

'Indeed it was.'

I get up from the armchair and move to the sofa. He puts his arm around me.

'She likes getting a rise out of people,' he says. 'You stood up to her well.'

'Did you really document your relationship in your books?' I ask.

'People always read their own meanings into books,' he says.

'I hope you're not documenting anything about us in *A Caribbean Calypso*.' I make a face at him. 'Especially as you've cast me as a murderer.'

'Only that appearances can be deceptive,' he says. 'Which was the theme of *Springs Eternal* anyway.'

'You're amazing.' I kiss him.

'So are you.' He kisses me back.

And then we stop talking and start doing far more interesting things instead.

Later, when we're lying in bed together, I can't help returning to his relationship with Ariel. I can tell he's irritated by my questions, but I say that I need more than 'we wanted different things' and that he might have been 'a bit jealous'.

'I thought she was having an affair,' he admits. He tells me about the author Cosmo Penhaligon, who I've never heard of, and Ariel's visits to him in Cornwall.

'She was having an affair with him? Wow.'

'She insisted she hadn't slept with him,' says Charles. 'But later, after we'd argued about it, the two of them went to Canada for a festival. When she came back, I discovered a pair of his underpants in her laundry.'

'Why on earth were you rummaging around in her laundry?' I ask.

'I like doing the laundry.' His tone is defensive. 'It relaxes me.'

'If she knew you liked doing laundry – interesting info, by the way – then why on earth would she leave a pair of his underpants in there?' I ask.

'Who knows.'

'What did she say when you confronted her?'

'I didn't,' he replies. 'I shoved them in the bin.'

'Maybe Cosmo put them in her stuff to cause trouble,' I suggest. 'I can't believe she left them there on purpose.'

'There was no need for him to do that,' says Charles. 'He was having the time of his life with her anyway.'

'If I was having an affair, I'd be very careful to cover my tracks,' I say. 'I'd be especially wary of leaving stray under-garments lying around if I knew my husband liked doing the laundry!'

'Oh, look, I accept entirely that there may have been some innocent explanation,' he admits. 'Not that I'm convinced. But by that stage we'd gone past the point of no return. She was fed up with me, and I . . .' His voice trails off and he doesn't finish the sentence.

'Did you still love her?' I ask.

'I sometimes wonder if I ever did,' he replies. 'I admired her hugely, and still do. We were a great couple. We were together all the time. I thought we should be in love, so I proposed.'

'Right.' I lean my head on his chest and mull over what he's said. I can't help thinking it's a bit like me and Steve. I thought we should be in love too. I dropped a million hints about getting engaged before he actually proposed to me. Perhaps I pressured him into it. And his calling it all off was a lucky escape.

Charles's body moves beneath me, and I realise he's laughing.

'What?' I ask.

'The first thing I thought after I saw his feckin' jocks was that they were too small to be mine,' he says. 'That and the fact that they were M&S. I never buy M&S underpants.'

'You mean you were comparing size?' I start to laugh too.

'It's a man thing,' he says.

'Ooh – you could use it in your next murder mystery,' I suggest.

'You're right.' He sits up, dragging the duvet with him. 'My detective could wonder why there's a pair of Calvin Kleins in the drawer when the hero only wears Hugo Boss.'

'Exactly!' I drag him back down to me.

'You're giving me all my best ideas,' he murmurs as he kisses me.

'I do hope I'm more than an ideas machine to you.'

'You absolutely are,' he whispers. 'You absolutely are.'

Charles brings me breakfast in bed the next morning, as I don't have to be at the port until the afternoon. As I munch on toast and marmalade, I ask him about his divorce settlement with Ariel.

'I told you there's no issue with any of it.'

'I know. What I meant was – this house? You both lived here and we're going to live here. But if you're not actually divorced yet . . . she's entitled to half, isn't she? Are you getting a loan to buy her out?'

He explains that they've already agreed all the financial details and that the only thing she gets is the mews at the back.

'The mews?' It takes a moment, then I push the duvet back, get out of bed and stand naked at the window looking down over the garden. 'That mews? I thought it was *your* office.'

'You've been in my office. My study. Why would you think the mews was my office too?'

'I just assumed . . . So that's why she was here last night. All she had to do was stroll up the garden path.'

'Not why,' says Charles. 'Like I said, she sometimes drops by to talk about stuff like the edits informally.'

'It's not very . . . appropriate.'

'Now you're being silly.'

'Seriously, Charles.' I begin to get dressed. 'She's your ex. It's bad enough that you have to work with her. And worse that you're still married to her and that she's wearing her wedding ring even if it is a unique piece of jewellery. But having her working in the garden and thinking she can pop by for a chat . . .'

'She doesn't,' he says. 'We got into the habit of doing it from time to time. I'll tell her not to.'

'Can you move her out of the mews?'

'No. It was part of the separation agreement. It'll be part of the divorce agreement too.'

'For feck's sake. Is she going to be living in our ear day in day out?'

'Honestly, you'll hardly ever see her.' He puts his arm around me. 'Ariel is a good woman and she only has my best interests at heart. And seeing as you're part of my best interests, she'll take you to her heart too.'

He's so sincere, I almost believe he's right about her.

Almost.

Chapter 26

Ariel

*One sure window into a person's
soul is his reading list.*
Mary B. W. Tabor

I can't stop thinking about her. I don't want to, but I am.
Those big brown eyes might be appealing, but she's nothing
like his usual type. She's too short and too . . . well, sturdy,
I guess. Charles doesn't go for sturdy; he prefers slim, willowy
women. I was slim and willowy when we first met, although
that was partly because in those days I was existing on
lunchtime salad bowls from Pret and warm white wine at
evening book events. After I started going out with him
and learned about his preferred female shape, I was on
constant flab alert. In my twenties, it was easy to keep slim,
but it was a lot harder in my thirties, and now, in my forties,
it's a battle. That's why I wear shapewear whenever I'm
meeting anyone. I can't afford to look anything other than
perfect. And I especially want to look good any time I meet
Charles, because I don't want him to think that I let myself
go after we broke up. I want him to see that it's made no

difference to me. And I know he still finds me attractive. Why shouldn't he? After all, handsome as he is, he's put on a few kilos himself. Why does that never matter for a man? Why aren't they bombarded with messages about how to look good in your forties, fifties and sixties? Why are women expected to do all the work?

My mind is spinning around in circles. I know I'm spending far too much time thinking about someone with whom my most intimate relationship is in the past. Yes, we care about each other. And yes, there have been the occasional friends-with-benefits moments. But no matter what Ellis might think about us being the perfect couple, he's not in love with me and I'm not in love with him.

Yet I'm struggling with the thought of him and Iseult. I know I told him she was what he needed, but I was being . . . well, polite isn't the right word. I said it to make him think I didn't care. He's a complex personality and it's clear to me that she's not. It's a holiday romance, and when it goes wrong it'll throw him into a fit of not being able to write (again) because he can't write when he's upset. He's only in love with her now because she got him out of his writing funk with her mad suggestion about a mystery novel that may have worked but isn't really Charles.

None of this is Charles.

He'll realise it soon enough.

Although I sometimes go to the mews office at the weekend, I decide that it's better to stay away for the moment, and instead do some work at home sorting the unsolicited emailed manuscripts that are cluttering up my inbox. I move them to folders arranged in date order, and when I've finished, I highlight the ones that came with a literate email and bin the ones telling me that I'd be a complete loser to pass on a book of such great importance and brilliance. I haven't got the strength to work with someone who uses the word 'loser' in the subject line of an email.

On Monday, I have an appointment with Josh Carmody, the accountant who's looked after me and the agency ever since I set it up. We meet in his office and he goes through a new system he wants me to use for generating payments for my authors, which will be slightly more expensive but significantly clearer. I give the go-ahead for the switch and he asks how things are going, which he already knows as he filed my taxes at the end of the year.

'I meant with you,' he says. 'How are things between you and the Big House?'

He always calls Charles 'the Big House'.

'He's getting married.'

'I thought I saw something about that after Christmas. Are you OK with it?'

'It's fine by me,' I say, but then add that I'm a bit conflicted because his fiancée is very young and I can't help thinking it's a big mistake. 'Which will mean more of his money going on a divorce settlement and him getting stressed out and not being able to write.'

'You're leaping over the actual wedding and going straight for divorce?' He sounds amused. 'When you haven't even got divorced yourself yet?'

Josh is one of the few people who knows everything about Charles and me. He looks after my money, so he needs to.

'We're working on the divorce. As for her . . .' I give him a slightly shamefaced look. 'Josh – you're a man. Do you all really believe that pretty young women fall in love with older men because of their looks rather than their bank balance?'

'You think she's a gold-digger?' He frowns. 'Charles is a catch, but not that much of a catch, surely?'

Josh is well aware of how much Charles earns. He sees the royalty statements, after all.

'There's a new book this year, which will bring in more money,' I remind him. 'And potentially another TV series. Admittedly Charles spent a lot of his cash when he first did well, but he's much more frugal now. Except for his six-week Caribbean writing holiday and his New Year's Eve party, of course. And the wedding. He'll probably spend a fortune on the wedding.'

Josh laughs, and after a moment, I do too.

'I'm sorry,' I say. 'His finances are none of my business.'

'His income is,' Josh says. 'But his expenditure is entirely a matter for himself.'

'And his new wife.'

'Exactly.'

'You didn't answer me,' I tell him. 'Do you really believe it's love, not money, in this kind of age-gap relationship?'

'I suppose all men like to think they can attract a pretty young thing,' he replies thoughtfully. 'We want to believe we're still macho and manly. Though I don't suppose any young woman falls for an older man who's unattractive and insolvent. In Charles's case . . . honestly, he gets better-looking with age, the fecker. I cnvy him. And I say that as a straight man.'

This time it's me who laughs. Josh is around the same age as me and isn't unattractive – he's shorter and less well built than Charles, but he takes care of himself. His hair, which he wears in a buzz cut, is salt-and-pepper grey. His eyes are grey too. He wears decent suits, although his shirtsleeves have buttons, not cufflinks as Charles prefers. On the other hand, I've never seen Josh in casual gear, while Charles can occasionally look positively feral when he's writing, happy to wear the same worn-out T-shirt and trousers for a week. The two men know each other because they worked at the same company for a short time, and Charles recommended Josh to me when I was setting up. He said that much as he found it therapeutic to do his own accounts, it would be a nightmare for him to do the agency's too, and I agreed on the basis that it would be a massive conflict of interest for him to know what my other authors were earning, and would spark too much paranoia in him for me to deal with.

'Want to grab lunch?' asks Josh.

I nod, and we head to an upmarket deli close to Baggot Street, where I order a warm chicken salad and Josh asks for a steak sandwich. The deli is full of business people, and I feel a sudden sense of belonging. I'm a business person too. At a business lunch. With my accountant. Josh is good company, and his conversation about the agency is upbeat and positive. He tells me I'm doing better than a lot of small businesses and I should be really proud of what I've accomplished. For some unaccountable reason his compliment makes me well up, and I pretend to choke on a crouton so that I can wipe the tears from my eyes.

'I'd be lost without Charles, though,' I say, after I've assured him I'm not going to choke to death and have taken a sip of my mineral water.

'It'd be a serious hole in your income,' he agrees. 'But who knows for how much longer he'll write?'

'Years, I hope.'

'I'm amazed he's written so many already, to be honest. Unlike your Lucy Conway and Janice Jermyn, with the books as regular as clockwork, the Booker people tend to take their sweet time about it.'

'Because they're polishing their work.'

'Yet Charles manages to get one out fairly regularly.'

'I know. I think he believes that if he stops, he'll lose it,' I say. 'Even though he also believes he's an absolute genius.'

'Charles makes you money because you get him really good advances for his books and because of all the other rights you sell for him,' says Josh. 'But Janice and Lucy provide a very dependable, regular source of income. As an accountant, I like dependable, regular sources of income.'

'They're both wonderful,' I agree. Then I dig into my handbag and give him proof copies of their next books. He's a fan of Janice, and his wife, Paula, loves Lucy.

'Thanks,' he says, as he puts the Janice Jermyn in his case. 'You can keep the Lucy Conway, though.'

'Why? Has Paula gone off her?' I'm shocked. Nobody goes off Lucy. Even though some readers describe her as a guilty pleasure, once they've read one, they read them all.

'Paula and I have split up,' says Josh.

'What?' I'm even more shocked. Josh and Paula have been together for twenty years. 'I thought you two were the perfect couple.' It occurs to me that I'm using the same phrase people used about me and Charles, and I think how nobody really knows what goes on in a relationship.

'No such thing.' Josh pushes the uneaten portion of his steak sandwich to one side. 'She's found someone else.'

'Oh gosh.' I give him a sympathetic look. 'Here I am banging on about divorces and remarriages and you've got this to contend with. What happened?'

'She met him at her book club.' Josh snorts.

I wince. I don't like to think of a book club being something that broke them up.

'Their eyes obviously met over a romantic read and she decided I didn't match up.'

'I'm really sorry.'

'So you should be.' This time he gives me a rueful look. 'It was one of Charles's books.'

'Not really?'

'That damn novella of his that I thought was rubbish but the book club decided was beautiful.'

It'd be funny if it wasn't such a horrible thing for him, so I say nothing. In any event, whatever was going on with Josh and Paula was deeper than Charles's novella.

'When did this happen?' I ask eventually. 'You didn't mention anything when we were doing the taxes.'

'November.' He shrugs again. 'It was a bleak Christmas.'

'Have you moved out?' I ask.

'Living over the office.'

'You should've told me. I would have . . . you could have called me.'

'You were in Mallorca for Christmas, remember?'

'Only for a few days. You should've got in touch if you were at a loose end.'

Although I understand why he wouldn't. We get on well, but we're not close friends. I remember Charles once saying that men don't have close friends in the same way women do. Not friends they can cry with. But I don't cry. Not if

I can help it. Besides, my closest friends are in London, and that's a long way to go for a few tears.

'Maybe we could meet for a drink sometime,' says Josh. 'Compare divorce notes.'

'I'm not sure how helpful I'd be, but happy to meet whenever you like.'

'I'll give you a shout,' he says. 'I'm juggling stuff at the moment.'

'I'm flexible,' I assure him. 'Whenever suits.'

Josh gets the bill and we leave the deli. He heads back to the office and I hail a cab back home.

There are another five unsolicited manuscripts in my inbox when I return.

Maybe one of them will turn out to be the mega author who replaces Charles as my main income stream in the future.

Though none of them will ever replace him as a person.

Chapter 27

Iseult

Fiction is the truth inside the lie.
Stephen King

The next time I visit Riverside Lodge, Charles and I FaceTime my parents. It was his idea, after I told him that they'd shortly be going on their Asian cruise. We do it early one morning after a cosy night spent eating pizza in front of the TV.

Charles is charming towards Mum while being relaxed and friendly with Dad. He jokes that it's important for him to get on the right side of the prospective in-laws and hopes that they'll appreciate how much he loves me and how well he's going to look after me. He takes them on a virtual tour of the house, and they're impressed by the beautiful living room and library, the stunning entrance hall and enormous kitchen.

'What I wouldn't give for a kitchen like that,' says Mum, and Charles tells her – as he told Celeste – that she can use it any time. It deserves the love of someone who knows how to cook, he says, and I see Mum fall for him a little more.

He then assures them both that his divorce is his main

295

priority. I know Mum wishes it was done and dusted already, but Charles tells her that he hopes it'll all be sorted very soon, and is so amiable and charismatic that both my parents hang on his every word.

'I know I might not have been your first choice for Izzy,' he says. 'But I assure you that nobody could love her more than I do.'

'There won't be any nonsense about changing your mind so?' Dad's face fills the screen.

'Not a chance.' Charles holds the phone away from him, as though doing that will make Dad back off.

'Are you planning a big wedding?' It's Mum who takes over the screen now.

'We haven't decided on that yet,' I say.

'Whatever Iseult wants she gets,' says Charles.

'Ah here.' Dad laughs. 'Don't make yourself a hostage to fortune.'

We end the conversation with promises to meet up as soon as they're home.

'You could sweet-talk for Ireland,' I tell Charles when they've gone.

'As a rule, only on paper.' He grins. 'But nothing I said to them is untrue. Especially that part about loving and protecting you for ever.'

I kiss him.

'To that end,' he says as he makes coffee, 'what d'you think about moving in with me now?'

'I'd love to, but not yet.'

'Why?'

'Partly because I don't want to leave the house in Marino empty while Mum and Dad are away, and partly because . . .

because I think we should make some changes to Riverside Lodge before I move in.'

'What sort of changes?' He frowns.

'I want to redecorate. I love this house, I really do, but the style is yours and Ariel's, and I'd like to make it a bit more mine. Nothing drastic,' I add quickly. 'Just a bit of refreshing. I won't go near your study or the library.'

'If that's all you want, it's fine.' He sounds relieved. 'I'm happy to let you loose on it. I remember having never-ending discussions on shades of green when we were first renovating, and it did my head in.'

'I promise not to have colour conversations with you,' I assure him.

'Does it all have to be finished before you'll even consider moving in?'

'No.' I shake my head. 'As long as you agree to do it, I'll move once Mum and Dad are back.'

'I can't wait,' he says as he pulls me close to him.

I glance over his shoulder towards the mews. I suppose Ariel is there already, doing whatever it is literary agents do.

She's always there. That's going to have to change too.

The sun has come out by the time I arrive at the port, the breeze is light and the salty tang of the sea hasn't yet been overpowered by the stench of diesel from the trucks. I'm on form-filling duty, although I keep getting distracted by the spectacular view over the bay, where the sun is glinting off the waves while the seabirds wheel and shriek against the blue sky. I'm betting that if Charles had a view like this he'd find it inspiring. All the same, it doesn't inspire me to fill in the forms any quicker. When I eventually finish, I check the screen to see if the ferry due in is on schedule. It's about to dock, so Natasha and I drive to the terminal, where we take up our positions and wait for the cars and trucks to roll off.

It's routine. There's a lorry with inadequate paperwork and an overladen minivan, both of which I send to be checked, but there's nothing that needs to be scanned and nothing to set our spidey senses on edge. I return to the office and some more form-filling, and await the next arrival, a cargo vessel from Rotterdam, which might be a little more challenging.

The longer evenings are becoming very noticeable now, and although it's dark by the time my shift is over, I don't feel as though the day is completely done. Because I spent the night with Charles, I drove Dad's car to Terenure and into work today. I'll definitely need to consider my transport options when I'm living in Riverside Lodge because the cross city traffic is always a nightmare, but at least next week is an early shift so if I stay with Charles, there won't be any problem getting in to the port for 5 a.m. The commuters will still be in bed.

As it turns out, I don't stay with Charles the following week. He's deep into his edits and rewrites, and as he likes to work at night, it wouldn't be convenient for either of us for me to be there. But he asks me to come to his on Friday afternoon and stay for the weekend. I'm finished at lunchtime, so I pick up a takeaway sandwich and eat it at home, then have a shower and change into my comfy jeans and a sweatshirt. I think about using Dad's car again, but the council is doing its best to discourage cross-city traffic, and every route across the river is horrible, so I get the bus instead. It's definitely not any quicker, but I put my earbuds in and listen to music, so I'm quite chilled by the time I get to Riverside Lodge.

It takes Charles ages to answer the door, and he apologises, saying that he's in the middle of a Zoom call with Sydney and telling me to make myself at home. I lug my overnight bag to the bedroom, and then go back downstairs again to make coffee for both of us.

I tap on his study door and he looks around in surprise. As I leave the mug beside him, I can see and hear Sydney talking about Ursula, who's the grandmother and the final corpse in Charles's manuscript. She's suggesting that Ursula be a little less hateful, but I really liked her as a horrible character, and I'll say that to him later. Sydney might be his editor, but I'm his beta reader and his fiancée, which surely counts for something! Charles thanks me for the coffee, then waves me away. I leave him to it.

As I walk into the living room, my eye is caught by movement in the garden, and I see Ariel stepping out of the mews. My fingers tighten around the mug as I watch her talking on her mobile while also looking up at the house. She's probably putting a deal together for one of her authors. Or maybe even finalising that TV series for Charles. I step back a little from the window so she can't see me. We haven't spoken since the time she came to the house to talk to him about his edits, and I've no desire to speak to her now. I appreciate that she works very hard for him, but she's still his agent-slash-ex, and not as ex as she should be. I wish she wasn't working from Charles's back garden, but I've no idea how to change that. At least, not yet.

I finish my coffee, then stretch out on the comfortable sofa. I put my earbuds in my ears, and despite the fact that I've ingested a mug of caffeine, Adele lulls me to sleep within minutes.

I wake up with a start when I sense there's someone in the room, watching me.

'I'm sorry,' says Ariel. 'I did say your name when I came in, but there was no answer. I didn't mean to wake you.'

'Were you looking for something?' I sit up and slide the buds from my ears.

'Friday wine moment.' She raises the bottle of red she's holding. 'Freedom Friday is a bit of a tradition between me and Charles. And now you, of course.'

'I'm not sure we'll be having wine moments every Friday.'

'It's nice to unwind after a long week,' she says. 'I'm sure you feel the same. You were asleep after all.'

'Because I started work at five o'clock this morning.'

'Poor you.' She gives me a sympathetic look as she goes to the sideboard and unerringly finds a silver corkscrew. 'You could definitely do with a glass in that case.'

I'm about to say no, but she's already opening the bottle.

'I bet you're hungry too,' she says as she hands me the glass. 'Stay there. I brought some cheese. It's in the kitchen.'

Before I have the chance to say anything, I'm alone again. I'm not pleased that I've allowed Ariel to go downstairs to the kitchen and fetch the cheese as though I was her guest. I should have told her I'd get it myself.

I'm properly alert by the time she returns with three varieties of cheese, neatly arranged on a large plate, alongside a selection of crackers and some grapes.

'Thanks,' I say as she sits opposite me.

'So how's it been going?' she asks.

'Work? Very busy.' I wilfully misinterpret her question.

'You and Charles,' she says. 'It's all very exciting.'

'It will be when we set a date,' I say. 'And that depends on your divorce.'

'Now that the solicitors are on the case, I'm sure it'll happen pretty soon. Then time will whizz by to your wedding. As soon as you start planning, it comes at you like an express train. Oh, but you know that already!' She covers her mouth with her hand. 'I'm sorry, I forgot. You called off your own wedding. It must have been a difficult time,' she adds.

'It wasn't what I expected,' I admit. 'But subsequently it became a relief.'

'All the same . . .'

'And if it hadn't happened, I wouldn't have met Charles, so there's a silver lining,' I continue. 'Anyway, like everyone says, better to call it off before than have it go wrong after, like you.'

Her eyes narrow.

'It's amazing, really, that you're such good friends,' I add. 'Steve – my ex – wanted us to be friends, but quite honestly, once it's over, it's over, don't you think? Otherwise it becomes a bit controlling.'

'I suppose it depends on how mature you are about it.' She places a sliver of cheese on a cracker. 'And given our professional relationship, Charles and I have to be mature about it.'

'I guess so.'

'After all, we talk almost every day.'

I say nothing.

'It's good that we all get on.' She smiles.

They might. *We* don't. And we don't have to. There's nothing that says I'm obliged to like her, or speak to her, or have her in my home. I'm aware of a charge between us, a crackling tension that seems entirely about who has the greater claim on Charles. I'm annoyed at myself for feeling it, because nobody should have a claim on anybody. But I definitely feel like Ariel is staking out some kind of territorial advantage here.

'I can see you might think it a bit awkward that I'm in such close contact with him,' she says. 'But it's only while he's working on his book. After that, you'll hardly see me.'

That's good. I don't want to see her.

'So Freedom Friday ends once it's done?'

'Well, we do tend to have a glass or two in the summer,' she admits. 'It's nice to sit on the patio and crack open a bottle of bubbly. He's always thrilled when I sign a new client, and we like to celebrate our mutual successes. But it'll be even more fun with you there too. You'll be good for him, I know. Charles can get very self-obsessed sometimes. Oh, by the way . . .' She reaches into the enormous bag she left beside the sofa. 'As promised, that signed Janice Jermyn. And a proof copy of her new one too.'

'Oh.' Despite myself, I feel my eyes light up. A signed copy is lovely to have. And a proof of the new one is a real treat. I see from the cover that it isn't out until the summer, and I feel privileged.

'Thank you,' I say, and mean it.

'You're more than welcome. If there are any other books by my authors that you'd like, just say the word.'

'I don't want to impose on you.'

'Next time you're here, drop down to the mews,' she says. 'It's a bit damp outside to go there now, but you can take anything you want.'

'You're very kind.'

'Not at all.' She smiles at me, then lifts her glass. 'We're friends, right?'

'Friends,' I say, although I wonder how true that is.

It's nearly an hour before Charles joins us. We've made quite a dent in the bottle of wine, although Ariel has drunk more than me. She's been telling me stories of her life in London and giving me titbits of gossip about celebrities she's met. She's a good storyteller and she knows quite a few famous people who've written books. Or had them ghostwritten, she says. It's a bit of a thing for celebs now. Some have done very well. Many, she confides, have sunk without trace.

'Which is why it's important to nurture an exceptional talent like Charles,' she says as she fills a glass for him. 'He's the real deal, you know.'

'Thank you.' Charles sits beside me on the sofa. At least Ariel wasn't able to claim it this time, what with me having been asleep on it earlier. I move a little closer to him.

'Are you going to the Seán Óg launch next Thursday?' Ariel asks him. 'It's in the National Library.'

'Another tome about the Famine?' Charles groans.

'It's very good,' she says. 'So I've been told.'

'That man loves exploiting misery. I suppose I should turn up, though. I'm guessing all the usual suspects will be there.' He looks at me. 'You'll come?'

'I'm working from eleven till seven next week,' I say.

'That's a shame,' says Ariel. 'It starts at six thirty.'

'Get a cab,' says Charles. 'There'll be at least half an hour's schmoozing before Seán says anything. Besides, he'll go on for ages and then read from his book. If you're unlucky you'll catch the end. Please come.'

'OK.' I don't really want to, but at the same time I have to support Charles. Besides, I don't want him there with Ariel by his side.

'I'm glad you can make it,' she says.

#Friends #Enemies #Frenemies

Chapter 28

Ariel

*A woman must have money and a room
of her own if she is to write fiction.*
                                    Virginia Woolf

The following week, I have lunch with Janice Jermyn. Many readers seem to think that writers of cosy crime are somehow cosy themselves. Not Janice. She's tall, blonde and statuesque, with a shrewd business brain and a quiet confidence about her success. She delivers her manuscripts on time and with a minimal need for editing, and she doesn't give a damn about reviews. She gets on with writing her next bestseller without any fuss whatsoever. Yet while all my male novelists (who seem to take up far more of my time) have had in-depth newspaper pieces written about them and their work, Janice's main feature was all about how lucky she was to be able to chuck in her job as a dental technician after her first novel (where the murderer was a dentist) was a solid bestseller in five countries.

She's brilliant, of course. She's also great fun.

'What's this I hear about Charles Miller muscling in on

my territory by turning to crime?' she demands when we get to the dessert stage of our lunch. 'It's a big change for the Undisputed King of Tearjerkers.'

I laugh. That was a headline used on a book blogger piece about Charles last year. He was furious when I told him. He said it made him sound like some kind of romance novelist. When I joked that he sort of was, I thought his head would explode. I tell Janice that he has indeed written a crime novel, though it's nothing like hers.

'It better not be.' She smiles at the waiter, who's placing a huge slice of lemon meringue pie in front of her, but her expression when she looks at me is fierce.

'It's an enjoyable book,' I say. 'Would you like to read a proof? Maybe give a quote if you enjoy it.'

'Me? Quote on a Charles Miller novel?' Janice splutters. 'You're having a laugh.'

'I have it on good authority that it was reading one of your books that inspired him to switch to crime.'

'Feck's sake.' She stabs her pie. 'Tell you what, Ariel. You get some of your literary reviewers to give me the kind of fawning reviews they give Charles, and I'll say something wonderful about his crime novel.'

'Yes, well.' I smile. 'You know how it is, Janice.'

'I bloody do.' She takes a moment to demolish the dessert. 'Delicious. Anyhow, leaving reviews and quotes and all that sort of thing aside, they're not going to bump me for him at Harrogate, are they?'

Harrogate is a prestigious literary crime festival and Janice is scheduled to be on a panel. It's the first time she's been asked, and she's very excited.

'Of course not,' I tell her. 'They specifically want you.

Anyhow, he's very nervous about his foray into crime, so I'm not sure he's ready for Harrogate yet.'

She snorts and say he's got nothing to be nervous about. It's about respect, she continues. Men are always respected more than women, no matter what area of life it is. Business, arts, entertainment – you have to be exceptional to be noticed as a woman. A man expects it.

She's not entirely wrong. In fact, in my experience she's entirely right.

'We'll be talking to your publisher about a contract soon,' I say.

'Yes.' She nods. 'I have some ideas for a new series.'

'Oh? Not Crispin Devereux?' This is both good and bad news. It's fun that Janice is considering a new series, but her readers love Crispin. He's a throwback to the gentlemen detectives of the 1930s and 40s. The son of an earl who's fallen on hard times and is selling off the country estate, he is now a detective inspector on the police force. Janice and I often joke that the beautiful countryside in which he lives is an absolute hotbed of murder, blackmail and dark deeds.

We chat for a while about her idea for a female detective and I like what she's outlining. The character's warm, empathetic exterior masks her brilliant deductive reasoning, and I think she sounds like a very modern Miss Marple.

'That's the idea,' says Janice. 'Although she's living in an apartment in a new town, not a gorgeous cottage in the Home Counties.'

'I like her already,' I say.

'In my head, she's a bit like you,' she tells me.

'How?' I frown.

'You're such a lovely person to talk to, but all the time I

can see the wheels spinning inside your brain. Working out what'll work and what won't. Working out how to shape things to the best advantage.'

'I don't know whether to be flattered or not,' I say.

'Oh, be flattered.' She grins at me. 'I couldn't have a better agent.'

'That's good to know.'

And it is. In a year where things haven't always gone exactly to plan, it's nice to hear that my bestselling crime novelist appreciates me.

I feel equally appreciated when I meet Josh that evening for the drink we eventually managed to schedule. When I arrive at the Cellar Bar at the Merrion Hotel, he's already there, a pint of Guinness in front of him. I sit down opposite and apologise for being ten minutes late.

'No worries.' He signals to the barman and I order a gin and tonic.

'How are you doing?' I ask when we clink our glasses together. 'Any progress on . . . well, whatever you're going to do.'

'Divorce,' says Josh. 'There's no chance of a reconciliation. She's mad about Ivan.' He almost spits the name out.

'Are you sure it isn't . . . Sorry, Josh, I hesitate to say this because I hate the term and always edit it out of a manuscript, but are you sure it isn't some kind of midlife crisis for her?'

'Even if it is, she can't throw me out and expect me to come back whenever she feels like it.'

'Do you think she might?'

'I doubt it.' He sighs. 'Apparently this Ivan guy is bringing her to arty events and theatre and stuff like that, and she says it's enriching her life immeasurably. We used to go to the pub and maybe occasionally a blockbuster movie with popcorn. Mostly we stayed in and binge-watched TV dramas. She said she couldn't be arsed to go out. Now I gather she never wants to stay in.'

'What about the kids?' They have two, a boy and a girl.

'They're at home with her, of course,' says Josh. 'It's not like I could have a twelve-year-old and an eight-year-old in the flat above the office, is it?'

'I guess not.'

'I thought we were building a good life together,' he says. 'She never said there was anything wrong. She seemed happy. I suppose I'm totally clueless for not realising that she wasn't.'

'How serious is it between her and Book Club Man?' I ask.

'Apparently he understands her in a way I never will.' He makes a face. 'I swear to God, Ariel, I feel like I'm a character in a romance novel myself. A minor character. One that gets forgotten after Chapter One.'

'Oh, Josh.' I reach out and catch him by the hand. 'The overlooked characters in Chapter One sometimes make a triumphant return at the end.'

He laughs.

'Have you got a good solicitor?' I release his hand.

'If nothing else, I know lots of good solicitors,' he says. 'How about you and the Big House? Now that he has someone else, I presume you've got that in motion yourself.'

'Working on it,' I reply. 'It should be fine. Everything's already agreed.'

He orders another drink, and when he's finished it, he says he'd better get home as he had a couple before I arrived and is now feeling the effects. He apologises for being a boring old drunk. I tell him he's certainly not boring or old, even if he is a little drunk. He tells me I'm kind. I order a cab and we share it as far as his office.

'Would you like to come in for coffee?' he asks, and then immediately says, 'No, don't, sorry. That's such a cliché. Besides, we're both still married to other people, and anyway, you're my client, Ariel. A good client. I don't want to mess that up. I'm sorry.'

I make soothing noises and ease him out of the cab while the driver pretends he's not listening to us. I wait until I'm sure he's safely inside before telling the driver to carry on. But I'm thinking about Josh's remark about us both still being married to other people.

We won't be married to other people for much longer. Yet as much as I'm Josh's client, Charles is still mine. And that complicates things in ways that, at this hour of the night, I can't really get my head around.

I'm on a Zoom with Shelley when the door to the mews opens and Charles walks in. I look up in surprise, because he rarely comes to my office.

'Why haven't you returned those signed documents?' he asks.

'Charles! You can't just walk in here. I'm in the middle of—'

'I texted you. You didn't answer.'

'I'll get back to you, Shelley,' I tell my assistant, and end the session.

Then I turn to Charles.

'Never, ever interrupt me when I'm talking to someone again,' I say. 'You could have ruined a deal, for yourself or someone else.'

'You were talking to Shelley,' he says.

'You weren't to know that. Now, I have a heap of things to do that are really important—'

'The most important thing is telling me you've signed the papers I know you received the other day.'

'Everything is in hand,' I say.

'I don't want it to be in hand,' says Charles. 'I want it to be with the courts. Iseult and I would like to get married as soon as we can.'

'What's the big rush?' I ask. 'Is she pregnant?'

'Of course she isn't pregnant!' He gives me a horrified look. 'Why would you even say such a thing? And not that it would matter if she was, but . . . are you jealous?'

'Oh, please.' I roll my eyes. 'How could I possibly be jealous of her?'

'Well, you not getting on with things is affecting my work. I can't think of anything till it's done. Sydney sent me more – more! – suggestions for *A Caribbean Calypso* . . . You'll have to talk to her and tell her to lay off on them. I can't concentrate properly until I know those papers have been filed. Iseult's parents will be home from their cruise soon and I want to be able to tell them that I'm a divorced man.'

'Even if I'd hand-delivered the papers to the judge himself, it wouldn't make things happen faster.'

'Well, if you haven't bothered, if you're too bloody busy to walk to the post office, give them to me now and I'll post them myself.'

'Here you are.' I pull open the bottom drawer of my desk and take out a large envelope. 'Everything that's needed is in there.'

'Why you couldn't have . . .' He shakes his head. 'At least I know we'll be up and running after today. I'm going to send them by registered mail right now.'

'Fine,' I say. 'Takes something off my plate.'

'Anything to help,' says Charles, and walks out of my office, slamming the door behind him.

Fuck, I think as I watch him stalk up the garden. I should've sent the papers the day I got them. But every time I took the envelope out of the drawer, I put it back in again. Something was holding me back. Perhaps it was the feeling that the invisible bond between him and me is necessary for both of us. Or maybe it was simply that I don't want him to have that bond with someone else.

I'm being silly. I know I am.

I turn back to my laptop, but my concentration has been shot to pieces.

I glare up at the house, then snap the laptop shut.

I'll work from home, where I won't be interrupted.

Chapter 29

Iseult

All writers are lunatics.
Cornelia Funke

I go directly from work to the Seán Óg book launch. I texted Charles and asked him what to wear, because I don't know how posh it will be. His response was to dress for the weather. Given that it's tipping it down by the time I leave the port, I'm hoping that my ankle boots, black jeans and sparkly top are OK.

When I arrive at the National Library, I realise that the ankle boots and jeans are perfect, and it's the sparkly top that's a little bit too much. Most of the guests are rocking a traditional Irish look of corduroy trousers and woolly jumpers, and quite a number of the men are sporting tweed caps. The woman at the lectern is making a speech in Irish, the general gist of which is that Seán Óg's book is an important piece of work about a seminal period in our history.

I'm guessing that he hasn't spoken himself yet and that I haven't arrived at the tail end of proceedings. I accept a glass of rather warm white wine from a passing waiter, and look around for Charles. But it's Ariel I see first, looking smart and businesslike in slimline trousers, a red jacket and high heels. She's wearing her copper hair in what seems to be her signature style of a loose knot, while the drop earrings that match her ring sparkle in the light. As I look at her, she turns and sees me, and immediately walks over.

'You made it,' she murmurs so as not to distract from the woman who's speaking. 'In plenty of time too.'

'My boss knew I had something on and let me leave early,' I tell her. 'Is Charles here?'

'He was chatting to Seán Óg earlier,' she says. 'I'm sure he'll scoop you up when Seán's finished speaking.'

'I haven't missed it so.'

'No. Even though you were given every opportunity.' She shrugs. 'Seán tends to . . . Ah well, you'll hear for yourself.'

The woman at the lectern is introducing the author now, and there's enthusiastic applause from the crowd.

I remember him from the party: a tall, somewhat unkempt man with a fearsomely bushy beard. Then he was wearing what I reckoned was an ancient green velvet jacket over black trousers. Today he's in jeans and a tweed jacket with elbow patches. He reminds me of Mr O'Hanlon, my old history teacher. Poor Mr O'Hanlon spent three years trying to interest me in the past when all I cared about was the future.

Seán Óg begins by thanking what feels like every single person in the room, then starts to talk about his book. I tune out and survey the guests instead. I still can't see Charles and I want to go looking for him, but Ariel is standing close beside me and I don't feel I can walk away. I wonder if her feet are killing her in those heels. At least my ankle boots are low.

Seán speaks for about fifteen minutes and then reads from his book for what seems like an hour but is probably another fifteen minutes. When he finishes, the woman who introduced him thanks him and says he'll be signing copies for anyone who wants one. An orderly queue forms at a desk set up for that purpose.

'You should buy a copy,' says Ariel. 'It'll make a great gift.'

'What!' It's a massive hardback, and despite the fact that it's being sold at five euros off the recommended price, it's eye-wateringly expensive.

'You've got to support him,' she says.

'I don't even know him.'

'You're in the book world now.'

Maybe Dad would like a copy, I think. He's interested in history.

'How are the wedding preparations coming along?' Ariel changes the subject.

'It's kind of tricky until we can set a date. And Charles is reluctant to set a date until he's divorced. From you,' I add, as though she mightn't be aware she's part of the whole thing.

'It's all under control,' says Ariel. 'He came into my office the other day demanding to know if my part of it was on schedule.'

I've no idea how divorce works in practice, so I say that I hope it is and she says that of course it is and that one day soon I'll be free to waltz up the aisle with Charles.

'I read some of the old pieces from years ago about you and him,' I say. 'It must have been a real flurry of love and success.'

'Our feelings for each other grew over time,' she says. 'It wasn't as speedy a love story as yours seems to be.'

'It was a fun thing in the Caribbean,' I tell her. 'I didn't expect to feel the same when we got home. But I did. I do.'

'I hope you'll be very happy together.'

Her words sound automatic, but I say that I hope we'll be happy too.

'I'm sure you thought you and he would be for ever,' I add, 'but sometimes things go wrong and it's best to accept that fact. I guess finalising your divorce from him will give you permission to move on.'

Her eyes narrow. 'In what way?' she asks.

'I simply mean that you can be professional without being around all the time. He admires you a lot,' I add. 'As a professional.'

'Indeed.'

Charles himself arrives at that point and puts his arm around me before kissing me on the cheek. Then he says he wants to introduce me to Seán Óg, and I say I don't really need to meet him, which makes Charles laugh.

'He's a bit of an acquired taste all right,' he says. 'But a good-hearted man.'

'Did you see Mairin McGettigan?' asks Ariel, who's still hovering around. 'She wanted to have a word with you.'

Even I've heard of Mairin McGettigan, who's a broadcaster with a weekly arts show. Charles perks up on hearing she wants to talk to him.

'Can you find her for me?' he asks.

Ariel nods and walks off, while I lean closer to Charles.

'I'm glad you came,' he says.

'So am I.'

'We'll give it another ten minutes or so and then head off,' he tells me. Then a photographer stops in front of us and asks if he can take a photo. Charles releases me and stands straight. The man takes a photo of him but not me. I'm wondering if it would be really bad form to ask him to take one of the two of us together with my mobile, but even as I'm thinking it's probably a naff idea, the phone starts to ring.

I frown at the unknown number, but answer it anyway.

'Is that Iseult?' It's a female voice.

'Yes.'

'I'm calling from Beaumont Hospital. I have Steve Carter for you. Hold on.'

I don't have time to ask her what the hell she's talking about, because Steve is talking and it's something about a broken arm or leg or . . .

'Slow down,' I say. 'What's the matter?'

'I came off my bike,' he says. 'Some effing eejit opened his car door and I slammed into it.'

'Oh my God. Are you OK?'

'Hardly.' I hear him take a deep breath. 'I've broken my collarbone and my ankle and I've sprained my wrist and thumb.'

'Oh dear,' I say.

'They want to discharge me from hospital now but I can't go home.'

'Why not? Are there no cabs?'

'Yes, but there's nobody home. They're away 'til next week. I wouldn't even be able to put the key in the door and turn it, let alone look after myself, I don't know what to do.'

I suggest that Dessie, one of his friends, could help.

'Are you out of your mind?' he says. 'He'd probably kill me by mistake.'

He has a point. Dessie is worse than useless when it comes to practical matters.

'I thought . . . I know this is a bit of an imposition, Izzy, but I thought maybe you could put me up for a couple of days. Until the folks are back.'

'I can't possibly put you up, Steve, don't be daft.'

'There's nobody else,' he says. 'I wouldn't ask if there was.'

'But I'll be at work. I can't take care of you.'

'It'd be better than nothing,' he says.

I don't know what to say. I glance over to Charles, who was initially listening to my conversation but who's now been nabbed by a woman in a multicoloured knitted dress and matching wool hat.

'I'm not sure—' I begin.

'Please, Izzy. When you see me, you'll understand. The broken collarbone is on the other side to the wrist and thumb. I'm a mess.'

He's putting me in a really difficult position, but what else can I do? I tell him I'll be there as soon as I can.

I drop my mobile back in my bag. The crowd around me has shifted and there's no sign of Charles and Woollen Hat Woman. Or Ariel. I spend a minute or so scanning the room for him, but with no luck. I walk out into Kildare Street, and with the kind of good fortune that rarely happens in real life, there's a cab approaching. I hail it and hop in.

Ariel

Charles is helping himself to another glass of the frankly horrible wine when I return with Mairin McGettigan, who immediately begins to talk to him about a potential new show she's thinking of, featuring outstanding locations in Irish literature. *Winter's Heartbreak* was set in Mayo, and she thinks it could be a stunning place to include.

'Although,' she adds, 'I'm not sure if we'd get the chance to film it under a blanket of snow like in the book.'

'We haven't had a heavy snowfall in a long time,' says Charles. 'Maybe it's due.'

'We'll be filming in April.' Mairin grins. 'I'm hoping it won't be snowing then. But you're interested?'

'Of course,' he says.

'You might like to have him on your show before then,' I say. 'His new book, out later this year, is brilliant.'

'I heard it was a murder mystery,' says Mairin. 'Interesting. And I'd love to talk about it, but we've got everything we need for this season. I'll definitely keep you in mind for next season, though,' she says to Charles. 'And we'll be in touch about the new programme.' Then she moves off into the thinning crowd.

'That's great,' I say. 'A slot for both her book show and the new one.'

He doesn't answer. He's staring at his phone and frowning.

'What's up?'

'Iseult,' he says. 'She had to go.'

'Not her thing? I didn't really think so, to be honest. Even for me, Seán Óg—'

'It's not that.' He gives me an impatient look and shows me his texts.

So sorry. I got a call about a medical
emergency and had to dash. Couldn't find
you to explain. I'll give you a shout later

'What type of emergency?' I ask.
He taps the question into his phone.

Motorbike accident

Someone you know?

Steve ☹

There's a sharp intake of breath from Charles, and he begins to type furiously.

Doesn't he have someone else to call? It's
hardly appropriate for you to help him

Apparently his parents are away this week. He needs
some help. I'll fill you in when I've seen him

I look at him and raise my eyebrows.
He starts to type, then erases it. He starts again. Erases it again. Eventually he types:

Call me asap

Iseult replies with a thumbs-up emoji. Charles snorts, then puts his phone into his pocket.

'I hate that she texts me all the time,' he says. 'I'd have a better idea of what was really going on if she'd call.'

'That's Gen . . . God, what Gen is she?' I ask. 'Gen X? Y? Z? Another letter of the alphabet?'

'I've no idea.'

I take out my own phone and search.

'Charles! You and I are Generation X,' I tell him. 'She's . . . How old is she again?'

'Twenty-nine.'

'She's a Millennial.'

'They're nothing more than labels.' He shrugs.

'But a label is useful in determining how people behave,' I say. 'Presumably Millennials are the ones who hate speaking on the phone and only communicate by text. Or maybe she finds it easier to text you when she's rushing to the side of her ex-fiancé like a ministering angel so that she doesn't have to answer awkward questions.'

He ignores my comment and looks at his phone again. There are no more messages from Iseult.

'Come on,' I say. 'No need to be here any longer. Let's grab a bite to eat while we wait for her to call you.'

I think he's going to say no, but he doesn't. He follows me out of the library and towards Dawson Street, where I usher him into a small Italian restaurant that's a favourite of mine. Even midweek it's busy, and I worry that there won't be a table, but Gennaro, the head waiter, finds us a lovely little booth at the back.

'Perfect,' I say as I slide into the banquette opposite

Charles. He seems to think so too as he unwinds his scarf from around his neck and almost visibly relaxes.

He places his phone on the table between us. We order some antipasti, then rigatoni for him and linguine for me. We're both drinking water, our palates having been destroyed by the horrible wine at the launch.

We talk about books in general, a conversation I'm always happy to have. He keeps checking his phone, even though it hasn't pinged once with a notification.

'I heard back from Laurence earlier,' he says when our pasta arrives. 'Now that all the paperwork is in place, he thinks he'll get the divorce done quickly.'

'Excellent.'

'I'm glad we're being sensible about this,' he says.

'What other way is there to be?'

'You're one in a million.' His words are heartfelt.

Then his mobile buzzes.

Chapter 30

Iseult

If you can't annoy somebody,
there is little point in writing.
Kingsley Amis

When I arrive at the hospital, I'm directed to a waiting area. Fifteen minutes later, Steve arrives, pushed in a wheelchair by a porter. His left arm is in a sling and his right wrist is in a support. He has a cast on his leg and a plaster on his cheek. He looks terrible.

'Wow,' I say. 'You really are a mess. Have they given you good painkillers? Did you get the details of the car owner?'

'I'm drugged up to the eyeballs,' he says. 'Even so, I ache all over. The Gardaí have my details and the car owner's details as well as witness statements. I can't believe it happened. It totally wasn't my fault.'

'I never thought it was.'

Steve is a careful motorcyclist. I always felt safe on the back of the bike with him.

'I'm sorry I called you, Izzy, but I couldn't think of anyone else.' He attempts to rub his forehead but instead hits himself on the nose with the wrist support. He winces. 'If there was any other option, I'd take it,' he tells me, 'but as it is . . .'

'You'll have to come home with me,' I concede. 'When are your folks back?'

'In a few days,' he replies. 'I won't be in the way, I promise.'

He absolutely will be in the way. And I'm not sure how he'll manage when I'm at work. I'm not going to be able to slip away a bit early like I did today. Besides, I have other things going on in my life. Like Charles. Who'll be really pissed at me for abandoning both him and the launch. He's already pissed at me. I can tell from his texts. I want to call him, but I can't right now, not with the taxi pulling up and Steve trying to manoeuvre himself inside.

Steve is painfully aware of every bump in the road, but fortunately it only takes us fifteen minutes to get home. It takes nearly as long again to get him up the stairs. He says he's happy to sit in the armchair by the TV for a while, but I say he'll be better off in bed, where the painkillers can do their job. Besides, I have to call Charles, and I'm not doing it in front of Steve. I put him into my bedroom, since he's familiar with it; I'll move into my parents' room while he's here. When he's finally sorted, I bring him tea and biscuits. I have to help him drink the tea because he can't move the arm in the sling and he has no strength in his hand with the support bandage.

'To think that I nearly had to kill myself to get you to look after me again.' He smiles weakly at me.

'I'm very glad you didn't kill yourself,' I say. 'And I'm happy to have you here tonight. But I'll be out of here by ten thirty tomorrow and I won't be back till after seven.' I give him a worried look. 'I'm not sure how you'll manage on your own.'

'Can't you change shifts?' he asks. 'You've done it before.'

I tell him that it's not feasible. I'm not going to change my shifts just to suit Steve. I can't help thinking that this makes me seem mean and unreasonable, but I'm already doing him a massive favour by letting him stay here. I add that if I was on nights I'd be sleeping during the day and not able to look after him either, then I close the bedroom door firmly behind me and go downstairs.

I make myself a cup of tea and bring it into the living room, where I flop into the armchair. It takes a while before I summon up the energy to call Charles.

'I wasn't expecting to hear from you,' he says with a chill in his voice. 'I thought the best I could hope for was a text.'

'I'm really sorry,' I say. 'It was all a bit of a mess.'

'Tell me.'

He listens without saying anything.

' . . . and so if we can't find somewhere else for him, he'll have to stay here for a couple of days,' I conclude.

'What exactly is your current relationship with this guy?' Charles's tone remains cool.

'I told you. He's my ex.'

'Doesn't seem all that ex to me,' he says. 'You're the first person he calls when he's in trouble, and now he's installed himself in your house.'

'Rather like you and Ariel,' I say.

'That's a completely different scenario,' he tells me after a moment's silence.

'Is it?' I ask. 'She was with you tonight, for heaven's sake.'

'She was working!' exclaims Charles. 'And she's not bloody well staying in my house.'

'She doesn't need to. She hangs out in your back garden all the time,' I retort.

'Because that's where her office is.'

'Yes, and when I said I was uncomfortable with it, you dismissed it. Now you're uncomfortable with Steve staying with me, and I haven't dismissed it but simply drawn a comparison.'

'It's not the same,' insists Charles.

'Well, no,' I agree. 'Because Steve has his arm in a sling and his foot in a cast and he can't move without assistance. Whereas Ariel can roam wherever she pleases and you do nothing to stop her.'

'Ariel is my *agent*,' says Charles.

'She's still your wife,' I point out. 'But I haven't thrown a strop about it.'

Although I'm throwing one now.

'Look, I'm sorry about Steve being here,' I say, a little more calmly. 'Believe me, the last thing I want is him in my house. But he can't manage by himself and he needs some support. What was I supposed to do?'

There's a pause before Charles replies, and then he tells me that it was very unfair of Steve to put me on the spot, but that he understands, though he can't help feeling jealous.

'Jealous?' I laugh. 'You've nothing to be jealous about.'

'My beautiful fiancée is shacked up with a younger man,' he says. 'Of course I'm jealous.'

'A younger man who can't actually move without help,' I point out.

'Oh, all right,' he concedes. 'Let's talk in the morning.'

'I love you.'

'I love you too.'

I breathe a sigh of relief as I end the call.

Ariel

I get into the office early because I've lots of emails to answer and calls to make. I'm always happiest when I'm working, when I'm doing good deals for my authors and spreading the news of their achievements as far and wide as I can. Today I'm thrilled to tell Penny Blackwater that I've got a great offer for her next book from a really prestigious US publisher, and I'm just as excited as her when she shrieks with joy down the phone. Penny's news puts me in a great mood for the rest of the morning, and I've been working for four hours without a break when my phone rings. It's Josh Carmody. We haven't spoken since I dropped him home in a cab, although he did text the following day to apologise for drinking too much.

He's brisk and businesslike as he talks about a glitch in the accounts programme that has been sorted, and says that even though I didn't really need to know about it, he likes to keep me in the loop. I thank him for that and ask how things are going with Paula. He says he's got a solicitor, and I laugh when he tells me the name, as it's the same woman I've got looking after my own divorce.

'Sheedy is great,' says Josh. 'So smart.'

'Efficient for sure,' I agree. 'In our case, most of the work is already done. It's getting it over the final hurdle that matters.'

'Don't you find it difficult while you're still working with Charles?'

'No, because we've been amicable about everything.'

'I wish Paula and I were amicable,' he says.

'You're not?'

'She's looking for so much, and I don't . . . Oh, feck it, Ariel. Maybe I'm so angry with her that I'm making it more difficult than it needs to be.'

'Charles and I worked out the finances very quickly,' I told him. 'If you tell yourself you're paying for a peaceful life rather than giving her something for nothing, it's easier to deal with.'

'You got a good deal out of him,' Josh points out.

'That's because I'm a good negotiator.'

'Would you be available to meet for lunch again?' he asks. 'Perhaps point me in the right direction?'

'I'm sure Sheedy is already doing that,' I say.

'All the same, it'd be nice to get another viewpoint,' he says. 'Also, I promise to stick to water. I'm mortified that I drank too much the last time we met.'

'Oh, don't worry about it,' I say. 'We're all entitled to drown our sorrows from time to time. Let me check my diary and I'll send you some dates.'

'Perfect,' says Josh. 'Looking forward to seeing you, Ariel.'

I realise as I put my phone away that I'm looking forward to seeing him too. Josh is a decent guy and I want to help him if I can.

I make myself a coffee. The sky is bright and the rectangle of lawn is lush and green. I step outside with the hot Americano, revelling in the weak warmth of the sun and thinking that although it's technically winter, the last few days have held the promise of spring. Spring, when the leaves begin to unfurl and the evenings grow lighter, is my favourite time of year. It's full of promise for the months ahead, and I tell myself that it's full of promise for the agency too.

I glance up at the main house and Charles's writing room. I wonder if he's sitting at his desk working on his edits. He's still complaining about Sydney's continuous amendments and suggestions, and I decide to give her another call and ask if she isn't micromanaging him too much. If some of the changes she wants to make aren't simply for the sake of it.

Before I get the chance, my mobile buzzes again.

'Ellis,' I say in surprise. 'How are things?'

'Fine, fine,' she replies. 'I'm in town today and thought you might like to meet up.'

I mentally run through my to-do list.

'Later this afternoon?' I suggest. 'Are you planning on seeing Charles? Do you want to come here?'

'I texted him, but he hasn't answered.'

'He's editing,' I explain.

'In that case, yes, I'll drop by your office after I've finished my shopping and call up to him afterwards. He's not going to be shut away all day, is he?'

'Who knows,' I reply. 'But if he's been working all morning, he'll probably be up for a break by the afternoon.'

'Great,' she says. 'I'll see you around four.'

I walk back into the office and put my cup in the slimline dishwasher. Charles freaked out when I said I was buying a dishwasher. He wanted to know why a sink wasn't good enough for me.

'Because I can hide cups and plates in a dishwasher,' I explained, and he shook his head and told me I was ruining him. I gave him a dark look, and he backtracked and said that if I wanted to throw good money away on a dishwasher, that was entirely up to me.

I return to my emails.

A short time later, my phone buzzes with a text message.

Fed up with editing. Syd is a slave driver. I've had to completely rewrite Chapter 20 now. I'm going out for a sandwich. Want to join me?

I can't. Expecting a call. Need to be here

Will bring one back for you if you like

That'd be great, thanks

OK, see you later

Charles hardly ever goes out to get sandwiches. I need to take advantage of it when he does. Meanwhile I get in touch with Sydney and ask about the amount of rewriting Charles is having to do. She concedes that she's been very demanding, but insists it's only because she wants the very best for him. We chat about holding off on any more suggestions for the time being, and I end the call pleased with myself for fixing something else for him.

It's much later by the time he comes back with a rather sad-looking wrap that he tells me he picked up in the petrol station.

'Sorry,' he says. 'Iseult called and I got distracted, and then there was a huge queue at the deli and I couldn't be bothered to wait, so I popped into the pub and had a quick toastie.'

I briefly think about murdering him, but I take the wrap (chicken Caesar; where would fast-food outlets be without bloody chicken Caesar) and put on the kettle.

'Do you want a cup of tea?' I ask.

'Coffee,' says Charles.

'Make it yourself so,' I say. 'The machine is on.'

He busies himself with the machine while I make myself tea and tear open the wrap. It's actually not as bad as it looks, though the mysterious dressing drips onto my desk and forms an unappetising puddle.

'How's things?' Charles flops into one of the armchairs as I wipe it away.

I tell him I've been talking to Sydney and she hasn't seen any more major changes to be made in his novel.

'Praise the Lord,' he says.

'No. Praise me.'

He grins.

'D'you think it would be naff to have my wedding in the garden?' he asks suddenly.

'Charles, I really don't want to discuss your wedding.'

'Why not?' He looks surprised 'I thought you'd be interested. And pleased to get me off your hands.'

'You're not on my hands any more,' I say. 'At least, not in the personal sense.'

'D'you think there's a chance we could make a drama series out of *A Caribbean Calypso*?' He veers from the personal to the professional again.

'I'm not sure it lends itself to an entire series.'

'They could use the main character in other settings, though. It'd be fantastic. I'm sure you could sell it if you try hard enough.'

I think again about murdering him, and wonder how Janice Jermyn would plot it.

'Iseult's mum is anxious for her to set a date.' Charles returns to the subject of his wedding. 'She and her husband will be back from their cruise soon. I'll have to meet them.' He grins. 'The future son-in-law meeting the parents-in-law. A great dramatic moment.'

'I'm sure you'll get on fine,' I say.

'We did on FaceTime.' He drains his coffee and then goes back to the machine to make another. 'Are you in bad form?' he asks. 'You seem snarky.'

'I was a long time waiting for my sandwich,' I reply.

'Sorry,' he says again, although without a hint of apology in his voice.

'What's the situation with Iseult's ex-fiancé?' I wasn't going to bring it up, but I'm pissed off with Charles and want to annoy him. I'm perversely glad to see his face darken.

'He's holed up in her house waiting for her to come home,' he replies. 'She should've told him to eff off.'

'I would've.'

'I know. But Iseult is such a softie.'

'Is she? I'm sure you don't get to be a customs officer by being soft.'

'I presume she does her job well. But personally I think she was too soft in letting her ex stay with her,' he admits. 'I don't like that he managed to persuade her just because he cracked a rib or something.'

'You're jealous?'

'A bit.'

'It's not your best character trait.' I click on my computer screen. 'Anything else?'

'No.'

'In that case, can you take a hike? I'm really busy.'

'All right, all right. It was just . . .'

'What?'

'I need to be friends with you, Ariel. I know I've upset you with Iseult, but you and I . . . Well, you'll always be important to me.'

'And for as long as you're writing your bestsellers, you'll always be important to me,' I tell him without looking up from the screen.

'You're being very hard on me today.'

He leaves the office and walks up to the house. I see the light go on in his study.

I'm glad he's working.

I go back to work myself.

I'm absorbed in the finer details of a new contract for Lucy Conway (who, despite being violently ill in the early stages of her pregnancy, has almost finished her current work-in-progress and has already sent me a synopsis for the next) when there's a tap on the door and Ellis walks in.

I'd forgotten she was calling by.

'Am I interrupting?' she asks. 'You look very fierce.'

'Busy.' I push my chair back from the desk and lead her upstairs to the library area. 'How are you?'

'Not bad,' she says. 'Getting quite a lot of overseas orders for my stuff, which is great.'

'Fantastic. I'm delighted for you.'

I make us both coffee, though I really shouldn't have any more caffeine. I'm jumpy enough as it is today.

333

She chats away about her work and her designs, and when she's finished her cappuccino, she asks for an update.

'On what?'.

'The divorce. The wedding. Everything.'

'Ask Charles.' Even I can hear how abrupt my tone is.

'Are you OK, Ariel?'

'I'm fine. Just fed up with all the drama around him. It's distracting me from real life.'

'Oh dear. What's the latest drama?'

I tell her about Iseult and her ex and that Charles was in my office earlier looking for reassurance.

'He's probably madly jealous. And suspicious,' says Ellis.

'His jealousy's not endearing,' I remark. 'It never was. Though if the ex is too badly injured to look after himself, he's too badly injured to make a play for Iseult.'

'Oh, but you know how women are with helpless men. Fluttering around them and fulfilling their every wish.'

I laugh.

'Charles is still a feckin' eejit for breaking up with you,' says Ellis.

'We broke up with each other,' I correct her.

'Even so. I bet you'd have stayed with him if he'd been better behaved.'

'Depends on what you mean,' I say. 'He never really got over me having other clients in the agency. I think he thought it was strictly for him only.'

'That was part of it. But that whole thing with your other author . . .'

'It wouldn't have mattered if we'd been in a good place ourselves at the time.'

'Huh,' she says. 'As far as I'm concerned, Charles was

being a selfish pig. You had a little flirty thing that didn't come to anything. He should have cut you some slack.'

'I'm not sure I would have cut him any in the same circumstances.'

'Of course you would. Anyhow, regardless of the past, when it comes to the present you need to remember that you're an independent woman. Like me. We deserve to work hard, enjoy our triumphs and be supported. And that support should come not just when Charles or some other man has time for it, but always.'

'Goodness,' I say. 'You're totally embracing your inner feminist today.'

'Possibly.' She smiles. 'And you're possibly better off without my brother, even if I'm not so sure he's better off without you.'

'Who knows?' I shrug, then glance up at the study window of Riverside Lodge. The light is still glowing. I tell Ellis that I hope he's working right now.

'I texted him a short time ago,' she says. 'He's expecting me. I have to warn you, Ariel. We're going to meet her. The fiancée.'

'You and Charles? Now?'

'No. Me and Mum. On Saturday night. He's invited us to dinner.'

'I hope your mother likes her better than she liked me.'

'Mum respected you,' Ellis tells me. 'That's far more important than liking you.'

She might be right about that.

Chapter 31

Iseult

You can fix anything but a blank page.
Nora Roberts

Steve is staying with me until his parents return. I can't turn him out of the house when he needs help to do even the simplest of tasks, and although I'm out at work during the day, at least I'm there at night to look after him. Also, I asked Trisha Castle next door if she'd mind popping in from time to time, and she was delighted to help out.

Charles asks if Steve couldn't book himself into a nursing home for a few days.

'Even if we could find one at short notice, I doubt very much he could afford it,' I say when he calls me to say this. I'm doing some form-filling so welcome the distraction, even though I don't really want to talk about Steve again.

'Doesn't he have health insurance?' Charles asks.

'I don't know.'

'You were going to marry him and you don't even know if he has health insurance?'

'I don't know if you have it either,' I point out.

'I do.'

'Oh good. Because it's a deal-breaker, you know.' I make a face at the phone. It's a voice call, so he doesn't see it.

'I'm sorry,' says Charles. 'I'm pissed off because our night was ruined, and you're saying that freeloader will be with you for a while, and I'm betting you won't be able to come over to me because you'll be looking after him.'

'It's only a few days,' I say. 'Then I'm all yours again.'

'It's as well that I love you.'

'What's not to love?'

I hear the sound of a buzzer and he tells me he has a visitor. I feel my heart sink as I jump to the conclusion that it's Ariel, but he tells me that it's his sister, Ellis. I'm meeting her and Charles's mum on Saturday night. He's organised dinner at his house. I'm looking forward to it in an anxious sort of way.

He's getting a chef – an actual chef, for heaven's sake – to cook the meal for us. I've heard of dinner parties where people hire chefs, but it doesn't usually happen with the people I know. When he told me about it, I suggested Celeste could do it for him instead. He looked as though he was thinking seriously about it for a moment, then said it was better to stick with the chef he knows. 'We could ask Celeste another time,' he told me. 'Try her out.'

I was a little offended on Celeste's behalf, because she most certainly doesn't need to be tried out, but as Charles seemed anxious about the dinner, I said nothing.

I leave him to his sister and complete my form filling. Then Natasha tells me that the latest ship has arrived, and we drive down to it together. My mind switches to work mode and I stop thinking about Charles and his family and his catering arrangements.

Today's drama is an overloaded white van that tries to evade the barriers and ends up stuck outside the foot passenger building. Ken and Mateusz detain the driver, who has a large supply of power tools and four black sacks full of cash in his van. Not surprisingly, he hadn't made a declaration that he was travelling with a substantial amount of cash, as he was supposed to do, and given that he seemed to be trying to make a getaway, Ken seizes the cash and calls the Gardaí.

These are the kind of dramas I like in my life. Not ex-boyfriends nearly getting killed in motorcycle accidents and taking up residence in my house, or having dinner with my new boyfriend's mother and sister for the first time.

Steve is in a cranky mood when I get home, and I put it down to boredom and pain. I don't have the mental energy for him on my own, so I call Celeste.

'You're kidding me,' she says when I tell her about Steve. 'He's actually in your house right now?'

'Yes.'

'Do you want me to come around?'

'Could you? I'd be really grateful.'

'I'll be finished here in an hour,' she says. 'Then I'll be with you. I might reek of fish and chips, they were very popular tonight.'

'Ooh, could you do a takeaway for us?' I ask.

'I could.'

'You're an angel.'

Steve thinks so too when she turns up with foil containers of food. She's added in some mushy peas, lemon and tartar sauce too, and quite honestly, it's one of the best meals I've had in ages. Celeste is always self-deprecating about being a chef in a pub rather than a restaurant, but their standards are very high. I definitely should have insisted Charles use her instead of his own chef.

'Bloody brilliant,' says Steve, who has washed his meal down with a tin from the slab of beer that Celeste very thoughtfully brought with her too. She and I are drinking the bottle of Sauvignon Blanc I had chilling in the fridge.

'Izzy runs the best care home in the country,' Celeste tells him. 'You're lucky she was able to bring you here.'

'She's a jewel,' says Steve. 'And I'm an idiot for letting her slip through my fingers.'

There's a rather uncomfortable silence.

'You did me a favour,' I tell him. 'We wouldn't have worked out.'

'Why?' he demands. 'We're compatible, you and me.'

'When I'm doing what you want,' I tell him. 'When I'm looking after you.'

Both he and Celeste give me startled glances. I'm not surprised. I've startled myself. But it's true. Steve and I were a great couple, but only because I always fell in with his plans. We went to the places he wanted to go, we watched the TV he wanted to watch, we did the things he wanted to do. And I thought that was fine, because I thought I wanted to do those things too. In the time after Steve, I made my own choices. And I liked it.

I don't say all this, though. Instead I go into the kitchen and return with another beer for him.

Celeste is the one who changes the subject and asks Steve about his injuries. It's a good topic. He can talk about his shoulder, his wrist and his leg for hours.

*

He hasn't improved that much by Saturday, not that I was really expecting him to. The doctor said it would take about eight weeks for his collarbone and wrist to heal but that the leg could take longer. Not being mobile is really getting him down, and although I'm doing my best to stay cheerful, he's worried about his job as well as his broken bones. I reassure him as much as I can as once again I help him wash.

'This is so bloody undignified,' he complains. 'As for my face . . .'

His designer stubble is growing into a beard, and he doesn't like it.

'I'm sure your dad will be able to help with the male grooming,' I say. 'Sorry, it's not my forte.'

'And I'm sorry for grumbling,' says Steve. 'It's just . . .'

'What?'

'I keep thinking that if I hadn't broken the engagement, you'd be doing all this stuff for me because you were my wife and not as a massive favour.'

'You mean I'd be obliged to because I was married to you instead of from the goodness of my heart.' I burst out laughing. 'I'm not sure that's the flex you think it is, Steve.'

'I didn't mean . . . Oh, hell, I'm useless. Absolutely useless.' He buries his head in his hands, and I realise he's crying.

I slowly fold away the towel and tidy up the bathroom, but I don't say anything. After a while, he sniffs and sits up straight.

'Sorry,' he says. 'And sorry for keeping on saying I'm sorry.'

I shrug.

'And sorry for being the biggest idiot known to man.'

'You're not an idiot,' I tell him.

'I am,' he says. 'I'm in love with you, Izzy.'

'No you're not.'

'I am. And every time I see that ring on your finger, I want to choke the guy who put it there.'

'You'd struggle in your current condition,' I point out. He makes a face at me.

'Seriously, though,' he says. 'Do you really love him?'

'Of course I really love him.'

'But he's ancient.'

'He's only forty-nine.'

'Listen, old people can say fifty is the new thirty all they like,' says Steve. 'But it isn't. It's fifty. And that's nearly twenty whole years older than me.'

'Twenty more years of learning how not to be the biggest idiot in the world.'

'Touché,' he says. 'Izzy?'

'What?'

'Kiss me?'

'No.'

I pat his face dry and help him downstairs, leaving the remote control beside him.

Fortunately he says nothing more about being sorry he dumped me or wanting to kiss me. I know that both these things are only because he's here in my house, forced to be close to me. If he hadn't had his accident, he'd be happily going about his life not thinking about me at all. Except . . . and the thought makes me uncomfortable, he was kind of shadow-stalking me already. He was texting me. He was keeping the connection there. So perhaps he really does feel that he made a terrible mistake. I feel good about that, to be honest. Like the nerd in school who turns up to the class reunion as the most successful and beautiful person there. I know that doesn't ever happen in real life. But Steve is making me feel like it does.

When I come downstairs later in the evening, dressed for my dinner at Charles's, he looks at me with real desire in his eyes. I'm wearing the butterfly Ted Baker again, but this time with my high heels and the cute pink cardigan that Celeste bought me for Christmas. I'm also wearing more eye make-up than usual and am rocking a Selena Gomez look, if Selena had short spiky hair.

'I won't be too late back,' I tell him as I slide on my coat. 'I'll help you up to bed later.'

'I'd like to go to bed right now,' he says.

'I could get you there if that's what you want.'

'That's not what I mean.'

'I know it's not. And you've got to stop talking to me like this. I'm going to dinner with my fiancé.' Even if I've been anxious about it all day. I pick up my keys and tell him to enjoy the movie he's about to watch. Then I let myself out of the house.

The cab is waiting.

#NotLookingForwardToThis

Chapter 32

Ariel

*Talent is helpful in writing but
guts are absolutely essential.*
Jessamyn West

I didn't really have to come into the office today. I could have worked from home if I'd wanted to work at all, given that it's Saturday. But one of my authors sent a message about a misprint in their latest edition, and I don't have a hard copy of the book at the apartment, so I came to the mews to check it out. It could have waited, of course. It's not like I can do anything about it now. But I'm nothing if not efficient.

The author is right about the misprint, so I take a photo of it and send it to the publisher. Then I sit at my desk and work my way through a list of minor tasks I didn't get around to during the week. I like working on a Saturday when I know I'm not going to be distracted by phone calls and emails and sudden publishing emergencies. When I've finished, I take a few photos of my tidy desk and overfilled bookshelves and post them to the agency's Instagram account: #LiteraryLife. I'm not as good as I should be on social media, even though I do Charles's for him. Thinking of him distracts me and I look up the garden towards the house. I don't know if he's there. He might have met his mother and Ellis in town before their dinner this evening. But if so, will Iseult have met them then too? Or will she be unveiled, so to speak, later?

The dinner is at 7 p.m. I know that because he asked if I could get a chef from our usual catering company to cook it for him. I was very tempted to say that his personal life was nothing to do with me any more, but I didn't want to be petty, so I contacted Ash O'Halloran, who arranged for someone, although she said that given the short notice, the meal couldn't be from their premium menu selection, which needs additional prep. I told her that whatever menu they had was absolutely fine, so Charles and his family will be having salmon with garlic potatoes and green beans, a meal I could have cooked for him myself with my eyes closed. But there you go. If he wants to spend a fortune on getting someone to do something that's quick and easy, it's entirely up to him.

I close down my laptop and take my jacket from the back of the chair, then look up at the house again. I feel a sudden desperate need to walk along the garden path and go inside, but I clamp down on it. As I pick up my bag, it vibrates with my ringing phone.

It's Ash. I ask if everything is OK and on schedule.

'I'm really sorry,' she replies. 'We have a problem. James's father passed away today. He's been ill for a while so it's not entirely unexpected, but it was sudden. James can't make it.'

James is the chef.

'I'm very sorry for his loss.' The words are automatic. 'Who have you got instead?'

'That's the problem,' says Ash. 'We're catering for a really big party this evening and I have two other events as well. James was doing this job as an extra, and I don't have another spare chef. I thought . . . well, it's only for four people, isn't it? The starters are individual quiches, the main is salmon and the dessert is a tropical trifle. It's all very easy stuff. I wondered, if I brought everything ready prepared, would Charles be able to do it himself?'

After a moment of shocked silence, I erupt into laughter. Ash doesn't know that the absolute limit of Charles's culinary abilities is oven chips. And even then he frequently scorches them so that they're rock-hard sticks of black crunchiness.

'Not an option?' she says.

'Oh, Ash. It'd be funny if it wasn't such a disaster.'

'How about you?' she asks. 'I can have everything prepped for you and deliver it in a box on my way to Wicklow. I'd give you a printed list of timings and instructions. It couldn't be easier, Ariel, I promise you.'

'I can't . . .' I begin, and then I hesitate. Because I can. I was only thinking earlier that I could cook the salmon with my eyes shut. The tropical trifle doesn't need cooking. I'm not sure about the individual quiches, but if everything is ready to go, and Ash leaves me with clear how-to instructions, how hard can it be? All the same, it's cooking for Charles and Iseult, Ma Miller and Ellis. Cooking is not in my job description. Why would I even consider it?

I suddenly think of the plot line in Janice's latest cosy crime, where dinner guests are poisoned one by one by the cook who's catering for a party. There's only one intended target. The others are red herrings. Though obviously dead red herrings. Naturally I've no intention of *poisoning* Iseult or Ma Miller myself. All the same, if I have control of the kitchen, I could . . . Stop it, I say to myself. Just stop.

I ask Ash to explain the prepping and the recipes.

'It's dead easy,' she assures me.

'Even the quiches?'

'They're a doddle,' she says.

And so I agree to cook dinner for Charles, his sister, his mum and his fiancée.

I must be out of my mind.

I look more like a waitress than a chef in my white T-shirt and black jeans. Fortunately I have my comfy Skechers with me, so I can wear them while I'm cooking. I let myself into the house, where I check the dishwasher and see that it's full of dirty cups. I put it on a quick wash cycle and then investigate the cupboards. I doubt Charles has moved anything, but it's a while since I spent any significant time in this kitchen. When we were married, I used to cook either on Saturday or Sunday, depending on our mood. I wasn't always someone who could afford to eat in fancy restaurants, after all.

I've got all the utensils I need in place when I hear the front door open. Ellis and Ma Miller's voices waft down the stairs – Charles's mother is talking about Dublin traffic and Ellis is agreeing that it's a nightmare. Charles then tells them to go into the living room and says he'll get them a drink. I wait, immobile, in the kitchen, wondering if he's going to come downstairs. But he doesn't. I take out my phone and send him a message. A minute later, he's standing in front of me.

'What the actual . . . What's going on? Why are you here?' he asks.

I explain about the culinary crisis.

'They had no one?' He's incredulous. 'No one at all?'

'Apparently not.'

'I should've asked Iseult's cousin,' says Charles. 'Iseult suggested her, you know. She said she's a great chef, but I wanted to be loyal to Ash's company. We're never using them again, by the way. Incompetent fools. I'll make arrangements with Celeste in future.'

'We've used that company dozens of times, and this is the first occasion something has gone wrong,' I point out. 'It's hardly James's fault his father died.'

'They should have had backup,' he says.

I decide not to argue with him, but instead remark that as Iseult will be looking after the New Year's Eve party in future, she can be the one to find an alternative. (She can try, but despite today's disaster, there isn't a better company in Ireland.)

'In the meantime, I'm your best hope,' I tell him. 'Unless you want to ask Ellis to cook? Or Iseult herself?'

'She's not here yet. I told her not to come until half-six. I wanted to give Mum and Ellis time to relax.'

'How is she?'

He knows I'm talking about his mother. He knows my relationship with her was always tricky.

'She's fine. She's older, Ariel. Not as prickly.'

'Astonishing.'

'You need to go easy on her.'

'I don't. I need to stay hidden in the kitchen. Which I promise I'll do.'

'What about serving?' He looks at me in sudden horror. 'You can't serve. Iseult and Mum mustn't see you.'

'I'm sure they'd be thrilled to see me demoted to being your waitress,' I say.

'Ariel.' He gives me a hurt look. 'It isn't like that.'

'You can serve it yourself,' I tell him.

'I can't. Maybe Ellis. You could hide in the pantry when she comes to collect the plates.'

I laugh.

'Oh, OK, maybe not.'

'Can I point out that I'm doing you an enormous favour?' I say. 'Otherwise you'd be ordering takeaway from the Golden Pond or El Molino.'

'Maybe we should go out instead,' he muses.

'Like you'll get a table for four in Dublin on a Saturday night without a reservation.'

He sighs.

'It'll be fine,' I assure him. 'It's always fine when I'm in charge.'

'That's true,' says Charles.

I smile at him, and he smiles back.

Although somewhat reluctantly.

Iseult

I arrive at Charles's house at exactly 6.30, a floral arrangement in my arms. It only occurred to me as the cab crossed the river that I hadn't brought anything for his mum, so when we drove past a large Spar shop in Milltown, I asked the driver to stop. I'd been thinking of chocolates, but the floral arrangements at the doorway were pretty and so I bought one of those instead. Unfortunately, some pollen from the tiger lilies has come off on my pink cardigan, and as I wait for Charles to answer the door, I make matters worse by rubbing it.

'You're here!' He beams at me. 'And precisely on time.'

It's as well we stopped for flowers. Otherwise I would've been early.

'Am I first?' I ask.

He shakes his head. 'Mum and Ellis are here already. We're having cocktails in the living room. Are those for me?'

'Your mum.' I show him the pollen mark on my cardi, but he shrugs and says it doesn't matter.

'I'll warn her in advance, though,' I say. 'I wouldn't like my gift to destroy her clothes.'

'Don't sweat it,' he tells me. 'It's fine.'

He pushes open the door to the living room and I step inside. The two women turn to look at me.

Seeing his mother, it's very clear where Charles gets his looks from. She's an angular woman, very thin, though that's probably because of her age, but with the same arctic-blue eyes and the same chiselled features. Her iron-grey hair, flecked with silver, is scooped back into a chignon that's finished off by a black velvet bow. She's wearing a houndstooth-check skirt and jacket, and a cream blouse. Her nails are varnished in ruby red.

Slight though she may be, she's dominating the room.

Beside her, Ellis, who I recognise from Charles's Christmas photos, is dressed more casually in an emerald-green silk shirt over skinny jeans and a lot of funky jewellery. Her mother has a lot of jewellery too, but it's recognisably expensive – probably, I think, from Warren's.

'So you're the new fiancée,' says Mrs Boyd-Miller. 'I'm glad we finally get to meet.'

'Me too.' I thrust the floral arrangement at her. 'Be careful of the tiger lilies.'

'Thank you.' She takes it from me and immediately puts it on the sideboard.

'I'm Ellis,' says his sister. 'Good to meet you.'

'And you.'

'What would you like to drink?' asks Charles. 'Actually, scrub that. We have champagne. I should've served it first.'

'There's really no need—' begins his mother, but Charles has already left the room, leaving the three of us standing looking at each other.

It's Ellis who tries to get the conversation going by asking if I've come directly from work. I'm taken aback by the question, given that I'm wearing my prettiest clothes rather than my hi-vis jacket, even if there is pollen on my cardigan.

'I wish I could dress like this for work,' I say. 'But I'm not sure how effective I'd be.'

'Of course, you're at the front line of securing our borders.' Her eyes twinkle. '*Border Patrol* is one of my favourite TV programmes.'

'It's not quite as exciting as it appears there,' I say.

'Aw, don't say that and shatter my illusions.' She smiles at me.

'Do you read at all?' demands Mrs Boyd-Miller.

I tell them about my love of crime.

'I heard you were responsible for Charlie's shift in genre,' says Ellis. 'What an influence you've had on him!'

Her words are kind, but Mrs Boyd-Miller purses her lips and says she hopes I haven't caused him to ruin his career. 'All that effort establishing himself as a proper, serious author, and for what?' she adds. 'To be laughed at.'

'He won't be laughed at,' I say.

'Who won't be laughed at?' Charles returns with the bottle of champagne. Nobody tells him we were talking about him, and he doesn't pursue the question. Instead he fills four glasses and hands them around. 'To Iseult,' he says, raising his. 'The love of my life and my wife-to-be.'

'You have to get rid of the old one first,' says Mrs Boyd-Miller. 'Though that's not a hardship.'

'It's all in hand.' Charles sounds irritated, but I like that his mother isn't an Ariel fan. Though given what she said about me potentially ruining Charles's career, I'm not sure she's a fan of me either.

'Anyway,' he continues, 'tonight is about moving forward and letting you get to know my darling Iseult.'

'Tell us about yourself.' Mrs Boyd-Miller looks at me. 'How did you move from being with the revenue inspectors to helping Charles with his book.'

'I work in Customs, not Revenue,' I tell her. 'And I didn't help Charles with his book.'

'Oh, but to listen to him, you practically wrote it for him!' cries his mother. 'He credits you with everything. Which is great if it goes well, not so good if it's a terrible flop.'

'It won't be a flop,' I say.

'I love your confidence in it.' Ellis raises her glass.

'The success or failure of my book has nothing to do with Iseult,' says Charles. 'It's all down to me. I'm the author, after all. Do you want to see the proposed cover?'

There's a chorus of yeses, and he takes out his phone to show us a Caribbean location with a corpse on the beach. It's bang on trend for cosy crime, though Pamela thinks it could be more noir.

'Xerxes are doing a good job,' concedes Charles. 'Now come on, everyone. Time to eat.'

We walk across the hall to the dining room, which overlooks the garden. Charles has turned on the outside lights and they illuminate the bare branches of the trees. I can't quite believe that very soon this will be my house and my garden. As I take my seat at the polished mahogany table, I feel my phone buzz in my bag. I check the messages and see Steve's name.

This movie is crap

I don't reply.

Ariel

Even though Ash has provided ready-baked pastry cases, I'm nervous about the quiches. I've never cooked quiche before, and something in the back of my mind tells me it's probably like a soufflé and could go horribly wrong. I'm peering in through the glass door of the oven watching them anxiously when Charles comes into the kitchen.

'Something smells good,' he says.

'I hope they taste as good as they smell.' I check my watch even though the oven is on a timer and there's three minutes to go.

'I'm sure they will.' He walks around the kitchen island

looking at the plates onto which I've already placed the accompanying rocket, pecan and cranberry salad. The salad is bright and vibrant against the plain blue plates, and the quiche will only add to the colour.

'Don't touch them,' I warn him. 'Everything is exactly so.'

'I wouldn't dream of it.'

'You can bring up the bread,' I tell him. 'It's in the basket, along with some pats of butter. Then come back for the quiches.'

He nods and disappears with the bread, and I release a sigh of relief. I'm not comfortable with him looking over my shoulder, and I'm terrified that if he stays in the kitchen too long, someone will come to see what's going on. I really don't want to be outed as tonight's chef. The mortification level would be huge.

The oven pings and I take out the quiches. I allow them to cool slightly before arranging them neatly on the plates. I'm pleased at my efforts, even though one of them has far too much bacon and another has hardly any. I think of the cosy crime again and look at the quiche with too much bacon. I tell myself that everything will be fine.

Where the hell is Charles? I told him to come back straight away; he's obviously chatting to his guests. I take out my phone and message him, but it's nearly a minute before he returns.

'Sorry, sorry,' he says. 'We were talking about book covers and interior design.'

I raise an eyebrow. Charles and I had many interior design conversations in which I tried to interest him in fabric and colours but failed miserably.

'Iseult wants to redecorate. She follows some woman on Instagram and likes her stuff.'

I make no comment, but tell him to get upstairs with two of the plates then come back straight away for the others.

The one in your left hand is your mother's. The other is for Iseult,' I say.

'What difference does it make?' he demands.

'Just do what I say, for heaven's sake.'

'I'll be knackered running up and down like an eejit,' he complains. 'I don't see why you couldn't have got someone to serve. I'm sure if you'd insisted, the catering company would've managed it.'

I think about hitting him over the head with the baking tray, but I don't. Instead I get the salmon ready for the oven by pouring Ash's glaze over it. The garlic potatoes have already been cooking for a while, so they should be ready at the same time as the salmon. I don't need instructions for the green beans.

I pour myself a glass of sparkling water. I'd really like to raid the wine, but I need a clear head, at least until the main courses are upstairs. I sit on the sofa and allow myself a sigh of relief. The things I do for my clients. Admittedly this is exceptional, but I've been known to rush out and buy Strepsils for an author who suddenly developed a sore throat before a reading (in the middle of a forest, a half-hour drive to the nearest village and back again), or lend one of my female authors my own bra when the strap on hers broke at a literary festival. Not exactly as crazy as celebrities' agents, I know, but problem-solving all the same.

The oven pings and I check the salmon, which is perfectly done. The potatoes are done too, and the garlicky smell is making me hungry. I'm about to text Charles, but then remember I haven't done the green beans. I swear under my breath and turn on the hob.

'Ariel? What on earth are you doing here?'

I spin around and see Ellis standing in the doorway with two empty plates and the accompanying cutlery.

'Shh,' I hiss.

'Are you *cooking*?' Her voice is a whispered squeak of disbelief. 'You can't be. Not our dinner.'

'It was an emergency.' I fill her in, and she stares at me.

'Are you mad? We could have eaten out. Or ordered in. You shouldn't be cooking for us, for heaven's sake!'

'It was far too late to get reservations. Besides, Charles wanted a proper dinner for you.'

'To meet his fiancée?' Ellis snorts.

'How's it going up there?' I definitely wish I'd opened the wine.

'Mum is giving her the third degree, but she's holding up quite well.'

'Charles said you were talking about the book cover.'

'Oh yes. Mum thinks it should be more noir. The fiancée is pretending to agree with her.'

'For feck's sake!' My cry isn't because of the stupid book cover (although it could have been) but because I'd forgotten about the beans and the water has boiled over.

'Sorry, I'm distracting you,' says Ellis. 'I didn't think you were such a great cook. Those quiches were wonderful.'

'Not all my own doing,' I admit as I turn off the hob and deal with the water spillage. 'Why are you down here anyway? It's Charles who's supposed to be helping.'

'He was chatting away to Mum and Izzy. He told me not

to bother, but you know what he's like. I thought I'd help. You can't cook and wait tables. You shouldn't be doing it at all, for God's sake.'

'I know it's a bit mad, but I've done worse.' I shrug. 'I did actually wait tables when I was at college. I'd probably be better at that than Charles.'

'Mum was a bit surprised when he turned up with the starters all right.' Ellis grins. 'He said the kitchen was short-staffed.'

'He'll get the short end of my staff in a minute,' I mutter.

'Let me give you a hand.'

Between us, Ellis and I set up the plates with the main course. She says she'll bring two up and send Charles down for the others.

'Tell him to bring down the other plates and cutlery too,' I say.

'Izzy didn't eat the quiche,' Ellis informs me. 'She says she's allergic to eggs. But she ate the salad.'

I allow myself a slight sigh of relief. In a moment of madness, I'd added extra jalapeño to hers. Not enough to make her ill or anything, but enough to make her splutter all the same. I regretted it the moment Charles went upstairs with the plates. All the time I've been cooking, I've been waiting anxiously to hear if she's OK, (a) because it was a horrible thing to do and I'm really not a horrible person; and (b) because I realised that it wouldn't be me who'd get the blame for the spicy quiche, it'd be Ash, and that wouldn't be fair.

Clearly I'd never make the cut as a murderer. Maybe it's just as well.

Chapter 33

Iseult

*You can't blame a writer for
what the characters say.*
Truman Capote

I'm a little embarrassed I couldn't eat the starter of quiche
because of my egg allergy. It's not the worst allergy a person
could have, but I come out in hives almost immediately and
every part of my body itches like crazy. The last thing I want
is to have an allergic reaction in front of Mrs Boyd-Miller
(she's asked me to call her Pamela, but it feels all wrong and
so I'm trying not to use her name at all). I don't feel she'd
be totally sympathetic to uncontrollable scratching at the
dinner table, so I pick at the salad instead, which is very, very
tasty. I say this to Charles, who's still a bit flustered about
me not wanting the quiche, and the fact that some kind of
kitchen emergency meant he had to bring up the starters
himself, not that this is any big deal in my book given that
our kitchen and dining room at home are the same space.

When Ellis says she'll help by taking the empty plates to
the kitchen, Charles jumps up and tells her that she's not

to bother and that he'll do it himself. His mother comments on the inconvenience of it and he agrees, saying he's considering asking Celeste to cook in the future. Though he adds that it's not as though he entertains so often that he needs catering staff anyhow.

'I keep telling you you should have more soirées,' says Pamela.

'Soirées?' He raises an eyebrow and I muffle a giggle.

'Scoff all you like, but there's nothing wrong with great writers hosting evenings where people can talk about literature and discuss the important matters of the day,' she says.

'We usually do that in the pub,' says Charles. He looks around. 'Oh hell, where's Ellis?'

'She went to get the mains while you were talking,' I tell him, and am surprised to see an anguished look pass over his face.

'Maybe I should—'

'Hey, everyone.' Ellis walks in with two plates of salmon. 'Here we go. Chas, can you nip downstairs and bring up the others.'

'Is everything OK?' He looks at her anxiously.

'Fine,' she says. 'Your substitute chef is working away happily, doing a great job.'

He walks quickly out of the room while Ellis puts plates in front of me and her mother. I look at it in relief. I can eat salmon.

'Charles tells me you have a book club,' I say to Pamela 'And that you're on the radio.'

'I'm the chair of a small but influential gathering, yes,' she says. 'And as such, I'm sometimes asked to share my reviews and expertise.'

'Mum's club was on that TV book programme with Mairin McGettigan last autumn,' says Ellis. 'Did you see it?'

'No.' I shake my head. 'I don't watch much TV, to be honest.'

'That's nice to hear,' says Pamela. 'Too many people spend too much time watching television these days.'

'But there are some great series being made,' says Ellis. 'Particularly on the streaming services.'

Pamela holds up her hand. 'I don't need to know. I have one cable service and that's more than enough. Because no matter how often I search the programmes, there's never anything worth watching.'

'Did you watch the movie of *Winter's Heartbreak* on TV?' I ask.

'We went to the Dublin premiere,' says Pamela. 'It was a wonderful evening.'

'I hope the new book is made into a movie,' I say. 'I'd love to go to a premiere.'

'It can take years.' Pamela sounds like she's had lots of experience with movie deals. 'And even then, something can throw it off course.'

'It's an exciting prospect all the same,' says Ellis. 'And I'm sure Ariel . . .' she pauses. 'I'm sure his agent is working hard on his behalf as usual.'

'You can say her name,' I tell her, then turn my attention to the salmon in front of me, even though Charles hasn't returned with the other two plates yet and I should really wait until he does.

'This must all be quite overwhelming for you, Iseult,' says Pamela. 'Mixing in these circles.'

'If you mean the movie business, I haven't met anyone to do with it yet,' I say.

'Not only the movies. Important writers like Charles.'

I'm not sure how I'm supposed to respond to that.

'Have you worked out your living arrangements?' she asks.

'Our living arrangements?' I look at her in confusion.

'How you're going to manage when you're getting up in the middle of the night to catch drug smugglers,' she says. 'You can't disturb Charles. He needs his sleep. And you can't disturb him if you're off during the day either, because he needs his creative space.'

'I'm sure we'll manage. After all, I need my sleep too and sometimes that's during the day. I don't spend my whole life catching smugglers either,' I add. 'It can be more mundane than that.'

'You've got to understand that being married to Charles isn't like being married to an ordinary person,' Pamela says.

'No, it's like being married to a man-child,' Ellis pipes up.

I laugh.

'Seriously,' she says. 'For someone who's supposedly so brilliant at writing women, he can be an absolute pain to live with.'

'You're being very harsh,' says Pamela.

'Oh, come on, Mum. Ariel did her best, but it was difficult for her. He was always interrupting her at work. Drove her nuts.'

I say nothing. Pamela tells Ellis that Ariel was the one who did all the interrupting.

'No she didn't,' says Ellis. 'She gave him more than enough of your so-called creative space. He was the one who was under her feet.'

'Nonsense,' says Pamela.

'Anyhow,' Ellis turns to me, 'don't let him walk all over you. He's the kind of person that if you give him an inch takes a few miles. Start as you mean to go on.'

'I'll keep that in mind.'

'Have you met Ariel?' asks Pamela.

'Yes.' I keep my voice as relaxed as I can, but I stab my salmon like a victim in a Janice Jermyn book.

'What did you think?'

'She's very focused.'

'Multi-talented,' says Ellis. 'Can turn her hand to anything for Chas, and often does.'

I don't know why she smiles when she says this.

'I'll admit she's done well for him as an agent,' says Pamela. 'But really and truly, he could've had a better wife.'

'In what way could she have been a better wife?' I ask, delighted that the conversation has turned towards dissing his agent-slash-soon-to-be-divorced-ex.

'You can't have two very ambitious people in a marriage,' says Pamela. 'Something's got to give.'

Everyone seems to have the same view about Ariel's ambition. Even though I don't want to sympathise, I can't help feeling a little sorry for her. Why shouldn't she be ambitious?

'If she wasn't so driven, she wouldn't have got him all those deals,' I remark.

'All she ever thought about was how good he was for her agency,' argues Pamela. 'She forgot he was her husband too.'

And they're off again, making the case for and against Ariel as a wife. I'm thinking they'll start on me next, but fortunately Charles returns with the other plates of salmon.

He puts one in his place and one in front of Ellis and asks what we were talking about.

'Ariel,' says Ellis.

Charles, who'd popped some potato in his mouth, starts to cough.

'Hot,' he says. 'Sorry.'

'The potato? Or Ariel?'

'For crying out loud, Ellis.' He glares at her.

'I was just wondering,' she says.

'Well don't.'

There's a definite atmosphere whenever Ariel's name is mentioned, and it's not because they're being sensitive around me.

'Did you like her?' I ask Ellis.

'She always, always did her best for Charles,' she replies. 'Still does. Goes above and beyond. No job too big or too small. Or too personal.'

I glance at him. He's glowering at his sister now and says that it's in Ariel's best interests to make sure his life is hassle-free.

'You'll be expected to keep it hassle-free too,' she says to me. 'If you run into problems, just let me know.'

'It *will* be hassle-free with me,' I tell her. 'I'm low-maintenance.'

'What about your wedding?' she asks. 'Is that going to be low-maintenance too, or something grand and glamorous?'

'We haven't really talked about it much.' I glance at Charles. 'He's been so busy with his book . . .'

'Oh, for feck's sake, Chas!' Ellis gives her brother an exasperated look. 'Get with the programme. You need to start planning.'

'Not before his divorce,' says Pamela.

'Why not?' asks Ellis. 'Are you expecting him to back out?'

I shoot her a horrified look.

'Sorry, Izzy. I didn't mean that he would. I'm sure he can't wait to tie the knot with you.'

'For your information, I have a meeting with Laurence on Monday.' Charles's tone is frosty. 'So there's no issue about the divorce, and yes, darling Iseult, we'll get on with our plans straight away.'

'Great.' I smile at him. He reaches for my hand and holds it tightly.

'So what happened to the original caterer that meant you needed a substitute chef?' I ask, deciding a change of subject is a good idea.

'It's not important.' Charles doesn't look at me.

'The stand-in is excellent.' Ellis beams at him and he gives her another glare. 'This salmon is wonderful.'

'I'm definitely using Iseult's friend in future,' he mutters.

'Does she have her own company, or does she work in a restaurant?' asks Ellis.

'In a pub,' I say.

'A pub!' Pamela looks at me with genuine interest. 'So she does sandwiches and lasagne, that sort of thing?'

'It's a gastro-pub,' I say. 'It's a very diverse menu and the food is great.'

'Mum thinks every pub is like Miller's.' Charles shrugs. 'Honest Food for Honest People is our motto, although not all the regulars there could be categorised as honest. Joey Harte was done for tax avoidance a few years ago, and wasn't Mattie McDonagh jailed for that scam with the animal feed?'

'Really, Charles, there's no need to speak about our clientele like that,' says Pamela. 'Yes, some of them have had difficulties in the past, but I always say let bygones be bygones. Besides, the pub food is different to the restaurant's offering.'

'We're always happy to take their money, no matter where it comes from,' agrees Charles.

'You shouldn't be saying this in front of someone who works with the Gardaí,' remarks Ellis.

'I don't—'

My words are drowned by a loud clatter from downstairs, and a muffled swear.

'I'd better check what's happened,' says Charles, who's on his feet immediately.

'I'll go with you.'

Ellis pushes back her chair and both of them hurry out, leaving me sitting with Pamela, who shakes her head and says that no matter what Charles thinks of his caterer, you can't get good staff any more. She asks about my friend the pub chef, so I tell her about Celeste, how great she is, and then add that she's my cousin, in case Pamela puts her foot in it by saying something disparaging about pub chefs again.

'You're close?' She looks enquiringly at me.

'Like sisters,' I confirm.

'I wish my family was closer,' she says, and there's a real sense of regret in her voice. 'Charles and his brother are chalk and cheese, and Ellis . . . well, she's a good girl, but she lacks ambition.'

'I thought you didn't like ambitious women,' I remark.

'Excuse me?'

'You didn't seem to like Ariel's ambition.'

'Because she put it above Charles.'

'Wasn't she entitled to?'

'She was certainly entitled to be ambitious *for* him. That brought her success. It should have been enough.'

'And Ellis?' I ask. 'What should she be doing?'

'She should move from that airy-fairy arty-farty stuff she's doing and be more commercial,' says Pamela.

'Surely if she's happy, that's all that matters?'

Pamela snorts.

'And *you* have your literary circle,' I add. 'Clearly you're ambitious enough for all of them if you're on the airwaves.'

'I'm not ambitious for me, only my sons,' she says.

'Not Ellis?'

'No point any more.'

I feel sorry for Ellis, who's being so completely dismissed by her mother. But I suddenly understand where tensions could have arisen between Charles and Ariel. Because if he's inherited his mother's way of looking at things, I can see why he thought she was too ambitious for herself and not ambitious enough for him. Even though she clearly was.

My phone buzzes.

I'm going to turn into a pot of tea. I've had at least half a dozen cups already. Are you having fun?

Steve loves his tea. Half a dozen cups is nothing to him. I tap out a quick reply saying that meeting the future in-laws is never exactly fun.

Maybe it's you, not the future in-laws

I grimace as I recall meeting Steve's mum. Although

significantly younger than Pamela Boyd-Miller, Lorraine Carter has a lot in common with her. Mostly the belief that her son is a genius and no woman is good enough for him. I reply with a non-committal emoji and put my phone back in my bag.

'You know that's immensely rude,' says Pamela.

'Yes. But a sick friend is staying at my house, so I needed to check up on him.'

'Him?'

'Yes.'

'And Charles is agreeable to this?'

'It's not up to him to be agreeable or not,' I say.

Her eyes narrow. 'You're not dissimilar after all,' she says. 'I thought you were. You're quieter. Younger too, obviously. And more in awe of him. But you're like her in some ways.'

'Like who?'

'Ariel, of course,' says Pamela.

She's comparing me to the first Mrs Miller.

That's surely not a good thing.

Chapter 34

Ariel

Only a mediocre person is always at his best.
W. Somerset Maugham

I'm nursing my burnt hand when Charles bursts into the kitchen, followed by Ellis.

'Are you all right?'

'What happened?'

They speak at the same time.

'I forgot the hob was on and left an empty pot on it,' I reply. 'Burnt my hand on the handle.'

'Let me see.'

Ellis gently unclenches my fist. The burnt strip across my palm is red and angry. She turns on the tap and holds my hand under the cold water. I whimper.

'Any tea bags?' she asks Charles.

He goes to the cupboard and takes out a tin.

'Used tea bags, you idiot,' she says.

He takes the lid off a ceramic pot on the low shelf behind the sink and wrinkles his nose.

'Are you sure?' he asks. 'I'm never convinced about your home remedies.'

'The tannic acid in the tea is an analgesic,' says Ellis as she dries my hand then puts a cold tea bag on the burn. It does help a little, but I tell her there might be some Savlon in the first-aid box in the cupboard. Charles takes it down, and it's pretty much as it was the day I left, with neatly rolled bandages, a selection of plasters and a few ointments.

'Check the best-before date,' I tell him as he takes out a tube of cream.

'Three days to go,' he says. 'You should be safe.'

I remove the tea bag and apply the cream. My hand is throbbing.

'The things I do for you,' I say to Charles.

'You didn't have to,' says Ellis. 'He could've cooked that meal himself.'

'I couldn't,' says Charles. 'My relationship with the oven is casual at best.'

'Like all your relationships,' she retorts.

'Whoa!' He looks at her. 'Where did that come from?'

'I don't know,' admits Ellis. 'And it's not true either. Your relationships aren't casual. They're . . . they're . . .'

'What?' he demands.

'You're the feckin' writer!' she exclaims. 'What exactly do you call a relationship when your wife is in the kitchen cooking dinner for your fiancée?'

'That's not entirely accurate,' says Charles.

'I think you'll find that Ariel, who's still your wife, has just spent an hour slaving over a hot stove while we're entertaining Izzy, who's your new fiancée. So it's exactly accurate and you're an absolute pig, Chas. It's not respectful to Iseult to have Ariel here, and it's not respectful to Ariel to treat her like the hired help either.'

'But she *does* work for me,' he protests.

There's a sharp intake of breath, and I realise it's from me.

'Sorry, sorry,' he says. 'I didn't mean it like that. I meant we have a working relationship.'

'I think you've made it very clear what you mean.'

'Ariel, for God's sake. I was provoked. Ellis always bloody provokes me. And I didn't mean . . . I'd never . . .' He puts his arm around me. 'I love you, you know that.'

Which is when Iseult walks into the kitchen.

Iseult

Pamela and I have run out of conversation. We sit opposite each other without anything to say. I check my phone again, but there are no more messages from Steve. I rearrange the cutlery in front of me – a spoon and a cake fork, which makes me wonder what dessert is. Then I fold my linen napkin and tell Pamela that I'm going to check that everything's OK downstairs.

'The chef dropped something, that's all,' she says.

'He might have injured himself,' I say. 'I'm trained in first aid.'

'Whatever.' She shrugs, so I get up and go down the stairs to the kitchen.

As I push open the door, I hear Charles's voice saying, 'I love you, you know that.'

When I walk in, I see him hugging the chef. Who is Ariel. The agent-slash-ex-to-be.

My stomach spasms, and I throw up my barely digested dinner all over the beautiful tiled floor.

'Oh Christ.'

I can hear Charles's words, but they're not registering properly. All that matters are his words to Ariel. *I love you, you know that*. But I feel his arms around *me* now, not her, and he's asking me if I'm all right.

'How can she be all right when she's been sick?' demands Ellis.

'I'm fine,' I gasp as I wriggle from his hold. 'I'm sorry.'

'Don't be,' he says. 'It's not your fault.'

'Here.' Ellis thrusts a glass of water in front of me. 'Sip that.'

She leads me to the sofa, and I drink the water while Charles clears up the mess. I'm utterly mortified at having him clean up after me, but I can't do it myself.

'This is an effing disaster,' says Charles. 'Ellis, will you tell Mum that we'll be back up in a moment.'

'No need,' says Pamela Boyd-Miller from the doorway. 'Mum is already here and surveying the scene of destruction.'

'Why on earth didn't you wait upstairs like I asked?' Charles whirls around to face her.

'Because I was abandoned upstairs,' says Pamela. 'And it seems all the fun is happening down here. Hello, Ariel. So good to see you again.'

'Hello, Mrs Boyd-Miller.' Ariel's voice is flat.

'And you're here because . . .?' Pamela raises an eyebrow.

'Because she was helping me out,' says Charles. 'My chef let me down at the last minute and Ariel stepped in.'

'You're going above and beyond, surely,' says Pamela. 'You're his agent, not his housekeeper.'

Even though I'm feeling rotten, I hide a smile. I can't put myself in the PBM fan club, but she's quite acerbic when she wants to be, and I like it, especially when it's lobbed in Ariel's direction. I glance up. Ariel's back is towards me and I send her some acerbic thoughts of my own. Charles told me he'd arranged for a professional chef for tonight, and his ever-bloody-present agent certainly isn't a professional chef, although cooking does seem to be another one of her talents because the food was great even if I passed on the quiche and left the rest of it on the kitchen floor.

'This has all been a mistake,' she says now as she turns to face us. 'I thought I could cook the meal for you and be out of here without you knowing.'

'I told you it was mental to have Ariel as your fallback instead of simply ordering a bloody takeaway,' Ellis says to Charles.

'I couldn't do that,' he says. 'This was meant to be a family dinner.'

'There's nothing more family dinner than a takeaway,' she retorts.

'I can't believe we're standing around talking about takeaways when the most important thing is that your first wife is injured, your soon-to-be-second wife has thrown up, and both of them are in your kitchen,' says Ellis.

'Lots of first wives and current wives get on well together,' says Charles.

'When they've been properly introduced.'

'We *have* been introduced,' Ariel says. 'We met at his New Year's Eve party. And again here. So Iseult knows who I am and knows that Charles and I have a completely professional relationship.'

But how can it be a completely professional relationship when he was hugging her and telling her he loved her as I walked into the kitchen? I might have a ring on my finger, but Charles has unfinished business with his not-yet-ex-wife. Who is still wearing the multicoloured eternity hoop. I feel sick again.

My phone buzzes.

When will you be home?

Ariel

This is a monumental clusterfuck. I'd like to say it's all Charles's fault, but it isn't. I was the one who stepped in to save the day and I'm the one who very much didn't. For once in my life, I'm at a complete loss as to what to do, and I'm relieved when Ellis suggests that everyone goes upstairs while she puts the kettle on for a cup of tea.

'I think we could do with something stronger than tea,' says Pamela.

'Ellis is right,' says Charles. 'Come on, Mum, Iseult.'

He takes both of them by the arm and leads them out of the kitchen. With their departure, I feel the throb of my hand and the hammering in my head lessen.

'You should go upstairs too,' says Ellis.

'Are you kidding? I'd only fan the flames again.'

'You've had a shock,' she says. 'You need tea.'

'I'll have it here.'

Ellis says nothing, but fills the kettle and takes a patterned teapot from the shelf. I bought that teapot. I'd planned to have it in the mews, but Janice Jermyn gave me a pretty teapot as an office-warming gift, so I left this one in the house.

'Where did it all go wrong?' I sigh.

'Nothing's really gone wrong,' says Ellis. 'The meal was great, by the way. I know it was pre-prepared, but you did a fantastic job anyway. Honestly, Ariel, you're amazing!'

Amazing. I wish. I recall the desserts in the fridge and tell her about them.

'I'm not sure anyone is up for dessert,' she says.

'Maybe not,' I concede.

'Are you sure you want to stay here?'

'I might sneak over to my office.'

'I meant down here,' says Ellis. 'Don't even think about going to your office. It'll be cold, and you don't want to be cold. Don't go anywhere until I come back down to you.'

I'm too wrung out to do anything. I sit on the sofa while Ellis makes tea and pours a cup for me before going upstairs again. I sip it as I imagine what they're saying about me and how Charles is going to salvage the situation. I know Iseult heard him say he loved me. What I don't know is if she believes he means it. Or, indeed, if I do.

My stomach rumbles. Despite having cooked the meal for them, I haven't had anything to eat myself, and I'm suddenly ravenous. I put down my tea and open the fridge door. I take out one of the mango and lime trifles and eat it sitting at the counter. Ellis made a mistake by not bringing them upstairs. It's delicious.

Feck the Miller family, I think, as I lick the spoon.

Then I take out another trifle and eat that too.

Iseult

We don't return to the dining room, but go instead to the living room, where Ellis pours tea from a pot. I'm with Pamela Boyd-Miller in thinking that something stronger is called for, but I take the tea anyway and warm my inexplicably cold hands on the delicate cup.

Nobody speaks. We're probably all struggling with what to say. All I want to know, though, is if Charles meant it when he told Ariel he loved her. Maybe that's why they haven't yet got their divorce. Maybe it's because deep down he truly doesn't want to divorce her. And she doesn't want to divorce him. Who in the wide world cooks dinner for her ex's fiancée? I don't want to be the one to bring up the whole tangled relationship scenario. I don't want to be the one who says anything.

In the end, it's Charles who speaks.

'If I write another murder mystery, that's a scene I'll use,' he says.

'Huh?' Ellis stares at him.

'It's so good,' he tells her. 'Everyone gathering in the kitchen. High tension. First and second wives – almost. And maybe a hidden murder weapon. A cleaver, I suppose.'

'For crying out loud.' She shakes her head. 'Do you think of everything as a story to be used? Ariel burnt her hand and is in pain while I'm quite sure Iseult is upset at learning that your ex-wife cooked dinner. If,' she added, 'and I very much mean *if*, anyone was writing a murder mystery, Iseult would be found poisoned and Ariel would be the chief suspect.'

'Or Ariel would be poisoned and Iseult would be the chief suspect,' says Pamela. 'Makes it a better story.'

'In fact, me being poisoned and both of them being suspects is the most likely,' says Charles.

I can't quite believe they're discussing a storyline when they're talking about my actual life. What is wrong with these people?

Ellis glances at me and probably sees the expression on my face.

'I'm sorry, Iseult,' she says. 'It's our way.'

'What is?'

'Being flippant about things. Turning them into stories. We're very much a story-telling family. It's how we get through life.'

'Really?'

'Yes, really.' Charles, who'd remained standing while the tea was being doled out, finally sits down on the sofa beside me. He takes my hand, but I shake it off, and a pained expression crosses his face. 'Iseult, darling, I'm really sorry about all this. It wasn't what I planned, I assure you.'

'What part wasn't planned?' I demand. 'The part where she burnt her hand or the part where you told her you loved her? Oh, or the part where you're still bloody well married to her?'

'I don't love her,' he replies. 'Not how I love you. You know that. I've told you often enough. But I do love how she always tries to help me out, no matter what.'

'Why on earth did you allow her to cook?' I demand. 'Especially after I suggested Celeste?'

'It seemed like a good idea at the time,' he says. 'I'd paid for the dinner, after all, and the caterer was supplying the food.'

375

He'd allowed his ex to cook because he didn't want to waste money?

'What if I'd gone to the kitchen myself? Before everything blew up?' I ask.

'Why would you have done that?' Charles looks bewildered.

'*I* did,' Ellis reminds him. 'I brought down the plates, remember?'

'Which means you knew.' I shake my head. 'When we were eating, you knew. And you didn't say anything.'

'I felt bad about it,' admitted Ellis. 'But what could I say?'

'You're all mad.' I stand up abruptly and nearly knock over the half-finished cup of tea on the table beside me. 'You think this is normal? It's not.'

'Oh, look, every family has a slightly mad moment from time to time,' says Pamela. 'There's no need to get your knickers in a twist.'

'I think anyone would get their knickers in a twist if they heard their fiancé telling his ex that he loved her,' I return.

Pamela and Ellis exchange glances.

'Is that the crux of the problem?' asks Pamela.

'I didn't mean it,' Charles tells me as he gets to his feet and this time tries to put his arm around me. I move away and face him.

'In that case, why did you say it?' I demand.

'It's just something you say.'

'It's not something *I* say,' I snap. 'Not unless I mean it.'

I take my phone from my bag and flick through the apps.

'Sweetheart, let's talk this through.' Charles gives me a pleading look. 'I understand it's upsetting. I wouldn't have had it happen for the world.'

'I'm not talking anything through,' I say as I order an Uber. 'This has been the worst night of my life.'

'You've had a sheltered life in that case,' remarks Pamela.

'Wouldn't the night your fiancé broke off the engagement have been worse?' asks Charles.

'I'd forgotten about your previous fiancé,' says Pamela. 'You're in the same boat as Charles, aren't you?'

'A previous fiancé is not the same as a previous wife,' I retort. 'And he's not bloody well here for me to tell him how much I love him, is he?'

'No,' says Charles. 'He's waiting for you in your house.'

Pamela and Ellis stare at me.

'Your *ex-fiancé* is your sick friend?' asks Pamela.

'It's a long story,' I say.

'I'm sure we've time to hear it,' says Ellis.

My phone beeps. I tell them my taxi is outside. It's not, although it can't be far away. The beep was alerting me to Steve's message. It's a picture of his empty plate.

Chapter 35

Iseult

The road to hell is paved
with works in progress.
Philip Roth

Traffic is light and it takes half an hour to get home. As I put my key in the lock, my phone buzzes. It's Charles. I don't answer.

'That you?' calls Steve.

'Who else?' I open the door to the living room. His empty plate is on the side table along with a can of lager. 'Everything OK?' I ask.

'Sure. Though I'm totally fed up with TV at this stage. Not even motorsport is exciting any more. I'm glad you're back. I didn't expect you this early. Was it a good evening?'

I could tell Steve the reason I'm home before 9.30, but I don't need him picking over my relationship with Charles. Or Charles's relationship with Ariel. Or indeed any of the deeply weird relationships that seem to exist in the Miller family. So I simply say it was fine and ask if he wants tea, even though I recall he's already had half a dozen cups.

'I'd love one,' he replies.

I go into the kitchen and boil the kettle, throwing two tea bags into proper mugs as opposed to the designer china cups that Charles has. I let the tea brew for a lot longer too, before bringing it to the living room.

'So,' says Steve. 'What's your prospective mother-in-law like?'

'I don't want to talk about her.'

'Jeez, you have form on mothers-in-law, Izzy. You didn't like my mum either.'

'Don't be silly.'

'You said she was a lightweight.'

I wince. That wasn't the best moment in my relationship with Steve, who took it as an insult but fortunately didn't share my ill-chosen description with his mum. The thing is, Lorraine is very different to me. She's into all the latest products when it comes to fashion and beauty. And in fairness, she looks great. But she was forever suggesting a 'touch of Botox' and a 'few mils of filler' as solutions to what she described as my 'over-expressive' forehead and my 'too-thin' lips. When I got engaged to Steve, she gave me a voucher for her favourite beauty aesthetics salon, which, she told me, was totally up to speed with the absolute latest tweakments. And not that I don't think everyone could probably benefit from a decent self-care regime, but I'm scared of needles and I *need* an expressive forehead! I want to be able to frown at some of the drivers coming through the port.

'Whatever,' he says. 'You were always a bit snippy about Mum.'

I feel my equilibrium, already under immense strain from dinner, begin to crack.

'You're in my effing house, eating my food and drinking

my drink because I'm the only one who'd look after you,' I retort. 'I really don't think that dissing me over your mother is the way to go here, Steve.'

'I'm sorry, I'm sorry.' His tone is contrite. 'It's probably the painkillers.'

'The beer, you mean?'

'Don't let's fight, Izzy. I was out of line.'

'Yes, you were. You always bloody are.'

'You've been wonderful to me. You really have. I appreciate it very much. And that idiot you're engaged to doesn't appreciate you half enough.'

'What makes you say that?'

'If he did, he wouldn't have let you come home on your own.'

'I'm not sure he would've wanted to walk in and find you here.'

'He already knows I'm here.'

'Nonetheless . . .'

He reaches out his hand and catches mine. 'I made a right mess of things, didn't I? Can I put it right?'

'I hate to have to remind you yet again, Steve, but you cancelled our wedding. As a result, I met someone else. If "putting it right" means interfering in my life, you can forget it.' I slide my hand free of his.

'I don't want to interfere. I want—'

'Steve, I don't care what you want,' I say. 'You didn't want to be with me, but you're pissed off that someone else does. I'm with Charles now and we're engaged.'

'Do you love him the way you loved me?'

It's a good question and I don't know the answer. My feelings for Charles are very different to my feelings for Steve.

Steve was love at first sight. Charles . . . well, falling in love with him was a gradual, unexpected thing. I thought I was having a fling and it turned into something much deeper. When I'm with him, I feel complete in a way I didn't with Steve.

But I don't know how I feel now. When I left his house earlier, I was furious with him. But that was because the key question wasn't whether I loved him.

It was whether he loved me.

Because I can still hear his words to Ariel.

I love you, you know that.

Steve is looking at me enquiringly. I don't bother replying to him and walk out of the room.

Ariel

I've eaten all four mango trifles, and now I'm sitting on the sofa in the kitchen thinking that I should go home but without the energy to get up and make it happen. All I want to do is put my head down and sleep for a week. Not that I have time to sleep for a week, because I've got new contracts to negotiate and new deals to do and new authors to sign. But for the first time in my life, none of that makes me feel any better.

I keep hearing Charles's words. *I love you, you know that.* What I know is that he once loved me but that he doesn't now. And that he said what he said to comfort me. But what really bothers me is that I needed to be comforted. Because usually I don't. Usually I can comfort myself, thanks very much.

I feel like a character in an Edwardian novel, where the downstairs staff gossip about the upstairs drama and a cook or a parlourmaid falls hopelessly in love with the lord of the manor, who leaves her pregnant and marries a third cousin to keep the stately home. I always thought I should be an upstairs sort of person, but here I am, huddled in the kitchen nursing my sore hand and scoffing food meant for the toffs.

I definitely should go, although the kitchen is still a mess and I hate to leave it like this. But it's not my kitchen, is it? Nothing here is mine. Not even the eaten trifles.

I retrieve my coat from the utility room and am putting it on, gingerly avoiding my sore hand, when I see Ellis at the kitchen door.

'You're leaving?' She sounds surprised.

'Of course.'

'Come upstairs and have a glass of wine with us first.'

'Are you joking? I can't imagine Charles wants his ex and his fiancée in the same room. Besides, I have to drive home. I can't drink wine.'

'Iseult has gone.'

'She has?'

'She was a bit overwrought by everything.'

'I'm not surprised. I'm a bit overwrought myself.'

'I don't blame you,' says Ellis. 'Seriously,' she adds. 'Leave the car. Have a glass with us. We need to talk.'

'Why?'

'Charles is a mess. He needs sorting out. And you're the only one who can do it.'

'Charles made his choice,' I say. 'He can sort himself out.'

'He needs closure, Ariel.'

So do I. I drop my coat on the sofa and follow her up the stairs.

Charles and his mother are sitting opposite each other,

tumblers of whiskey in front of them. He gets up when I walk into the room.

'Are you OK?' he asks.

'I will be.'

'What d'you want to drink?'

'I'll have a whiskey too,' I reply.

He pours a generous measure for me and then mixes Ellis's requested gin and tonic.

'So,' says Pamela. 'The night of the long knives.'

'Don't be ridiculous, Mum,' says Ellis. 'It was a misunderstanding, that's all.'

'Yet Charles's wife is here and his fiancée has gone,' she observes.

'I called her. She's not answering,' says Charles.

I can't help thinking that this seems to happen a lot between them. And I suddenly wonder if she's the one who's in control of the relationship, not him. In which case, she's doing better than me, because I always come running when he calls. Even tonight.

'Can you blame her?' asks Ellis. 'I'm sure it wasn't the sort of evening she was expecting.'

And that's my fault. I stepped in to help Charles because I always do, but this was a step too far and I don't understand why I didn't see it before now. I'm so used to being his fixer that I thought I should fix this too. Although that wasn't the entire reason, I admit to myself as I recall spiking Iseult's quiche with jalapeños. What has happened to me? What have I become? *Who* have I become?

I take a tissue from my bag and blow my nose.

Charles has his phone in his hand and is composing a text. I'm sure it's to tell Iseult that he loves her more than anything and that he's going to fire me as his agent. Maybe that's a good thing. Maybe we should never have stayed together in a professional capacity. He glances up and sees me looking at him. I can't read the expression in his eyes. He can't love both of us. At least . . . he can't be *in love* with both of us.

He's not in love with me. He's used to me. He depends on me. But he's not in love with me.

'I really do have to go.' I drain the whiskey and take out my own phone to call a cab.

'I'd feel better if you stayed,' says Charles.

'I don't honestly care how you feel,' I tell him.

According to the app, the cab will be here in fifteen minutes.

I decide to wait in the hall.

Iseult

Dearest darling Iseult – Izzy. I don't blame you for not picking up my calls. I'm really sorry for tonight's debacle. I'm horrified it all went so horribly wrong. I realise I shouldn't have allowed Ariel to cook for us. I'm so used to her rescuing me that I wasn't thinking. I know you must hate me right now, but please don't. Because I love you. I love you more than life itself. Charles xx

What takes my breath away is that as well as calling me Izzy, he's put two kisses at the end of the text. He never does that, even though he knows I like it. So he's clearly really upset about tonight. Which he should be. *I'm* really upset.

I'm sitting in Mum and Dad's bedroom after helping Steve up the stairs and putting him to bed. He kept trying to worm the night's events out of me, wanting to know what had gone wrong in paradise, and I'd finally told him to shut the fuck up because he was driving me insane. I reminded him that he was in my house and taking up my space and my time and that he was walking on the thinnest of thin ice. And so he eventually did shut up and agreed to go to bed. But I know he was enjoying himself because he could tell there was something wrong.

Once he was out of the way, I poured myself a glass of wine (another Lidl special) and brought it up to the bedroom. I heard the ping of my phone and I knew by the tone that it was from Charles, but I didn't look at it. Instead I got undressed and threw my pink cardi into the linen basket for washing, though I'll have to do a hand-wash and even then I'm not sure the tiger lily stains will come off. Then I went downstairs and fetched the bottle of wine. One glass was never going to be enough to see me through Charles's text.

So he loves me more than life itself, does he? I mutter as I scroll through it. How much is that relative to his love for Ariel? More? Less? About the same? That's the reply I want to send him, but I don't. Instead I switch off my phone, take a huge mouthful of wine, then lie back and look at the ceiling. I think of the first time I saw Charles at the White Sands hotel, and how even then, seeing him alone at his table, I was attracted to him. And how much more I was attracted to him when I saw him dive into the pool at his villa. And then how rude he was on the beach and in the bar when he almost spilled his drink over me, but how charming he was afterwards. And how much fun we had talking about his novel and turning it into a cosy crime. (Well, it's not that cosy, but it's still very good.) I think of how grateful he was and how I liked his gratitude, and then how fantastic the sex was between us. How much better it was than with Steve. How much it made me feel that Charles was the one because he cared for me and wanted to cherish me. How much I wanted to love and cherish him too. I don't want to lose that. I think about how grown up I feel when I'm with him. And how grown up he is compared to Steve. At least, how grown up we usually are. Because tonight we were like children.

Nonetheless, I'm in love with him as much as he claims he's in love with me.

But is it enough?

I roll over and turn out the light.

#LoveConquersAll #OneForTheProblemPage

Chapter 36

Ariel

Unwritten thoughts slip away
like last night's dreams.

Marcus Aurelius

Surprisingly, I wake up early the next morning, with a reasonably clear head, and after a run alongside the river followed by a vigorous shower, I feel renewed. My hand is still raw and sore, but a couple of painkillers and more burn ointment is keeping the pain at bay. I don't spend any time thinking about Charles, Iseult and the disastrous dinner but instead settle down in my favourite armchair with a manuscript from a writer named Tamara Bondarenko that's both funny and moving and keeps my attention for longer than the first three chapters. I make a note to call Tamara in the morning. She could be one of my new signings for this year.

I'm going to need a lot of new signings to replace Charles.

Because if last night has proved anything to me, it's that I need to stop representing him.

My phone rings.

'How are you?' asks Ellis.

'Pretty good. I've been for a run, I've found a new author and my hand is much better.'

'I'm glad to hear it,' she says. 'Mum and I are heading home later. I was wondering if you'd like to meet for coffee.'

'I really don't want to see Pamela,' I say.

'Not Mum. Just me.'

I've missed Ellis's friendship over the last few months, but I'm not sure that having coffee with her is the right move for me. If I'm cutting Charles out of my life, surely I should be cutting his sister out too. And yet it's always good to have female friends. So I agree to coffee, and half an hour later we're in a smart café in Clonskeagh.

'Are you sure you're OK after last night?' she asks when we're both seated with frothy cappuccinos in front of us.

'Last night was a massive mistake on my part,' I say. 'The more I think about it, the more I think I was actually quite crazed to even consider cooking for you all.'

'It was a bit mad,' agrees Ellis. 'But then I was equally mad to go along with it and not tell Chas he's a fecking eejit. Which he is.'

I add sugar to my coffee and tell her I don't think I can represent him any longer.

'You're right to let him go,' says Ellis. 'Better for your mental health.'

'I thought that before, but he wanted me back and I guess I was flattered. As well as which, I got some brilliant deals for him, so it seemed a good decision. But I know it wasn't. God, I'm such an idiot.'

'No you're not,' says Ellis.

'What did you think of Iseult?' I ask.

'Am I allowed to like her?'

'No.' Then I laugh. 'Yes. Of course.'

'Well, she's a lot younger than me and we don't have much in common, but I think beneath it all she's a nice girl . . . woman. I don't honestly know if she's right for Charles, but he does seem to be smitten.'

'Did he go racing across town to her last night?'

'No,' replies Ellis. 'He called and sent a million texts. She didn't reply to any of them and he dithered about what he should do. He was afraid of appearing to be – and I quote – "embracing toxic masculinity" if he went over while she clearly didn't want to see him. So he's waiting for her to make the first move.'

'Gosh. I wonder if she will.'

'Hard to know.'

'Poor Charles.' I sigh. 'He's got himself into a right old mess.'

'Let's not feel sorry for Chas,' says Ellis. 'He's a grown man and should be able to look after himself. I'm as bad as you for always trying to fix things for him. Let's focus on ourselves instead. Will your agency be OK without him?'

I can't blame Ellis for thinking that Charles is the be all and end all of ABA, because I've behaved as though he was myself. I recite a list of all my bestselling authors and tell her that I'm working on even more deals. So that although Charles will be a blow to the bottom line, I'll make it up eventually.

'I've every confidence in you,' she says. 'I know we kind of drifted apart this last year or so, but we've always got on well together, you and I. Let's stay in touch.'

'Won't you be too busy being friends with Iseult?'

'I wouldn't be able to keep up with her.' Ellis laughs. 'All that youthful prettiness.'

I grin, then tell her about my conversation with Josh regarding the reasons young women went out with older men.

'It's not necessarily money,' says Ellis. 'Not all older men are rolling in it. I firmly believe it takes men a lot longer than us to grow up – if they ever do! Let's face it, it's a struggle to put Charles in the grown-up category yet.' She shrugs. 'How is Josh, by the way? I remember meeting him at one of your do's years ago. He gave me some sound financial advice.'

'In the throes of a divorce.'

'Bloody hell,' says Ellis. 'Everyone I know seems to be getting divorced. I'm glad I never bothered to get married.' She gives me a quizzical look. 'Anything likely between you and him?'

'He's lovely, but no,' I say. 'I'm going to be like you and stay single.'

'It doesn't suit everybody.'

'I've been nominally single for quite a while,' I remind her.

'Not the same.' She glances at her watch. 'I'd better go. Mum will be waiting for me, and you know what she's like. Take care, Ariel. Hopefully we'll see each other again soon.'

'Take care yourself.'

We hug, and she heads off in one direction while I take the other.

It's been nice to sit and talk with her.

We definitely won't leave it so long in future.

Iseult

Thankfully, Steve's parents arrive home on Sunday evening. Lorraine comes to my house to collect him. I'm not sure I could've put up with him for much longer. He's a truly terrible patient, demanding and complaining in equal measure while also madly inquisitive about me and Charles. He was expecting Charles to call around at least once while he was here. I think he was hoping to confront him and tell him that he wasn't treating me properly, not that Steve has a great track record in that department either. But he knew there was something amiss between us and he desperately wanted to find out what it was. In the end, I told him that Charles was jealous of him staying with me, and he looked positively pleased with himself and said it wasn't surprising, him being a young, attractive man and Charles being over the hill. I remarked that Charles was in better shape than him right now, but Steve, who had perked up considerably over the last twelve hours, said that he'd soon be on his feet while Charles probably needed to put his up every few hours.

I couldn't help laughing. I wonder why it is that men always compare themselves favourably to other men, yet women usually compare themselves unfavourably to other women. Steve thinks he's a way better catch than Charles, whereas every time I look at Ariel, I wonder why on earth he let her go. I mean, I know why in theory. But in practice she's so much more glamorous and sophisticated than me that it's not surprising he likes having her around.

I check my phone. Another half-dozen texts from Charles, the last one asking if he can call to Marino.

I need time alone, I respond. Please stop messaging me.

OK. Call me soon. I love you. Cxxx

Three kisses!

I leave the phone to one side, bundle Steve's medication together and put it a paper bag. He's wearing the same clothes as he was the night he came to me, which I've washed and ironed, although I haven't been able to do anything about the rip in his shirt. Not that it bothers him. Ripped is his look. He's been living in Dad's tracksuits and T-shirts since coming to the house, and he's glad to get rid of them. Dad isn't known for his street style.

'Thanks for everything, Izzy,' he says. 'You were great.'

'Indeed you were,' says Lorraine, more warmly than she's ever spoken to me before. 'We all appreciate how much you've done for him.'

'I hope we'll keep in touch.' He gives me a meaningful look. 'Any time you need me, any time at all.'

'I won't need you, Steve,' I say. 'But I'll always remember you.'

I wave them off and close the door. Then I flop into the armchair he's vacated and close my eyes. It's good to have the house to myself again. It's good to be on my own again. I've got used to living alone since Mum and Dad went to New Zealand. It'll be hard to adapt to their return. Just as it'll be hard to adapt to living with Charles, always provided that that actually happens. That we'll get married like we're supposed to.

I pick up my phone and scroll through his multiple text messages and voicemails.

What is it with men? I wonder. When they want something, they keep on and on at you until you give in. Like Steve persuading me to let him stay at the house. And like Charles over the last twenty-four hours. Or maybe it's me. Maybe I'm the sort of person who encourages them to keep trying. Maybe I don't know how to say no. #PeoplePleaser

Ariel

It turns out that Tamara is a lovely Ukrainian woman who came to Ireland as a refugee and decided to stay. She works in the health service and volunteers with a care organisation at weekends. In her early forties, she has two children, and her book, *Yellow Fields*, is a sweet family story beautifully told. Her actual personal story is a lot harder, but she says she didn't want to write it, at least not yet, though I can't help thinking it has potential. It turns out that her family had a bookshop in Kherson, but of course the building no longer exists.

'I'll do my very best for your book if you sign with me,' I tell her over coffee. (Not the Shelbourne this time. Tamara lives in Rathmines and we meet in a café there.) She nods, and I say that I'm a member of the Association of Authors' Agents, which has its own code of conduct, but if she wants to get legal advice on the contract that's absolutely fine.

'No need,' she says, taking out a pen and signing the paper in front of her. 'I like you, Ariel Barrett.'

'I promise you won't regret it,' I say.

We order two cream cakes to celebrate.

When I get home, I dance around the apartment. I know

this woman is going to be a success. I will do everything I can to make it happen, but even without me, there's something about her that sparkles.

I go onto my Instagram account and put up a picture of a printed manuscript with a cover page that says *Untitled by Anonymous*. I add the hashtag #WatchThisSpace.

Chapter 37

Iseult

*It sounds plausible enough
tonight but wait until
tomorrow, wait for the common
sense of the morning.*

H. G. Wells

The flowers arrive at the office, the biggest bouquet in the history of the port and a display that's immediately snapped by people to put on their social media with a selection of #WishTheyWereForMe hashtags. I sort of wish they *weren't* for me, because the bouquet is so absolutely enormous it takes up my entire desk. Every time someone wants to talk to me, they have to push the foliage to one side. There's no doubt that Charles is making a statement, and there's no doubt that the statement is he's very sorry, but honestly, he's turned the office into a garden centre!

Anyway, I don't need flowers to be ready to forgive him. I've thought it all through and I accept that he's so used to Ariel making things easy for him and smoothing out his life that the notion of her cooking the family meal seemed more or less normal to him. And to her too. More worrying is his comment about always loving her. I'm currently rationalising that by recalling that she'd burnt her hand and was very upset, and telling her he loved her was . . . well, something to make her feel better. I don't really think he loves her. Not any more.

I can put the dinner debacle behind me. But I do have a red line. And that's her coming to the house uninvited ever again, for their Freedom Friday drinks or anything else. I'm going to make it clear to him and he has to make it clear to her. Because if she dares put one foot inside the house – *my* house-to-be – without my permission in the future, that's it. Over. For ever.

I say all this to him on Monday night when he comes to Marino after I finally sent him a text saying I was ready to talk. Before he arrived, I gave the place a deep clean (the area around Steve's armchair was an absolute pit!), leaving it super tidy and smelling of irises, anemones, amaryllis, orchids and all the other flowers from his over-the-top bouquet. I divided the flowers among an assortment of vases because it was far too big to fit in a single one.

'You're absolutely right,' he says when I finish speaking. 'I realise how insensitive I've been. I guess it's because I'm a gnarly old man who hasn't a clue, while you're a young, intelligent woman in touch with your feelings.'

'I thought the USP for your books is that you're totally in touch with women's feelings,' I remark.

'Fictional women,' he says. 'I can make fictional women feel what I want, do what I want and think what I want. It seems I'm not quite as successful with real-life versions who have minds of their own and think differently to me.'

I laugh, and so does he.

'You can't imagine how pleased I am that you're laughing again,' he says.

'I'm laughing now, but I absolutely won't be if Ariel comes into the house again.'

'She won't,' he assures me. 'You have my word.'

'I'd really like it if you two weren't in touch at all,' I murmur as I snuggle up to him on the sofa.

'It's tricky when she's my agent,' he says. 'But I won't be writing another book for at least a year, so any contact between us will be minimal.'

'Except she's working at the bottom of your garden.'

'I realise now that it's not ideal,' he says. 'But honestly, Iseult – Izzy – I usually don't see her that often.'

'Fortunately you don't have to. It's not like you have children to co-parent.'

'My books are my children,' he says.

'Hmm. What about actual children?'

'What about them?'

'You said they weren't a priority for you and Ariel, that you weren't in a hurry. But what about now, Charles? You're approaching fifty and I'm nearly thirty. Even though I'm not in a rush myself, it's something we need to think about.'

He's silent. I don't say anything either.

'I never saw myself as good dad material,' he says eventually. 'Even before I wrote books, I was very caught up in my career. But being with you – even though I'm making a terrible hash of being with you – has made me realise there are more important things in life. I think I'd be a better dad now than I would've been ten years ago. I hope so anyway. And I'd love to have children with you.'

I snuggle even closer. His arm around me is comforting.

'Oh, there's something I forgot to mention,' he says after a while.

I feel my heart jolt. If it's something about Ariel and the divorce, I'll kill him.

'I told Mum I'd do her next literary festival. I hope you'll come. It's in a few weeks. I've never done one for her before,' he adds. 'She never asked me.'

'She never asked?' I sit up and look at him. 'I'd've thought you'd have been her first author.'

'She didn't want it to look like favouritism,' he says.

'Wow. She seriously thought asking her Booker-winning son to read would be giving off nepo-baby vibes?'

'It's her way,' says Charles. 'She bigs me up in public but likes taking me down a peg or two at home. There's a part of her that thinks I let her down by not managing the pub with Nick.'

Honestly, what's wrong with the woman? Both her sons are doing well, aren't they?

'Oh, she's very happy that I became a literary success,' says Charles when I say this. 'She just thinks I should remember my roots. She's . . . well, she marches to the beat of her own drum.'

I can see now why she and Ariel didn't get along.

I wonder will I fare any better.

Ariel

Penny Blackwater, my Northern Irish author, has been short-listed for another literary prize, and we celebrate by meeting up in Belfast and having lunch in the Titanic Quarter. She tells me she's thinking of writing about a fictional descendant of one of the world's most famous shipping disasters, and we chat about how that might work. By the time I'm getting the Enterprise train back to Dublin later that evening, I'm quite excited about the idea. I'm also excited that Avery Marshall has sent me what he's calling 'a very, very rough first draft' of his next comedy, and that Shelley has called to say that the new contract has come through for Cosmo Penhaligon. Given that I negotiated a steep increase in his advance, I'm very happy about that, and happy that my fifteen per cent will soon be nestling in the agency's account, which will look good on the monthly figures.

The train is crossing the Malahide estuary when my phone buzzes with a call from Josh.

'I was just thinking about you,' I say, and let him know about the Cosmo deal.

'Excellent.' And yet I can hear from his voice that that's not the most important thing for him. I wonder if he and Paula have got back together. There's a lightness to his tone that hasn't been there in weeks. 'There's something I wanted to put to you,' he says. 'Would you like to drop by the office tomorrow?'

'I have online meetings scheduled throughout the day,' I say. 'Why can't you tell me now?'

'Not over the phone,' he says.

'Curiouser and curiouser. Can you come to my office instead? Say two thirty?'

'I'll be there. Don't worry,' he adds, clearly picking up on the hint of anxiety in my tone. 'It's a positive thing.'

It must be that Paula's coming back, I decide when he ends the call. But then I remember that he said he wanted to 'put something' to me, and that would hardly be anything to do with Paula. I'm intrigued, but I decide to let it go until tomorrow.

I'm having a coffee break when he turns up, looking very smart in a navy suit and crisp white shirt.

'I've another meeting after yours,' he replies when I remark on how snappily dressed he is. 'I've found a shirt-laundering app and the service is great. Paula always hated ironing.'

'Not that there was anything stopping you from ironing your own shirts,' I point out, and he gives me a chastened look.

'D'you think that's what went wrong?' he asks.

'Did you share things at home?' I ask in reply. 'Did you do more than put out the bins?'

'Of course!' He looks affronted.

'It wasn't the lack of ironing skills so.' I smile at him. 'Trade secret, I use a laundry service too.'

We go upstairs to my library area and I make us both Americanos. Then I look expectantly at him.

'I've had an approach on your behalf,' he begins, and my heart sinks. These approaches are usually by friends, or friends of friends, who want me to critique a manuscript. Well, they say critique, but on the rare occasions I do, they nearly always get upset when I suggest changes.

But the approach Josh is talking about isn't a novel by a friend. It's a business proposal. A bigger agency is looking to buy me out and has made an extraordinarily high opening offer.

'You have a great list of authors,' Josh points out when I say this. 'Why shouldn't they pony up for them?'

'They absolutely should,' I agree. 'But this is an offer way above any I've ever had before.'

There have been a few over the years but none that have piqued my interest enough to sell. And of course, I haven't wanted to let myself be brought into the fold of somewhere bigger where my business relationship with Charles might have changed. That's not an issue now, though. As for the money, it's a massive step up.

'And me?' I ask. 'Do they want me to stay on?'

'Of course.' He looks shocked. 'That's why they're making such a great offer. They want you and your authors and your potential authors too.'

The agency is an international one that manages some very well-known actors and celebrities both in the UK and Ireland and globally. They have an office in Dublin where they mainly look after TV celebrities, and now want to increase their presence in the literary market. From what Josh is telling me, they have a lot of money to splash around. It's all very exciting, except for the fact that the ABA agency wouldn't be mine any more.

'No,' concedes Josh. 'But the proposal would have you as a management consultant with them. If you didn't want to do that, you could move somewhere else. There's a non-compete clause, of course, so you wouldn't be able to do it immediately, but you'd have the option eventually.'

The offer is very tempting. I need to think seriously about it.

'I wish we could talk about this a bit more,' I say. 'But I have another Zoom in fifteen minutes.'

'That's why they want you.' He grins at me. 'You're hot-wired into hard work, Ariel. They know you're worth it, and so do I. Don't forget – there's always room for upward negotiation.'

Naturally, I know that. It's how I get the best for my clients. It's a long time since I tried to do it for myself. I'm already looking forward to the challenge.

Chapter 38

Iseult

The world breaks everyone and afterwards they are strong at the broken places.
Ernest Hemingway

We go by train to Waterford for Pamela's literary evening. The family pub and her café are close to both the station and the city, with views over the River Suir. I can't remember the last time I was in Waterford, and I reckon we're seeing it at its best, because it's a glorious day with a crisp blue sky and a surprisingly warm breeze. The boats on the river make it ideal for an Instagram photo, and I insist on taking a selfie with Charles. It's a good photo and (despite not being entirely accurate) I post it with the hashtags #RomanticBreak and #SummersOnTheWay. I tag him in it.

We're staying in a local hotel, as Ellis, who's helping Pamela with the event, has already claimed the spare room at her mother's bungalow on the outskirts of the town. Charles said he'd prefer to be at a hotel anyhow, and not distracted by whatever preparations Pamela might have to make. We're going to the pub afterwards to meet Nick and Rachel. #MeetTheInLaws

I'm actually quite looking forward to that. I want to get to know his family, and Nick and Rachel sound like ordinary hard-working people with no notions about themselves – unlike Pamela, who's full of them.

When we get to the hotel, Charles retreats into the Author-with-a-capital-A version of himself and spends his time poring over the passages in the book he plans to read. (Why, I don't know. Surely he knows them by heart already!)

I take my Kindle from my bag and curl up in a chair beside the bay window. I'm reading a crime novel by someone I haven't read before. It popped up in a deal and the great news is that the author has a backlist of half a dozen other books that I'll download if I like this one. It's started off well – the first wife is a suspect in the murder of the second. I'm trying not to draw parallels with my own life, even if Ariel hasn't featured in it lately. And not in Charles's either, as far as I can tell. He assures me there have been no more Freedom Fridays – in fact he calls over to me most Fridays now, and last week he came to the pub and met the gang.

They were a little in awe of him at first, but he got on well with everybody. It seems to me that there are definitely two Charles Millers. One is the literary Charles who's happy to be feted by those around him. The other is normal Charles, who doesn't take himself half as seriously and who's genuinely interested in other people's lives and finds out everything about them without seeming to try.

'I can see why you fell for him,' Katelyn said to me when we were freshening up in the loo. 'He's such a gentleman.'

I'm glad I forgave him for the Great Dinner Debacle, as he and I now call it. Anyhow, maybe it wasn't such a debacle after all. Maybe it straightened out a few things between us. #SilverLining

We've been in the hotel since almost 4 p.m., but Charles doesn't want to get to the café until nearer the start time of 6.30. I thought that would mean time to spend in the rather sumptuous king-sized bed, but he's now reading aloud the excerpt from *A Caribbean Calypso* that he's chosen to share with the audience. It's not the best piece to choose in my opinion – there's rather too much about the beautiful island setting and the azure seas and not quite enough about the bludgeoned body on the terrace, but I get that his readers like his descriptive writing and that they'll probably enjoy this bit. It certainly makes you feel as though you're sitting under a tropical sun with palm fronds waving overhead and brightly coloured birds calling to each other from the trees. He's read it so many times now, though, I'm sick of hearing it, and I take myself off to the bathroom, where I have a shower and wash my hair before putting on more make-up than I'd normally wear for a visit to a café.

Books and Bakes is smaller and prettier than I expected. It has a duck-egg-blue facade and a large plate-glass window with the name etched into it, while an old-fashioned hanging sign in blue wood tells potential customers that the café serves sandwiches, pastries and Waterford blaas, which are local bread rolls. Inside, there's a counter with stools in front of the window, while half a dozen tables fill the rest of the space. One wall is taken up by an asymmetric bookshelf with a notice to *Leave a book, take a book*, and another is adorned with Pamela's (mostly male and mostly dead) literary greats photographs. A young woman, her white T-shirt and taupe jeans protected by an apron in the same duck-egg-blue as the outside, is busy wiping down the pretty oilcloth tablecloths and placing a small vase of flowers on each one.

'Any sign of . . . Oh, Charles, you're here.' A door at the back of the café opens and Pamela Boyd-Miller walks in.

'Sorry I'm late,' he says. 'This looks great.'

'It better be,' she says. 'I had to hurry a big group out fifteen minutes ago. Doesn't leave a lot of time. People will be arriving shortly.'

Even as she speaks, the door opens and a couple of women who I guess are in their mid fifties walk in.

'Charles Miller!' The taller of the two beams at him. 'It's so exciting to see you home at last. How are you?'

Charles hesitates for a moment, and then his eyes light up in recognition as he greets the woman and says she's changed her hairstyle.

'It'd be a sad day if I hadn't, given that you haven't seen me in at least twenty years.' She smiles. 'This is my cousin Lynsey. She's come specially for the event. Do you remember her at all? She lived with us for a few months when we were kids. She came off her brand-new scooter outside your front gate one Christmas morning. Your mother bandaged up her knee and gave us both lemonade and chocolate Santas.'

'He won't remember,' says Lynsey.

'Of course I do.' Charles smiles at her. 'You bled all over your pretty dress and you were so upset about it. I tried to kiss you to make you better and you cried even more.'

Lynsey laughs, and it suddenly occurs to me that she's the girl who broke his heart on Christmas Day. I wonder if she even knew.

Charles shakes her hand, and then more people start to arrive and I sidle out of the way.

'You OK?' I jump as someone taps me on the shoulder. It's Ellis.

For a horrible moment I thought it might be Ariel, even though I know Charles has taken my ultimatum very seriously. To be honest, I feel slightly guilty that I've interfered in their professional relationship as well as their personal one. I remind myself that it's not my problem.

'It's nice to see you in less fraught surroundings,' says Ellis. 'Can I get you coffee and a scone?'

'That would be lovely. Thank you.'

She goes behind the counter. When she's finished making coffee for both of us, the young employee, who's been joined by another girl around her own age, begins making it for the customers.

'This is a lovely place,' I say as I take the cup from her. 'It's really warm and welcoming.'

'She may be prickly with those closest to her, but Mum is very clued in about what people want,' says Ellis. 'If she'd been born a little later in life, she probably would've been a bigger entrepreneur. But back in the day, when she wanted to open a small farm shop in the town, she couldn't even get a loan in her own name. The bank manager told her to come in to see him with her husband, even though everyone knew that Mum was much smarter than him.'

'Charles told me she was the one who opened a restaurant in the pub.'

'Yes.' Ellis nods. 'Back in the seventies, lots of pubs didn't want women coming in and could refuse to serve them. Mum reckoned if there was a restaurant attached, it would make a difference. Of course, by the time she actually got it going, things were starting to change, but she was a bit of a feminist in her own right.'

'So why didn't she and Ariel get on?'

'Too much alike,' says Ellis. 'Too argumentative.'

'And yet Ariel works so hard for Charles and his books, you'd think your mum would love her.'

'I'm surprised you're championing Ariel's cause after that awful night,' says Ellis. 'And I'm not sure Mum and I were as nice to you as we could have been either.'

'It was a disaster,' I acknowledge. 'But hopefully also a turning point. D'you think your mother will like me more than Ariel? Not that it actually bothers me,' I add. 'But am I perhaps less threatening? After all, she thinks I should be grateful to be moving in her circles.'

Ellis laughs, and it's so infectious I can't help laughing too.

'Just because you're not as outspoken as Ariel doesn't mean you aren't perfectly capable of holding your own with my mother,' she says. 'And I'm impressed at how you hold your own with Charles too. He's mad about you, you know.'

'He is?'

'Jeez, doesn't he tell you enough?' She grimaces. 'He never stopped talking about you at Christmas. I've got to confess that I thought it was just an infatuation at first. And I was very unsure about you. But I think you make a good couple.'

'Am I supposed to be relieved?'

'*I* am,' says Ellis. 'To be honest, I was in the Ariel camp initially. We were good friends. I still want to be friends with her. But . . . I'm not saying we're going to be best mates, Izzy. All the same, I'm sure we can get on.'

I hope so. I like her. She's far less complicated than I first thought.

Charles, who's been busy shaking hands with people and making small talk, comes over to us and says he's going into the back room to practise his reading again. Pamela takes over the greeting duties. The arrivals are mainly women, though there are a few men. They take their places at the tables, coffees and scones in front of them.

Pamela makes a short introductory speech about the book club, mentions how to leave the café in case of an emergency and then introduces Charles as the international bestselling Booker Prize winner and local author.

There's rapturous applause as he walks back into the room.

He's good, no question. He reads the excerpt from *A Caribbean Calypso* beautifully, and the applause is warm and genuine. He's bombarded with questions about his books and his writing, and in particular, what made him write a murder mystery. I'm waiting for him to mention me and wondering what he'll say, but he doesn't. Instead he talks about going to the island and finding himself in a different 'creative space'. He says that he was inspired by the concept of introducing murder into such a beautiful, tranquil environment. There's no mention of cocktails on the beach or sex in an expensive villa with someone he's just met. Or of her telling him to jettison the book he was writing for something else. Or of him getting engaged to her.

I shouldn't be hurt, but I am. After all, he wouldn't have written the book without me. Then I tell myself that tonight isn't about me and Charles as a couple, it's about him as a writer. The people here don't want to know about me. They're all a little bit in love with him.

'You wouldn't think he'd be so good at stuff like this,' murmurs Ellis beside me. 'He's a loner at heart, but as always, they're eating out of his hand.'

'However, in addition to all of the above, the major inspiration for *A Caribbean Calypso* is the woman sitting in the audience beside my sister,' Charles continues. 'My fiancée, Izzy, who told me that my original attempt at a murder mystery was too wordy and forced me to write something better. So for that, I thank her.'

Everyone turns to look at me, and I feel my face flush as, led by Charles, they applaud me.

I'm embarrassed, but I love that he acknowledged me.

Ellis squeezes my arm.

It's going to be all right, I think, as a warm glow envelops me. Charles and Ariel are over. He loves me. Ellis likes me. And his mum – well, I'm sure we'll manage to get on eventually.

When he's finished, people take photos of Charles and me together. Ellis takes one too, which she sends to me. Then I take a video of him signing books for his adoring fans, and post it on Instagram along with the photo of the two of us: #BestsellerAlert #ACaribbeanCalypso #BetaReaderFiancée. I tag him again.

Ariel

Josh has been in touch about meeting the MD of the company that's looking to buy my agency. I asked a few questions about the initial proposal and he wants to answer them in person, so we're going to meet him and some of the board in London next week. Josh offered to come with me for moral support, and I agreed, even though I'm someone who's used to doing things on her own. But this is a monumental decision and it would be good to have another perspective. I ask him to set it up with an overnight stay, because I'll try to meet some other contacts while I'm there. I never waste a trip to London if I can help it.

A ping on my phone notifies me of an update to one of my social media accounts. I'm surprised to see it's a mention on Charles's account. A photo of him with Iseult smiling beside him and the beautiful backdrop of Waterford behind them. My stomach tightens. I hadn't forgotten that he was in Waterford for Pamela's literary evening tonight. I'd asked him if he wanted me to go with him – I usually accompany him to all his events. But he told me that Izzy would be coming because he wanted her to meet the family.

And now here she is, beaming in a selfie with him. It feels . . . odd.

There's another ping, this time Josh sending details of our London visit and asking if there's anything I need clarification on.

I pick up the phone and ask if he has time to meet this evening.

'Sure. Fancy a bite to eat?'

I haven't eaten all day, so I tell him this sounds like a plan, and we elect to meet in a small diner close to him.

I don't bother going home to change first, and regret not having made the effort when I realise that the diner has undergone a recent refurb and is a lot trendier than I remember.

'You look fine,' Josh tells me when I apologise for my jeans and baggy jumper combo. 'You're right, though, this place has poshed up quite a bit.'

He insists on two glasses of Prosecco to start, and we order off the well-judged menu.

We've almost finished our main course before he gets around to asking what part of the deal I want to talk about.

'Charles,' I say.

He looks at me enquiringly.

'Things have been a bit tricky since he got engaged,' I tell him. 'I've been thinking about him getting new representation. Obviously he's one of the authors the new agency will want to have on their books.'

'He's not talking to another agency at the moment, is he?'

I shake my head.

'Seems to me you have a great opportunity to move him to another agent in the expanded organisation,' says Josh. 'Obviously that would have to be in London, because the only literary agent in the Irish office would be you.'

'Y'see, I thought that, but it would depend on what he wants.'

'I'm sure you could work out a transition with him,' says Josh.

'You've got such faith in me.'

'Of course I have,' he says. 'I thought you had great faith in yourself, Ariel.'

'It's been knocked about a bit this last while.'

'I don't see why.'

'Oh, just Charles getting engaged again. It sort of flattened me.'

'It always flattens you when an ex moves on,' says Josh. 'Flattens you more when the wife you've been living with moves on without you even knowing it.'

'We're a right pair.'

Our eyes meet. I'm pretty sure we're both thinking the same thing, but I'm really not sure if it's a good idea.

'Finished here?' he asks.

'Yes.'

'Want to come back to mine?'

'No strings,' I say.

'Not even a thread.'

He pays the bill and we walk quickly back to his building. We don't even bother going upstairs.

Chapter 39

Iseult

Make sure you marry someone who
laughs at the same things as you.
                    J. D. Salinger

It's easily an hour after the end of Charles's event by the time we get to Miller's, where his sister-in-law, Rachel, greets us and brings us to a reserved table in the adjoining restaurant.

Both the pub and the restaurant are old-style, with interior brick walls, dark furniture, gold fittings and an enormous fire blazing in the hearth. Although it's a gas fire, there's a big basket of peat on the granite hearth and a faint background smell of peat that's warm and homely. The walls of the restaurant are covered in old posters from Irish travel and transport companies, some extolling the virtues of touring Ireland by coach and others suggesting that passengers allow the train to take the strain. I'm fascinated by them and by the times they evoke.

The table is set for four – Pamela, Ellis, Charles and me – but Rachel takes a chair from an unoccupied table and sits down to chat with us while one of the waitresses brings pitchers of iced water.

'So, Izzy, tell us about yourself.' Both her voice and her expression are warm and friendly.

I embark on my well-worn life story and am gratified that she seems genuinely interested in my job at the port.

'It sounds fantastic,' she says. 'I'd love the power.'

'I'm not that powerful.' I laugh.

'Oh, but you are,' she insists. 'Being able to stop a six-axle lorry. Being able to search it. Being able to arrest someone.'

'I don't do any arresting,' I correct her. 'But if a case is brought, I often end up having to give evidence in court.'

She's hugely thrilled by this.

'It's like a TV drama,' she says.

I don't want to burst her bubble by saying it's far less streamlined than a TV drama and that I'm always terrified I'll say the wrong thing. You have to be really careful to answer questions exactly the right way so that the case doesn't get thrown out on a technicality. It's happened, though thankfully not to me.

'There's so much material there for your next crime novel.' She turns to Charles, who shakes his head and says he's not sure about another crime novel.

'Don't be stupid,' says Rachel. '*A Caribbean Calypso* will sell millions.'

'You haven't read it yet,' he says.

'But it sounds fantastic,' she tells him. 'And you know how much I like crime fiction.'

'Who are your favourite crime writers?' I ask.

'All of them.' She grins. 'My mum has a huge collection of Ngaio Marsh passed down from her own mum. I love

Ian Rankin, and Jo Spain too. And Corinne Doherty and Janice Jermyn.'

I'm pleased she likes the same writers as me. I tell her that I have a signed copy of two of Janice's novels, and she's envious.

'You never get signed copies of anything for me,' she says to Charles. 'Hopefully Izzy can be my gateway to my favourite authors from now on. I'm really looking forward to Janice's next one,' she adds, turning back to me. '*The Mystery of the Missing Mallet* was great.'

'Wasn't it?' I beam at her. 'Did you guess the murderer?'

'Not until two thirds of the way through. And even then—'

She's interrupted by the waitress asking if we're ready to order, and Pamela says that we really should, because the kitchen will close shortly, so Rachel excuses herself and goes back to the bar while we choose our food. I opt for lasagne. Everyone else orders the hake.

I'm sorry Rachel can't stay, but I can see that both pub and restaurant are busy and she has better things to do than sit with us. But I can't help feeling pleased that at least one member of the Miller family seems perfectly normal, both when it comes to books and reading, and in general conversation. There's nothing hidden about Rachel. She's a nice person.

The lasagne when it arrives is good, and so is the garlic bread that accompanies it. As I eat, I listen to Pamela, Ellis and Charles talking about the event and about people they know, and I feel like I've finally been accepted into the family.

I feel even more accepted later in the evening when Charles's brother, Nick, joins us for a drink. Although it seems unfair to say it, he's like a lesser version of Charles

– less intimidating, less handsome, less interesting. But he's good company and tells some amusing anecdotes about being a pub landlord that keep the conversation flowing. He also talks about his two daughters, Emily and Louisa, telling Charles that he'll have to give them plenty of notice so they can be back home for the wedding.

'Chas still has to get his divorce first.' It's Ellis who says this, although in an entirely practical way.

'I forgot about that.' Nick gives Charles a gentle thump on the back. 'Got to disentangle yourself from one Mrs Miller before making it legal with the next.'

'Indeed,' says Charles. 'It's all in hand.'

I excuse myself and go to the Ladies'. I give myself a few minutes there and see that I've got a message from Celeste asking how things are going.

Pretty good. The event was successful and the rest of the Millers seem normal

Yay!

TBH I kept thinking Ariel would show up. But she didn't. I'm hoping she's been put in her place once and for all

Celeste had been both horrified and highly amused at the notion of Ariel having to cook for me. We'd had a long conversation about the entire situation and she'd suggested that Ariel might be trying to win him back. I said that women fighting over men was so last century and that he wasn't a prize. She laughed and told me to follow my heart, but that even if I broke it off with him I should keep the beautiful Ice Cube engagement ring.

We exchange a few more texts, then I decide I'd better get back to the group. But before I do, the door to the Ladies' opens and Ellis walks in.

'Are you OK?' she asks.

'Why shouldn't I be?'

'You've been gone for ages.'

'Were you sent to find me?'

'No. I'm the only one who noticed you'd disappeared. The others are deep in conversation about Charles's potential next crime novel. Even Nick, who has zero interest in books, is keen on another murder mystery. He wants Charles to set it in the pub.'

'Rachel suggested a customs setting earlier,' I remind her. 'And Charles himself wasn't against the idea when I brought him around the port. Though I'm not sure how we can tie it in to the Caribbean. I have a feeling he enjoyed the research there a lot more than he enjoyed wandering around Dublin Port with me.'

'Good point.' Ellis grins. 'Look, I admit I was sceptical about you and him at first. But you're good for him. Both because you helped him out of his writing funk and because you make him live in the real world.'

'His world is the real world too,' I say.

'Not entirely,' she tells me. 'He makes most of it up, after all.'

We both laugh.

'But Ellis,' I add, 'my relationship with your brother shouldn't be defined by what I can do for him. It should also be what he can do for me. Love is a two-way stream. We should be supporting each other.'

'Oh, wow.' Her eyes widen. 'You're more like Ariel than I thought.'

Pamela said that to me too. They can't both be right, surely? I ask Ellis why she thinks we're alike.

'She and Charles . . . it was always about what they could do for each other. She made him the success he is. He's the leading light in her agency. It's symbiotic.'

'I didn't mean supporting each other's careers, though obviously that's part of it. I meant supporting each other's lives.'

'You're deeper than I gave you credit for,' she says. 'I'm so sorry I underestimated you. Mainly because you're young and pretty.'

'I'm nearly thirty,' I say. 'Not that young. And thanks for saying I'm pretty. It's not something you ever think about yourself.'

'We've all underestimated you,' she says. 'We thought you were overwhelmed by Chas. But now I wonder if it's Chas who's been overwhelmed by you.'

I smile at her and say I should get back to the table, even if nobody has missed me.

But at least one other person has, because when I slide into the seat beside Charles, he puts his arm around me and says he was thinking of sending a search party out for me.

'I was afraid they'd frightened you off,' he whispers.

'Not at all,' I tell him. 'I think I'm getting the hang of the Millers at last.'

He laughs and kisses me on the cheek.

From across the table, Ellis winks at me.

#HappyFamilies

Chapter 40

Ariel

Anyone who ever gave you
confidence you owe them a lot.
            Truman Capote

The offices of the Denton-Marr agency are located in a red-brick building off the Marylebone Road, and are far more impressive inside than out, as Josh remarks when we walk into the foyer. We've come directly from the airport, having caught a morning flight to London and spent the time talking about the takeover proposal. We haven't yet spoken about our night together (well, three hours – I would have liked to stay, but needed to be home early the next morning), but there's no awkwardness between us and we've slipped into our usual roles of accountant and client. Nevertheless, Josh has always been a good friend to me, and I don't want to mess it up because I slept with him. I'm pretty sure he feels the same way.

I like business meetings and I feel very comfortable sitting at the boardroom table talking to the MD and financial controller about ABA and how it might fit into Denton-Marr's future plans.

'Of course we'd be Denton-Marr-Barrett if we agree terms,' says Christian, the MD.

There's something immensely satisfying about that, and I bask in a warm glow for the rest of the meeting.

When Josh and I leave, after having raised a few more issues that Christian seems to think will be easily resolved, we make our way to a local wine bar, where he orders two glasses of Prosecco.

'You always seem to be ordering me glasses of Prosecco,' I say.

'Because I'm always celebrating with you.' He raises his glass.

'We haven't finalised the deal yet.'

'You will,' he says.

'There's still the issue of Charles,' I point out. 'I have to do the right thing by him.'

'I'm sure he'll be well looked after at Denton-Marr-Barrett.'

Every time I hear the name, I smile.

'You're not letting your concerns about him hold you back, are you?' He frowns.

'No,' I say. 'I'm very excited, although nervous too. I've been working on my own for so long that I'm not sure how I'll be as part of a big team again.'

'Brilliant, I suspect.'

'Josh, you don't have to keep bigging me up.' I laugh. 'You were amazing at that meeting, throwing financial projections at them whenever there was a pause and making me seem like an absolute genius talent-spotter.'

'Well you weren't doing enough of it yourself,' he points out. 'My aim is to make sure you get the best possible deal.'

'We do almost the same job,' I remark. 'Except in this case I'm the client.'

'And a very gorgeous client you are too,' he says.

'Josh . . .'

'Yes?'

'The other night . . .'

'I guess we should clear the air about that,' he says.

'It was absolutely lovely, and you've no need to worry. I'm not looking for anything meaningful.'

'Dearest Ariel, I'm not worried, and nor do I need anything meaningful, although if I did, you'd be an excellent choice. But I'm in the middle of a messy divorce, remember?'

'Well, exactly. And I've a lot on my plate. I just didn't want you to get the wrong idea.'

'There's no wrong idea to get,' he assures me. 'Nothing needs to be said. It was great, though,' he adds. 'I really enjoyed it. And I'd like to do it again sometime if you would. But strictly no strings.'

'Strictly no strings,' I agree.

We finish our Prosecco and go back to the hotel.

Despite hoping I'd get to see some other publishers on our visit, or at least Maya or Ekene, I only managed to arrange an hour with Sydney Travers, who's coming to the hotel later. Maya is in Birmingham doing a publicity tour, but I take out my phone and text Ekene in case she's suddenly become free for the evening. She replies to say that she can't get out of the business dinner she's going to, but that the next time I'm in London we'll definitely meet.

422

So with Josh out and about, meeting an old friend, I'll be on my own tonight. I can't help feeling it's a bit sad to be alone when I'm about to sign a major deal that will bring me a lot of financial freedom. A few months ago I would have celebrated with Charles, and although I accept now that Charles and I are over, it feels odd that he's not the one I'm texting with my news.

It occurs to me, as I refresh my make-up, that after my split with him, I never really considered he might find someone else to marry. I never thought of any of his relationships since I left as consequential in any way, just as mine have never been consequential either. I wonder if that's because we didn't get divorced. Because deep down I always saw myself as a married woman, even if I was a married woman who was no longer living with her husband. Somehow it wasn't the actual fact of our separation that mattered. It was how I perceived it. How he perceived it too, I think. We were a husband and wife who didn't live together but were still a husband and wife. And now we're not.

There's a sense of freedom in that thought, even if I feel slightly like a hot air balloon that's been released into the sky. Nobody has a grip on me any more. I can go wherever I like.

Which right now is downstairs to meet Sydney to find out how the publication plans are coming along and make sure that no matter what happens, *A Caribbean Calypso* is Charles's most successful book yet.

The meeting with Sydney is fun. Beneath her rather severe exterior is a smart, witty woman who takes no prisoners. She says she thinks the work Charles has done has improved the book a thousand per cent and she's eager to make it a massive success. It is, she says, a privilege to work with him and she's glad he's had enough faith in her to fall in with her suggestions. I don't say that I made sure I echoed all of them in my own notes to him to reinforce the message. Her suggestions were excellent, even if they drove him to distraction.

When we finish talking about Charles, she asks if I've ever considered expanding the agency or moving back to London. I look at her anxiously in case news of the Denton-Marr offer has leaked.

'Not immediately, but you never know,' is my non-committal answer.

'I admire that you run your own business,' she says. 'It's something I'd like to do myself one day.'

'Oh? As a publisher?'

'I know there are niche publishers, but it's hard to be up against the big guys. I might move into agenting.' She gives me a grin. 'Though I don't think you have to worry about me as competition.'

'I'd worry a lot about you as competition,' I assure her.

She smiles, and we chat a little more about authors we've worked with and the choices we've made. She's so enthusiastic and positive about her career that it rubs off on me, and when she leaves, I sit back in the banquette seat of the hotel bar and remind myself that nothing ever stays the same. Why should it? Life moves on. The trick is moving with it. Being open to change. Accepting what happens and making the most of it.

Like an amazing offer to buy my business.

Like not having to answer to anyone.

Like being footloose and fancy-free in London for the night.

Even as I'm thinking this, Josh walks into the bar.

'I thought you were out for the evening,' I say.

'I was only meeting Greg for one pint,' he says. 'He had to get back to the family. They've a new baby, born last month.'

'Oh.'

'So here we are in London, with nothing to do.'

'It's London. There's hardly nothing to do.'

'Anything you fancy?' he asks. 'A cultural event, perhaps.'

'Get a grip, Josh,' I say. 'I'm here to sell my business. I've already had a glass of Prosecco with you and another with Sydney Travers. Who sees me as a bit of a role model, by the way, which is very satisfying. I'm so not here for cultural pursuits.'

'More bubbly?' he suggests. 'I certainly think London and bubbly go together.'

'You couldn't be more right.'

Josh orders a bottle of Bollinger, which, I tell him, is totally over the top. A couple of glasses would have been fine. But when the barman eases the cork from the bottle with a gentle pop, I sigh with satisfaction and take a photo for my own Instagram account. I won't put it up until everything's signed and sealed. Don't want to tempt fate.

When the champagne is poured, we make a toast to brave decisions. I wish Josh the best of luck with his divorce, and he says that he had a call from Sheedy earlier and things are moving along far more quickly than he expected.

'Which is good in lots of ways,' he says. 'It's made me have to face up to the fact that it's happening.'

'Charles and I did it all wrong,' I tell him. 'We put it on

hold because of being too busy. Now that I can think about it more clearly, there was nothing more important than getting ourselves into the right place personally.'

'Can't get everything right,' says Josh.

'I was too comfortable with being half in and half out of our marriage. Maybe I even grew to like it. I'm such an idiot.'

'No you're not,' he says. 'You're a wonderful business-woman who's selling her company for a life-changing chunk of money. You've been totally validated, Ariel.'

'I always think being validated makes it sound like you're a parking ticket,' I say.

He laughs and pours more champagne.

I'm light-headed before we finish the bottle and I say that I'm going to bed.

'I think I will too,' he says.

We get into the lift together.

He's on the third floor. I'm on the fourth.

When the doors open on level three, he steps out, then turns to me.

'Anything else you want to do while we're here?' he asks.

I follow him out of the lift and along the corridor to his room.

He opens the door and we fall onto the king-sized bed. We're a tangle of clothes and limbs, laughing and giggling like a couple of teenagers, and then I'm lost in the sheer pleasure of him.

#LoveLondon #NoStrings #CelebrateSuccess

Chapter 41

Iseult

You have to take risks. We will only
understand the miracle of life fully when
we allow the unexpected to happen.

Paulo Coelho

Back in Dublin after the Waterford trip, my boss, Ivor, calls me into his office.

'Congratulations,' he says immediately. 'You've been promoted.'

I look at him in astonishment. I'd applied for a more senior position before I went to the Caribbean, but upward mobility within the Civil Service can be slow and tortuous, and with everything else going on in my life I'd almost forgotten about my application. Or at least I'd deliberately pushed it to the back of my mind because I didn't want to think I wasn't getting it.

'Oh my God! That's great. Will I have my own team?' I beam at him.

'Not here,' he says. 'They're moving you to the airport.'

'There isn't a chance of anything here, is there?' I ask. 'You know how much I love the port.'

'Not immediately,' he replies. 'Of course you can apply for a transfer back here when a position at your level becomes available and we'll be delighted to have you, but you should get the experience there too, Izzy. It's good for your CV to move around a bit.'

He's right. Like him, many of the more senior people at the port have come from other areas within Revenue and Customs. It took a while to get him up to speed on how things happened here. But he's a good boss and he looks out for all the staff. It'll take me time to get used to the airport. Besides, I like a challenge.

Nevertheless, I'm dazed when I go back to my desk.

'What did Ivor want?' asks Natasha as I sit down.

I tell her about my promotion and about the move to the airport.

'You'll love it,' she says. 'At least you won't be standing in a force ten gale hoping an irate driver doesn't mow you down.'

'I'm excited, but I'll miss being here.'

'Don't be daft.' She grins at me. 'You've got to climb the greasy pole, Izzy. We all do. Until we decide we want to give it all up and live the simple life.'

I think about the promotion all day. It'll be some time before my transfer comes through, so I'll be working with the gang for a while yet. But things will shift between us. They'll know I'm going and I won't feel part of the team any more. It's the way it is. As I scoot back to Marino at the end of my shift, I also think about the impact moving to the airport will have on my personal life. The commute there from Riverside

Lodge will be even worse than the commute to the port. I'm going to be spending half my life getting to and from work.

I know it's highly unlikely, but I wonder if I could persuade Charles to move somewhere closer.

I dismiss the thought almost immediately. I couldn't even ask him to consider leaving his beautiful home, especially as he's totally committed to redecorating it and making it ours. (He's actually been in touch with the interior designer I follow on Instagram. She's coming to see us next week.)

As I park my scooter and let myself in the front door, I think that perhaps I should move to Terenure now rather than waiting for Mum and Dad to come home. My life is changing. It's time for me to embrace that change and be positive about it.

I say this to Charles when I call over to him later that evening. I've brought a change of clothes for the morning, but I now keep a selection of cosmetics and other bits and pieces at Riverside Lodge so that staying over doesn't seem like a major event any more. He's delighted that I'm talking about moving in permanently, but is also taken aback when I tell him about my promotion and that it means working at the airport.

'Congratulations,' he says. 'You deserve it. You certainly work hard enough. I honestly couldn't cope with the shift work myself.'

'Thank you.'

'I bet you're thinking about the commute,' he says.

'It did occur to me,' I admit.

'You do know that you don't have to keep working?' he says. 'I mean, I know you love it, and I'm not asking you to stop, but it's not essential.'

'I've just been promoted,' I point out. 'It's pretty essential to me, don't you think?'

'What about when we have children?' he asks.

'I was thinking that you'll be a perfect stay-at-home father.' His eyes widen. 'Are you serious?'

'Why shouldn't I be? You told me you thought you'd be a great dad. Why not a great stay-at-home dad?'

'I wouldn't be able to look after a child and write a book!' He looks aghast.

'What about all the women who write books and have children?' I ask. 'What do they do?'

'I . . .'

'I'm not saying you have to be full-time looking after the baby,' I say. 'But you'll definitely be on hand, won't you?'

He still can't speak.

I go to the bathroom, and when I come back, Charles takes a deep breath and tells me that I have a point, and that if and when we have children, he'll certainly do his share. But, he says with a slight tone of terror in his voice, we'll have to plan it so it doesn't coincide with him being in the depths of writing. Or editing. Because he doesn't think he could do both.

'Maybe your next murder mystery can be a domestic noir,' I suggest. 'Where the wife murders the husband because he doesn't understand the nature of childcare.'

'I do!' cries Charles. 'That's why I'm so anxious about it.'

I laugh. After a moment, he does too.

I really think I'm starting to turn him into husband material.

Ivor tells me that it's going to be a month before my move happens, which means I'm still working at the port when

Mum and Dad arrive home. I've been using Dad's trusty Ford to commute from Charles's house while I wait for the arrival of the new electric Kia he ordered.

'You've bought me a car?' I looked at him in complete amazement when he told me.

'I'm lucky that I only have to walk up the stairs to work,' he told me. 'I want you to be able to do your commute in ecological comfort.'

I flung my arms around him and kissed him.

The day after my parents' return, I park outside the house in Marino and feel a thrill of delight at seeing the warm glow of light through the window that tells me they're home. I ring the bell, then put my key in the lock and shout to tell them I'm here.

'Izzy!' It's Mum who hurries out from the kitchen and throws her arms around me. 'How wonderful to see you again, dearest darling. I'm sorry it's been so long.'

She's followed by Dad, who joins the group hug and the general delight at us all seeing each other again, though I hasten to assure them that I've been fine in their absence and that Adrian and Cori needed them more.

'They did need us,' agrees Mum as she leads the way back into the kitchen, where she immediately puts on the kettle for a cup of tea. 'But, oh, Izzy, you needed us too.'

'You can't be everywhere at once,' I tell her. 'And I've managed on my own.'

'You've certainly managed to surprise us,' agrees Dad. 'Breaking up with Steve, getting engaged to Charles. Where is he, by the way? We need to meet him.'

'He didn't want to muscle in on our first hello,' I say. 'We can get together at the weekend.'

'You certainly look happy,' says Mum.

'I am.'

'And you've been promoted.' Dad beams at me. 'You deserve it, of course. There were loads of online stories about that drugs haul you were part of. Impressive stuff.'

'It was,' I agree.

'So tell me everything.' Mum puts mugs of tea and a large plate of chocolate Kimberleys on the table. I pull one of the mugs towards me, unwrap a biscuit and proceed to give her a reasonably full run-down of my life since I met Charles Miller.

'He's certainly splashed out on the ring,' observes Dad. 'It doesn't look like it came cheap.'

'He's one of the most generous men you could ever meet,' I tell him, and then add that he's bought a brand-new car that will mainly be for me. Dad nods approvingly.

'And the age gap?' Mum gives me a wary look. 'That's OK?'

'I don't even notice it,' I say. 'What I do notice, though, is that he's a mature person. Appearances don't matter to him. He's not a slave to fashion. The only thing he's obsessed with is his writing.'

'And his divorce?'

'Coming along,' I assure her. 'He's hoping it'll be signed and sealed by the summer. And we could have the wedding at his house. It's gorgeous,' I add. 'I love it there. The rooms are amazing, and there's a fabulous garden.'

I don't say anything about the mews at the back of it. I'm suddenly imagining Ariel working from home on the day of our wedding, staring out of the window at the celebrations. I shudder.

We haven't heard anything from her in ages, and there's been no sign of her any time I've been at Riverside Lodge. She hasn't come out of the mews to take phone calls as she used to, and there hasn't been any hint of a Freedom Friday bottle of wine. I don't like to think I've vanquished a love rival, but I most certainly have put my foot down, and it seems to have worked.

We talk about Charles and the wedding for ages, then the topic switches to my brother and his family, and Mum and Dad produce photos and videos of the boys and Azaria that melt my heart. I say that I'll definitely have to visit and meet my niece and nephews, although it'll probably be next year by the time I can do it.

'Have you and Charles discussed a family?' asks Mum, when Dad leaves the kitchen for a moment. I tell her about his terror of being a stay-at-home dad. She laughs, but when I say it won't be for a while yet, she advises me not to leave it too late.

'Not that I'm advocating having a baby straight away,' she says. 'But you can let it drift and then it's a bit more difficult, and, well . . .'

'Are you telling me I'll be too old to have a baby?' I say. 'Cori's older than me and she's popping them out.'

'She was only very slightly older than you when she had the twins,' Mum reminds me. 'And twins are in our family you know. They skipped mine and Jenni's generation, but your grandmother was a twin, don't forget.'

'So now it's twins I'm having.' I make a face at her. 'Oh, Mum. Let me get married first.'

'Sorry. Sorry. I'm letting things run away with me.'

'You are. And we do still have to wait for Charles's divorce.'

Because no matter how comfortable I am with moving in with him before it's made final, I'm certainly not going to have his children until he's well and truly disentangled from his agent-slash-ex.

Chapter 42

Ariel

*If you can meet with Triumph and Disaster
and treat those two imposters just the same.*
Rudyard Kipling

It's Friday, and I have a bottle of champagne in the fridge. It's good champagne, a Laurent-Perrier that Penny Blackwater gave me when she won the emerging writers award she was shortlisted for. I went to Belfast for the day and we had a great time at the Linen Hall, where everyone was in good spirits and Penny did an absolutely amazing reading from her book. She gave me the champagne as I was leaving, saying that if it wasn't for me she wouldn't be a published author at all. This is patently untrue: Penny is hugely talented and I've no doubt she'd have found a publishing home, but I'm glad to be part of her success story.

The champagne has been sitting in the fridge ever since, but it seems to me that today might be a good day to open it. I look up at Charles's house. With the longer evenings, the sun is reflecting off the windows, and the red brick of the walls looks warm yet stately.

Interested in a one-off Freedom Friday
Special? I have business news that needs to be
shared. Obviously not if it's an issue for you
and Iseult. And it'll be quick, I promise

I send the text and wait for a reply. I'm not sure there'll be one. Charles and I have been communicating by email these last few weeks, and we've kept all of them brief and businesslike.

If it's absolutely essential to talk to me face to
face. We did say no more Freedom Fridays

In and out, no worries

I take the bottle from the fridge and walk up the garden path. I'm expecting Charles to be waiting at the door for me, but he's not. I push it open and step into the house.

'Anyone home?' I call.

There's no answer, so I begin to climb the stairs. Charles is in the living room, standing by the window.

'Were you watching me walk up the garden?' I ask.

'Only after you texted. What's the news?'

'Let's open this first.' I hand him the bottle. I've always allowed Charles to open champagne, even though I'm perfectly capable of doing it myself.

'You said in and out,' he says.

'There's time for a quick taste first.'

'Good news, then?' he asks.

'Yes.'

He doesn't say any more, but fills two Waterford crystal flutes with the fizz.

'Congratulations, whatever it is.'

'Thank you.' I look around. 'No Izzy this evening?'

'She's at a farewell do,' says Charles.

In some ways that's a relief, because it means she won't barge in throwing wild accusations around the place. On the other hand, it might have been good to have her here tonight.

'She was promoted,' he adds. 'She's transferring to the airport. It's a big change for her.'

'Congratulations to her. I know you said she works hard,' I say. 'The reason I'm here is that things are changing for me too. As a consequence, they'll change for you. But ultimately it'll be very positive,' I add as I see his face darken.

'How?'

I tell him about the offer from Denton-Marr that I've accepted and signed, and that the ABA Agency will be moving from the mews behind his house to their Mount Street offices. Then I add the most important part – that I'll be a consultant agent and spending the next six months based in Los Angeles, though making frequent trips to Dublin and London.

'What!' He looks at me in disbelief. 'You're leaving me?'

'Not at all. I'll be getting to know another aspect of the business.' I take a deep breath before continuing. 'Obviously these are big changes, but then there have been big changes for both of us in the last few months already. Our divorce will be done any day now, you're moving on with your life, and I think it would be better to move on with your agent too. Denton-Marr-Barrett gives you the opportunity to do that. One of the senior agents in particular is passionate about your work and would love to represent you. It's your choice, of course, and you may want to move to another agency, but I honestly think Tristan Marr would be a great fit for you.'

He stares at me. 'You don't want to be my agent any more?'

'I've loved being your agent, Charles. It's been an absolute privilege. But I think it's best for both of us, and for Izzy, if we're not involved any more.'

'But—'

'Seriously, Charles. Carrying on as we are isn't a good idea. You must see that.'

'I know it's been tricky sometimes—'

'And it'll be nothing but trickier when you're married. And not . . .' I hold up my hand to stop him interrupting me, 'not because of any feelings I have for either of you. Simply that I'm your ex and she'll soon be your wife and you don't need both of us in your life.'

'What about the deals you're working on for me?'

'I'll conclude any deals that are currently out there but will liaise with Tristan on them if you're agreeable to working with him. You'll like him, Charles. He's very knowledgeable and has brilliant contacts on the movie side of things, which is a big bonus.'

'You did all right with adaptations.'

'He'll do better.'

'You think?'

'I do.'

'Do you want to set up a meeting with him?'

I nod. I've been cool and calm about this until now, but it's suddenly real. Charles and I are properly breaking up in every sense of the word. I finish my glass of champagne and he begins to top it up, but I stop him and say that I have to go.

'What about your office?' he asks suddenly, looking out of the window. 'The mews is part of our settlement deal. Are you looking for something in lieu now that you're moving out?'

'Only your good wishes.'

'You have them, of course,' he says. Then he gives me a half-smile and says he always knew it would happen one day. That I'd sell the business and send him a letter telling him what an exciting time it was for the company and for him. Except that he thought we'd still be together as a couple when it did.

'I might get you to write that letter for everyone else.' I smile at him. 'You'd phrase it much better than I could. OK, I've got to go now, Charles. I'll set up the meeting with Tristan, and of course we'll be in touch before I leave for the States.'

'I'm glad for you, but I'm not good with change,' he says.

'And yet since *Winter's Heartbreak*, there's been lots of change in your life,' I point out. 'You became a massive bestseller. Your work has been made into movies. Everyone in the trade loves you. I love everything you've achieved. Where we went wrong, you and I, was getting involved romantically. I fell for you, but I shouldn't have.'

'I fell for you too,' he reminds me.

'We were high on success,' I say. 'That wasn't the right basis for love.'

'But I did love you.'

'I loved you too.'

'Yet not now?'

'This might sound a bit crazy to you, Charles. I do still love you, in a way. But I love myself more.'

'I see.'

'For a while you absolutely were the most important man in my life and for a long time I hung on to that,' I tell him. 'It's taken time, but I've got over it. And I'm glad you've found someone else. Someone who can't wait to share the rest of your life.'

He takes up the champagne bottle and pours some more champagne into my glass. 'To us,' he says, raising his own glass.

'To us,' I echo, as I tip mine against it.

Iseult

We're in the pub for my leaving drinks. A lot of people have come to wish me well in my new job at the airport, and even though I'm really sad to be leaving the port, I'm very excited about the move and the opportunities it might bring.

'Here you go.' Natasha puts another bottle of beer in front of me.

'This is my last,' I tell her. 'Senior executives like me can't get pissed with the plebs.'

She sticks out her tongue and we both laugh.

I haven't had that much to drink. I've mixed quite a few non-alcoholic beers with the alcoholic variety, and although I'm tired, it's because it's been a long day and I was out last night with Charles. We went to dinner after yet another book launch – who knew there were so many writers in Dublin – and stayed up late when we got back to Riverside Lodge because there was a documentary on TV about Ian

Rankin, who Charles has met a number of times and which he wanted to watch. I asked when there'd be a documentary about Charles himself and he told me that Ariel had tried to get someone interested after the Booker but that he probably wasn't exciting enough.

'You're exciting enough for me,' I said, and promptly yawned, which made him say that the excitement of knowing him had clearly worn off.

'Not entirely,' I said. 'But I think I'll head up to bed. I'm knackered and I have a busy day tomorrow.'

'I'll be up later,' said Charles. 'And I promise not to wake you.'

He lied about that, because he put his arm around me when he got into bed and I snuggled up against him, and then I turned around and kissed him, and next thing I knew we were making love, and honestly, it's so good with him that I feel elated every single time. We talked about inconsequential things for a short time afterwards, but, like every man I've ever known, it didn't take him long to fall asleep. To be fair, I nodded off soon afterwards too. He was still out for the count when I got up this morning, and although he's texted me twice, I've been too busy to do anything more than send emojis in reply.

'Any news on the wedding?' asks Natasha, who's plonked herself down beside me.

'We're working on it,' I say. 'I was too scared to do anything before their divorce came through, but his solicitor said it should be done and dusted by next week. And then it's full steam ahead.'

'You're so lucky,' she says. 'He's the sweetest guy, even

if he is on the older side. I'm reckoning that means lots of the kinks are already ironed out.'

'Oh, he has some of his own.' I grin. 'But no better woman than me to sort him.'

'Absolutely. I'm going to the bar. Would you like another drink?'

I glance at my watch and shake my head.

'I'm not cut out for late-night sessions any more,' I say. 'I'm going home.'

I get up and begin my goodbyes, telling everyone that I'll miss them madly and insisting that we'll stay in touch. There are lots of hugs and good wishes and it's nearly twenty minutes later before I actually leave the pub. Although night has fallen, a faint light remains on the horizon that lifts my spirits and says summer is on the way.

Despite being tired, there's a real spring in my step as I begin the walk back to Marino – I'd decided it was better to stay with Mum and Dad tonight rather than schlep across town – but then I see a taxi approach with its light on and I stop it.

'Terenure,' I tell the driver as I climb into the back seat and close my eyes.

Ariel

I know I shouldn't have allowed Charles to refill my glass again, but there's a lightness in the atmosphere between us that hasn't been there for months, and I can't help feeling happy about it.

'Perhaps all we needed was for you to dump me as a client,' he says when I tell him this.

'Oh, don't say that. We've made mistakes, Charles, but we've got over them.'

'To us,' he says again. 'Thank you for everything. For being such a great agent. For being a good wife, even if it didn't work out in the end. For always pointing me in the right direction. For putting up with me.'

'You're welcome.' I take a sip. 'I really do have to go after this. I'm meeting my accountant later. There are a few outstanding bits and pieces about the deal I want to check with him.'

'I thought it was signed.'

'Trivial things,' I say.

'It's Josh you're meeting?' he asks.

I nod.

It looks as though he's going to ask me something else, but in the end, he doesn't. He pours himself some more champagne and asks Siri to play jazz. As always, the playlist starts with 'I Fall in Love Too Easily', but then it moves on to Duke Ellington's 'Mood Indigo', which is one of my own personal favourites. I tell him to turn the volume up and I twirl around the room, the glass of bubbly in my hand.

I suppose it's because of the music, and because I've let my guard down, that neither of us hears the door opening. But both of us hear Iseult's sharp exclamation of 'What the actual fuck!'

I turn around so suddenly that I stumble into the table and send the champagne glass skittering across the room. It bangs into the wall and shatters into pieces.

'It's not what you think,' says Charles to Iseult. 'It absolutely isn't.'

I wince. Even written down, 'it's not what you think' is a cliché. Coming from his lips, it smacks of desperation.

'You know what I'm thinking, do you?' Iseult is spitting fiery rage. Her dark eyes are positively black and her spiky hair looks like sharp nails on her head.

'Neither of us knows what you're thinking,' I say. 'But if it's anything along the lines of Charles and me disrespecting you in some way, you're totally wrong.'

'I don't have to *think* you're disrespecting me,' she snarls. 'I can see that for myself.'

'Look, Ariel called up to the house to share some important news about her business,' says Charles. 'That's all.'

'Important news that you celebrate by having champagne and dancing around the living room.' Iseult gives him a look of disgust. 'The same way you celebrate *un*important news with her.'

'That's not true.' I speak softly and calmly. 'Honestly, Izzy, when you hear—'

'Oh fuck off,' she says. 'I'm not listening to you and I'm not listening to him. I've had enough of whatever weird psycho drama you guys are playing. You're far too invested in each other to give a shit about anyone else.'

'If you'd just—'

'I won't just!' She glares at him. 'I won't be taken for an absolute fool any more. I've had enough of it.'

'Nobody thinks you're a fool,' I say. 'And if you'd give me thirty seconds of your time—'

'I don't care if you think I am or not,' she snaps. 'Your opinions don't interest me in the least. And I don't have a single second of my time to waste on you.' She turns to Charles. 'Or you. I'm off. And so is this.'

She practically rips her beautiful engagement ring from her finger and hurls it at him. He ducks, and it flies across the room, coming to rest among the debris of the champagne glass.

'Iseult – Izzy – for God's sake . . .'

But she ignores him and storms out of the room, slamming the door behind her.

In the silence that follows, Julie London begins to sing 'Cry Me a River'.

Iseult

What an absolute idiot I've been. How could I have believed him when he said it was over? Their not being divorced should have been a massive red flag. The fact that they're still not divorced should have been an even bigger one. And there they were together drinking champagne and dancing to sultry music as though they were in a fecking nightclub.

Celeste had her doubts. Mum had her doubts. Even Steve, not that he was ever entitled to them, had his doubts. But I didn't. Oh no. I was too convinced that I was right, that Charles had fallen in love with me and that I was in love with him. Well, I *was* in love with him. But not now. Now he can rot in hell for all I care. Him and his agent-slash-ex-not-ex. They're welcome to each other.

They deserve each other.

I deserve better.

Ariel

'Oops,' I say into the silence. 'You'd better go after her.'

'Again?' he asks.

'What d'you mean?'

'How many times has she walked out on me?' he asks. 'At the dinner. At Seán Óg's launch. And now. Maybe she's telling me something.'

'All she's telling you is that she's upset.'

'But I seem to upset her all the damn time!'

'She's young. She's emotional. She needs reassurance.'

'I'm old. I'm emotional. I don't know if I can give her the reassurance she wants.'

'Oh, Charles.'

'Maybe I'm not cut out to be married,' he says. 'I made your life miserable, and I seem to be making her life miserable too.'

'You didn't make my life miserable,' I tell him. 'Things went wrong, that's all. It happens. And this time what's happened is that, understandably, Izzy's got the wrong end of the stick. I'm sure when she calms down she'll feel differently.'

'But I promised.' He gives me a mournful look. 'I promised no more Freedom Fridays. I promised not to see you in the house. I meant it. Yet I broke that promise.'

'I made you break it,' I say. 'I'm sorry.'

'You didn't,' he says. 'I should've told you not to come. To tell me whatever news you had over the phone. Or somewhere else. But you'd said it was good news and I thought . . . well, for a split second I thought maybe I had been nominated for another award. I wanted to hear it from you face to face.'

'You made a bad decision then,' I agree. 'Make a good one now. Go after her.'

He hesitates for a moment, then nods and walks out of the room, leaving me alone with Bryan Ferry and 'These Foolish Things', another of my favourite songs. I tell Siri to mute the music, then go to the kitchen and return with a dustpan and brush. After removing Iseult's engagement ring from the debris and leaving it on the sideboard, I sweep up the shards of glass and put them in the bin. I recall that the set of Waterford champagne glasses was a wedding present to Charles and me from Saxby-Brown. There were six. We broke others over the years. With this one smashed, that only leaves the one Charles was drinking from.

I leave it on the kitchen counter, and then I go home.

Chapter 43

Iseult

Your will shall decide your destiny.
Charlotte Brontë

I know it's the summer season because people in the baggage hall are dressed for the holiday destinations they're returning from rather than the grey drizzle that's been falling on Dublin on and off since yesterday. This morning's flights have come in from Malaga and Lisbon, Alicante and Tenerife, and there's a general end-of-holiday stress among those crowding around the belts, anxious for their luggage to appear. When it does, they'll wheel their cases through the blue EU channel, clamping down on vague feelings of guilt, even though they're perfectly entitled to bring home the booze or cigarettes they've picked up while they were away. As for anything else, there'll be one or two random stops, but we don't have any specific intelligence for the recently arrived flights, so I'm not expecting any problems.

As I walk past belt number 5, I do a double-take and stop in my tracks. I recognise the man hauling a large red suitcase from the belt, even though he's wearing a blue polo shirt, cream shorts and navy Skechers. As I watch, he puts his arm around the young woman beside him and kisses her on the cheek. She's much shorter than him, and dressed in pink leggings, a white top and pink flip-flops. A pair of enormous sunglasses perched on top of her blonde curls confirms they've come off one of the sun destination flights.

He hasn't seen me, and I'm tempted to let him go by without saying anything, but I can't. As they head towards the customs channels, I step in front of them. I sense their immediate nervous reaction to my uniform before Steve realises who I am.

'Izzy.' His voice is full of relief. 'What are you doing here?'

'I've been working here for the past two months,' I tell him. 'You're looking well. Nice holiday?'

'Yes, me and Taz went to Santa Ponsa for a week.' He turns to the girl with him. 'Taz, this is the old flame I mentioned before, Izzy. Izzy – Taz.'

'Nice to meet you,' I say. 'Have you known each other long?'

'Taz works at the clinic where I've been getting my scans.' Steve answers for her. 'She's made sure I've been well looked after.'

'And how are you doing now?' I ask.

'It's been tough.' His face darkens. 'I thought I'd be back on my feet quicker. But the holiday has helped and I'm feeling good.'

'I'm delighted to hear that.'

'You looked after him when he had his accident.' Taz finally speaks. 'That was nice of you.'

'Oh, Steve knows I'm a softie at heart.' I smile at her.

'We'd best be going,' says Steve. 'We pre-booked a cab.'

'Don't let me delay you,' I say. 'And don't worry, Steve, I'll tell my colleagues not to stop you.'

He gives me a slightly hunted look, and I grin. I know he probably has a small amount of weed in his luggage, and it's against the law to bring any of it into the country, even for personal use. He nods, but as he and Taz walk off, he diverts to the bathroom, where I'm pretty sure he'll flush it down the toilet.

I continue my stroll through the baggage area. Taz is obviously the reason Steve's calls stopped. I'm glad he's found someone else, and amused that she's been able to get him out of black, something I singularly failed to do, even when we were on holiday. It's hard to believe that this time last year we were planning our wedding in the Caribbean. In the time since I went there with Celeste instead, he's been on holiday with someone else and I've been engaged to someone else. From being all-important in each other's lives, we're strangers who exchange pleasantries in a crowded baggage hall.

At the end of the hall I see Killian O'Keefe with Betsy. Killian is one of the dog handlers at the airport and Betsy, like Chips at the port, is a gorgeous English springer spaniel. Even when she's working, she exudes friendliness, and Killian has his hands full making sure the passengers don't try to pet her. She's an absolute demon at sniffing out drugs, no matter how creatively they're hidden, and we all adore her. The pair of them are off to do a routine check, and I leave them to it, making my way to my office to deal with a backlog of administration. It's never my favourite task, and I delay myself slightly by standing at the window and gazing out at the airport. I do miss the view over Dublin Bay, but I've grown to like watching the planes moving around the airfield, while there's a certain beauty in seeing them arrive and depart with power and grace.

When I've finished the admin, I sling my bag over my shoulder and head for the staff car park. I put up my umbrella and think of all those returning holidaymakers, some disappointed at the grey skies after the continental heat, and others delighted to be back to the soft rain and ever-present greenery.

I get into my car and drive to Marino. It's quiet in the house. Mum and Dad have gone to Galway for a week – Dad spotted an amazing-value deal online and booked it without even telling her. But as he said afterwards, it was too good to miss. The hotel has a golf course and a spa, so their joint holiday needs will be catered for. I love that they know exactly what's right for each other and that they still love each other after all these years.

I've just finished changing from my uniform to a plain top and jeans when my phone beeps.

See you there OK?

I send a thumbs-up emoji in reply. Celeste and I are going to the Taste of Dublin food festival this afternoon. It's held in the Iveagh Gardens every year and is a Mecca for people like her. Even though I'm not a foodie, I enjoy it too. I'm hoping that the drizzle eases off, however, because although there are plenty of tents, it's an event that's best enjoyed in warm sunlight. It seems that the gods are on our side, because almost as soon as I arrive at the gardens, the rain stops, and Celeste, who's waiting for me, lowers her brightly coloured umbrella.

'Let's go,' she says, leading the way.

She's booked in for one of the masterclass sessions, and I'm happy to watch a celebrity chef prepare and cook a main course with locally sourced ingredients. Afterwards, I buy a couple of cooking sauces at an artisan stall. Despite being impressed by the chef, I honestly can't be bothered with all that make-it-from-scratch palaver when I can get it in a jar. Celeste ignores the ready-made stuff in favour of buying some herbs and spices, then both of us spend a happy couple of hours checking out the stalls and the samples before she says that we should go into town for some drinks.

'Seriously?' I look at her in astonishment. 'We've had enough food and wine here to last us a week.'

'We had one glass of wine,' she corrects me. 'And . . . well . . . Darragh texted. He's in the Bailey.'

She's still going out with her bookseller. I know it's only a few months, but it's the longest she's gone out with anyone in years.

'I don't want to be a gooseberry,' I say. 'I'll head home.'

'Oh, do come, Izzy. We haven't been out together in ages.'

'We were out last week,' I remind her.

'I mean you, me and Darragh,' she says. 'I can't even remember when we last got together.'

The fact that she wants me to have drinks with them makes me think this relationship is serious. Although to be fair to them both, they're always trying to include me. I usually say no.

'One drink,' I tell her. 'Then I'm going home.'

'Excellent.'

Despite the tiredness in our legs from walking around the food fair, we head on foot to Duke Street, where the pub is located. I don't tell Celeste that I've actively avoided this part of town in recent times because Warren's, the jewellers where I chose my engagement ring, is nearby. Every time I remember picking out the ring, and every time I think about flinging it at Charles, I want to cry.

I will *not* cry, though. I absolutely will not.

'Oh.' Celeste stops abruptly outside the bookshop in Grafton Street. She looks at the poster and then turns to me with an anxious expression.

I recognise the picture on the poster – the dead body on a tropical beach. And the title of the book above it with the author's name below: *A Caribbean Calypso. Charles Miller*. Copies of the book make up the entire window display. I have to admit that it looks good. If I hadn't read it already, I'd be tempted to go in and buy it.

'I forgot it was out now,' I say, although I didn't forget, I shoved it to the back of my mind.

'Do you want to go in and have a look?' she asks.

'Why? I can see it perfectly well from here.'

'But maybe . . .' She points at a notice in the other window. *Reading and book signing today with the author, Charles Miller.*

'It's probably over,' I say. 'The shops will be shut soon,'

'Thursday evening,' says Celeste. 'Late opening. And the reading doesn't start for half an hour, it says so there.' She nods at the notice.

'Not for me,' I say.

'If you're sure.'

We walk past the bookshop to the Bailey, where Darragh is waiting. He gives me a brief hug and Celeste a much longer one, then asks what we want to drink. I tell him I'll have a gin and tonic, and when he returns with it, I drink about a quarter before telling Celeste I'll be back in a while.

'Are you going back to the bookshop?' she asks.

'For a moment, that's all.'

'I'll come with you.'

I shake my head.

I need to be by myself.

Ariel

It's great to be back in Dublin. Not that I haven't loved every minute of LA (it's a city that can definitely break you or make you), but it's nice to cut back the pace and walk through St Stephen's Green and along Grafton Street again.

I stop in front of the bookshop and assess the signage for Charles's reading tonight, although it's nothing to do with me any more. Tristan Marr, his new agent, has already texted me to say that everything is looking great. He and Charles are getting on famously, and I couldn't be happier. It was Charles who asked if I'd like to come to the reading. He said I'd been very involved in the book and it would be nice to see me there.

But it's Tristan I see first, on the upper level of the store where the event is taking place. There are already a few super-fans waiting for Charles, which is heartening.

'How is he?' I ask him.

'Practising away in the stockroom,' he says.

'He'll be fine. He always gets good sales at events.'

'Yes, the manager says they've sold a load of books already. She told the buyers that Charles would be here later, but they couldn't wait.'

'That'll keep him happy.'

'He needs to be told he's good, doesn't he?'

'Don't we all.'

I smile at Tristan and then take a seat at the back of the room, where I'm partially hidden by a display of Irish history books. As the room begins to fill up, I recognise the young woman sliding into the seat in front of me. I hesitate for a moment, then tap her on the shoulder.

'Oh,' she says when she turns around and sees me. 'Ariel.'

'Francesca.' I smile at her. 'How are you? How's the book going?'

I didn't hear anything more about her after our meeting at the Shelbourne, although for a while afterwards I kept an eye on the trade news to see which agent her father had deemed good enough to represent her.

'No news,' she says. 'I've been busy at work.'

She's in hotel administration as far as I remember.

'It takes time,' I say. 'I hope you're still writing.'

'Oh, I'm not sure about that any more.' She shrugs. 'I don't think it's me really.'

'Francesca! It's absolutely you. Your book is marvellous. Did you get an agent?'

'It didn't work out.' She makes a face. 'Dad feels he can do it himself.'

'Look, I don't want you to take this the wrong way, but please don't let your dad influence your future career. I know he means well, I know he thinks he's doing his best for you, but he doesn't have the knowledge or the contacts or the experience.'

'A friend of his knows someone in a small publishing company who might be interested,' she says.

'And have they made an offer?'

She shakes her head.

'Even if you want to go to that publisher, you can still have a chat with me first,' I tell her. 'I'm not trying to muscle in, I promise. I just want to be sure you're doing the right thing. I'm in Dublin for a couple of days, so get in touch if you feel it's appropriate.'

She hesitates, and then tells me she has my number and might give me a call. I say that's fine and settle back in my chair. She turns around, then a moment later turns back again.

'Could you meet me tomorrow?' she asks. 'The morning would be best, but whatever suits you.'

'Ten thirty? At the Shelbourne?'

'That'd be perfect,' she says. 'My dad won't be with me.'

I smile to myself. Sometimes the things that seem to pass you by are simply waiting for the right moment.

The room is now full, and Charles walks out to a warm round of applause. After being introduced by the store manager, he opens the book and begins to read.

He's so, so good at this. He has them in the palm of his hand. I look at all the rapt faces and then catch my breath. Because I recognise another young woman, this time sitting in the back row, shielded behind a table display.

It's Iseult O'Connor.

Charles's beta-reader-slash-ex-fiancée.

Are they back together?

*

Charles finishes his reading and the applause is enthusiastic. People immediately start to form a queue to get their books signed. Iseult stays where she is, watching them.

I go over to her.

'Hello,' I say. 'Welcome to Charles's reading.'

'Oh. It's you.' She looks at me in surprise. 'I should've known you'd be here.'

'I flew in specially.'

'Of course you did. I heard you'd moved to the States.'

'That's right, although it's a temporary move.'

We sit in silence for a moment, and then I ask if she and Charles are an item again. Because the last I heard from him was that she'd point-blank refused to see him and had blocked his number. He was devastated and said that he'd lost the person who mattered most to him in the whole world. I felt a twinge when he said that, but it didn't hurt the way it once would have. Ellis had tried to talk to her too, but Iseult was having none of it. The woman has an absolute iron will. She would've made a great agent.

'I'm not with Charles, but I spent a lot of time with that book,' she replies. 'I wanted to see the final copies.'

'Are you going to get one signed?' I ask.

She shakes her head.

'Did you buy one?'

'Not yet.'

I reach into my bag and take a book from it. I hand it to her.

'It's already signed,' I say. 'I was sent some for publicity purposes.'

She takes it and studies it, running her hands over the dark blue cover with its embossed lettering.

'It looks good,' she says. 'He was so worried about it.'

'He worries about all of them,' I tell her. 'It's nothing new.'

'I guess you know him better than I ever did.'

'That part of him, yes.'

'How's he managing without you?' she asks.

'Perfectly well,' I reply. 'He has a new agent.'

'I always knew he needed a different agent. No offence,' she adds.

'None taken. You were right. How d'you think he's managing without *you*?'

'Equally well, I guess.'

'You know, nothing happened between him and me that night,' I say. 'Nothing was ever going to happen. I hadn't seen him for ages and all I wanted to do was celebrate my good news.'

'He explained all that in multiple voicemails. Over and over. A one-off, he said. Toasting your big business deal. That's when he told me about the States.'

'So why did you break it off?' I ask. 'If you knew it was perfectly innocent, why didn't you stay with him?'

'You still came and he still celebrated,' she says. 'It wasn't what I asked of him.'

'I'm sorry. It's my fault. I told him I had news, and—'

'It doesn't matter. He promised not to see you but he did.'

'And yet he loves you,' I say.

'He loves the idea of me,' she says. 'In the same way my ex-fiancé loved the idea of me. In Steve's case, it wasn't till we split up and I started doing my own thing that he wanted me in his life again. He couldn't believe I was managing fine without him. As for Charles – I was someone, something different for him. I wasn't part of the whole book tribe thing. It was fun for him at first, but even if I hadn't come back that evening and found you with him, something would have triggered our split. We were too different.'

'I don't know about your first fiancé, but I think you're being a little hard on Charles.'

She shrugs.

'He said he tried everything to convince you he loved you,' I say. 'He went after you that night, but you'd already got a cab.'

'I wasn't going to hang around waiting for him to run along the street and lie to me again. I haven't seen him or spoken to him since I handed back the engagement ring.'

If you can call flinging it across the room handing it back. I glance down at the multicoloured ring on my own finger. Izzy glances at it too.

'Our divorce came through,' I say.

'Oh.' She looks surprised. 'I thought perhaps . . . well, it doesn't matter to me any more, of course.'

But it matters to me. It matters a lot.

I didn't expect to feel different after the divorce, but I do. I feel as though I've been released. And as far as our professional relationship goes – well, when I met Charles earlier, I was seeing him as a client and not as a man who's been part of my emotional life for over fifteen years. It was unexpectedly wonderful.

Perhaps I've grown up. It's a bit of a blow to think it's taken me so long.

The queue of people waiting for him to sign their books is thinning out.

'Sure you're not going to say anything to him?' I ask.

She shakes her head.

'I'm sorry,' I say. 'I behaved badly towards you. I didn't mean to, but I did.'

'How did you behave badly?' Her dark eyes seem even darker.

'By not respecting your boundaries.' I give her a half-smile. 'By being self-centred. By not understanding Charles despite the fact that I should have had plenty of experience in understanding him. Since moving to the States, I've had a crash course on boundaries. I've realised that perhaps I'm not very good at reading signals.'

'I'd've thought it's pretty easy to read "my ex is getting married to someone else so I should keep out of their way",' she says, and for the first time she sounds animated.

'I didn't think,' I tell her. 'Or at least . . .' I sigh. 'I thought I had more of a right to him than you. Not necessarily to be in his life and in his bed, but I thought you were . . .'

'Too young and too stupid.'

'Not stupid!' I exclaim. 'Never that. It's that you *weren't* part of the book tribe. I was dismissive of that. I shouldn't have been. I'm sorry.'

'It's fine,' she says, even though from her tone I know that it isn't. Not really.

'Ellis told me that you and I were more alike than I thought,' I say.

'She told me that too,' says Iseult. 'So did Pamela. I didn't know whether to feel insulted or complimented.'

And then she starts to smile.

'Who'd've thought it,' she says. 'We're alike because we

both let Charles take over our lives. We both wanted more for him than we did for ourselves. And now we've both decided enough is enough.'

'I think Charles loves you in a way he never loved me,' I say.

'He loves himself more,' she remarks.

'Oh, Izzy, I know he can be self-centred, but—'

'But you still defend him.'

'It's been my job. I can't help myself.' I grin. 'I heard about your promotion. Congratulations.'

'I do a lot of the North American flights. Just to warn you.'

I laugh, and so does she.

'I'll be going.' She stands up. 'It was . . . good to see you, Ariel. I'm sorry we never got to know each other in better circumstances.'

'Maybe there's never good circumstances for an ex and a wife-to-be.'

'But we're both exes now.' She smiles again, and her face lights up. 'So you never know.'

'You never do.'

She heads for the stairs.

She's disappeared from view when Charles comes up to me.

'Great reading,' I say. 'Congratulations.'

'Never mind that.' He gives me an impatient look. 'Was that . . . did I see Izzy?'

I nod.

'Where's she gone?'

'I don't know.'

'What did she want?'

461

'To hear you read.'

'Why didn't she wait?'

'I don't know that either.'

'Why didn't you stop her?'

'Because she said goodbye.'

'I've been trying to see her for months!' he cries. 'Absolutely months. With no success. It's impossible to see her at work and I can't hang around her house, not with her parents there. They'd report me to the police.'

'Are you still in love with her?'

'You always thought it was some stupid fling, didn't you?' he demands. 'But it wasn't. I do love her, Ariel. I think I loved her from the moment I first saw her. I never properly showed it, because even though I thought I was the mature person in the relationship, I absolutely wasn't. I kept thinking it was OK to mix it up with you and her, that it didn't matter because I knew how I felt. I was able to keep you apart in my head. But she didn't know. Not really. I love her and I lost her and I'm an absolute fool.'

A few months ago, I would have been devastated by those words. Now, I'm simply amazed. Amazed that he's said them and amazed that he sounds so sincere.

'I patronised her,' he says. 'I treated her as though she were young and foolish instead of the clever, capable woman she is.'

'We both did,' I murmur.

'Yes, but she wasn't engaged to you! I shouldn't stand around here talking. I should be out looking for her.'

'If you think that's a good idea. But Charles, I got the impression talking to her . . . I don't know if there's a way back for you.'

'Maybe not. But I want to hear it from her.'

He turns away from me and clatters down the stairs.

I stay where I am and add the appointment with Francesca to my calendar. Then I say goodnight to Tristan, who's been schmoozing with the bookseller and is now heading off to another event.

After that, I text Josh to say that if he wants that drink he asked me about earlier, I'm free.

Iseult

The ice has melted in my gin and tonic when I get back to the Bailey. Darragh offers to get me another.

'Did you see Charles?' asks Celeste while he's at the bar.

'I saw him do the reading and sign books. And I met Ariel.'

'The agent-slash-nearly-ex.'

'The actual ex now,' I say, and tell her that the divorce has come through.

'Does that make any difference?' Celeste has been my absolute rock ever since I broke up with Charles. She hasn't tried to make me think one thing or the other, to believe that I made the right choice, or to persuade me to give Charles another chance. She's backed me up every moment of every day just as she did when Steve and I split up. She also helped to sell my wedding dress online. I actually got quite a good price for it. One day I'll find someone and get married and she can stop looking out for me and simply be my bridesmaid instead of breakup support. However, the way things are going, I'll be her bridesmaid first.

I tell her that Charles and Ariel's divorce means nothing to me, that she means nothing to me and that he means nothing to me. That the entire episode means nothing to me. It's not entirely true, of course. We're all affected in some way by the things that happen to us. But I don't feel the same visceral pain now as I did the evening I arrived at Charles's house and saw her there with him again. It seems I'm actually quite good at getting over broken engagements.

Then Charles walks into the bar.

He looks around and sees me. Celeste spots him at the exact same moment and clutches my arm just as Darragh returns with my gin and tonic. Charles looks at him, clearly wondering how he knows him. It's Darragh who speaks first.

'Charles Miller. Good to see you. I hear your reading was a tremendous success.'

'I . . . It was good, thanks.'

'Can I help you at all?' asks Darragh. 'I'm from Delaney's Bookshop.'

'Oh, yes, Delaney's.' Charles nods. 'Um . . . I wanted to talk to Izzy, if she doesn't mind.'

'We're a little busy here,' says Celeste. 'I'm not sure she has the time.'

'Do you?' His blue eyes look straight into mine. 'Do you have five minutes?'

'There's not a lot we can discuss in five minutes,' I say.

'Please,' says Charles.

Celeste asks if I'm sure as I stand up, and I tell her I am. Because I am sure. I can't avoid Charles any more. It's worked for a long time, but sooner or later I have to face him. And myself.

'Do you want to stay in here or go outside?' he asks.

'Outside.'

We step out into the fresh air. The street is thronged with tourists, many of whom are wearing brightly coloured caps against the possibility of more rain. I forgot to bring my umbrella. It's still in the pub.

'Thank you for coming to my reading,' says Charles.

'I was walking by. I saw it was happening.'

'Nevertheless, it was nice to know you cared enough.'

'I was with that book from the start. Of course I cared.'

'You made me write it, after all,' he says.

'No I didn't.'

'You did,' he insists. 'I'd still be faffing around with *Springs Eternal* if it weren't for you. And it would've been a shit book, I know it would.'

'Oh, I'm sure you'd have turned it into something brilliant. You always do.'

'Always?' He raises an eyebrow. 'I thought you'd only read *Winter's Heartbreak*.'

'I had to read the others. Especially after Ariel said you put real people in them.'

'I don't,' he says. 'I might . . . borrow events, but that's all.'

'So your next book?' I ask. 'Crime or a tear-jerker?'

'I haven't decided yet.'

'A jilted fiancé who goes on a murderous rampage? Or a fiancée whose heart is so broken she can't function in normal society. Until she gets her hands on poison.'

'You should write a crime book yourself,' he says. 'You have the best ideas.'

'I could never, ever write a book. Though I'm better at my reports since I moved jobs.'

'How's that going?'

'Good. I like it.'

'And an easy commute from Marino.'

'Yes.'

'I know you don't believe that Ariel coming to the house that night was completely unexpected,' he says. 'But it was.'

'Whether it was or wasn't doesn't matter,' I say.

'It matters to me.' His tone is fierce. 'A lot. Even if I never see you again after today, it matters that you believe me. That I hadn't invited her, that she only came because she had news about her company and—'

'And you didn't say it's not appropriate to come to the house tonight, let's meet somewhere tomorrow instead,' I finish for him. 'Instead you poured her a glass of champagne and danced with her.'

He stops walking and turns to me. 'I agree that would have been the right thing to say. I'm sorry I didn't say it, and I'm even more sorry about the champagne and the dancing.'

'So am I.'

'But you really do have to understand that it was impromptu.'

'I understand. It's fine. I forgive you.'

'Oh.'

We begin walking again.

'You and I were always a romantic fiction,' I tell him. 'A younger woman. An older man. Falling in love on a tropical island. Me with an already broken heart. You . . . Well, your heart was fine despite your agent-slash-ex, but you were struggling with your book. Throw in cocktails on the beach and sex in your poolside villa. It'd be more surprising if we hadn't fallen for each other.'

'But we were in love even when we came back.'

'Dublin in the snow,' I say. 'Your fabulous party. Fireworks at midnight. Your amazing proposal. How could I say no?'

'Did you want to say no?' he asks.

'Not then,' I admit.

'So if all the things that went wrong are fixed, with Ariel in the States and our divorce finalised, would you reconsider?'

'It wasn't only Ariel,' I say as we reach the end of Grafton Street. 'She was a great excuse, but it was about me too. What I wanted and what you couldn't give me.'

'What couldn't I give you?'

'The confidence to be myself,' I say. 'I was always the less experienced, less sophisticated person in the relationship. An appendage to your more glittering life.'

'You were my beta reader, not an appendage.'

'Charles! That's exactly what I'm saying. I was supposed to be the woman you loved, not your beta reader. I was always involved in your stuff. Trekking down to Waterford to support your reading even though I had to change a shift to do it. Going to book launches for people I'd never heard of. Tiptoeing around the house so as not to disturb you when you thought it perfectly fine to wake me up if I was sleeping after a late shift . . . If that's not being an appendage, I don't know what is.'

'I never thought of it like that.' He looks genuinely contrite. 'I thought you coming to things was fun for both of us. And it's not like you didn't have the confidence to tell me my book was terrible, by the way. Though I'm glad you did.'

'I never said it was terrible.'

'You didn't pander to me, though,' he says. 'You told me

I should be more like Janice Jermyn, an author I used to sneer at. Much to my shame. I've read all her books now, and they're great.'

'I'm so glad I introduced you to her.' I give him a half-smile. 'Charles, I'm not blaming you for how things turned out. It's as much on me. I wanted to think the age gap didn't matter, but you *are* a different generation. You have another perspective on life. You're already hugely successful in what you do. I'm building my career. You like fine dining and your expensive wines. I'm still a Nando's girl at heart.'

'You've been promoted at work. You're way more successful than I was at twenty-nine.'

'I'm thirty now,' I remind him. Not that I needed to. He sent me flowers for my birthday. Another massive bouquet that took over the house. Even Mum asked me then if I was really sure I didn't love him any more.

'More successful than I was at thirty,' he amends. 'Yes, there are differences between us. But there are also things we both want.'

'Such as?'

'A loving relationship. Someone who understands us. Someone to share our lives with. Someone to laugh with. We had some good laughs, Izzy.'

'I'm sure I'll find all that in the future. I'm sure you will too. Right now, with two failed engagements on my CV, I need time to be me.'

We walk up Dawson Street in silence and are almost back at the pub when he stops at Duke Lane, where Warren's have their store. I recall the day he brought me there, the excitement of trying on the Ice Cube diamond ring and the fun of celebrating with champagne afterwards. I remember, too, that Steve had called me. I never told Charles that.

'I still love you as much as I did then,' he says as we look towards the shop. 'After everything you've said, I don't expect you to wear this, but I do want you to have it.'

He reaches into the pocket of his jacket and takes out a box. It's the box that Warren's gave us for my ring. He opens it, and there's the Ice Cube, glinting in the evening light.

'Why have you got that with you?' I ask. 'You weren't expecting to meet me today.'

'I expect to meet you every day,' he says. 'I have it with me all the time. Just in case.'

I stare at him.

'It may have gone wrong for us,' he says. 'I didn't change for you and I wanted you to change for me. Maybe that's because I *am* an old fart. But I'm willing to work at change, because I've never stopped loving you. Also . . .' he takes a deep breath, 'everything you've said is absolutely right. It was only after you'd gone that I realised how difficult it had been for you. And how difficult living in Riverside Lodge would have been for you too. Difficult for getting to work and your family – yet you were prepared to do it for me. I should've told you I'd move on day one.'

'It wasn't all about the house, Charles. Though,' I add, 'not having Ariel in the back garden would have helped.'

'Would you have felt differently if I'd offered to move closer to the airport as soon as you were promoted? Because it wouldn't matter where we lived. It really wouldn't.'

'Don't be an idiot.'

We stand looking at each other. We've run out of things

to say. But I'm mulling over his words in my head and I can't turn away from him. I remember once thinking that I was always the girl who gave in to men because I couldn't say no. I've learned to be stronger and tougher thanks to Charles.

I'm vaguely conscious that Celeste has come out of the Bailey and is staring up the street. She sees me and waves. I wave back.

'Everything all right?' she calls.

I glance at my ex-fiancé. He's wearing one of his vast collection of polo necks over faded denims. His eyes are the same arctic blue behind his glasses. He looks fitter than ever, if that's even possible.

We had some good times and I've missed him. It's been hard not to pick up the phone and dial his number. But I've stayed strong. And that was the right thing to do. All the same, I can't help wondering if saying no to him is still the right thing to do.

'Everything's fine,' I call back to Celeste. 'I'm . . . I'm making a decision.'

'Make the right one!'

I don't know if I can.

I take the box and look at the ring. It's the most beautiful piece of jewellery I ever owned.

I close the box again and hold it in my hand.

Today is unexpected. It's also romantic.

Romance doesn't endure. Love does.

I do love Charles, but do I love him enough? Would it be different this time? Should I take a chance? I don't want my heart to rule my head. I don't want to make another stupid mistake.

I remember how happy I was when I first put the ring on my finger. I remember how he'd laugh at me moving it in the sun so that the light reflected off the stones in a rainbow of colours. I remember how right it felt with him then.

It's not about a ring.

It's not about a house.

It's about people.

Who we are.

I'm a different person to the one who first saw Charles when I should have been on my honeymoon. He's a different person too. We've changed. And we've changed each other.

I wonder if he knows that. And I wonder if, as different people, we have a future together.

If it's worth taking a chance.

#BraveDecisions #DoTheRightThing #BeYourOwnPerson #TheNextMrsMiller #WhatNow

Acknowledgements

I always start my acknowledgements by thanking the two women who have been closest to me when writing a book: my wonderful editor, Marion Donaldson, and my equally wonderful agent, Isobel Dixon, both absolute rocks of support and common sense as well as creative encouragement. Thanks also to Jen, Imogen, Zara and Sian, who have all been part of *The Honeymoon Affair* journey, along with the entire teams at Headline Publishing and the Blake Friedmann Literary Agency.

Big thanks to the fantastic Irish team, with another strong woman, Breda Purdue, at the helm, and her brilliant sales manager, Ruth Shern, who has accompanied me on so many 'glamorous' publicity tours.

Further thanks to the Hachette teams around the globe who put my books into bookshops and libraries, and to the booksellers and librarians who then get them into the hands of readers. I appreciate you all. Additional thanks to the translators who do such fantastic work to bring my stories to so many people.

Thanks and appreciation also go to my copyeditor, Jane Selley, who finds all the silly mistakes and queries them so

472

kindly and thoughtfully that I don't feel half as daft as I should for making them.

Massive thanks to my husband, Colm, who puts up with me during the writing process, also does a final proof edit and then gives his verdict. (Which, so far, has always been good, and he's definitely not biased!)

Special thanks to Rita O'Hanlon and Edel Finn – another pair of formidable women – for the information on customs procedures and the fascinating trips around Dublin Port. Naturally any factual errors are entirely mine.

This is the first of my books that my mum and my younger sister have not been here to read and to champion as they have done so magnificently over the thirty-three years of my writing career. Very sadly, both of them passed away before I finished writing *The Honeymoon Affair*, but I still draw on their positivity and strength even when I falter. I'm lucky to have a family that has each other's backs, and I thank each and every one of them for their continued unstinting support.

And of course a heartfelt thanks to my wonderful readers, whether you've been with me from the start or have recently begun reading the books and discovered a huge backlist . . . It's always a privilege to know that you've bought one of my books and an even greater privilege to know that so many of you recommend them to family and friends. The reading and writing community is a haven of kindness and goodness in a difficult world. I'm lucky to be a part of it.

SIGN UP TO SHEILA'S NEWSLETTER

Keep in touch with the world of

SHEILA O'FLANAGAN

For up-to-date news from Sheila, exclusive content and competitions, sign up to her newsletter!

You can sign up on her website, www.sheilaoflanagan.com

We will never share your email address and you can unsubscribe at any time.

REVIEW